Moscow Madness

Book 3 of the Moscow Nights Series

By

Beth H. Macy

Edited by Kevin Ryan

Acknowledgments

I also want to thank again my wonderful first editor, Dori Harrell, who brought me so far as a writer.

Prologue

2 June 2019

Elda Ainsworth could feel the sweat soaking the back of her shirt where it pressed against the cotton cloth-covered armchair. Her arms pressed into the wood of the chair's arms. She struggled to think and to shake off her lethargy. Her feet were heavy and seemed glued to the ground.

Why what?

Words swirled around in her head. She chased after them.

It hurts to breathe.

She rubbed her eyes to clear her vision. *Why can't I see?* She drifted in and out of the fog that surrounded her. She could faintly make out shapes in the room.

Where am I?

She heard a voice as if she was underwater. It was asking, "Do you know why?"

Tell them nothing. Only disclose your name, rank, and serial number.

She shook her head to clear her vision. Droplets of sweat flew off her face. Her arms felt like lead, but she wasn't restrained.

I'm not tied up. Did they drug me?

She opened her parched mouth to talk, but nothing came out. Her brain hurt as she tried to coordinate her thoughts and lips.

What do they want?

The gentle touch of a hand on her arm burned.

What is this? Good cop/bad cop? Focus! Who are they?

Elda looked around the room. Her vision blurred as she struggled to recognize where she was. Nothing seemed familiar. She worked to orientate herself and bring herself into the present. *Breathe. Clock, pillow, desk, breathe. Rug, shoe, Dawn... Dawn? What was her wife doing there?*

She glanced at her Garmin watch: June 2nd, 1400. The date and time seemed wrong. She looked in confusion at Dawn and then turned to the other woman in the room. *Ah, my therapist. We're in couple's counseling...*

The therapist's voice floated to her ears, "Welcome back, Elda." Elda nodded to show she was no longer in a dissociated state.

Dawn reached out and touched Elda's hand. Elda saw the love and concern in Dawn's blue eyes as they bore into Elda's brown ones. Dawn softly said, "Are you okay, honey?"

Elda nodded and asked, "What was the question?"

The therapist said gently, "It was: 'Why do you hate yourself?' but we have done enough for today."

***

12 April 2019

Nigel recoiled from the spyhole in his front door. His heart raced. Beads of sweat broke out on his forehead. A man with a gun was standing there. *If I don't open the door he could shoot his way in. If I open it, perhaps he'll see he has the wrong place.* With trepidation--knowing he had no other options—Nigel Davies slowly opened the solid metal door of his large apartment in Moscow. He stepped back on shaky legs as the man pushed his way inside and stated, "Your father, Henry Davies, is dead."

Nigel sunk to his knees onto the marble floor and wept out of fear for his own future.

"You were our leverage against your father. And now you are useless." The man raised his pistol.

Nigel held out the palm of his right hand and implored, "Wait. Please. I can still help you."

The man dropped the pistol barrel downwards. "How?"

Nigel gulped and his eyes darted all over the room as he searched his brain for a way out.

"Make it quick," snarled the gunman, raising his pistol again.

"N-no, no, …," Nigel stuttered, desperate to save his own life, "W-w-wait, wait, wait,…" He blurted out, "I can get you a United States senator on the Intelligence Committee."

The assassin snapped, "What is his name?" He lowered his weapon again.

Confident that he had given the right answer, Nigel slowly stood, straightened his glasses, smoothed his wiry black hair, and squared his shoulders. He stated pompously, "I will handle him myself. He will be my protection."

The assassin contemplated the white ceiling. He returned his weapon to his leather shoulder holster before responding, "*Da*. Yes. You will still be useful. You may live …for now. But you better deliver. We will contact you." He quickly exited the apartment, slamming the door closed behind him.

Nigel collapsed in relief, sliding down the inside of his now closed apartment door

Chapter One

THEY ARE COMING. SHUT IT ALL DOWN AND GET OUT NOW! ADRIK. The words flashed across his screen. Anton Morozov shouted to the rest of his group, "Leave now. I will handle the machinery." Three Russians jumped from their stations and dashed out the door.

Anton, remaining behind, copied the team's files onto a portable hard drive. While the data was being transferred, he rushed to set the timer on explosives that he had placed in strategic spots about the building. He typed into his computer. *ALL SET, LEAVING IN 3 MINUTES.* Although he knew that it was against orders, he packed his personal laptop into his backpack. Seeing that the transfer was complete, he disconnected the hard drive and added that to the backpack. After one more look around, he dashed out the side door.

He turned the corner to the front of the building as three black SUVs pulled up, and armed Federal Agents, with FBI printed on their vests, poured out of them. Leading them was a woman with closely cropped hair. Anton took off at a run, darting through a parking lot and heading towards a nearby chain link fence.

Without hesitation, the woman was after Anton. She shouted over her shoulder at the rest of the team, "Check for bombs before you go in." Just then a loud retort sounded, followed by another, and another. The FBI scattered and took cover behind their cars as the building lit up on fire. One agent called for a bomb squad and fire department assistance.

Anton leapt onto the chain link fence and was climbing it, when his leg was grabbed from behind. He kicked at the impediment but was yanked off the fence and fell onto the ground on top of his backpack. "*Nyet*! No! Not my computer!" He started to rise when he felt the barrel of a gun pressed to his forehead. He knelt and put his hands in the air. The woman deftly cut his backpack off of him and cuffed him. He started crying, knowing that by being captured he had just signed his own death warrant. No matter where the Americans took him, his boss would find him and have him killed.

Two agents separated from the pack and grabbed Anton, half carrying him to a waiting vehicle.

"They will kill me!" Anton sobbed.

"If you're lucky," snarled one of the FBI agents.

The frantic sound of a jingling bicycle bell rang. Anton turned to see a young man on an out of control bike heading towards the three men and heard the rider yell, "My brakes don't work!" Anton felt the tire rim hit his leg and a sting as something jabbed his arm. He fell into an agent and toppled him.

The second agent tripped over the bike as he reached to help everyone up. The group fell into a pile by the car. The agents quickly untangled themselves from the mess and drew their pistols. Anton put his hands in the air, and yelled, "Please don't shoot me." His cry was echoed by the bike rider, "Hey, hey! Don't shoot! You can see for yourselves, my brakes are toast!"

One agent looked at the bike, with the now bent front tire, and retorted, "That whole bike is unrideable. Carry it with you and get out of here."

Anton's chest hurt and he started rubbing it and moaning. The bicyclist picked up his bike and hurried away.

"Get in the back seat." The agent opened the back door of the black SUV and roughly assisted his prisoner inside. Having difficulty staying upright and breathing, the pain overwhelming him, Anton toppled over onto the back seat.

***

Charlie Burlamachi grabbed at her phone. Her boss at the FBI was calling. "Excellent job nabbing that cyber terrorist, Charlie. We've passed the information along to another department for further analysis, but Ed Wilson has informed me that there appears to be some data that could implicate the Russians. And thanks to your fast thinking, no-one was hurt at the scene when the bombs went off..."

Uninterested in praise, Charlie inquired, "What happened to the prisoner?"

Her boss answered, "Unfortunately, he died from a heart attack before we could transfer him to interrogation. So that makes the equipment you found even more important. I'm putting you in for a promotion."

Frustrated by the lack of excitement in her job, Charlie requested, "I would prefer another field assignment."

Her boss responded, "Unfortunately there is nothing for you right now. Take a few days off."

Charlie sighed and hung up. Despite the promotion and praise, this job was not what she had hoped for.

Chapter Two

"You wanted to see me, *ser*?"

Dust hung in the rays of sunlight streaming through the only office window. Wooden chair creaking, Adrik Lebedev slowly swiveled his large frame around to glare at Nadia Belov, who calmly returned his stare. "Obviously I did or you wouldn't be here. I hope you are smarter than you appear. Also, it is customary to knock," he stated icily.

Thus warned, Nadia drew herself up to her full height of 5 feet 8 inches and stood at attention. She responded politely, "Yes, *ser*, it is, but your door was wide open and your secretary indicated that I could just come on in."

Adrik narrowed his eyes and sat silently observing her. Nadia did not blink and stood rock solid. Tension filled the air between them.

Finally, Adrik broke the silence, "As you know, I head up the cyber-attack group here in Moscow. That is the war of the future. These old-fashioned ops of your boss's will serve us no purpose. Nor will he in the end. Unfortunately, he has gathered high-level support from his past successes. I need him to fail so that my cyber ops take priority." Adrik raised an eyebrow and looked directly into Nadia's eyes. He continued, "I suspect you are ambitious enough that you can help me in this effort. Is that correct?"

Nadia answered without moving, "*Da, ser*. I will gladly help you."

Adrik cocked his head and put his hand down under his mahogany desk. His hand found the trigger for the gun built into his desk. The trigger was located close to the back of the desk and easy to access. It was wired to fire a specially constructed pistol hidden in the front of the desk and pointed at whoever was sitting there. Adrik whispered, "You agreed rather quickly. Have you no loyalty to your superior?"

Nadia stood taller and answered in a level tone, "May I speak frankly, *ser*?"

Adrik raised both eyebrows, narrowed his eyes, and replied in a cautious tone of voice, "Of course."

Nadia leaned slightly towards Adrik. She kept her face expressionless and stated, "I am loyal to the Kremlin and to Mother Russia. However, I need to work for someone who appreciates my abilities. Tosh does not use me as often as I would like and has demoted me in the past for no fault of my own. I feel he has aged out of the service and should be removed for the greater good." She returned to an upright position of attention again.

Releasing the hidden trigger, Adrik brought his hand up to the top of his desk. He nodded, acknowledging her message, "*Ochen' khorosho*, very well. Then we are going to get along. Just know that if you cross *me*, it will not be a demotion. If you ever fail me or turn on *me*, I will ensure you die a slow, painful death."

***

Toshchiy Chelovek, aka, Tosh, glanced out his office window and noticed that one of his operatives was striding quickly away from the building. He muttered to himself, "*Interestnyy*. And why would Nadia be here today?"

***

Rip. Adrik tore open a candy bar and took a large bite. He read his encrypted message again. *Subject terminated before interrogation. No information given to those who captured him.* Adrik wondered if that was true or if his subordinate was covering his own *zad*. He decided to leave it be. The appearance of success for his team was enough for him. He liked the straightforwardness of cyberterrorism. He thought of his meeting this morning with that woman, what was her name? Ah, Nadia. Yes, he was well on his way of getting rid of that annoying team. Spies. Such old-fashioned, slow work. And messy. He didn't want those complications. He devoured the rest of the candy bar. Crumpling up the wrapper, he threw it at his trash can. *That will be you, Tosh.*

The paper missed the can and fell onto the floor.

***

How much longer will we be together? Tosh mused as he studied his sleeping partner. He crept out of bed, slipped on his black and white checkered robe, and padded barefoot into the bathroom. Tosh dropped the robe and kicked it to one side. *I got rid of the first one of these but then got a replacement for my birthday! I really dislike this robe. I never should have said I lost it on a trip. Perhaps I should just buy myself one I like.*

Contemplating his aging frame in the mirror, he stood taller and tightened his abs. He addressed his image, "If I were 20 years younger, I wouldn't select you as a lover, you old *bolvan*." He wondered why his partner stayed with him. He hit himself up the side of the head and repeated his admonishment, "*Blockhead*!"

He grabbed for his blood pressure cuff and pumped it up. He was surprised to see it was in the normal range. "*Interestnyy*," he muttered as he stepped into the shower. While soaping up, he wondered how many more years he would be able to retain his job. He believed there was still much to be done and also a dire need for his Cold War skills. However, his new boss, Adrik Lebedev, was not a fan of his abilities. He chastised himself while toweling off, *I should have kept my temper in check and not had my top assassin, Anatoly, murder my previous boss, Alexei. But it was necessary. I could not work for a traitor that put my people second to his ambitions and needlessly risked their lives. But you, old man, you knew that the devil you know is often better than the one you don't. Be wary of Adrik.*

Tosh wandered into his kitchen for a cup of tea. He popped open his laptop to check his emails. Before him was a command to meet with Adrik that very morning. *Speak of the devil.*

Thirty minutes later, Tosh sat calmly in a hardback wooden chair with a slightly padded maroon leather seat, waiting to meet Adrik for the first time. Through the dirty window in Adrik's office, Tosh could view the red brick and green top of the Kutafiya Tower, accenting the yellow and white of the nearby Kremlin buildings. His pale gray eyes glanced at the large round analog clock hanging on the wall over a dingy, ripped printed calendar.

9:05 am on Monday the 17th of June 2019. *He's late,* Tosh thought.

Just then Adrik plodded in and plopped his flabby, obese body in his chair behind the large wooden desk opposite Tosh. Tosh looked him up and down, committing the image of Adrik to his photographic memory. Adrik spoke abruptly, without any formal introduction or social niceties, "My predecessor met an untimely end."

Tosh displayed no emotion as he replied, "Yes sir. I was sorry to hear that Alexei had moved on."

Adrik's belly rolled, signifying an internal laugh. Finally he snorted. "Moved on. An interesting way of putting it. Well, I am thankful, since I had my eye on this job for a while. It seemed he would never die." Adrik leaned forward in his chair, his right hand gripping the chair arm. "And you, Tosh. Do you have ambitions?"

Without flinching, Tosh evenly replied, "My goal is to live a long life and to serve you and Mother Russia, for as long as I can."

***

Satisfied with Tosh's answer, Adrik's face relaxed into his jowls. Adrik leaned back and released his grip on the one-shot gun that was built into the chair arm. Adrik thought, *Too bad, old man. That would have been the quick and easy way to remove you. But you have many friends in high places so I will have to finesse your downfall. I will set you up on a mission where your old-school techniques will fail.*

Adrik tapped his computer and declared, "I have read the files on operation Bittman and, although you handled that mission well, I feel you may have been too invested in your relationships with the British and Americans. It was unfortunate that Henry Davies, our mole in the communications department of MI6, was found, but the usefulness of moles has passed. We are now beating the United States through cyberattacks. You need to let go of all of looking under rocks for traitors and move forward into the new world order. Do you understand?"

Tosh assented, "*Da, ser. Ya ponimayu.* I understand. I will ensure that your success is closely tied to mine, *ser.*"

Adrik sat silently contemplating Tosh's answer and then moved forward in the discussion. He spoke again, "*Ochen' khorosho.* I have a new mission for you. As you know next year is an election year in the United States. We have many plans to help move that along. We will need you and your team to help us. Some of these assignments will stretch your team's abilities and be outside their normal realm of operating. Can you handle that?"

"I aim to serve." Tosh appeared to be waiting patiently for additional information.

Adrik cocked his head, knotted his brow. *Is he serious or placating me?* He continued to fill Tosh in, "*Khorosho*. We have an asset who has recently relocated to London. He claims he can get us a United States senator on the Intelligence Committee. I wish to know who that is, and if this informant is needed. If he isn't, then feel free to cut out the middleman and manage the senator directly." He slid a battered brown unlabeled folder across the desk to Tosh and started cleaning his nails, while waiting for Tosh to read the contents.

Tosh quickly flipped through it and pushed it back. "*Da, ser.*"

Adrik frowned. It appeared as if Tosh had not fully read the file. "Did you memorize that information?"

"*Da ser.*"

Adrik had heard of Tosh's photographic memory but had never witnessed it. He put his nail file down and shook his finger at Tosh. Lecturing Tosh on the seriousness of his role in the mission, Adrik declared,

"I am selecting you, Tosh, because we must be discrete here. No electronic traces may be detected. It needs your light touch and Cold War skills. *Vy ponimayete?*"

Silence.

Adrik repeated himself. "*Vy ponimayete?* Do you understand?"

Tosh replied flatly, "*Da ser.* Yes sir. I understand."

Adrik glared at Tosh.

Tosh gazed back with an inquisitive expression. The silence grew in the void between the two men. Adrik wondered if Tosh saw through Adrik's ploy to cast Tosh as unable to embrace the new technology. Tosh's successes were positioning Tosh for promotion and were a barrier to Adrik's rapid ascent up the ladder. Adrik would not let that happen. He drummed his fingers on his desk as he contemplated his next move.

Finally Adrik continued, "*Assuming* that you and your team satisfactorily handle this first operation, I have another mission that is related. I need a strong message to be sent to a group of senators who are visiting Moscow in a few weeks. We need to recruit them so that each individual is in our pocket. Any senator that that refuses our overtures will be quietly disposed of, once they are back on United States soil. This will make an unquestionable point to the other senators and demonstrate that they cannot escape our reach. However, there must be *no* way to trace the assassination back to us. Your team has been very successful in their missions. I expect you will be able to handle this one too."

Tosh hit the center of his chest with a closed fist and strongly asserted, "*Da ser. Spasibo ser*. Thank you. I work for the greater good of Mother Russia and will not fail in my duties."

Adrik raised an eyebrow. *Is he putting me on or serious?* Adrik then nodded. "*Khorosho*. You are dismissed." He pointed his finger at Tosh's head and added threateningly, "*But know this*. If you are caught, we will disavow knowledge of you and your team. The price of failure will be death." Adrik added silently, *And I will ensure you fail.*

Burp. After his meeting with Tosh, he had gone down to the canteen to see what goodies they had. His stomach was churning. Adrik glanced around to see if anyone had noticed that.

Adrik knew he was not a spy. He had clawed his way up the Kremlin hierarchy by blackmailing or killing those who stood in his way. However, it was unfortunate that these techniques could only be used effectively at the lower levels. Now he was up against others who had friends in high places and had more experience than he had. Adrik knew that Tosh was better connected than Adrik was and could easily have Adrik removed from his position.

Adrik was confident, however, that he could find a way to remove any obstacle to his ascent. He needed to consolidate his power base and saw Tosh as a threat to that. Tosh's success using Cold War skills threatened Adrik's positioning as the expert in using new techniques in spycraft. All he had to do was set Tosh and his team up for failure. Then bring on the right minions and show success using his own teams in contrast to Tosh and others whom he wished to remove. The age of technology was his ally.

"Your days are numbered," he muttered to his large dish of ice cream, covered in whipped cream.

***

Plop. Tosh dropped a pile of blue and green folders onto his meticulously neat desk. *Try hacking into these files.* Tosh did not believe in relying on computer backup, since electronic files could be so easily hacked, stolen or destroyed. He didn't trust who else had access to his computerized data. His paper files even contained information that he would not commit to online.

Tosh sat down in front of the folders and rapidly sorted them into Team A (green) and backup team B (blue). Although he had every file memorized, he briefly glanced at each one, speed reading the contents to ensure he had all of the details fresh in his mind.

Tosh had been active as a field agent for the Soviet Union during the Cold War. He had heard the lore about him. Others in the profession said that he was legendary - a ghost who could slip into a location, successfully accomplished his mission, and disappear without a trace. *I have done well, but I am aging and cannot afford to slip up now.*

His mission in 2018 against the United States operative, Elda Ainsworth, was the first time he had ever come close to failing. Although he and Elda had worked on a joint mission last year, he welcomed a chance for a rematch as adversaries.

Tosh tapped his fingers on his desk and mused, *This is a mission against the United States. And Adrik was rather khitryy when he mentioned letting go of operation Bittman. I have to watch out for that deviousness of his.* He pulled a red file labeled *Bittman,* and quickly reviewed it. He muttered, "Something's missing." Aware that his office might be bugged by Adrik, he went silent. Adrik would be livid if he knew Tosh was staffing with newer technical skills. *I know you are looking for me to fail, you bastard. I will beat you at your own game. I need to get someone computer savvy to gather more information.* He thought about who he could recruit. *Aga! Stas Garin! Stas helped us immensely in our last mission. His computer skills are unmatched.*

He returned the folder to the file cabinet.

He continued to ponder, *I wonder if any of the American agents will get involved? I best add to the team, just in case.* He returned to his ancient wooden file cabinet, pulled open a creaky drawer, and selected an additional two blue folders. He tossed each onto the top of the two piles on his desk. *Now which American might be involved?* Carefully closing that drawer, to keep it on its tracks, he opened the one above and pulled out a slender red folder labeled, *Elda Ainsworth.*

Tosh slowly opened the last folder and reviewed his handwritten notes on Elda. He reached for his pen and added a few notations. He kept his private notes unwritten. *Ah, Elda. You are extremely skilled at the spy business. Your analytical skills are actually better than mine. Plus, you have your additional insights as a therapist. I thoroughly enjoyed our time in Florence and our mutual love of art and fine food. There is much that we could have learned from each other. You sharpened my skills sparring with you. I wish we were not on opposite sides. In another lifetime we would have been friends. Unfortunately, that is not the case, and only one of us will be left standing in the end.*

Tosh placed the folder on top of the 'Team A' pile. Patting the folder he told it silently, *Pray that we don't meet again, Elda. It will be the last encounter you have with me.*

***

Tosh slipped through the darkness of the night, hiding in the shadows and periodically checking to ensure he was alone. *This recruitment needs to be done without any electronic trace back to me. In person is best.* Taking out his lock set he silently opened the door to Stas' apartment and entered. He saw Stas typing rapidly on his computer. The glow illuminated Stas' face as he scowled at the screen.

Tosh stood behind Stas and tapped him on the shoulder. "Are you playing a game?" he inquired of Stas.

Stas jumped up and wheeled around holding his arm in the air and his mouse in his fist. Tosh burst out laughing. "Are you going to mouse me to death?"

"Tosh! You scared the shit out of me!" Stas lowered the mouse, looked at it in his hand and joined Tosh in laughter.

"How would you like to join my team?" inquired Tosh.

"Really? As a spy? Can I still do some side projects? Can I get more equipment?"

Tosh laughed again. *They always want that special gun, eavesdropping device or I suppose in Stas' case, computers.* He answered, "As long as they don't interfere with your ability to perform your job for me."

"Da!" said Stas.

"Fine. Wait to hear from me for your first assignment. We will communicate only through a specially encrypted message chat or in person," Tosh instructed.

Stas' computer binged. Tosh exited while Stas was turned away, leaving no trace that he had ever been there.

Chapter Three

In her Maine farmhouse, Elda sat facing Dawn across the old wooden kitchen table. Dawn pushed back her chair to leave.

"Please don't go, honey," pleaded Elda.

Dawn held up her hand, signaling Elda to stop. "You know I can't stay, Elda. We are not in a good place. You're still working at that spy stuff, and I can't even stand the concept of guns and deceit. If we are to work out, you *must* retire from that job."

Elda bit her bottom lip and clenched her fists. She knew it was useless trying to explain yet again to Dawn how important her job was to her and to the United States. She glanced at Vee, her small Coton de Tulear, who was lying under the table gazing back with her large brown eyes. *At least Vee gets me. Why do I stay with Dawn? Why do I want her back so badly?*

As if reading her thoughts, Dawn asked, "Do you want a divorce?"

The silence that followed that question pressed heavily on the two of them. Elda wiped a tear that was forming at the corner of her eye. Finally she took a deep breath and answered, "No, honey. I want both of us to be happy and living together. But I also want to be accepted for who I am. I want the full *you, me, us* of a healthy relationship. I want couple's counseling to work for us. Is that too much to ask?" Elda searched Dawn's face for some trace of understanding.

Dawn pulled her jacket from the back of her chair. She looked Elda in the eyes and stated flatly, "It may be, Elda. It may be." Turning, she walked away.

Elda sat listening to Dawn's footsteps retreating and then the front door slamming closed. She reached under the table and picked Vee up. Hugging her, Elda sat and silently cried.

***

Elda sat quietly in a puddle of raw feelings. Finally, an hour later Elda received a message that her boss, Ed Wilson, wanted to chat with her. *Saved by the bell. I hate this emotional crap.*

With Vee trotting behind her, Elda paced across the wide pine plank floors to a windowless secure room in the lower level of her old farmhouse in

Maine. She was careful not to knock over the webcam she had situated on a tall tripod. Pausing by her computer, she started the secure messaging app, pressed a button on her keyboard and maximized the window containing Ed's image.

"We need you, Elda." Ed looked at Elda pleadingly from a small window on her battered laptop. He ran his hand over his square clean-shaven jaw, then attempted to slick down his salt and pepper cowlicks.

Elda replied emphatically, "No Ed. I am done." She responded sharply to his look of disbelief, "I *mean it* this time. I *must* stay here and continue to work on my relationship with Dawn. Anyway, there is no-one to look after Vee for me." She rapidly continued, "And, really, Ed, give it up – that hair is meant to stick up." Elda ran her own fingers through her curly salt and pepper hair, making it even more unruly than before. "See? Hair does what it does."

Ed smiled. "I wish I had your disregard for your looks." He then frowned. Elda's face was tired and gaunt. Ed asked with concern, "Are you getting any sleep, Elda?"

Rubbing her red rimmed eyes, Elda sighed heavily, and responded, "Here and there. I miss Dawn so very much. It's just not the same in this house without her."

"Then come to DC. I think that the Russians are up to something and I am suspecting that Tosh and his crew may be active. We came across some computer equipment. The portable hard drive had a file on it that pointed to Tosh. It seemed a bit convenient and not quite his style but that's why I need you in on this operation." Ed paused, and softly continued, "Are you happy, Elda?" Elda could see the compassion in his eyes.

Elda stopped looking at Ed's eyes, in order not to tear up. She halted her pacing and sat down heavily in her office swivel chair. "No, I'm miserable. And I'm lonely." She looked down sadly at her bare feet, where her small black and white dog, Vee, had just curled up, warming one set of toes. "I'm failing at my relationship. I can't do all of this, Ed."

Ed reached out his hand to his camera and pleaded, "Then come on down. Throw yourself back into your work. You once told me that your work was who you were. And, if Dawn loves and wants you, she will need to accept all of you, not try to mold you into someone you are not."

Elda despondently gazed at the camera, and stated in a flat, dead tone, "Part of me thinks that's true. I can't be anyone else than who I am. But, am I wrong? I also see how patient and loving she has been, while I have just gadded off doing my thing, leaving her here, waiting and wondering if I will return."

"It's what we do, Elda," reasoned Ed, "And we do important work."

"I know," responded Elda heavily.

"So come for just a week," Ed cajoled. "You remember our master of misinformation and data analysis, Jackson Taylor? Help Jackson and myself look at the information we have, and then decide if you want to return to Maine, or, stay and help me save the world again."

Elda dropped her chin into her hands, and murmured, "Let me think on it."

"I'll book you a room and send the chopper on Friday. You have until Thursday evening to say no." Ed's window flashed off into blackness.

"Damn." Vee stood and put her paws and head on Elda's knees. "Come on Vee, let's go for a walk."

***

Slap. The sounds of crying filled the air. The grownups sighed a collective breath of relieve. Elda Ainsworth had been prematurely brought into the world and was not happy about it.

Having grown up in a rough area of a city in the United States, and the child of a single mother, Elda was self-sufficient at an early age. She worked three jobs and had obtained a scholarship to get herself through a state college and had graduated on the Dean's List with a double major. Unsure of what to do next, Elda joined the Navy, obtained her Masters and, after the Navy, practiced as a therapist until she was recruited by the CIA. No longer with the CIA nor a practicing therapist, Elda was now working for a small intelligence agency known only to a selected few in the United States government. It had no official name but a clear international charter to protect the interests of the United States by any means. Elda loved what she did. The thrill of the missions, her love of puzzles and ability to analyze human behavior, her deep intellectual curiosity, all combined to keep her fascinated and happy with her job.

***

The door slammed behind Elda as she marched into her house. *Damn, I need to fix that door so it swings gently shut.*

"Is that you, honey?"

"Dawn! What are you doing back here?" Smiling, Elda strode into the kitchen.

"I needed to pick up some things. I still have my key so thought you wouldn't mind if I let myself in." Dawn was standing in the kitchen with a Corningware white and blue casserole dish and cover. "You know I love this old casserole dish that was your mother's. I was hoping you wouldn't mind if I borrowed it for a few days."

Elda worked to control her look of disappointment. She was hoping Dawn was returning home. "No problem, honey. Can we talk about something while you're here?"

Dawn carefully placed the dish on the wooden kitchen table. She warily eyed Elda. "It's not like you to want discuss something. What's up?"

"Ed called."

Dawn scowled and snapped, "No, Elda. *No*. You know the conditions of us getting back together. You told me you had retired."

Elda replied beseechingly, "I know, Dawn. And I told Ed exactly that. He's just asking me to come to DC to help train a new analyst. It would only be for a week. I owe it to Ed."

After closing the cabinet door, Dawn hung her head, put one arm around her middle and her other fist on her chin and snorted. She tapped her foot rapidly. Elda braced herself for the explosion. None came. Dawn looked up at Elda and gave a huge sigh. "Ok, call me when you get there." She grabbed the casserole dish and stomped out of the house.

Elda looked after her sadly. Vee came over to Elda and plopped her well-loved purple ball toy onto Elda's foot. Elda reached down to pat Vee's curly head. "Vee, mommy has to go on a trip. National security is more important than my or Dawn's own needs. Plus, damn it, Dawn needs to accept all of me. She doesn't need to like it, but if she truly loves me, she will see how important this is to me. I'm going to DC."

***

Struggling with a sense of guilt over forcing Elda's hand, Ed thought back to the day he first met her. His father was in the CIA and had recruited Ed for an undercover mission for the CIA in Wales.

It was a raw day in the outskirts of London. Ed had been waiting at a burn facility for a United States Navy truck to give him a ride to Wales. Tall and slender, teenage Ed tried to pass himself off as older by wearing a grey greatcoat and leather driving gloves. However, his voice cracked as he introduced himself to the Naval Officer. Her dark brown eyes bore into him. He felt that she had correctly sized him up.

Ed silently observed Elda as she kept her cool through being diverted to London and deftly handled being rear ended by a farm truck. Although he was young, he had recognized Elda's abilities could be used by his father and passed one of Ed senior's cards. He had no clue that someday he, Ed junior, would become Elda's handler. Over the years of running Elda, he and she had become friends.

Lately the missions had become more complicated with a greater dependence on intelligence gathering, electronics and cyber security. Although Elda was unmatched as an analyst, he also needed her skills in the field, and there was just too much information to analyze. So he had proactively brought onto his team a researcher and data investigator, Jackson Taylor. Plus, after seeing on the last mission how Stas Garin, the Russian hacker had proved so invaluable, Ed had hired Ashok Bhatt to help round out his own team in that area. Despite all the recent hires, he worried that he was still missing a greater breadth and depth in his team and made a mental note to expand it and eliminate all single points of failure. That included his dependence on Elda as his star agent.

***

Anxiety rose up within Elda. She could feel her chest tighten. She looked down at her open go-bag. *I have no clue what I just packed.* This relationship building with Dawn was taking her concentration and focus away.

She wondered if she could handle another mission, especially one against Tosh. *What if I have to go to Moscow? I have a love-hate relationship with Russia. There is a part of the culture that is now part of me. But I'm fear it somehow, despite the beautiful metro stations, delicious Georgian red wine, and the familiar language. Fear of being dragged off to a place no one would ever find me. Fear of being tortured. Fear of always being watched and followed.*

And it's cold there! It's a cold that comes at you through the wind, the soles of your boots, and intensifies the fear inside.

"Stop it, Elda," she berated herself. "Go sharpen your skills at the shooting range and then pop over to the gym and build up those reflexes." She decided should also ask Ed to get her a sparring partner when she was in DC. Putting thoughts of Russia and any inadequacies out of her head, she grabbed her gun box.

***

The pungent smell of nitroglycerin hung in the air. Elda pushed a button to bring forward her target and swiftly replaced it with a new one and sent it back downrange. She switched from her Smith & Wesson revolver and snapped a magazine into her M&P 380 SHIELD EZ pistol that Anatoly Petrov had given her last year. She rapidly emptied the clip and finishing, she brought the target whizzing back and tore it off. She lay both targets side by side to analyze the bullet holes around each bullseye. On target number one, two of the five bullets had missed the bullseye by ¼ inch. The other three shots had gone through the bullseye, ripping the middle of the target into a larger hole. She was still getting used to her newer gun and her first shot had missed the bullseye to the left by ½ inch. She had corrected her aim and the remaining shots were dead on. Satisfied, she packed up her gear and left the range.

In the parking lot, she ran into her old friend, Jim Martin. Jim was a tall, lanky New Englander who had served in the war with a mutual friend, Fred Perry. Fred had committed suicide a few years after the Vietnam war. Fred had been like an older brother to Elda, and his loss had made her friendship with Jim even more precious.

Jim waved hello at Elda. "Howdy, Elder. Did you leave any tahgets for me?"

Elda smiled at Jim's thick Down East accent and replied, "One or two, Jim. I was going to call you today. Can you look after Vee for me? I have to pop down to DC on Friday for a day or two, but you never know how long these things actually take."

Jim fell into step with Elda as she continued walking to her car, inquiring, "Ah you off to skate or play yoah spook games?"

Elda jested back, "You know I'm just going to be sandbagging it, Jim."

Jim grinned and responded, "No worries then, Elder. Whatevah you need. Go shootin' with me when you get back from yoah goat rope?"

Elda stopped at her car and shook Jim's hand firmly. "You're on, Jim. Thanks much."

Elda turned to get into her car. Jim uncharacteristically put his hand out and touched her shoulder. She turned slowly back to face him, knowing what he would say.

His brows knitted over his eyes, Jim asked with concern, "You okay, Elder?"

Elda shrugged. She knew her friends worried about her. "I got a pulse, Jim."

Jim filled in the expected refrain, "Beats the alternahtive."

Elda gave a hollow laugh in reply.

Chapter Four

Plop. Plop. Nigel Davies sat with his feet up on Douglas Clark's battered wooden coffee table and surveyed the squalor of Doug's flat. The ceiling was peeling and periodically dropping chips of paint on the floor. The brown and gold speckled linoleum was cracked and starting to curl at the edges, and the kitchen stove, with one remaining working burner, was on its last legs.

Nigel had recently relocated to London, to try and escape the Russians who were threatening him. He had a fair amount of money from inheriting after his father's death and from doing insider trading when he was in Russia. Most of his money was hidden offshore in Cypress but he had also stashed a large amount of cash and his passport in his home safe. Luckily his Russian wife had not been able to access the safe. Nigel had snuck away from her in the dead of night. He hoped neither she nor the Russian handlers could find him.9

When he had arrived in London he had contacted his old college roommate, Doug, figuring he could involve him and his father as a safety net, if the

Russians found Nigel again. Nigel mentally made a note to thank his friend in Russia, Aurelio Ainsworth, for suggesting Nigel look for leverage.

Bored while sitting and watching Doug type at his computer, he decided to get Doug's attention. "Hey Doug, how would you like to make a lot of money?"

Doug looked up from his Windows laptop, "Doing what?" His pudgy hands unwrapped a Bounty candy bar and he took a large bite, displaying his slightly crooked teeth. They were framed by pink lips and topped by a scraggly mustache.

Nigel ran the fingers of one hand through his short cut wiry black hair and gestured around the room with his other. "First of all, move out of this slummy bedsit and move in with me. I have a ton of room in the house I just bought here in London near Hyde Park. You don't need to pay rent and you can just split the utilities with me. You might even save up enough to get those braces you told me you wanted."

Doug's wide face brightened behind his wireframe glasses, which perched crookedly on his nose. "Cor! Your place is posh. I'd love to live there. Are you sure?"

"Sure, just until you get back on your feet again. I know you're down on your luck."

Doug shut down and closed his computer, straightened his glasses, and gave Nigel his full attention. "You mentioned making money. Do you have a line on a job for me?"

"Of sorts." Nigel knew what Doug's answer would be even before he had asked the question. Doug had less regard for his father than Nigel had had for his own. Nigel had been incensed when his dad disowned him. And Doug felt like a beggar each time he asked his father to send him more money. It had been a commonality that bonded Nigel and Doug when they were roommates at Oxford. "How would you like to make a complete fool out of your old man?"

"Of my father, John? Of course I would! How?" asked Doug.

"Well, you know how straight and narrow your dad is. He's always preaching to you to do the right thing and telling you how good he is at his job and what a failure you are." Nigel inwardly smiled, knowing that his comments would get Doug's dander up and he'd be even more ready to agree to Nigel's plan.

"*Cor*, you know him well. *Yes*, count me in."

Nigel continued, "What if your dad got caught with his hand in the candy jar?"

Doug brightened, "How do we do that?"

"We just need him to get us some information that can be traced back to him. The scandal will most likely be short lived but he'll never be able to be *holier than thou* with you again."

"That's Brill, Nigel" Doug beamed his admiration for his friend.

"Of course it is. I thought of it. Stay tuned." Nigel strutted out the door.

***

After Nigel left, Doug surveyed his surroundings. "It *is* a dump," he said to himself.

Doug sat with a slightly warm ale at his side. He was beginning to have second thoughts about living with Nigel and Nigel's plan. He took a sip from his beer and mused that on the plus side he would no longer have to deal with a fridge that couldn't keep his food cold. He continued weighing his decision to set his dad up. *He never liked me*, he told his insecure self.

His dad had always signed him up for sports, only to be disappointed by Doug's lack of athletic abilities. He was constantly harping on Doug about his weight and slightly girlish looks. Doug knew his father was ashamed of his son. Doug rebelled against his father's constant harping by eating more candy bars and being even more sedentary. The upside was that Doug's rebellion drove him into books and his studies and he was able to get into Oxford. But even that upset his father.

He heard his father's sharp voice in his head: *Damnit, why couldn't you go to an American school. I'm a United States Senator. Now I have to explain this away.* His resolve toughened, Doug shook his fist at the peeling ceiling and shouted, "OK, Dad, you'll see what being a looser is all about. I'll show you."

A piece of ceiling paint fell down into his drink.

***

The weight of his body was suffocating. Nadia's nails ripped into Yaromir Kozlov's back, drawing blood. Yaromir shouted, "*Suka! Bitch!* We are just sparring. You better have not left me with scars." He rose from on top of her and looked at his back in the mirrored wall of the gym.

The smell of stale sweat was in the air. The black mat was scuffed and abraded in places. The gym was empty except for Nadia and Yaromir, two bicycles machines and one working treadmill set off to one side, waiting to be used. Black weights lay scattered by the weight rack.

Nadia jumped up. Taking advantage of Yaromir's distraction, she kicked him in the back of the knee, causing him to fall over. She laughed delightedly, only to be silenced as Yaromir rolled over and knocked her sideways off her feet. She landed hard on her hip and cursing him, spun her body away from his, narrowly avoiding a kick to the head.

Yaromir leapt on top of Nadia, knocking the wind out of her. He held her head back by her hair and whispered in her ear, "Enough?" She muttered back, "You know I never can get enough of you." He chortled and rose from her.

Nadia crawled to her feet and faced him, taking in his muscular torso glistening with sweat and licking her lips suggestively. She was rewarded by a growing bulge in his shorts.

***

In his apartment bedroom, Yaromir slammed Nadia's body down on the bed. Simultaneously she grabbed him behind his head and brought him crashing down on top of her. Her legs wrapped around his hips and she ground into him. She bit his lip, drawing blood. He swore and grabbed the top of her gym shorts and ripped them down, noting with satisfaction that she wasn't wearing any underwear. He pulled his penis out of his shorts and rammed into her, causing her to yell with delight. She grasped him tightly with her legs and they rocked together in a practiced battle.

Sated for now, Yaromir rolled off of Nadia, who reached over to the bedside table for a pack of cigarettes and a lighter. Yaromir reached for the bottle of vodka he had placed on the other bedside table and poured two shot glasses, handing one to Nadia. She knocked it back and handed him her glass for another. Yaromir poured and watched the second shot quickly disappear. Pouring again, he put the bottle down and held his hand out for her empty glass. "Again," she pouted.

He placed the glass aside, leered and said, "*Da*," rolling her over and forcing himself into her. She grunted and spread her legs further apart. He pulled out before she could come and went to wash himself. She reached down and used her fingers to finish up. When she rolled over, she saw Yaromir standing there naked, stroking himself while watching her. She crawled across the bed and put her mouth over his rigid penis, helping him come.

They lay side by side. Suddenly Yaromir said, "So how was your meeting with Adrik?" Nadia bolted up into a sitting position and stared down at him. Yaromir winked at her as he lay back calmly with his hands behind his head. "How did you know that?!" she asked defensively. Yaromir smirked and said, "I didn't. It was pure guesswork on my part. But thanks for confirming it."

Nadia hit him hard with both fists. Yaromir rubbed his chest and scowled at her, "*Blyad*'! *Fuck*! That's going to bruise," he snapped. Then he looked her in the eyes and said seriously. "Beware, Nadia, if I guessed it, Tosh will know about it. And you know he doesn't tolerate traitors."

Nadia flicked an imaginary piece of dust out of the air, stating, "I don't care what Tosh thinks." She looked down at her fingernails.

Yaromir rolled on top of her in a high plank position and pinned her arms to her side, "Look at me. This is important. What you do may affect me too. You should be worried."

Nadia raised her groin up to meet his and licked her lips suggestively, "Don't worry. His days are done."

Yaromir lowered himself down onto her and before he entered her muttered, "Yours may be shorter than his."

Chapter Five

"Ouch, your little nails and teeth are sharp!" Sitting on his black leather couch in his Moscow apartment, Yuri Kuznetsov pried the small orange ball of fur off of his hand. Katya curled up into his lap, purring, while Yuri scratched behind his ears. The sound of Yuri's phone ringing sent the cat flying off onto the couch next to Yuri. Yuri said softly, "*Papochka* didn't mean to scare you, Katya," and patted his lap invitingly. The cat jumped back and settled back down. Yuri stretched to reach the phone without disturbing Katya, but ended up falling off the couch and onto the floor. As he fell, Katya sprung off, hunched up, and hissed like a Halloween cat.

Yuri caught the call on the last ring. "*Privet,* Tosh." He listened to Tosh's command. "*Da. Kogda*? Okay, now then." He nodded and looked regretfully at his cat. "*Khorosho*. I am heading out. *Poka*." He placed the phone down and picked up his kitten with one hand. "It's okay, baby." He kissed Katya on the top of his head and then played with him for a few minutes. "*Chert*! *Damn*. Your claws are getting long. Remind me to cut them when I get back home."

Although his parents did not have a lot of money, Yuri had grown up in Russia in a family with a number of pets, two cats, a dog and a goldfish. His father was a construction laborer and Yuri—an only child—was a good student, expected to go to college. When Yuri was eight years old, both his parents died in a car accident and Yuri was sent to an orphanage. There, he picked up skills such as pickpocketing, lying, and orchestrating secret transfers of goods into the orphanage. As soon as Yuri could, he left to join the military and had become part of the Main Directorate of the General Staff of the Armed Forces of the Russian Federation, more commonly known as the GSU (*Glavnoe Razvedyvatel'noe Upravlenie*), transferring over to the Foreign Intelligence Service (*Sluzhba Vneshney Razvedki* or SVR) afterward. From his core family Yuri had a passion for learning and educated himself. He was a creative thinker with an expertise in logistics.

With an entrepreneurial streak, Yuri, while still working for the SVR, became a free agent, treading on thin ice since he acted as an agent for the CIA, and other United States agencies. He also did large job logistical planning for the Mafia. Recently, Tosh had recruited Yuri to work exclusively for him. Since Yuri's mistress, Natasha Ainsworth had left Moscow, and being in his mid-forties, Yuri had decided it was probably time to be more settled and had accepted a relocation to Moscow to take the job.

Yuri cleaned the cuts on his hand, selected a clean baby blue t-shirt from the bedroom bureau drawer, and drew it over his muscular chest. He tucked it into his black jeans and cinched his belt tight against his rock-solid abs. Yuri was a handsome man with a boyish charm and had no problems with the ladies. He texted his cat sitter and checked to ensure the cat had enough food and water, in case the sitter was late arriving.

"Be good Katya."

Holding his go-bag in one hand, Yuri locked his apartment door and jogged off in the direction of the Kremlin.

***

Poof! The black night swerved to avoid Stas Garin's sword and fell backwards into the volcano. With one click of his mouse Stas had just vanquished one of his enemies. He turned and ducked under a low bridge and ran a short way into a small cave. He reached into his backpack for a flashlight when across his computer screen flashed, TEKST. *Shtopat'*! *I was almost done with level 32 too!*

Stas paused the game and read the message from Tosh. Prior to being recruited by Tosh, Stas was an experienced hacker who lived in an apartment in a ramshackle multistory high-rise building that had been built in the Soviet era. It was dirty and filthy and had a broken elevator. With all his equipment, his electricity usage was rather high, but Stas kept the bill down by tapping into various neighbor's lines. The up side was walking the stairs to the 8th floor was the only exercise he had.

But now, with a regular paycheck and being an employee of the Kremlin, his living situation had improved. He glanced around his well-organized apartment with equipment humming, neatly aligned on a large wooden table, cords tie wrapped, leading to multiple outlets. He appreciated that the heat and electricity were covered as part of his employment agreement. Stas valued his job, and when Tosh called he dropped everything to respond.

He rapidly packed into his backpack his favorite laptop computer and checked the others, to ensure all of the processes he had initiated that morning were still on track. Leaving his equipment buzzing behind him, he headed off to catch the metro to the Kremlin.

***

In her Moscow apartment, Snezhana Chelovek pulled a tight black tank top on over her lacy black bra. She turned sideways to check her outfit in the full-length mirror on the back of her bedroom closet door. She drew herself up to her full height of 5' 7" and patted her tight belly. She ran her hands through her chestnut brown hair, automatically stopping at the nape of her neck, still feeling the shock of her missing ponytail. She smoothed the tank down over her pert breasts, feeling her nipples respond to her touch. Her tight black slacks showed off her long muscular legs and shapely hips.

Rummaging through a pile of shoes on the floor of her closet, she slipped her feet into a pair of black sandals. Restless with lack of activity, Snezhana picked up a well-worn card from the bedside table, and read again the words on the back, *Safe, but not boring. Enjoy, T.* She turned the card over to the number that she knew by heart and tapped the card on her other hand, while rocking slightly side to side, trying to decide whether to call or not. She threw the card back down on the bedside table and instead picked up her SR-1Vektor, to head out for some target practice.

Snezhana had followed in her great uncle's footsteps into the spy business. She was extremely patriotic and had shown in training that she was a good planner and had inherited the familial photographic memory. She also had lightning-fast reflexes, an excellent analytical mind, and could effectively kill when needed. Her ability to manipulate others, especially males, was unparalleled. That trait had initially worried her uncle, since Snezhana, while bored waiting for an assignment, was randomly drinking too much and picking up strangers for sex. These men could be anyone: even an American spy. If she picked up someone who was trying to elicit information from her, or use her to get more information about Tosh, she could potentially be a security risk. Hopeful that Snezhana could become his replacement, Tosh had warned her against continuing this practice and had set her up with a secure paramour who would satisfy her needs between operations.

Just then, Snezhana's phone brightened with an incoming message. Reading it, she ripped off her tank and pants and threw on a less revealing black button up shirt and pants that were stylish, but not as form fitting, and more suitable for work. She kicked off her sandals into the shoe pile and put on a pair of black sneakers. She paused, and, in the hope that Anatoly would also be there to spare with her at the gym after the meeting, she threw some workout clothes into a bag. Closing her apartment door and locking both locks, she set off for her uncle Tosh's office at the Kremlin.

***

On a rainy night on the south side of the Arno in Florence Italy, Anatoly Petrov waited outside the traitor's house. The traitor had sold classified information. Anatoly had been assigned to kill him in a way that sent a clear message to others who might think of betraying Russia.

He really should change his schedule. Every Wednesday he walks across the Ponte Vecchio bridge to the Il Tornabuoni Hotel to meet his lover.

The man exited his apartment and walked quickly down the street, glancing fearfully over his shoulder. Anatoly quietly followed the traitor, stopping in shadows whenever the man looked back.

Such a stupid man. He always glances over his right shoulder. Doesn't he realize that creates a blind spot for me to hide in?

Reaching the Via del Campuccio, Anatoly suddenly sprinted, catching the man and tapping him on his shoulder. The man startled and stopped. Anatoly asked in Italian, "Excuse me, but where is the Giardino Torrigiani?"

"No Italian, sorry."

The man turned to walk away but Anatoly put his arm around him and, while pulling the man into the nearby garden, he whispered into the man's ear, "Scream and you're a dead man. *Vy ponimayete?*"

The man opened his mouth to yell but Anatoly shoved a handkerchief into it. Anatoly held the man close to his body and slipped a garrote around his neck. Anatoly turned the struggling man around so he could see his eyes as Anatoly squeezed the life out of him. Wide eyed the man flailed and kicked at Anatoly while attempting to remove the garrote from his neck.

The traitor sagged in Anatoly's arms. Anatoly continued to strangle him to ensure he was dead. After a few minutes Anatoly dropped him onto the ground and checked his pulse. There was none. With gloved hands Anatoly searched the man and found his wallet. Anatoly removed and pocketed the handkerchief and inserted the wallet full of money and ID into the man's mouth. He positioned the arms at a ninety degree angle from the body and placed the man's feet together so that the corpse spelled the letter T.

Thank you. That was rewarding. Anatoly dispassionately looked at his own erection and waited until it went down before leaving the park.

*****

Click. The next day, back in his apartment in Moscow, Anatoly secured the loaded magazine in his newly cleaned MP-412 REX .357 Magnum revolver. He set it gently down on his kitchen table and patted it fondly. His guns were necessary tools of his trade, and Anatoly cared for each weapon as an extension of himself.

Anatoly was a trained assassin and he loved killing. For him there was nothing like the feel of a body struggling for its last breath as he held it close, strangling the life out of it. Anatoly was non-sexual and without any empathy for his fellow man. He felt it was an honor and a thrill to end a life. This, as well as his love of order and routine, combined with an aversion for drink or drugs made him the perfect soldier for the Kremlin.

An orphan, who bullied others in his youth, Anatoly grew up under the tutelage of the two arms of Russian intelligence. He began with the KGB, *Komitet Gosudarstvennoy Bezopasnosti* (Committee for State Security), which ended in 1991, and continued with the special forces in Russia's foreign military spy agency, the GRU, *Glavnoye Razvedyvatelnoye Upravlenie*, (Russian: Chief Intelligence Office). These organizations gave him structure and guidance, as well as a feeling of belonging. The strong killers in these organizations became father figures to him. His handler, Tosh, was the closest to family that he had ever known. His duty was first and foremost to Tosh, secondly, to his teammates, and thirdly to the Motherland.

Anatoly was carefully repacking his black leather kit bag with his weapons when he received a secure text from Tosh: *REPORT TO MY OFFICE AT 13:00 TODAY.* Anatoly glanced at his Rolex Cosmograph Daytona stainless-steel watch, a present to himself after his first kill. It was 12:30. He immediately grabbed his weapons bag. Leaving his *go-bag*, he shoved a clean change of underwear along with a spare t-shirt in the side pocket of the weapons bag. He carefully closed and double locked his apartment door, checked that his carefully placed piece of wire, the tell, was in place above the lock. Opening the door without first carefully removing the wire would set off a silent alarm, notifying Anatoly that his apartment had been breached by an unwanted guest. Satisfied, he jogged off towards the Kremlin.

***

Angelina lowered the scope from her eye and brushed a stray piece of black hair from her forehead. She instinctively felt the wind speed and direction and calculated the distance to Anatoly's door. "No. That would be too quick a death for you. I finally found you. *Svoloch',*" she whispered. Her tongue felt the gaps in her mouth where her molars had been.

She hissed, "I will make you pay for what you did to me, you bastard." Her three-month search was over.

51

Chapter Six

Whup-whup-whup. The helicopter landed on top of a roof in DC. Elda ducked under the rotating chopper blades and entered the federal building from the roof door. She let the heavy metal door slam shut behind her and jogged down the concrete stairs to Ed's floor, badged her way in, and trotted to his office.

As she entered the room, Jackson Taylor stood and rushed to greet Elda, exclaiming "Elda! It's great to see you again."

Jackson and Elda hugged warmly. Elda stepped back to take in Jackson. He had salt and pepper hair, a pitted face from childhood acne, and a hooked nose, which caused him to wheeze slightly when he breathed. Although he could not be considered handsome, he carried himself well, and had seemingly gained confidence since the last mission on which he and Elda had worked together. Elda could see Jackson's hazel eyes unblinkingly analyzing and observing her.

Jackson had been part of Elda's team on a joint mission with Tosh's team to defeat those who were out to assassinate the President of the United States. He had been instrumental in finding the assassins. His analytical abilities, combined with his deep love of research and solving puzzles made him an invaluable asset. In the previous mission, the combination of his skills, paired with Tosh's computer expert Stas' abilities, made them an ace team.

Elda looked at Jackson with compassion and sincerely replied, "It's great to see you again too, Jackson. How's the wife and kids?"

"Kids are growing up too fast. My oldest is off to college this Fall." Jackson held out his phone with a picture of his family for Elda to see.

Elda took it gently and winced. Masking her personal sadness at the loss of her own cozy life together with her wife, she replied, with a grin and cheery voice, "What a lovely crew," and handed it back. Elda sat down heavily in a chair on the side of Ed's desk and Jackson sat in one in front of the desk. "What do we have guys?" she asked, to refocus the conversation and her thoughts onto the work at hand.

"I noticed that a number of senators have suddenly booked a trip to Moscow, so I alerted Jackson and asked him to look into it," explained Ed, straightening his dark blue tie and brushing invisible lint from his crisply starched white dress shirt.

Jackson tipped his chair forward and propped himself on one forearm on Ed's desk where his laptop was sitting. He turned the computer towards Elda. Pointing at one of the open windows on the screen, Jackson continued the story, "And, I had noticed an uptick in disinformation on Social Media originating from Russia and being forwarded by these senators. They are amplifying the stolen election mantra and labeling democratic values as socialism, while they benefit from free healthcare and other benefits of the system. If they are not currently controlled by the Russians, they are ripe for the picking."

Elda took over the computer and rapidly browsed the information on Jackson's screen, memorizing it as she scrolled. Without pausing, she asked, "From your experience, Jackson, what phase do you think they are in the process?"

"Good question, Elda. I think they are ready to be turned. They have been primed with disinformation about the United States global actions that has been targeted to appeal to them and their quest for power through re-election. It will play well with the voters who believe in conspiracy theories. If Russia was controlling them now, then they would be more actively forwarding these posts and creating their own versions to send out."

Ed leaned in and spoke up, "I need your talents, Elda. You will be able to analyze which ones are all in and hopeless, and who we should focus on turning back around. Also, I would love to know what they have on these guys, or perhaps, will soon have, on them."

Elda scrolled down, scanning further into Jackson's information and inquired, "Do you have a full list of who they are?"

"Not yet," Ed answered, adding, "but by the time you land, we should."

Elda raised an eyebrow and queried, "I land?"

"Yes. In Moscow."

***

Elda popped her head into Frank Garcia's office. Football trophies took up an entire shelf of his bookcase.

"Hey Frank," she said cheerily, "I'm Elda. I work for Ed. Ed mentioned that you might be willing to work out with me at the gym? I would like to hone my reflexes."

Frank was a fit, 5 foot 10 inch, thirty-five year old from the agency. He worked out in the gym daily. Frank looked at the small, older woman in the doorway of his office. The set of his mouth signified he was holding back a laugh. He stated snidely, "I'm pretty aggressive, Elda. I wouldn't want to hurt you."

Elda smiled sweetly at him and replied, "Don't worry, Frank. I've got a good insurance policy."

Frank shrugged, "It's your funeral." He grabbed his gym bag and followed Elda to the locker room. Her back to him, Elda stripped off her shirt and pants and Frank noticed that her back muscles were well defined. Perhaps this *would* be a reasonable bout.

***

He crashed to the mat with a thud. In the company gym, Elda alertly stood a few steps away, waiting for him to get back up. He warily got up off the floor and looked at her in surprise. Elda gave him a sweet smile. "Beginner's luck," she jested. She stood in an athletic stance, with her feet solidly planted, knees slightly bent, hands up chest high, waiting for his next move.

Frank ran at Elda, who sidestepped his lunge, while sticking a foot out to trip him. He thudded down onto the mat face first. He rolled and rose up again and eyed Elda more seriously. She stood ready on the balls of her feet. He closed in on her. She stood her ground. Frank punched out at Elda, who deflected the blow neatly with her arm and landed an uppercut on his jaw, snapping his head back. He swung back at her only to connect with air. She bent over and neatly flipped him over her shoulder and down onto the mat again. Frank lay there on his back, trying to get his breath. Wheezing, he asked, "Who are you again?"

Elda replied with a smile, "Elda Ainsworth. I work for Ed."

Frank rolled onto his side and shakenly got up again. He walked around to Elda's side, and then to the back of her. Elda didn't turn around. Appearing confused, but taking advantage of Elda's position, Frank ran to tackle Elda, only to find himself flying through the air again. Missing the mat, he crashed down to the floor. Elda's moves were uniquely her own, a combination of many styles from a number of mentors over the years, as well as her own invented techniques. She mixed in the Peruvean street fighting style of Bakom with the Japanese martial arts, Aikido. She had been trained in boxing, was also well versed in the Brazilian fighting style, Capoeira, and was a Black Belt in the American martial arts system, Kajukenbo (ka for karate, ju for judo and jujitsu, ken for kenpo, and bo for Chinese boxing (kung fu)).

"Ouch. Damn, Elda. How did you know I was coming."

Elda stood and offered him a hand up. She replied, "The air pressure changed as you rushed at me. Sorry you missed the mat."

Frank grabbed her hand and yanked her down. She deliberately crashed down onto his chest, driving the air out of his body. She swiveled her body to the side and brought a knee onto his neck and grabbed his hair with one hand, stating, "You should cut this hair. Get a crewcut. This is a liability in the field." His arms flailed at her and she bashed his head back down onto the mat. His movements were starting to slow due to the lack of oxygen. Elda jumped back up. He massaged his neck, gulping for air.

Elda held out her hand again. "Next time, Frank, I won't be as lenient. Would you like a hand up and for us to declare the match was a draw?"

Frank nodded and held out his hand. "That is generous of you, Elda," he croaked. "You won the match."

She helped him up. "Yes, but we don't want the office to think you were bested by a little old lady, do we." Her eyes sparkled and Frank, now standing, looked at the doorway where a small crown had gathered to watch.

Chagrined he muttered, "So it was that obvious what I was thinking?"

Elda nodded. "Yes, Frank. Next time don't judge a book by its cover. Thanks for the match!" She slapped him on his back and strode out of the gym.

He coughed in response.

Chapter Seven

Anatoly glanced over his shoulder. The hair on the back of his neck was standing up. Something was off. He broke into a run, making a sharp turn at the next street corner and slid to a sudden stop. He waited, holding his breath to a quiet whisper to listen for footsteps behind him.

Silence.

He dashed back around the corner and whipped around to look up and then down the street.

No one.

Still he had the suspicion that someone was watching him. He took off again at a slower pace. Still the uneasy impression of being tailed remained.

He decided to make an unplanned stop at the Dobryakova Bakery to see if he could flush out anyone who might be following him. Once inside the bakery he was sorely disappointed that the stop wouldn't even yield sochniki, but decided to purchase chocolate blueberry muffins for the crew. Bag in hand, he stood at the doorway for a moment, scanning his surroundings. No-one. But the feeling still lingered.

He took off at a jog along Bol'shaya Nikitskaya Ulitsa towards the Kremlin. Running at a full tilt into the Alexander Gardens, he stopped at the main fountain on Manège Square and stood appearing to admire the horse statues. He could see no-one who matched anyone he had seen in his journey. He doubted many could have kept up with him on that last leg from the bakery to here. He decided to walk the rest of the way to Tosh's office in order to be cool and collected when he arrived.

His skin still crawled with the feeling that he was being watched.

***

Tosh pressed ENTER and sent the message to his grandniece, Snezhana Chelovek. Although it had only been a couple of months since he last saw her, it felt like much longer to Tosh. *Every time I see her she appears more mature, but she has only been on three missions. I wonder if she's ready to be groomed as my replacement. I best find someone soon. I am not getting any younger.*

Tosh thought back to the last time he had seen Snezhana. As her handler, Tosh had let her take the lead in a mission to neutralize an enemy agent.

Snezhana had left the safe house in St. Petersburg with Tosh trailing her.

Snezhana had memorized every detail available about the enemy and had quickly tracked him down in St. Peterburg. She jogged up to him while he was walking along the English Embankment near St. Isaac's Cathedral. As he turned to look at her, she reached out and stabbed him in the arm with a needle filled with a quick acting paralysis drug.

"Wha…?" He stopped mid word and as he wobbled, Snezhana hip checked him into the Reka Bol'shaya Neva canal. Snezhana watched as his lungs filled with water and he sank. It would be days before the body bloated with gases and floated up again.

Satisfied, Snezhana ran on to the Admiralteyskaya Metro station and slipped away on a train to the airport. Tosh met up with her again at his office in Moscow to debrief her.

She is turning into an excellent spy and assassin.

***

Which one of us will die on this mission? Shaking that unusually pessimistic thought from his brain, Tosh sat back in his office chair and surveyed the faces sitting in front of him.

Anatoly Petrov was sitting with a blank expression on his face, but his eyes were alert and he sat forward in his chair, as if to spring up at a moment's notice. A skilled killing machine, his large mass of muscles made his chair look like a child's playroom toy. He was dressed in a tailored and well pressed white shirt that stretched tight over his pectoral muscles. His blue jeans strained to contain his muscular thighs. His large hands that easily snapped necks, rested lightly on his legs. His feet were encased in steel-tipped black shoes. Tosh knew that Anatoly's belt doubled as a strangulation device. Anatoly had been well trained in hand-to-hand combat and spoke multiple languages. He could easily travel around the world to accomplish his assigned missions.

Yuri Kuznetsov, looking in size and musculature like Anatoly's twin, appeared happy to be with his teammates again. He was sitting upright in his chair with his hands folded in his lap. Yuri was a master at logistics. Although he looked threatening, he had washed out of the Russian assassin programs since he was a bit of a softy, especially when it came to animals and women. However, Yuri had no compulsions about working with the Kremlin, the Mafia, or anyone else who paid his salary. He had worked closely with the Americans and Elda for a number of years. Tosh looked him over and made a mental note, *I must ask him what those scratches are on his hands.*

Snezhana sat patiently, with an bright twinkle in her blue eyes, her short brown hair lay neatly around her ears and on the nape of her neck. Tosh silently approved of her well-tailored black shirt and black dress pants. Under Tosh's scrutiny, she reached up and checked her ponytail that was no longer there.

Stas Garin sat slumped in his chair, as if he still had a computer in front of him, but Tosh guessed that Stas' favorite T-Platforms rugged laptop was in the well-worn canvas backpack on the floor between Stas' legs. Stas was slender and pale, with dark circles under his eyes, and dressed in a wrinkled beige t-shirt and faded blue jeans.

Stas was a hacker who Anatoly had used in a previous mission to plant replacement DNA information into a woman's record, so that she would be successfully reported as dead. The DNA of the deceased was from a prostitute that Anatoly had taken the initiative to kill. Anatoly was impressed with Stas' professionalism and computer expertise and had reported it to Tosh. Tosh, recognizing the need for a greater degree of computer literacy on his team had brought Stas on board for Operation Bittman.

"It's good to see you all again," started Tosh. Anatoly raised his hand. "Yes, Anatoly."

Anatoly gestured to the sideboard with coffee, sochniki pastry and Anatoly's muffins on it. "I can hear better with a sochniki and coffee…"

Tosh motioned to the food. "Sorry, Anatoly, that was remiss of me. Let's all get a bite to keep our energy up while I brief you. I really don't know how you keep your weight down, eating the number of pastries that you do, Anatoly. It would make me pudgy," Tosh said while patting his flat belly.

"Da, Tosh, what a huge stomach you have there. I would worry if I were you." Anatoly jumped up with delight, patted his own flat, muscular, six-pack abdomen, and grabbed a pastry of each type. Teasingly, Snezhana tucked a napkin into his collar and poured their coffee.

Once they were settled, Tosh began again, "We have a mission that will pit us against the United States of America. There are a number of distinct parts of this mission. Phase One is to contact an asset who is currently in London and evaluate the need for an intermediary. If none is needed, or, if at any time this person outlives his usefulness, you will terminate him. Yuri, you will be his handler. And since you have the contacts and experience to do so, you will also handle the logistics for moving staff and weapons to London and, if we need to, also to the United States. Anatoly, you will ensure the asset's cooperation."

Stas sat up straighter and looked scared. Tosh looked at him reassuringly and consoled him, "Don't worry, Stas. Your mission will be to gather intelligence on a group of United States senators who are coming to Moscow for a business trip and briefing. You will look for any and all weak points that we can exploit. Snezhana, we will need your calculated charms to help on this part of our mission."

Snezhana's face fell. She appeared disappointed that there was no killing involved in her part, but dutifully answered, "*Da ser.*"

Stas exhaled a large sigh of relief. Tosh noticed with approval that Snezhana was watching each team member's reaction. He continued with the briefing, "Once we find who we can leverage in this group, Anatoly will give them a strong message to help with their cooperation. Our goal is 100% compliance, and, if we cannot get that, we will wait and eliminate the outliers after their return to the United States. Any assassination however, *cannot* be traced back to the Kremlin."

Anatoly nodded, acknowledging his role as the assassin.

"Now, here's where we will need to work very closely as a team and brush off some of the Cold War skills that you have learned, from me, and also in our last mission, from Elda. We hope to be obtaining information from one of the senators on the United States Intelligence Committee. There can be no digital trace of any of our work. Where we do need to use electronics, we will need you, Stas to ensure that we leave no trail. And we will use drop boxes and each other as couriers. So we will spend some time together here, brushing up on our note passing, sharpening our pick pocket skills, and setting up our communication protocols."

"What is our end goal?"

"Excellent question, Snezhana. We are to turn as many of the senators as we can into an arm of the Russian propaganda machine. There is an upcoming election year in the United States. We want to disrupt it as much as possible. And, we also want to continue to exploit their weaknesses in cybersecurity, intelligence and warfare. We want to pick their brains dry and start a hidden funnel of ongoing information from inside the United States to the Kremlin. It is all part of keeping Russia strong and Russia's enemies weak. America thinks the Cold War ended and we are now friends, but they are wrong. We have always worked to bring it to its knees. Khrushchev declared in 1956, "*My vas pokhoronim!*" These words, 'We will bury you,' still hold true to today. Our goal was, and still is, to weaken the Americans and to obtain a dominant position in the world."

The team nodded as they absorbed the mission. Tosh spoke again. "There has been an ongoing cyber misinformation campaign, mainly run through Russia's GRU Unit 74455. Our instructions are just a small piece of the entire plan to destroy American democracy. Others may take over after we burrow our way in, but if we fail, there could be a strong anti-Russia president elected. We *cannot* allow that to happen. Although this is a only a small part of the overall operation, anything is only as strong as its weakest part. That will *not* be us. Russia's future leadership in the world depends on our success. *Khorosho?*"

"*Ya ponimayu,*" answered Yuri. The others shook their heads in agreement.

"Good. Go home and get your go-bags and settle your affairs. We start in the morning."

Chairs scraped back in concert on the linoleum floor. They stood to leave. Tosh cleared his throat. "One last thing…" Hearing a catch in his breath, they turned as one and stared at him.

"Failure equals death."

***

The sunlight glittered off the towers of St. Basil's Cathedral. Certain that she was being followed, Snezhana picked up her pace. She ran into Zaryadye Park and headed to the floating bridge to get an elevated view of her surroundings. She looked back at the red wall of the Kremlin and along the banks of the Moskva River and then scanned the pathways leading into the Park. Turning she looked over at the Concert Hall and ice cave. Nothing stood out for her. She walked slowly down the ramp of the bridge. The feeling of being tailed had ebbed. *I know there was someone there. But who?*

***

The hairs on Anatoly's neck were standing up again. He wondered, *Who was following him?* He broke into a jog. He dashed into Alexander Garden and slowed respectfully as he went by the Tomb of the Unknown Soldier. Passing the tomb, he looked around to see if he could spy anyone. *Nothing.* He started to run again, heading to the Kutafya Tower. He scanned the top of the tower for anyone. While alertly surveying his surroundings, he abstractly wondered how the squat building like structure could have been named a tower. Personally he felt it lived up to the original translation of *ugly squat woman*. The bottom part just looked like a bunch of whitewashed cinderblocks. The top was more rugged and manly.

Anatoly headed away from the tower to the Aleksandrovsky Sad metro station. He stood with his back against a wall and surveyed the other passengers. No one looked familiar. Why couldn't he shake this sense that he was being watched? A train pulled into the station and Anatoly jumped on.

The doors closed. The feeling of being tailed immediately subsided.

***

Yuri ambled back to his apartment, unaware of the shadow behind him.

***

Alertly looking for anyone who might be following her, Snezhana received a text to return to Tosh's office immediately. She did an about face and settled into a slow jog back.

***

Anatoly dashed off the train at Pushkinskya a second before the doors closed. No one else had jumped off. He jogged under the vaulted ceilings and chandeliers of the station and rode up the escalator to exit into Pushkinskya Square. His phone binged. He was wanted back at Tosh's office immediately. He wheeled around and headed back into the station.

***

Yuri's phone buzzed indicating he had a secure message. He opened it up and saw that he had been ordered back to Tosh's office. Shrugging, he made a U-turn and started a slow run back.

***

There was no pastry, nor coffee and tea laid out. Anatoly knew that to be a bad sign. Snezhana, Yuri and he sat anxiously waiting for Tosh to enter the conference room. The door slammed open and Tosh appeared. He said grimly, "Who thought they were being followed just now?"

Anatoly put his hand up and glanced around. Snezhana had also raised her hand. Yuri looked sheepish with his hands folded in his lap.

Tosh paced in front of the room, continuing his interrogation. "And, did you detect who was following you?"

"*Nyet*," both Snezhana and Anatoly said in unison.

Tosh turned to Yuri and said sadly, "And you had no clue that you were being followed?"

Yuri shook his head and asked, "Was I?"

Tosh took a deep breath and addressed his team. "You three are operatives. I expect you all to be able to at least detect that you have a tail and be able to identify who is following you. That done, you should either shake that person or turn the tables on him or her."

Yuri rubbed the back of his neck and sat up straighter.

"Snezhana, going up onto the floating bridge to get a view of the entire area was a good move. But it also told the person following you that you were onto having a tail."

Snezhana nodded.

"Anatoly, very good evasive technique, jumping onto a train a few seconds before the doors closed. But you also could have had a front tail."

Anatoly rubbed the stubble on his chin and inquired, "Did I have a front tail?"

Tosh shook his forefinger at him and answered sharply, "*Nyet*, but the fact that you had to ask is telling, isn't it?"

Stung, Anatoly hung his head in shame.

Already in deep water, Yuri asked, "Who was tailing us?"

Tosh replied with satisfaction, "I was."

Snezhana looked at him wide-eyed and blurted out, "All of us?"

Tosh stood a bit straighter and his eyes glinted with pleasure, "Yes. I would have been surprised if any of you detected me. It would have meant that I was slipping. But I am going to have all three of you practice being tailed and detecting your tail. This may be considered an old-fashioned skill by people such as my boss, Adrik, but it is a key one that I want my team to master."

Anatoly asked in a downcast tone, "Where are we going?"

Tosh replied sternly, "There's a new advanced training academy outside of Moscow. Since you, Anatoly, and you, Snezhana, have graduated from the Institute already, this will take you to the next level. Yuri, since you were not trained at the Institute, this will be a struggle for you, but I am sure you can do it. I've arranged for you three to go there for 3 days, and, during the same timeframe, for Stas to get some advanced hacking and cyber surveillance training at the Conservatory. You will not need to take anything with you. Leave your phones and weapons on my desk. The bus is waiting for you outside."

***

Stas, Yuri, Anatoly and Snezhana piled into the bus for their trip to the training academy. Once on board, they were blindfolded. The last thing they heard before noise cancelling earphones were placed over their ears, was Tosh saying, "Stay Alert."

The bus swayed and made many turns. Finally it stopped. Yuri, Anatoly, and Snezhana were pulled off of the bus, bound, and thrown into a van. Stas was led into a building and once inside led to his seat in a training room. His mask and earphones were removed.

***

The clatter of the keyboards filled the room. Fingers flying, Stas sat opposite another trainee, working to be first to breach the firewalls of their target server. Stas' head swiveled as he checked the three monitors, with multiple windows opened on each one. The goal was not only to breach the firewall, but to detect and disable the other intruders.

"*Blyad*'" The student's exclamation signified Stas's first attack was successful. Stas noted the student frantically trying to re-engage after being

74

kicked off. Satisfied, Stas went after his next target while keeping his firewall attack going.

"Chert." Number two had succeeded. Not slowing down, Stas made mental note of his second conquest. Pivoting his cursor to one of his windows, he parried a strike from another student. It was exciting to be pitted up against those who were as good as, and potentially better than, he was.

Success. He broke through the first firewall. But there were additional firewalls and code that attacked any intruder to overcome. He suspected the second firewall was on a different machine and operating system. His own firewall system had a first firewall that was Windows based, the second was Apple's and the third was Linux. Only the expert coders could breach his machine. He dreaded the attack code, however. A good defense system could identify the IP address of an intruder and reach his machine, causing it to fail either through repeated DoS attacks, code injection, or even breach the protections around the Root and disable the computer. Stas was confident that his Root password was extremely strong and that there were no holes in his OS that would allow an intruder to get that far.

Stas had never had to type or think as fast as he was going right now. His adrenaline rush was intoxicating. *There!* He was through the second wall of defenses.

"*Govno*! *Shit*!" Suddenly he was dead in the water. His seatmate smiled at him. Stas immediately kicked off his macros that had been recording his progress and within minutes was back where he left off, only now he had the signature of his attacker. His fingers were cramping from going so fast. He cursed at the student, "*Idi na khuy*!," pausing briefly in his typing to emphasize his curse with his middle finger. His seatmate was no longer smiling. Stas gave him a friendly nod and set up a program to continue the attack on him, while working to punch a hole in the third wall. He got through and his monitors went blank. He tried to reboot and couldn't. His computers had been wiped clean. He couldn't wait to learn how they did that!

***

The van stopped. Anatoly, Snezhana, and Yuri were untied and their blindfolds were removed. In front of them was a large building. One of the academy's instructors was there to welcome them as they piled out of the van.

"You are here to listen and learn and practice what you have learned. On the third day you will be returned to the van and dropped off for your final exam. If you pass, you will be allowed to keep your current jobs. Study hard and do well."

***

Day three had arrived. Yuri, Anatoly and Snezhana were cuffed and blindfolded and thrown back into the van. They swayed as the van sped towards its destination.

The van's brakes squealed as it suddenly halted. Unable to see around his blindfold, Yuri perceived Snezhana and Anatoly on either side of him in the back seat of the van. He could feel the smaller presence, Snezhana, jiggling to get free of her cuffs. Suddenly there was more room on one side of Yuri. Apparently Anatoly had been moved. Yuri wondered if Anatoly had been dropped off at that stop. He whispered, "Snez, do you have any idea what is happening?" A voice from the front of the van shouted, "Quiet!"

The van started up again. Yuri sat in his same position and swayed into Snezhana as the van moved through the streets. It stopped again. Only Yuri was left. Yuri sat nervously, waiting for his drop off. The van stopped suddenly throwing him forward. He caught himself from falling off the seat by grabbing in the air and contacting the top rail of the seat in front of him.

A man tugged at Yuri's arm and pulled him out of the van. Yuri's blindfold was ripped off and his cuffs removed. Yuri blinked from the brightness of the grey sky. He glanced around and saw that he was in a city, which he assumed was still Moscow. The man spoke to him, "You will find your way back to the Kremlin. Along the way you may be followed. It will be your mission to detect and evade the tails. This is your final exam. Show what you have learned and make Russia and your instructors proud."

Yuri checked the grey sky to see where the brightness of the sun was. He glanced at his watch and calculated where the sun should be that time of day and what direction to head in. He took off at a run.

***

There! Snezhana had seen that man previously about a mile before. She dashed around a corner into an alley way and sped to the end where she climbed and jumped over the chain link fence and through an empty gravel lot to the next street. On the corner was a motorcycle. She dashed over to it and found the keys in the glove compartment. She roared off down the road.

***

Breathing hard, Anatoly stood with his back against the warehouse door. He heard a man run past his location and onward up the street. Anatoly looked around the warehouse and found a forklift. He drove to the door he had entered—blocked it with the forklift—and waited. The footsteps returned and the owner of them tried to open the door. Failing, he ran off in the direction that they had both come from. Anatoly got his bearings and crossed the warehouse to a door leading to a street parallel to the one he had entered on. He listened, then opened the door slowly. No-one was around. He jogged on towards the Kremlin.

***

Delivery day! Yuri wandered into a grocery store and slipped out back where the delivery truck was unloading boxes for the store. Yuri had a quick chat with the man delivering the items and fell into step with him, helping to unload the cargo. When they were done, Yuri hopped into the back of the truck.

***

A surprised Tosh stood up and clapped when Yuri was the first of the three to enter his office. "*Pozdravleniya*, Yuri. You are the first to make it back. Congratulations again. Please go to conference room number one to get your debriefing."

***

Yuri strutted to the small room to find out how he had done. The instructor motioned him to a chair and opened with, "I am surprised to see you come back first, Yuri. Although you did reasonably well years ago when you were first trained, detecting and shaking a tail were not your academic strong points. How did you do so well now?"

Yuri acknowledged the backhanded recognition of his success and stated, "I know I am not as good as Snezhana nor Anatoly, so I needed to outwit everyone, using what I know best, and that's how to get things from point A to point B. In this case it was me that needed to get there." Yuri went on to tell the instructor how he had befriended the delivery truck driver and had himself dropped off a short way away from the Kremlin. "Surmising that you probably had people at the last mile, I slipped under another truck that I knew made deliveries inside the Kremlin and dropped off just inside the gate before the inspection point."

"Congratulations, Yuri. You have graduated."

***

A loud knock on Tosh's office door alerted him to a large crate outside of his office. He grabbed his wrecking tool and scanner and walked around the crate, examining it. From inside he heard, "It's safe, uncle, please, just get me out of here." Tosh pried open the box to see Snezhana sitting on the bottom, of it with her knees tucked up under her chin. She maneuvered a hand out and extended it to Tosh. "Can you please help me out?" Tosh suppressed a grin and reached out for Snezhana's hand. "Yuri beat you here, but you are number two," he stated, pulling her up and lifting her out.

"Number two! *Chert!*"

***

Snezhana walked into the conference room to get her final debriefing from her instructor. "You're limping. Are you hurt?" he inquired.

Snezhana reached down to massage her thigh and answered, "*Nyet,* I am just cramped."

The instructor waved to a chair and motioned for her to sit. Anxious to be done with the training and onto the mission, Snezhana sat, moving her legs back and forth as they chatted.

The instructor tapped his pen on the folder in front of him. He opened it and laid out pictures from the surveillance test and pointed to each one as he told Snezhana, "You were very successful in detecting and evading all of the tails we put on you.

How did you get to Tosh's office? We had agents along the last mile."

Snezhana sat up straight with pride and informed him, "I mailed myself there via interoffice mail. I went to a building that I suspected you might not be watching and grabbed a shipping crate. I smiled sweetly at a clerk, and promised him I'd see him again if he would help me surprise my uncle. He willingly played along and used a dolly to roll me over to Tosh's office."

The instructor nodded his recognition of a job well done and added, "*Ochen' khoroshiy*. You have graduated."

Snezhana frowned with a question that had occurred to her. She blurted out, "*Spasibo*. But how did Yuri beat me? I was moving very fast and even stole a motorcycle to cover the last few miles."

The instructor filled her in.

"*Blayd'*. He is clever."

***

A soldier cut out of formation and marched over to Tosh's office.

Tosh looked the soldier up and down, commenting dryly, "The uniform suits you, Anatoly."

Anatoly smoothed down the sides of his uniform and stood straighter. He thanked Tosh, "*Spasibo, ser.*"

Tosh deflated him by adding, "Yuri and Snezhana are already here."

"*Der'mo!*" Anatoly growled, "I never should have spent that much time in the warehouse." He repeated his swear and stamped his foot, "Shit!"

Tosh said dryly, "As interesting a story as that probably is, Anatoly, please go to the conference room for your debriefing."

Spinning around, Anatoly rushed out the door to get his grade and to be able to leave and get some decent food.

***

Anatoly flew into the conference room and skidded to a stop, standing at attention. The instructor waved him to a chair. He referred to a folder and stated, "Despite your grumbling about schoolwork, you did extremely well on all your courses."

Impatient to leave, Anatoly briefly acknowledged the praise, "*Spasibo, ser.*"

The instructor placed pictures from the file upside down on the table so Anatoly could see each one. They showed Anatoly spotting a tail and shaking it. Anatoly glanced at each one and then looked expectantly at the instructor. The instructor continued, "You also did excellent in the final practical surveillance exam. You detected and evaded everyone we threw at you. We did see you march into Tosh's building, but we were too far away to intercede. Well done."

"*Spasibo, ser.*" Anatoly pushed back his chair and stood, waiting to be dismissed.

The instructor held up his hand to pause Anatoly's exit and asked, "Any questions?"

"*Nyet.*"

The instructor gestured towards the door, "*Pozdravleniya.* You have graduated. You may leave."

Anatoly was gone before the instructor had put the period on his sentence.

***

"Where is he?" Snezhana queried no one in particular.

Snezhana, Anatoly, and Yuri sat in the conference room waiting for Tosh. The table was bare of coffee and pastries. Anatoly growled, "What have we done wrong this time?" Just as he finished getting that out, the conference room door opened, and Tosh strolled in, followed by Stas. Behind them a man rolled a cart with assorted pastries, including Anatoly's beloved sochniki, and coffee, tea and water. Anatoly was helping himself even before the cart rolled to a stop.

"Congratulations all of you. You have done well at the school and passed your tests. Stas has also excelled at his computer cyber security school. You made me proud with all the hard work you put in. Enjoy the pastries while we refocus on the mission at hand."

They settled down at the table, each looking excited to restart their operation. Tosh continued his briefing, "In a few days the group of United States senators will be visiting Moscow and staying at the Crowne Plaza Hotel. Stas is working to obtain the list. He will stay here to work with me and you three will book yourself rooms at the hotel. You will report here each day for additional information until they arrive. *Ponimat*?"

"Ya Ponimayu."

"Da."

"Da, ser."

'Yes."

Tosh continued, "Yuri and Anatoly, we will need to work the asset in London too. Yuri, you will use your logistics expertise and stage the equipment there for that part of the operation."

Yuri gave Tosh a thumbs up, and replied, *"Da, ser!"*

Tosh waved at the pastries. "Take as many as you like, then go home, pack your bags, and take the afternoon off as a celebration of job well done." He handed a small white paper bag to Anatoly, and added, "This will keep your pockets clean."

"Spasibo, ser," Anatoly said, selecting some sochniki and dropping them into the paper bag. Giving a thumbs up signal, he jogged out the door. The rest of the team soon followed.

***

The music wasn't to Yuri's taste, but the scenery definitely was. Yuri sat back in his leather chair at a small round wooden table in the Night Flight club on

Tverskaya Street, near the Kremlin, waiting for his contact to arrive. The night was young but the scantily clothed women were wandering around stirring interest in the upcoming striptease act. Yuri sipped his expensive beer, noting that, to him, it tasted the same as the cheaper stuff.

His contact sauntered into the room, dressed in a denim long sleeved shirt, with the top three buttons open to reveal his chest hairs. He also wore tailored, tight-fitting jeans and leather cowboy boots. Yuri flagged him over to the table.

Yuri opened with, "Long time no see, man. What are you drinking?"

The man, who had been ogling one of the girls, said, distractedly, "I'll have whatever you're having."

Yuri waited until the waiter had come and gone with the drink before starting business. "I was wondering if you were doing any work in the United Kingdom lately, especially, say, London?"

The man glanced at him and replied, "*Da*, we are going there quite frequently." He returned to people watching.

Yuri pressed on, "If I remember correctly, there's a couple of favors that you owe me?" That got the man's full attention. Seeing the man stiffen, Yuri added, "I only have a small suitcase that I'd like delivered outside of the regular mechanisms."

The man visibly relaxed and inquired, "When?"

Yuri thought and then answered, "I could have it ready for you tomorrow, if that is convenient?"

The man took a sip of his beer and replied, "*Da.* That works. No problem. Is that it? I do owe you for the work you did for me."

Yuri smiled and assured the man, "Don't worry. I'll collect on the debts another time, but yes, that's it for now. *Spasibo.* I assume I drop it off at the same place?"

"*Da.*" The music swelled and died, and the announcer introduced the first act of the night.

Chapter Eight

Elda's gut tightened as she deplaned at Sheremetyevo International Airport in Moscow. She kept her head down to change the angle of her face for the facial recognition software, though the probability that she would be recognized was very low. Her current identity papers had never been used before. She had changed her hair color to black, her eyes to a blue-hazel, and had inserts in her cheeks. Even her eye shape was altered by Botox injections in her brows. Small lifts in her shoes made her appear taller and a heavy jacket added bulk to her torso. She inhaled deeply as she walked up to passport control.

A stern-faced officer stared down at her. "*Privet*, Miss… Violetta Coton?"

"Yes, *Privet*." Calming her churning insides, Elda kept her face composed and open.

He spied the Winnie the Pooh book that she was holding and raised his eyebrows. He held out his hand for her to give it to him. She passed him the book, watched, and waited. She always carried it with her into Russia, just to see the look on their faces as they flipped the pages, wondering if there was some sort of code or secret message hidden in it.

Elda got a kick out of playing harmless mind games.

The officer leafed through the book, but found nothing untoward and wordlessly handed it back. He looked down at her papers again, asking, "What brings you to Russia from your home city of Toronto?"

"Just some much needed vacation. I wish to see the world while I'm still young enough to do so." Elda casually brushed back the front of her hair so that her whitening temples showed.

The officer nodded and asked curtly, "And what do you do?"

When lying, it was always good to stick as close to the truth as possible. Being an ACE Certified Personal Trainer, Elda gave her partially true answer, "I am a personal trainer for older adults."

The officer looked her up and down, assessing her physical condition. Her physique matched her story. He nodded, stamped her passport and waved her through. Elda shouldered her backpack and walked out into the sunlight to wave down a taxi. As she expected, one was ready for her. She jumped into the taxi and ordered, *"Pozhaluysta, otvezite menya v otel' Crowne Plaza."*

Before leaving for Russia, Elda had traveled to DC, where she had been briefed by Ed and Jackson that a contingent of United States senators was arriving in Moscow and staying at the Crowne Plaza Hotel. By the time Elda had left the States, Ed had not yet obtained the final list of senators, but he had assured Elda again that he would send it to her the moment he had it. She was hoping to observe the group and see who was shadowing them. If Russia acted as they usually did, the senators' visit would include drugs, sex and blackmail. She wondered who would be controlling them. Would Tosh be in on it in any way? She shuddered at the thought of being his enemy again.

***

Anatoly glanced over his shoulder. *"Der'mo,"* he muttered. He picked up the pace. The uneasy feeling of having a tail persisted. His frustration at not being able to catch whomever it was, stuck in his throat and furrowed his brow. He whirled around. No one.

He still sensed that someone was following him so he started to jog and dashed down the Kitay-gorad Metro escalator as quickly as the steep descent would allow. At the bottom of the escalator he dashed around the imposing granite columns and over the matching marble floors, wheeling around and hopping onto the up escalator. He scanned the faces of the descending riders. None looked familiar. He popped out into the daylight and took off at a jog for Tosh's office at the Kremlin, arriving slightly out of breath. The rest of the team was already seated. They, and Tosh, looked at Anatoly with a frown of concern.

"Is there a problem, Anatoly?" inquired Tosh.

Anatoly was uncharacteristically shaken and hesitant as he answered Tosh, "*Nyet, da, mozhet byt'*, … I really don't know. I keep feeling as if I am being followed, but I can't detect anyone. When I got back to my apartment yesterday there was a bouquet of flowers at the door. I called around to the florists and one of the florists disclosed that he had received an order for a delivery from a female, who had requested that there be no note. She paid cash. It was a very busy day and he couldn't remember what she looked like."

Tosh's eyes narrowed. "It's not like you to have a fan, Anatoly. The tail must be good if you can't detect it after your additional training. Ten to one this is not good news. Stas, can you see if you can get any footage from the florist or any of the cameras that may be in the florist's neighborhood?"

"*Da*, Tosh."

Tosh ended the discussion of Anatoly's problem by bringing the team up to date on the mission status, "Meanwhile, let's get down to business. Stas has obtained the list of senators. They will be arriving tomorrow and staying at the Crowne Plaza Hotel here in Moscow. We will spend today memorizing the information on each senator, reviewing the hotel layout, practicing the exchange of information, using drop boxes, and picking pockets. Stas will ensure we have the proper security and software on our laptops and phones. Then we will review our operational plans for tomorrow."

The atmosphere in the room was electrified, each person perched at attention, like race horses at the starting gate. Tosh continued. "Tomorrow, Stas will stay here with me. Yuri and Snezhana you will go to the Crowne Plaza Hotel with Anatoly, but you two stay separate from Anatoly, so you can see if anyone is following him. *Khorosho?*"

A tense chorus of "*khorosho*" echoed in reply. Tosh tapped his laptop and the large screen monitor in the conference room brightened. He pressed another key and up popped a picture of a man in his 50's with a deeply dimpled chin, greying blond hair and bright blue eyes. He was the poster boy for a senatorial success story.

Anatoly looked quizzically at Tosh who answered the unspoken question, "This is John Clark, your number one target, a senator on the United States Intelligence Committee. John has tickets to go to London after this. I am assuming he is going to visit his son, Doug, who is currently living in London in his college roommate's house. His roommate, Nigel Davies, is Henry Davies' son. If you remember from our last operation, Henry was the MI6 mole that we ferreted out. I don't believe in coincidences. I suspect that Nigel was being used to exploit his father, but any information on *that* mission died with my old boss, Alexei – that traitor."

***

Elda, still in disguise, entered the Crowne Plaza Hotel. She heard the murmur of voices from a group of United States senators carrying across the bar. She spotted the group was mingling just outside the bar, waiting to be seated. The staff ran up and quickly pushed a few tables together and gestured for them to sit. Elda walked through the lobby to enter the bar. Spying the Russian team seated at the bar, she immediately did a 180 and entered the hotel gift shop. That sighting confirmed for her that she was in the right place. Elda peeked out from the gift shop to observe the action.

Yuri swiveled in his bar stool to face in the direction of the senators and sipped his cranberry juice in a cocktail glass. Snezhana sauntered by, swiveling her hips in her black leather pants. Anatoly sat a table facing sideways to the elevator with a shot glass filled with water and another eight ounce glass of water in front of him.

Elda watched the lobby traffic out of the corner of her eye, calculating the risk of entering the bar. She needed to avoid Snezhana with her photographic memory and ability to recognize faces. Elda's disguise had passed the airport scans, but both Snezhana and Tosh were as good, if not better, than the airport equipment. Just then Snezhana left the bar and sashayed across the brightly carpeted open area to the glass-fronted elevators.

After Snezhana entered the elevator, Elda strolled over to the bar and ordered a vodka and water chaser. Yuri looked briefly at her and then went back to observing the senators. Elda adjusted her glasses, activating a hidden camera, and scanned the group. The pictures were automatically snapped and stored in a small chip inside the frame. Elda casually glanced at Anatoly, who was sitting perched on the edge of his chair. He held his cell phone as if he was checking his messages, but he was also filming the senators.

A new senator joined the group. The group of senators gravitated to the latest arrival. The rest of the senators were deferential to him. Elda zoomed in on his face to send a good picture to Ed to find out who this man was. As Elda watched from the bar, the newest arrival separated from the group and paraded out into the carpeted open area, looking up at the women who were hanging out around an upper balcony. Elda saw Snezhana lean over the balcony, point her finger at him and motion for him to join her. In a jaunting manner, he struck out for the nearby elevators and ascended.

Elda paid her bill and slowly wandered to the elevators, looking casually up as she moved across the open area. The Senator was having a brief discussion with Snezhana, handing her some money and receiving a room key in return. *The sting is on.*

After entering her hotel room, Elda removed her shoes and placed them on top of the bedspread. With less than an hour remaining in the time window for uploading the data, Elda sat on the edge of the bed and removed the heel of her shoe. She gently pulled out and unwrapped a flexible antenna. She twisted one temple tip from her glasses to reveal a screw driver head and, using that, carefully unscrewed the back of her phone. From her phone she removed a spare circuit board. She connected a small adapter to the circuit board and removed the tip from the other eyeglass temple and plugged that end into the free end of that adapter. She snaked a 3.5mm headphone jack connector from under the circuit board and connected that to a headphone-to-Lightening adaptor for her phone. Then she connected the whole contraption to the Lightening port of her phone.

Pressing a few buttons on her phone, she waited as the pictures she took, along with additional information, were uploaded to the internet to start their circuitous and anonymous journey to Ed. She glanced at her watch. She sent up a short prayer that it had completed the upload in time to catch the satellite flyby.

***

Using a corner of Tosh's desk to work on, Stas typed rapidly on his laptop. Frustrated he exclaimed, "*Govno*. The flower shop had no cameras, Tosh."

Sitting at his desk, Tosh looked up from the contents of a manilla folder that he was studying and said blandly, "That's unfortunate, Stas. Did you find any cameras in the neighborhood?"

Stas, hunched over his laptop, quickly typed onto his keyboard. "There is surveillance at the nearby metro station, but there's a lot of traffic that goes in and out and I have no idea what the woman looks like."

Tosh closed his folder and pushed it to one side of the desk, giving Stas his full attention. "Can you queue that footage up for me? Perhaps I have seen her before."

"*Da.*"

With a few keystrokes, Stas set the video to the correct frame and moved with his computer to sit next to Tosh. Stas drove the software while Tosh scanned the recording of crowds entering and exiting the metro station on the day of Anatoly's flower delivery. "Stop. Go back a couple of frames. *Tam! There! Stop!*" He pointed at a shadowy figure whose face was almost obscured by a hoodie and wraparound sun glasses. He sat back in his chair and addressed the image, "What are you doing in Russia, Angelina Rodin?"

"How can you tell who that is?" Stas asked, confused and impressed.

Tosh rubbed his right upper arm and replied tersely, with a hint of anger, "I never forget an opponent. Especially when they left me with a large bruise from a tire iron."

***

Wondering if anyone was assigned to follow her, Elda glanced over her shoulder while jogging along the Moskva River. Appearing to catch her breath, she stopped with her hands on her thighs and looked around to see if anyone was following her. There was no-one to be seen. She felt almost nostalgic for Grisha, Konstantin and Timur, her tails from her last visit to Moscow. She at least had become familiar with their patterns and could easily shake them. Slightly disappointed that her cover under the name of Ms. Coton didn't even warrant their interest, but convinced she was alone, she flagged down a taxi and headed to Gorky Park.

Leaving the cab, she checked again for any surveillance. The coast was clear. It seemed almost too good to be true. She ran past the quaint, old fairy-tale carousel, with bright whimsical colors and a small horse rearing on its back legs on a ball on the top, and wove her way to the skating rink. She noticed people crossing the rickety wooden bridge over the rink. No one there appeared to be looking at her. Stretching her hamstrings with her foot on a nearby bench, she reached under the edge and extracted a small toy horse. She stashed it in the side pouch of her runner's water bottle and took off at a jog for the park entrance.

Silhouetted by the morning light, a large muscular statue stared at her as she approached. She slowed down and stopped in front of him.

"We are not on the same side any more, Elda," he growled.

Curious to know how Anatoly had tracked her, Elda replied, "Yes, I know, Anatoly. How did you figure out it was me?"

Anatoly sneered, "I wasn't sure, but I saw you leaving the hotel this morning, when I was going out for my own run, and your walk changed as you picked up speed. I wondered where I had seen that walk before. It's quite a distinctive walk, you know?"

Elda nodded as she registered that information. She ruefully acknowledged his observations, "Ah, that was an error on my part. No one followed me here, though. What made you come to Gorky Park?"

Anatoly's face reflected the obviousness of his deduction as he filled Elda in, "I took a gamble that you might be coming here. You and Tosh waxed poetic about this place. It seemed logical that you'd want to visit here."

Elda took a beat to register and analyze his answers before replying, "I see. It's becoming very clear that the joint operation we did now puts me at a disadvantage. I will have to be more mindful and change my habits. But you do know that I can't let you kill me."

"You have no choice."

***

"Thank you for giving me this by the way."

Anatoly raised his hand and shot a throwing knife out of his sleeve. His hand finished the swing and the knife passed through the spot where Elda had just been standing.

Elda rolled quickly to one side and down, sliding under and back out the other side of a bench. A second knife embedded itself in the back of the bench. Elda skirted around a couple pushing a baby carriage and disappeared from the park.

Anatoly nodded with satisfaction. From his past experience, he knew that she was a challenging opponent, but he was sure he could beat her this time. He collected his two knives and took off at a loping jog. Confident he could locate her again, he felt no need to chase her now. After all, this was his home turf. It was time for her luck to run out.

***

Elda ran through the streets of Moscow. She knew that Anatoly was out there searching for her. She realized that, since he was so much stronger and faster than she was, in order to beat him, she needed to outsmart him. And, she had to change her patterns and disguises. While running along, she typed an encrypted message on her phone, containing a list of required items, to an old contact in Moscow. She hoped he was still in Moscow, for there were few others who could get her what she needed as quickly as he could. She mumbled to herself, "Ed's going to hate that I'm blowing the budget so soon. This one will cost dearly." With that, she pressed SEND and ran onwards.

***

A short, white haired, elderly man with a cane in one hand and a shopping bag in the other limped into the Crown Plaza Hotel. Anatoly was in the lobby, seated at a small table, shaking his head, deep in discussion with Yuri and Snezhana. The man shuffled past them and into the glass elevators, keeping his back to the lobby as the elevator ascended.

Once in her hotel room, Elda dropped the shopping bag on the couch. She retrieved from her water bottle case the small toy horse and pulled it apart to reveal a Lightening connector, and uploaded the information from the toy to her phone.

Scrolling rapidly, she read that the senator of interest was John Clark, head of the United States Senate Intelligence Committee. No wonder they were targeting him. She quickly read his bio and scanned the data on the other senators. Having memorized the information, she deleted it from her phone. She placed the horse in an ashtray, carried him into the bathroom and lit him on fire with a cigarette lighter. She watched as the toy quickly melted into much smaller, and unrecognizable, heap. She flushed the remnants down the toilet and returned to the living room area, where she rummaged through her bag of newly obtained goodies. Ed would have a fit when he found out how much she spent to obtain these items. And she now owed a favor to boot.

She changed into a hotel waiter's outfit and slipped out of the room. Grabbing an empty tray from the floor outside a room with a *Pros'ba ne bespokoit'* sign on the door, she entered the service stairway and jogged up the stairs to the next level. She moved quickly down the hallway and knocked on a door.

"Obsluzhivaniye nomerov." She then repeated in accented English, "Room service."

When there was no answer, she tagged the door key reader with a master room key and slipped inside. The shower water was running and a voice groggily called out, "Just leave the coffee on the table." Efficiently searching the room she confirmed it was John Clark's. She secreted a listening device in his briefcase and another in the lapel of his jacket.

The sound of the running water stopped.

Breathing heavily from her dash back to her hotel room, Elda, having narrowly escaped from the senator's room, switched back into the disguise of the elderly man. She carefully applied the hairs for the grey mustache, smoothed on a cream that puckered her face into wrinkles, applied another cream that gave her a rather sickly pallor, greyed her hair and eyebrows, and donned a man's suit.

She entered the dining room area on the ground floor and sat facing the mirrored wall. From her vantage point she could see Anatoly leisurely eating breakfast. Yuri and Snezhana were nowhere to be seen.

John Clark, looking very tired and wan, dragged into the dining room area. He plopped down at an empty table. Anatoly rose and strode over to join him. Eld activated a recording app on her phone to receive the Bluetooth signal from the recording device she had placed on John. Elda could only hear snippets of their conversation, but she would have the entire conversation later, since John was wearing his jacket.

John objected as Anatoly sat down at his table, "I'm sorry, but this is my table."

Anatoly smiled and retorted, "No problem. I'll just be joining you for a short while."

"I am not in the mood for company. Please leave," John insisted.

Anatoly lowered his voice, and, as he spoke, John's face turned beet red. Anatoly passed a picture across the table. John stared at it and beads of sweat broke out on his forehead. Anatoly passed him a second image. John picked the paper up with shaking hands. The color drained from his face. Clearly John was viewing photos from the previous night's escapades. Anatoly stood up and leaned forward with his hands on the table. As he loomed over John, his neck muscles popped and his biceps flexed. His posture and bulk sent a message that his mouth echoed. Anatoly finished, smiled a frightening smile, and left the breakfast area. John sat still, staring at the papers in front of him.

Having seen enough, Elda signaled for her check and, after signing it, also left the area to return to her room to listen to the recording on her phone. She assumed that the Russians were blackmailing the senator.

Elda spotted Anatoly and Snezhana at the elevators. Snezhana turned to look and her eyes narrowed. Elda recognized that she had been made and cursed herself again for that last joint mission with the Russians. She swiveled and dashed into the stairway.

Elda rapidly ascended, hearing the door to the stairway open and footsteps resounding behind her. She sprinted to her room and ripped off the now useless disguise. Throwing on new clothing and her jogging shoes, she tossed some items from the bag into a backpack. She moved rapidly, calculating that they would soon have her room number from scanning the security footage. Peeking out her door, she saw that the coast was clear. She darted out and ran down the corridor and down the stairs. At the bottom, she flew out the side door.

Her breath heavy in her ears, aware that the Russian government ran the taxi cabs, Elda ran towards the metro stop to take the train to the airport. She formed a mental map of the streets of Moscow, in order to quickly navigate her way to the Krasnopresnenskaya station, and not have to stop to read the maps in the stations. If she headed along the river and up Konyushkovskaya Ulitsa, then she also had the option of passing through the American Embassy from front to rear doors. Even though the United States would deny her presence in Russia, and she could not stay there, she might be able to shake a tail that way.

Behind her, a car skidded to a stop. She heard a door slam and footsteps moving towards her. She glanced over her shoulder and saw that Anatoly had jumped out of a taxi and was sprinting her way. She accelerated her pace, hoping to reach the crowds at the Krasnopresnenskaya Metro station before he caught up with her. Her feet on the pavement synced with the pounding of her heart. She resisted the temptation to look behind her, since that would take seconds off her lead.

Elda twisted and turned to slip between people at the Krasnopresnenskaya station. Even in her rush, she admired the ornate simplicity of the white and red marble accented with gold filigree. Just as she flew onto the platform, a train pulled up. She hopped on and worked her way to the opposite door to be ready to jump off at a stop. She spied Anatoly leaping onto an adjourning car, just before the doors closed.

Elda slipped off the train at Kiyevskaya station and was dismayed to see Anatoly jump off behind her. She stood next to a couple with a stroller, pretending to marvel at their baby, while keeping an eye on Anatoly. Out of the corner of her eye she also appreciate the vaulted ceilings with chandeliers and the gold framed arches and artwork. She rued that she never had the time to really enjoy the beauty of the Moscow stations. She waited until the next train was about to leave and made a dash for the car. She was frustrated to see that Anatoly managed to catch the train too.

Exiting the train at Park Pobedy, she wove her way around people and slipped between two large men to ride the escalators to the top. The escalators in the Park Pobedy metro station, Moscow are the longest in Europe at 126.8 m (416 ft) long and 63.4 m (208 ft) high with 740 steps. Elda didn't dare turn around on the steep three-minute ride, but from the commotion behind her, she assumed that Anatoly had pushed his way onto the escalator. She breathed deeply and leaned forward slightly to ease her fear of heights and falling backwards. Although the escalator only had a slope of about 26 degrees, it made Elda nervous to be standing at an angle on a moving platform and at a height for any period of time. The vulnerability of being off balance and the possibility of being pushed down the stairs weighed heavy in Elda's mind. The ride felt like an eternity. At the top she turned around and, humming beneath her breath to control her fears, immediately headed back down the 318 foot descent to the platforms. Behind her, she heard shouts and angry words. She sensed that Anatoly was closing in. Reaching the platform, she again hurtled to the waiting train and cursed the delay in the door closings that allowed Anatoly to get onto one of the train's cars.

Elda waited through the next stop at Kievskaya and exited the train at the Vystavochnaya Metro station. She bolted up the escalator and dashed past the old entrance to the closed Tsentr Metro station, to find herself near the river again. Her legs felt like rubber and she willed herself to go on. She heard Anatoly's feet heavy on the pavement behind her. Elda knew from experience that she couldn't outrun him. She stopped, turned and waited.

Anatoly ran at her and lowered his head which would prevent Elda from using her old trick of bending and using her shoulders to toss him into the river. When he was almost on top of her, Elda threw herself onto her back and brought her feet up in a lying crouched position. His momentum carried him towards her as her legs exploded out into his chest. Off balance and moving forward like a bullet, Anatoly lifted into the air and plummeted into the Moskva River.

***

"*Der'mo!*" A sopping Anatoly dripped over the marble floors of the Krasnopresnenskaya Metro station. He checked the crowds for any sign of Elda. There was none.

Anatoly's phone rang. Although he was pleased to see his phone still worked, he was dismayed to see that Tosh was calling. He was not ready to admit

Elda had dunked him again. He pressed ANSWER. "*Privet* Tosh. There is no sign of her here."

"Yuri, searched the Vystavochnaya Metro station and Snezhana searched Elda's room at the Crowne Plaza. No sign of her in either place." Tosh sounded angry. "Go to the airport and search there. Find her!"

"*Khorosho*. I will go to the airport to see if she is there."

"Wait one second, Anatoly. I thought you had eyes on Elda. How did you lose her?"

"How did I lose her? Ah, well, *ser*, she managed to escape."

"What?!" yelled Tosh.

Anatoly held the phone away from his ear. "*Da. Mne zhal', ser*." Anatoly took a deep lungful of air, and apologized again, before confessing, "She threw me in the river." Anatoly bristled at the laughter emanating from his phone.

***

Tosh hung up the phone and tapped his fingers on his desk. *Elda.* He stared up at his ceiling and thought back to his encounters with Elda.

Early on in his career he had been tapped to shake down a woman suspected of being an American spy. A tourist on the surface, she had contacted a person at the Embassy and arranged dinner, which implied she had a greater range of contacts in Moscow and might be up to espionage. He searched her room and found nothing suspicious. He was intrigued by the Winnie the Pooh book she was reading and made a mental note to read it himself at a later date to see if there was anything that could be interpreted as a message to someone else.

In order to see if she really was a spy, Tosh decided to arrange a face to face with her so that he could evaluate her. He found her standing in a snow drift, waiting for a taxi after her dinner. He told her to get in and saw her slight hesitation. In itself, this was not incriminating, but it did signal that she potentially had a heightened sense of awareness.

During the drive she was pleasant and answered his questions, but he could tell that he would not get information from her easily, and he did not have enough conviction that she was a spy to hold and torture her. He had guessed that she was about ten years younger than he was, in her early twenties, military or ex-military, possibly CIA. He told her he would take her back to her hotel. She calmly thanked him. It was all quite civilized. He had sent a clear warning to her and assumed it had been received.

He liked her and thought that when she matured, with more experience, she might be a force to be reckoned with, but did not ever think he would see her again. However, after years of not running into her, he had seen her a lot the past two years. They met in Florence while undercover, then worked together on Operation Bittman, and now, here she was *again*. And again she had managed to neatly thwart Anatoly. She had definitely become the operative that he imagined she would.

Tosh smiled to himself. There were so very few operatives from the Cold War left. Tosh recalled those days as a time when spies cooperated with each other and only killed if necessary, not to cover their tracks or protect their careers. It was like the old days of Mafia and police. Gentlemen's agreements.

That was the way Cold War spies had operated. They helped each other unless they got in each other's way. And if one couldn't turn, temporarily remove, or scare off the other, the other spy was eliminated. But it was a sad occasion. There was a lot of respect for the other side in those days. Mutual respect, mutual cooperation, adversaries to the end.

Tosh spoke to his ceiling, "As much as part of me enjoys how you operate, I can't let you get in the way of this mission, Elda."

***

112

Elda was dressed as a small male Hassidic Jew. Although she had worn this outfit before when working with Tosh and his crew, she felt it was good enough to evade detection. She exited the Rechnoi Vokzal Metro and hopped on a bus to the Sheremetyevo International Airport in Moscow.

At the airport, Elda was grateful that the lines to go through customs were not long. She was glad that she had lifts in her shoes and had added pockmarks to her face, darkened her eyebrows, and changed the size and shape of her nose. She had also changed her hair back to dark black, topped with a hat and shallots on the side. She was wearing a suit with a long black coat that covered her slender body. She was satisfied that the coat was thick enough so that the beads of sweat along her back would stay hidden. Even with the short lines, it seemed like an eternity, waiting for the inspectors to slowly clear each person.

Chapter Nine

Having successfully fled Moscow, Elda sat hugging her knees in an oversized chair in Ed's DC office.

Ed addressed Elda and Jackson, "So we can assume that the sting they played on John Clark was played on the entire group of senators. Since the ladies there are run by the government, Snezhana was probably personally only handling John, and from Elda's snapshots of him that morning, I'd bet she slipped him a mickie and posed him for some pictures. From your recording, we made a transcript of the conversation that Anatoly had with John. It's the typical speech of: *we have the goods on you, stay tuned and we will ask for a favor and give you the pictures in return.* Only we know they never give them the photographs and the favors keep escalating."

Elda squinted her eyes and studied Ed before speaking up. "Ed, don't you personally know John?"

Ed nodded, "Yes. He and I were old friends but we haven't spoken in a couple of years. I don't know if his political success since our friendship has made him open to working with the Russians."

Elda continued, "Does he know what your job is?"

Ed nodded, "Yes, well not exactly. He knows I am in a government agency and somehow associated with the CIA and FBI. Why?"

"Well then, if John is a good boy then he should reach out to you for help. If not then he will play along, right?

"Most probably," acknowledged Ed. He addressed Jackson, "Jackson, can you put something where John Clark will find it and we can put him to the test?"

Jackson scratched an acne scar on his hooked nose and rapidly typed a message on his computer and received an immediate response. "OK, done. Ashok has planted the disinformation I sent him about Germany's weapon production. The Russians should find this interesting. This will be in a briefing for the Senate Intelligence Committee. We can trace it and see if it ends up at the Kremlin."

Disinterested, Elda swung her feet down. "Good. Meanwhile I will head back up to Maine. I doubt I've been missed by anyone except Vee. Keep me posted.

Let's see if the senators all head home after this trip or if they go anywhere else. I'll keep my bag packed." With that stated, she marched out of the room.

Jackson looked at Ed with raised eyebrows. Ed responded, shaking his head, "I know, Jackson. She is having problems at home. I fear she doesn't care if she lives or dies right now, and that isn't good."

***

The wind roared through the pine trees and the waves crashed on the rocks below Elda's Maine house. Alone in the house, Elda was working in her home office.

Sighing, Elda tossed her pen across the desk. Her small dog, Vee, curled up at her feet, picked up her head and looked up at Elda. Elda reached down and patted Vee. "I'm sorry to disturb you, Vee," apologized Elda. "The house just feels so empty. I miss Dawn so much and I know you do too. It's hard for me to focus. But I have to figure this out. Figure what out, Vee? Thanks for asking. I don't feel right after Operation Bittman, Vee,"

Vee considered Elda with her large brown eyes, then sighed and put her head back down on her paws, obviously disappointed that she wasn't getting any treats. Elda went on, "For me we ended up giving too many of our own techniques to the Russians and that's hurting now. They are able to see through many of my disguises and anticipate some of my next moves. Anatoly even recognizes me from my walk." Hearing the word, *walk*, Vee perked up and cocked her head.

"But, Vee, the real issue is I keep having this strange feeling that there's *something* we missed," said Elda slamming one fist into another. "It feels like there is more afoot in the background. I fear that this current operation with the senators is just to distract us from what the Russians and perhaps other players are really planning. The political disinformation is old news and the players in this game are all identified. That doesn't feel right." Vee looked at Elda with soulful eyes. There had been no mention of the word treat.

Elda stood and dug out a pile of folders from her file cabinet and dumped them on her wooden desk. She turned on the lamp and started leafing through the folders to refresh her memory and look for any tidbits that might confirm her suspicions. She continued to address her dog, "What am I looking for you ask, Vee? I don't know. I suspect that not everyone is who they say they are. Yes, of course Vee, that *is* the way it goes in the spy world."

She reached down and patted Vee on her head and scratched her behind her ears. Vee settled down at Elda's feet and Elda continued. "Ah yes, Vee, I do think there may be more Russian moles in the United States and in MI6. Why would the Russians plant just one mole in MI6? And why did we not also discover a mole here in the United States? That mission was wrapped up too quickly and neatly for my liking." She reached into her pocket and handed Vee a Cheerio as a treat and patted her side. "Good girl, Vee. And you may also ask, *What is really the goal of this current mission?* Excellent question. You'll make analyst yet." Vee wagged her tail.

Elda stood, stretched, and shook her head to clear her mind. "Disinformation and misinformation is running rampant in all levels of politics and AI with its deepfake media being distributed on social media is not helping. It's getting very hard to know what is real and what is gaslighting. Ed is such a straight shooter that it's easy for him to believe what he is told. But he once instructed me to trust no-one. I feel that applies more and more. On the surface we are dealing with a group of senators being turned. But what if under that the Russians are working to broaden their spy network and establish new moles. What if we never found all of the existing moles in the first place? Identifying these senators has been too easy. We need to dig deeper."

Elda sighed deeply. Vee looked up at her with concern. "I'm okay, Vee." Plopping back down in her chair, she picked up the first folder and went to work. The analog clock on her desk ticked by the minutes as she read.

***

The smell of beer hung heavy in the air. John Clark sat in a darkly lit corner of the Grosvenor Pub in London, drumming his fingers on the scratched wooden table, waiting for his son, Doug. He had booked this trip in conjunction with his Moscow trip when Doug had asked to see him, saying it was an emergency. After the events at the Crowne Hotel, John decided to cut his trip to Moscow short but still stop in London on his way to DC. John nervously spun around in his chair every time the pub door opened.

He wondered what Doug wanted of him and worried that, after ten years, he wouldn't recognize his own son. His mind wandered back to the previous day in Russia. He berated himself for his stupidity. Lost in his musings on how to figure out a way to get ahead of his situation and do damage control, he missed the pub door opening and closing.

John looked up and noticed a stranger walking towards him. He mentally shaved the scraggily mustache, took a few years from the man's face, subtracted pounds from the body, and matched it to his mental image of his son. John slowly stood and held out his hand. To his surprise Doug shook it.

"What are you drinking?" Doug inquired.

"I was waiting for you to arrive before I ordered. I'll have a pint of Guinness."

Doug nodded and strolled over to the bar. John frowned, observing that his son didn't look well. He wondered if this meeting was about Doug's health, or if Doug needed money again.

Doug returned with two pints of room temperature Guinness and sat down opposite his father. He started off the conversation in a low tone.

"They have threatened to kill me."

John leaned in to hear better. "Who?"

"The Russians."

John took a gulp of his beer, splashing some down his chin and onto the table. He wiped the drops off his face with the back of his hand and swallowed a few times. Noticing his hand was shaking, he put the pint back down on the battered wooden table.

"Tell me all."

Doug told his dad the story he and Nigel had concocted, which was very close to the truth. They had amped up the danger in hope that, as in the case with Nigel's dad, John would love Doug enough to follow along with their requests.

"What do they want?"

"I don't know yet, but they did say if I don't comply they will kill me."

John put his forehead in his hand and moaned. He couldn't believe that the Russians were so entwined in his, and now his son's, lives. He wondered how much worse it could get. He decided he needed to leave London and get back to DC, where he had connections, to figure a way out of the situation. He straightened up and looked his son in the eyes. "Come with me," he pleaded.

Doug reacted with anger, "You just want me under your thumb again. I have a chance at a new life here. I have my studies to finish. You need to help me out."

There was a long pause. The sounds of the pub felt overly loud to John as he weighed his response to Doug. His relationship with Doug seemed permanently broken. Doug was just trying to use him.

Finally he stated, "Contact me when you know. I will help you." Standing, he threw some British pounds on the table, squared his shoulders and marched away.

***

Doug watched his father walk off. His father stopped at the door and looked back. A trace of sadness passed through Doug, but it quickly dissipated and was replaced by a feeling of elation. Doug took out his phone and dialed up Nigel. "It worked," he said excitedly to Nigel's message inbox and hung up. His chair scraped across the battered wooden planks of the floor as he emphatically pushed it back and stood. *I need this more than any waiter does.* Doug picked up two of the bills from the table, leaving a single pound note.

A large, solidly built waiter immediately moved over to wipe down the table and palmed the listening device from underneath the table.

Doug, happy to have put one over on his dad, danced to his scooter. Jumping on and pressing start, he spun it around and headed back to the house he shared with Nigel. A few cars back, a motorcyclist mirrored his moves.

Impatient to be celebrating, Doug put down his kickstand, jumped off his scooter and ran into the house. He slammed the door shut behind him. He put his keys and helmet on the gilded side table in the marble floored entryway and called for Nigel. "It's time to celebrate."

Nigel yelled back from the study. "Right on! Be right down. Be a good roommate and grab us a couple of cold ones and I'll meet you in the living room."

Doug grabbed a couple of Newcastle Ales from the fridge and an opener from the counter and sauntered back towards the living room. "I got us a couple of Newkie Browns," he yelled.

Entering the living room, he spotted Nigel standing there with a large man holding a knife to his neck. He immediately dropped the bottles on the oriental rug. The opener clinked on top of them and bounced onto the rug.

"Sit down over on the couch and no-one gets hurt," Anatoly commanded, pointing at the black leather couch with his knife.

Doug scurried to the couch. Anatoly released Nigel, who, with the help of a not so gentle push, plopped down next to Doug.

Anatoly pointed at each with his knife. "Now out with your plans, you two. If I like them and determine you are useful, you will live. So leave nothing out."

"I don't know what you are talking about," croaked Nigel, his eyes roaming the distance to the bottle opener. Doug noted Nigel's interest but doubted the opener's usefulness as a weapon. Before either could act, the knife flew from Anatoly's hand and landed directly in front of Nigel's shoe, just missing his toes. Nigel sat at attention with his eyes on Anatoly, signifying he had ditched any plans for resistance.

Anatoly lunged forward and pulled the knife out of the now marred, highly polished wooden floor. "The next one won't miss your toes."

Nigel looked at him with wide eyes. Sweat beaded up on his upper lip. He swallowed hard. Haltingly he told Anatoly how he had used his own father, Henry, to obtain information from MI6, until Henry had been discovered and killed. "They then came after me. I had to come up with a plan quickly to save my own life. Since Doug's father is a United States senator on the Intelligence Committee, I promised the Russians I'd get them information through him. But I never told them who my source is," he concluded in a whiney tone.

Doug's mouth dropped open. He sputtered, "Killed! You never even told me your father was dead! What did you get me into, Nigel?" Doug looked at the man he had loved and admired. A tear rolled down his cheek. *Nigel seemed smaller and less handsome.* He asked in a bitter tone, "So the story you made up about the Russians is true? And I'm helping make my father a traitor?"

Nigel turned to Doug and shrugged, "Sorry Doug," he stated flatly, "but they were going to kill me unless I proved myself valuable. I remembered your father was a United States senator and decided to use my connection with you to save my life. Did you really think I wanted you as a housemate?"

Doug rose halfway off the couch to attack Nigel. "You bastard! You were my hero!"

With one hand Anatoly forcefully pushed Doug back down into his seat. He said dryly, "As touching as this is, tell me how you planned to get information from Doug's father, Nigel."

Nigel grimaced. Shifting uncomfortably in his seat he explained, "I figured he probably loved Doug in the same way that my father loved me, and if he felt Doug's life was in danger he'd co-operate."

"Obviously. So where do you come in?" interrogated Anatoly.

"I have not yet given the name of the senator to the Russians, so they need me to get the information." Nigel sat back with a smug smile on his face.

Anatoly growled at Nigel, "How did you plan to get the information."

Apparently eager to show his brilliance, Nigel volunteered, "Doug would start to visit his father in DC and bring the information back to me."

Anatoly continued to bore into Nigel's plan. "What data have you been told to gather?"

"I don't know yet." Nigel started to look worried.

Anatoly continued grilling Nigel, "Do you have any way to contact the Russians?"

Nigel slowly answered Anatoly, "No. They were going to contact me."

"So you are only of value to the Russians because they do not yet know about Doug, nor do they know his father's name? Is that correct, or *eto verno*, as your Russians might say?" summarized Anatoly, with a trace of a smile in his voice.

Nigel's face screwed up, signifying he was working to digest that sentence. "Ah, well, I guess if you put it that way…, uhm, yeah." His face fell. The flaw in his plan was apparent to all.

Anatoly had moved behind Nigel on the couch. With a swift movement he slung a wire noose around Nigel's neck and started to tighten it.

Terrified, Doug shouted, "Wait. Stop. I won't do it if you kill him. You'll have to kill us both. But I suspect you won't. I think you are here because you need me."

Anatoly loosened the wire and removed it. Nigel collapsed forward, sucking in air, wheezing and coughing. He touched his neck and his fingers came away bloody. He slumped back against the couch for support.

Anatoly stared at Doug. "*Da.* I would like you to cooperate, Doug." He shook his finger at Nigel, "Nigel, it seems like Doug Clark is the smarter one of you two, and has quite the affection for you. You may live…for now. But remember: you are of limited use to us and only alive right now because of your friend here. You will do everything we ask of you. *Khorosho*?"

Nigel looked up at Anatoly with fear and nodded.

"*Khorosho*. Await my orders." Anatoly strode out of the house.

Doug gave Nigel a disgusted look. "What have you done?"

***

Just then Ed's desk phone rang. "My secretary will get it."

A few minutes later the secretary knocked on his door. "I'm sorry to disturb your meeting, Ed, but there's a Senator John Clark on the line for you. He says it's urgent."

Ed picked up his office phone. "John my old friend. Long time no hear from. Is this business or pleasure?"

John answered Ed's query, "I know Ed, and I must apologize up front. This is not a social call, although we must have a beer sometime soon. I need your advice. Discretely I may add."

Without missing a beat, Ed answered, "Ah, I see. Let's go for a walk then."

***

Splash. A brightly colored male mallard duck landed in the water and gobbled up a piece of popcorn. Ed walked along the banks of the Potomac River tossing popcorn into the water. He stopped and sat on a bench next to a man, who was wearing a

128

baseball cap, dark sunglasses, and a sweatshirt with the hood pulled up over his cap.

"It's not the best disguise, John, but it will do." Ed continued to throw popcorn out in front of him to entice the nearby pigeons.

Senator John Clark snorted in frustration. "I thought it was a good disguise. How did you recognize me?"

"Remember I'm a spy, and we never give away our secrets. So, why are we meeting like this?" Ed reached down to retrieve a piece of popcorn, glancing around as he bent to ensure no-one was nearby. He turned and studied John. John was sweating and his hands were shaking. He looked as if he had not slept in days.

Voice quivering, John stated, "Ed, I need your help. I'm in trouble." He wiped the sweat from his upper lip with the end of his sleeve.

"Tell me."

In a low voice, John succinctly filled Ed in on his trip to Russia and his meeting with his son.

As John revealed his story, Ed rolled his eyes and groaned. He finally blurted out, "Gads. How stupid could you be, John? Sleeping with a prostitute while you were carrying confidential information in your briefcase. And in a country that is out to make trouble for America? What on earth were you thinking? Stealing from a mark and setting him up for blackmail --These are the oldest tricks in the books." In disgust, Ed flung a piece of popcorn at John. The popcorn harmlessly bounced off his leg into the beak of a waiting bird.

John recoiled away from Ed, as if he had been hit with a fist. Tearing up, he answered, "I know Ed, please, … I must turn this around. You and I go way back. Can you help me? I *cannot* be a traitor to my country. I know they will first request only a small piece of information that will cause no damage to our security." Ed snorted. John responded with, "I know. I know the drill. I understand that it will only be a test to see if I will cooperate. Next they will want me to retrieve some critical information that few have access to. I *will not* do that."

Ed stared deadpan at John and sarcastically commented, "Very noble of you, John, but what about your son? He's not in America. Unlike for you, a senator, it would be very hard for us to get him any protection."

John's face turned cold. He spoke icily with a tight jaw, "That little prick has done nothing but take my money and treat me like dirt, and now he uses me to save his own skin. I don't care what happens to him anymore." John dismissively waved the thought of Doug away.

Ed studied John's face and pressed further, to determine his veracity and resolve, and probed, "What about the pictures they have? We will have to report this incident and it may reflect badly on your political career."

John's face fell, but he remained resolute. "Worse comes to worse, I will have to resign. I just *cannot* do this."

Ed nodded. John appeared to be sincere, but Ed continued to drill John for information, "Whom have you told that you won't do it?"

"No-one, but I plan to tell my son."

"Wrong," Ed barked, "That will get you killed. One way to fix this would be to use the situation to set a trap for the Russians. We can capture those who are putting the sting on you. When Doug next calls, you will let him know you have had a change of heart. We will get you information that is safe to give them but will keep the game going."

Chapter Ten

Tosh sat in his office chair, with his eyes closed and his palms together, and mouth resting on his fingers. When Anatoly finished his report, Tosh raised his head and opened his eyes. He nodded to acknowledge Anatoly's briefing and stated, "Good information Anatoly. You are doing well with the UK marks. We have an issue with another one of the senators in the United States, however. His name is Senator Baker. He seems to need persuading to go along with us."

Anatoly perked up at the potential of a meaty assignment. Tosh gave Anatoly a packet containing his plane tickets, a passport and money. Anatoly glanced inside the packet, nodded and removed and placed each document in his inside jacket pocket, leaving the empty packet on the desk.

"You will handle him in Washington, DC. Yuri will ensure you have all the equipment you need there. Here is the information on the senator." Tosh passed across his desk a few photographs of the senator, along with a one-page bio.

Anatoly picked up each piece of paper, studied it and then returned the pile to Tosh, asking hopefully, "And if he won't?"

"You will have to send a strong message to the rest of the senators and remove him."

***

Checking his watch for the third time, Yuri reminded himself that his contact was always exactly five minutes late. Elda had explained to Yuri that keeping the other person waiting was a control thing to establish a position of superiority. This was a game that Yuri knew how to play well. He was the obedient foot soldier.

At 3pm, Yuri flagged a waiter who was wandering by in the outside seating portion of the café. "*Dva piva, pozhaluysta.*" He reckoned the two beers would arrive at the table the same time his contact showed up.

Exactly at 3:05pm, a very tanned, large man with a grey sweater straining across his chest and a pot belly walked through the inside door to the outside courtyard. A gold choker hung around his neck. His slightly receding hairline was accented by the slicked back hairstyle. Yuri stood to greet him. As they sat, Yuri slid an envelope across the table. The man smoothly brought onto his lap, peeked to verify the

133

approximate amount and smiled. "*Dobreyy den'*, my friend. What can I assist you with?"

Yuri waited for the waiter to set the two glasses down on the table and retreat before he spoke. He raised his glass and toasted, "*Budem zdorovy*." The man raised his beer in response. Yuri then answered, "I have a need to move a package of tools into the United States to be left in an assigned spot where a friend of mine can pick them up in order to do a job in the DC area. The address is in that envelope I gave you. It is my understanding that you would be able to arrange that for me?"

The man looked again at the amount of money Yuri had slipped him. He looked skyward mouthing various calculations. Yuri fully expected some bartering so had come in a bit low at the beginning. The man glared at Yuri. "I can do it, but this amount is an insult to my talents. I would expect, say, 400,000 rubles more."

Yuri stared icily at the man and said in a steely tone. "I know your men make regular trips over to the United States and smuggle in far more than this. This would be a grain of sand in an already existing pile. But since I respect you, I will increase the amount by 50,000 rubles."

The man squinted. Yuri tensed, expecting the man to attempt to get more money from Yuri. Yuri's eyes and facial expression did not budge and clearly signaled it was Yuri's final offer. The man took a deep breath and stated, "100,000 more and consider it done."

Satisfied, but not wanting to appear easy, Yuri's eyes bore into the man. He sat silent. The man reached up and wiped his sweaty brow. Finally Yuri broke into a large grin. He was aware that the man had to feel that he had won the match, and the amount was less than Yuri had estimated. He spoke in a beaten tone, "You drive a hard bargain my friend." He reached into his wallet, drew out more money and slipped it under the table to his contact.

The man checked and pocketed the money. He took two large gulps of his beer, wiped his mouth with the back of his hand and stated, "Drop it off at the usual spot and it will be there in three days."

***

The key securely in his hand, a disguised Anatoly strolled casually into the post office near Union Station in DC. Walking up to an XL size mailbox, he checked the number, inserted the key and withdrew a small rectangular black leather bag that was about a foot long. He dug a shoulder strap out of the side pocket, slung the bag over his shoulder, closed the box, and walked quickly away.

***

"I won't do it." Senator Baker threw the photo back across the table and adjusted his bulk in his chair. He brushed crumbs of the donut he had just devoured from his mouth and repeated, "As I have told the others, I won't do it. No-one will believe those images. I am a churchgoing family man. My reputation is impeccable."

Anatoly slammed his chair back and stood over the senator. "You will go along. You don't want to make your wife a widow, do you?"

The portly senator laughed at Anatoly and spit onto his plate. Still chortling he remarked, "She won't care. She will have enough money to continue her current lifestyle. I'm old. My work is done. Do what you need to do, but know that I will report this incident. Now pay the bill. I'm leaving." The senator pulled himself up out of his chair and waddled off.

Seething, Anatoly threw some money down onto the table and stomped off in the other direction. He paused at a deserted street corner to call Tosh. When Tosh answered, Anatoly blurted out, "He won't do it, Tosh. I don't believe we have any leverage on him either. He scoffs at his own demise. He's got guts but they are very misplaced. He laughed at me! He's a *zhopa*, a real ass. I would welcome killing him slowly."

Tosh gently soothed Anatoly, "Don't worry. Just eliminate him before he can report the incident. But do it and get out quickly before the Americans know you're in DC. Did you receive your *tools?*"

Anatoly nodded to Tosh's instructions, agreeing, "Yes, I did pick up the box of tools that were waiting for me. Thank Yuri for doing that. … I know I must move quickly and cannot stay in the United States too long." Anatoly tapped his foot and scowled. "Why don't we just eliminate the bunch of them and be done with this stupid operation?"

Tosh chuckled, "Tempting as it is, we cannot. I need to play along with Adrik."

Anatoly offered, "I could solve that for you too."

"*Nyet!*" Tosh barked, and then added softly, "You already managed to solve the issue of my previous boss, that traitor, Alexei. I need to find a better way to take care of Adrik. One that doesn't have the potential of having you imprisoned. We next will need to have Doug work more in DC for us. He's an American citizen so can easily travel back and forth under the pretext of seeing his father."

"….*Da*…. We do need to expand Doug's role here. Thanks, Tosh."

Tosh continued his instructions. "Use a delayed action drug that will cause a massive heart attack"

"That's too good a death for someone like him," Anatoly growled. He exhaled heavily, "*Da ser*. I will send the message." He hung up and spit on the ground.

A few hours later, Anatoly followed the chubby senator from his office, wondering where he was heading, since, while shadowing him he had observed that the senator usually took the metro from the Capitol South Station. Instead he was heading towards the Eastern Market Station. Anatoly pulled at his Patriot's cap so that the brim covered his eyes more. Surprisingly the senator walked past the station and took a left, heading north on 8th St SE. The senator reached into his pocket and pulled out a piece of paper with many items on it. *Aga. Shopping.* Anatoly noted that *Trader Joes* headed the list. *Perfect.* Anatoly stopped clicked his heels and a needle popped forward in the toe of his shoe. He clicked again and it retracted. He had it armed with a slow acting undetectable poison. Anatoly could stab the senator with it and be far away by the time the he collapsed. Although the poison would mimic a heart attack, the message to the rest of the senators who had attended the gathering in Moscow would be clear.

Anatoly pulled his sweatshirt hood up and tugged the brim of his cap down low over his eyes and jogged past the senator and into Trader Joes. He did a quick but controlled lap around the outside aisles of the store, noting the camera locations. Satisfied, he returned to the entrance and picked up a wire basket.

With the basket dangling from his arm, he shadowed the senator, selecting a few items along the way and placing them into his basket. In the far corner of the produce aisle he reached across the front of the senator and politely said, "Excuse me sir, I am going to grab some avocados." The senator who was just reaching for the avocados, drew his hand and torso back and glared at Anatoly, who gave him a friendly but solid, slap on the back, deflecting his attention from Anatoly's toe connecting with the senator's calf. Anatoly smiled and retreated back up the aisle with his avocados. He waved and said, "Thank you, my friend." A click of his heels retracted the now slightly bent and empty needle.

Chapter Eleven

At her monthly therapy session with Dawn, Elda closed her eyes and massaged her temples. Her head hurt. "No, no, that's all wrong."

The therapist leaned forward and gently said, "Then explain it to Dawn."

"First I need to explain to you that I don't hate myself. I may have at one time in my life, but I have finally come to the point in my life where I like who I am. I like what I have done with my life."

The therapist smiled and acknowledged Elda's statement, "I appreciate you correcting that. Now what about Dawn's statement that you love your job more than you love her?"

Elda opened her eyes and took a deep inhalation. She turned and addressed Dawn sincerely, "I don't love my job more than I love you, Dawn. I adore you and I'm miserable without you. But I need a sense of purpose in order for me to go on in life. My job gives me action, puzzles to solve, and a sense that I'm worthwhile. I don't expect you to understand, but I *do* wish you could see that I can love you, but I need to do my job too."

Dawn crossed her arms and shook her head. The therapist put her hand up to stop Dawn from responding and said, "Tell us more."

Elda squinted, her eyes searching inward. She hesitantly replied, "It's like I'm not a full person without Dawn, but I can survive without her, as long as I have a mission." She paused to search for the exact words. "But without my job, I am a shell of who I am and have nothing to give to a relationship."

The therapist nodded. Dawn was eying Elda as if she was seeing her for the first time. "And if you don't have either?" inquired the therapist.

Elda contemplated the therapist in disbelief and stated emphatically, "I will always create purpose." Just then Elda's cell phone beeped. She ignored it.

Dawn looked at Elda sadly and nodded at the phone. "It's all right. I know that beep well, Elda. I won't be angry if you look at it."

Elda punched in her security code and decrypted the message.

"Shit. This is urgent. I have to take a break and make a phone call. Duty and country do take priority over my personal wants and needs. It's the difference between the needs of a few and the security and lives of many. We can discuss that more when I return."

She stepped out into the hallway, closing the therapy office door behind her.

***

Elda stood near the therapy door, in the corner of the hallway, where she could see anyone approaching. Although there were noise machines outside each door, she kept her voice down and held her phone tightly to her ear. Ed's voice came through clearly, "Hank Baker, one of the senators who visited Moscow has had a sudden fatal heart attack."

"Interesting. What does the autopsy show us, Ed?" asked Elda.

Ed responded, "No trace of any type of poison. He was overweight and rarely exercised. It could have been natural causes."

Elda sneered at the phone, "I don't believe in coincidences, Ed."

Ed agreed, "Neither do I."

Elda glanced at the ceiling and noticed it could use a coat of paint. She thought for a moment and asked, "Do we have any other information?"

"No. We've obtained a police report. He had returned home from the store and was putting the groceries away. His wife heard a crash, ran into the kitchen, and found him collapsed on the kitchen floor, lying among the spilled bags of groceries. She called 911 immediately, but he was dead by the time the EMTs arrived on the scene."

Elda glanced regretfully at the closed therapy room door. "I'll fly down to DC ASAP. Can we get a computer expert involved? I'll fly down there," she repeated to convince herself. She sighed loudly.

Ed, ignoring the subtext, answered the overt question, "Sure. I'll send the chopper for you. What else do you need, and we'll pull it together for you."

Elda rocked side to side, her body encouraging her racing mind, "I want all available footage from Dulles Airport for the day before, the day of, and the day after his death. Include private planes. Look for any of our 'friends' in that footage, especially anyone matching Anatoly's size. Also, see if Trader Joes has security cam footage of the parking lot and inside the store. Look at any footage of the senator, and see if he brushes by, or bumps into, anyone. "

"Will do."

Her mind sped to pull the plan together, before she had to return through the therapist's door. She asked, "Can you tap Charlie Burlamachi for me? It's past time I had an understudy and according to my sources, she's currently stationed in DC and bored."

"You, the loner, are requesting an understudy?" Ed queried with genuine curiosity in his voice.

Misinterpreting his tone, Elda snorted and snapped, "No sarcasm, Ed. Just line her up for the next time I'm in town."

Ed calmly continued, "Why Charlie, Elda?"

Elda retorted, "It should be rather obvious, Ed. She's a known entity, smart as anything, has the right prerequisite training, extremely skilled, has no family or attachments, and is being underutilized at the moment. Talent like that needs to be nurtured, and I need to clone myself. Win-win."

Ed probed a bit deeper, "But there are many others that fit that criteria, Elda. What is it about Charlie?"

Elda cocked her head and thought before replying, "She's tough and a loner. And she doesn't fit in. So I doubt she will get into a relationship, at least one that is long term."

"Why do you call that out as important. Elda?"

Elda looked at her phone as she was wondering if Ed had two heads and snapped, "You know how hard this is on us, Ed, and that it's even harder for those who try to be in relationship with us. And being attached is a liability. It defocuses you from your mission and puts the other in harm's way. But most people want to be with another. They crave companionship. It's part of human nature. Not having that need is an asset to our profession. I sense that Charlie is perfectly fine on her own. And to boot, she'll throw herself off a cliff for a good cause. Frankly, she reminds me of me at that age."

Ed replied carefully, "As you wish... And Elda?... "

Elda snapped, "What?"

"That wasn't sarcasm," Ed replied compassionately.

Shaking her head, Elda looked down at her feet and exhaled. She ruefully answered, "Damn. Sorry, Ed. There's just a lot of pressure here. I'm really trying to hold it together. I apologize."

"No need, Elda. We're old friends. You know you can always talk to me about whatever is going on in your life."

"Thanks Ed. I do know that. Now is just not the time to talk it all out. Okay? I just feel as if I'm being pulled into somewhere I don't want to be. But I can't talk about it yet. I'll be better if I can just focus on the job at hand. So you can help by keeping me busy." Elda glanced at her watch and at the door again. "I have to run, but how is the sting going with John Clark?"

"The false information about Germany's weapons that we planted for the Intelligence Committee to find hasn't shown up in Russia yet."

Elda grimaced and reflected back to Ed the mood she had picked up from his tone, "That's frustrating." Her eyes roved the ceiling while she searched her mind to connect the pieces of the puzzle. She probed further, "Do we have any information on the rest of the senators?"

Ed responded in his professional briefing voice, "Well, obviously, one of them refused to play along with the Russians. And we missed the assassination. Now we have closed that barn door by installing bugs for the rest of the senators and are also shadowing each one. Better late than never, as they say. We are monitoring their communication and also searching the chatter on the dark web to see if we can pick up on any clues."

Elda scratched her head and adjusted her glasses while searching for a mental puzzle piece. "So do we have any other data to go on?"

"While looking for clues, Ashok did come across the movement of an old *friend*. Apparently Nigel Davies, Henry's son, had been living in Moscow, but just recently relocated to London. If you remember, Henry was the MI6 mole that we uncovered in that operation we did with the Brits and Russians. We had suspected at the time that the Russians had leverage on Henry by holding his son hostage."

Elda pumped for more information, "Yes I remember him. Hum. Interesting that Nigel is in London. Have you heard anything from MI6, Ed?" She heard Ed's intake of breath before he declared, "I don't entirely trust James since the last operation, Elda."

Elda felt her jaw tighten as she thought of James' probable duplicity and surmised that Ed also had his teeth clenched. She rubbed her chin and breathed deeply to relax herself before agreeing, "Nor do I, Ed. It seems that I have to go to London too then. I can back channel through Sophia Brown," Elda stated without enthusiasm.

"Consider it done, Elda." Ed, next responded to Elda's tone, asking gently, "What about your home situation, if you leave again, Elda?"

Elda sighed heavily and answered flatly, "It's going to be what it's going to be. Gotta run." She hung up on Ed and re-entered the therapy session.

***

Crash. The man came down solidly on his back onto the black gym mat and lay there for a moment. "Uncle?" asked his opponent sweetly. He rolled over and brought himself up to his hands and knees and shook his head and spit out, "Never!'

The other combatant stood patiently and rubbed one hand along the closely shaved side of her head, while waiting for him to rise. He slowly stood, shook himself, and rushed at her. She deftly sidestepped and stuck out her foot in front of him, while pushing him sharply on his back to help his downward movement. *Slap* his face hit the mat. He lay there absorbing the shock and pain. He pulled himself back into child pose and squinted, calculating the distance between them. He vaulted up and managed to reach her knees, causing the two of them to come thudding down together onto the mat. He hung on desperately, crawling up her body to get more leverage.

She spun herself to one side, bringing a knee up and into his chest, creating a gap between the two of them. She brought her second knee up and in and held his head in her hands, forcing him to follow as she rolled onto her back. Once there, she pushed sharply with her legs to throw him off of her. He fell awkwardly onto his side.

"Now?" she inquired, with a lilt in her voice. More slowly than before he stood and circled her. She smiled at him, "You know you never win, Kevin." His eyes blackened and his thick brows marched across his forehead to his nose. With his teeth set in a grimace, he leapt at her. She dove and rolled, coming up behind his legs as he fell solidly to the ground again. She leapt on his back where she knelt and pulled his head back by his hair. "Uncle?"

"No!"

She slammed his face on the mat and rose off of him. He lay there, breathing shallowly from the pain.

"I'm leaving, Kevin."

A muffled, "I will get you next time, Charlie," rose from the body on the mat.

***

Ed sat straighter in his office chair and breathed deeply. *I feel worn and tired in the presence of such youthful energy.*

"Elda requested me?!" Charlie sat excitedly on the edge of her chair in Ed's DC office. She ran her hand through the dyed blond hair at the top of her head, disturbing the carefully gelled spikes and then brushed both her hands along the darker and close-cut shaved sides. As she reached back, her bicep muscle strained at the short sleeve hem of her white, two-pocket shirt. Charlie was solidly built and in top shape. She ran and worked out in the gym daily.

"She's a legend in the service. Boy oh boy. What I could learn from *her*! How does she even know about me?" Charlie asked.

"Do you remember that Elda gave that speech for your graduation from the FBI academy?" Ed said.

Charlie nodded and smiled enthusiastically, replying, "Certainly! It was an inspiring speech. She really confirmed for me that I was doing the right thing for myself and my country. But, I was only one of a number of graduates that year."

Ed regarded Charlie fondly. He regretted that she would most probably over time lose that pure joy of learning the job and become jaded by what she did. "True, but you were also top in your class. Elda's been watching your career ever since. She often mentors exceptional women in the field, but she has never requested a partner, until now. She's a loner and that will be a tricky partner to work with. You will never be the same again. You will see and do things that were never taught at the academy. Are you ready for this?"

Charlie stated emphatically, "More than anything."

Ed stared at her for a few moments to assess her. He doubted that she fully understood what she had just agreed to, but then again, none of them had known what they were really getting into when they first started. And she would be trained by one of the best.

Was I ever that young and idealistic? Ed sighed heavily, suddenly feeling the weight of his role. Then, straightening his shoulders, he waved to dismiss her, instructing, "OK, get your affairs in order and your go-bag packed. I'll be in touch."

Chapter Twelve

"You promised you would help me, father," whined Doug into his phone, his bottom lip trembling.

His father answered, "Yes I did, son. But I won't be a traitor to my country."

"Please father, just wait to see what they want. They will kill me if we don't cooperate."

John barked at his son, "When did this become *our* problem?"

"Please, please father, I'm begging you, just see. There may be no issues for you. But you must save me. I am your only son." Doug realized that his father had hung up on him. Trembling he terminated the connection, put his phone down and reached for a candy bar to sooth his nerves. He turned to Nigel who was waiting expectantly, "He hung up on me!"

Nigel laughed, "Of course he did. It's your father's typical power play. You ask. He hangs up on you. You call back. And then he agrees. You two have played that game time and time again. He will come through for you. As you said, let's see what they want from him."

Doug looked at Nigel adoringly, "You always know how to calm me down, Nigel."

Nigel picked Doug's phone up and handed it to him, commanding, "Now that you're calm, call your father back. Apologize for being a problem, but plead with him to do what you're asking."

Doug put his phone on speaker and dialed. "Hello father. Please don't hang up on me. I know I've caused you a lot of trouble but I really need your help this time."

Silence.

Doug bit his bottom lip. Nigel scribbled on a piece of paper. Doug read it out loud. "Pleeease, father. Please.."

A loud sigh came over the speaker and then John said in an icy tone, "Just once. You understand? One time."

The connection went dead.

Doug smiled at Nigel for approval. Nigel beamed back and praised Doug, "Good job Doug. Now we just wait a bit and let him sweat."

***

As the two men walked up the street towards Nigel's house, Anatoly stopped suddenly and addressed Yuri. "Yuri, you don't have to do anything except look large and intimidating."

Yuri stuck out his chest and bared his teeth. Anatoly laughed, "That will do."

Anatoly, followed by Yuri, barged into Nigel's home. He saw Nigel and Doug sitting in the living room, drinking beer, eating chips from a large plastic bowl, and watching a football game on the TV. Doug promptly dropped his crumpled handful of chips back into the bowl, and Nigel quickly switched the TV off. In the silence, Doug started to sweat.

Anatoly threw a piece of paper onto the coffee table. "There's some preliminary information we want John Clark to get for us. You have five minutes to memorize the contents on this paper. Doug, Yuri here will show you how to be a courier and accompany you on this one trip. From then on, you will be on your own. Nigel, when Doug is traveling, you will stay here with me as a security deposit."

Doug picked up and read the paper, put it down, waited a few seconds and read it again. He handed it to Nigel who repeated the process and handed it back. Doug read it again, uncertain of his memory, and handed it back to Anatoly. He nervously picked at a pimple on his nose and whined, "My father said he'd help but he may change his mind and resist giving me information."

Anatoly reached into his pocket and dangled the wire noose in front of Doug's eyes. "Then you will have to find a way to overcome that resistance."

Doug recoiled and then, sighing heavily, he resignedly asked, "When do I leave?"

Anatoly repocketed the noose. "Tomorrow morning. If you get out of line we *will* kill Nigel. Understand?"

Nigel startled at the sound of his name so definitively coupled with death. He challenged Anatoly, "You wouldn't."

Anatoly, holding one end of the paper, lit it on fire and dropped the burning paper and ashes onto the glass topped table. He snarled, "Don't test us. We are not to be fucked with."

***

Nadia pulled the man by his tie into her apartment. He grinned broadly, his excitement about what was to come was clearly showing. She kicked the door shut behind them and started to undo his tie and shirt. He reached for her but she pushed his hands down, "*Nyet*. Not yet, my man."

"Radomir, *menya zovut* Radomir."

"Soon your name will not matter; tonight you are my man." She pushed him into the bedroom, and as he reached the bed, she stuck out her foot and neatly tripped him onto the bed. His breathing was becoming rapid and shallow. His eyes were glued to her chest and the low neckline that showed ample cleavage and led into the gentle curve of her breasts. She straddled him and as he reached for her again she took each wrist and secured it to the bed post with a padded cuff. She could feel him hard against her. Sitting on top of him she undid her blouse and threw off her bra. Her nipples showed her own excitement. She unzipped and yanked down his pants and guided him into her, riding him hard until they both came simultaneously. She rolled off of him and left the room.

Nadia returned to the bed holding a drink with a long straw. She held his head, helping him drink. "There you go, my man. You will find this refreshing." Within minutes, he was hard again and they were off to the races. Again and again she repeated this ritual until he was begging her to stop. With him still inside her, she agreed, "*Da*, my man, it is time you rested." She rocked back and forth and moaned. After coming again, she kept him inside and grabbed a pillow. "Goodbye my man. You did better than most."

Unable to move from the drug that Nadia had slipped into his drink, Radomir's eyes widened with horror as she put the pillow over his face and held it tightly there. She tightened her vaginal muscles to eke out her last bit of pleasure before he became flaccid.

Done, she rose off of him and, smirking, addressed the other presence who had entered the room, "Did you enjoy the show, Yaromir?"

Yaromir held his arms crossed over his chest and shook his head negatively, answering her, "*Nyet.* It is getting tedious, Nadia."

Nadia rolled her eyes and yawned at him, "I'm bored. What else should I do?"

Yaromir suggested, "Perhaps something that doesn't involve killing random strangers?"

Nadia laughed at him and brushed the concept away with a flick of her hand. "It keeps my skills sharp. And they are dog shit anyway."

"You'll be dog shit if Tosh finds out about your activities." Yaromir shook his finger at Nadia to emphasize his point.

Nadia laughed. "I am too clever for him to catch me."

"No one is that clever, Nadia."

***

Lurking in the shadows across from Nadia's apartment, Tosh observed Yaromir walking out with a large rug over his shoulder. He overheard Yaromir turn to Nadia and say through gritted teeth, "This is the *last* time, Nadia. Next time you clean up your own mess." The tinkling of Nadia's laughter reached his ears. Tosh, the ghost, disappeared into the darkness.

Later that evening, Tosh spotted Snezhana slipping out into the moist night air. He saw that she was wearing gym clothes. Switching to a front lead, he followed Snezhana and observed her meeting Anatoly outside the gym. He overheard her tell Anatoly, "I have the sensation that I am being followed, but I cannot detect anyone."

Tosh vanished into the gloom. He drove a nondescript van to his next observation spot. Arriving at Stas's apartment he saw the glow from the computer screens light up Stas' apartment. From a van outside, Tosh listened to the clicking of keyboards. He glanced at his watch: 02:30. It was obvious the apartment dweller was not going out, nor was he receiving company. The van pulled away from the curb and headed to the Kremlin.

Once back at his office, Tosh swiveled his chair and opened his file cabinet to withdraw a stack of files. Opening each file, he made a few notes and then closed and replaced each file. He leaned back in his chair and contemplated his ceiling. He had spent the last week observing each of the members of Team A and Team B. He sat up straight and thought, *I am glad that Snezhana has mended her ways. But I am concerned that Yaromir and Nadia have grown too close. What is Nadia covering up? What was Yaromir carrying in that rug?* He picked up the phone to make some calls to check on missing people around the neighborhood where Nadia lived.

***

I cannot stand this wanker. He's such a prick. Standing in James' office, Sophia Brown shook her blond hair and forced her voice to stay controlled. "But James, I think the Russians are up to something in the UK. Yuri Kuznetzov was just spotted at Heathrow immigration, and Anatoly Petrov was seen in London last week."

James Richardson sat tall in his leather chair. He ran his hand through one side of his salt and pepper hair as if to brush away the annoyance of Sophia's visit. His seat squeaked as he sat back, narrowed his eyes, and frowned at Sophia. Leaving her standing, he did not motion for her to sit in either of the chairs in front of his desk. In a upper crust, condescending, tone he replied, "I know you have a heightened sensitivity to anything Russian from that last operation, but we put them in their place then. There's nothing to be concerned about. I gave you those folders on the Chinese. That's where you need to be focusing your attention, Sophia." He shuffled a number of papers on his desk to signify that the conversation was done.

He is such a dolt! How did he get this job? Sophia's teeth ground together and her green eyes nearly popped from her head as she attempted to smile sweetly at James. "That will take me weeks to finish wading through. I can research the Russian situation in a day and *then* get back to the Chinese. I haven't found anything to catch my attention in what you assigned me to read about China these past few weeks."

James' lips pursed together. He ran his hands through his salt and pepper hair and inhaled deeply before responding pompously, "*I* know where the threats are, Sophia. You are overreacting and may be looking for a way to get revenge for what happened to Oliver. *Drop it* and get back to those files." James looked down at his computer and started rapidly typing on the keyboard, dismissing her.

How dare he mention Ollie! He should be actively trying to get revenge for what happened to my husband. If he really knew where the threats were, Ollie never would have been ambushed. I'll give this bastard an earful. Sophia stood and opened her mouth to speak. James looked up. "Anything else?" he inquired in a tone that implied there better not be.

I best not. He could fire me. Sophia slammed her mouth closed. She stood for a second and then bitterly said, "No, James." The door closed sharply behind her.

***

The sounds of children screaming filled the distant air in Lincoln Park in DC. With his nerves already on edge, John Clark was glad he wasn't standing closer to the playground. A voice cut through the remaining calm and a hand tapped him on his shoulder, startling him. "Dad, this is one of the Russians I told you about."

John Clark stood in the pathway looking across at the Mary McCleod Bethune statue. He breathed deeply to calm himself, turned and looked Yuri up and down. He directed his question at him, "And your name is?"

Yuri replied firmly, "My name is of no matter to you. Just remember my face. In the event that your son cannot be here, I will be here instead. You will do what he or I ask of you."

"And if I don't?" challenged John. *I can't appear to give in too easily.*

Yuri took a step closer towards John, causing him to flinch and step backwards. He held out a picture of John from his night at the hotel in Moscow. The contents of John's briefcase were in plain view. *How on earth did they do that? That briefcase was locked! God, it must have been that prostitute. So they apparently were holding this picture in reserve to show me to put more pressure on. Bastards.*

"You and your son will be of little use to us. And, as you have seen from your colleague's recent heart attack, our reach is long."

John looked again at the statue, hoping to draw strength from it for his own mission. Once he knew what they wanted he could get the proper assistance and protect himself and possibly his son. *Although I have no idea why I would protect him. He won't do what I say and will just run off and do something even more stupid.*

He shook his head, "No, no. I doubt that you will kill me. I am of no use to you dead. My son, on the other hand, serves no purpose now that he has brought you to me. Isn't that right?"

Doug looked at his father in horror, "Dad! How could you even suggest that?"

Yuri said dryly, "Because stupid one. It's true. We keep you around now because we have no obvious need to eliminate you. But you, John Clark, must remember that we have pictures that will terminate your career."

He handed John a second picture with a prostitute sitting naked on John's penis and John handcuffed to the bed. "And if you don't care about your son, you have been in the senate many, many years. You are happily married to the same woman you met in college. I assume you care about that part of your life?"

Resignedly, John inquired, "What do you want me to do?"

***

Elda passed by the elevator and ran up the stairs to Ed's office. She waved at his secretary, who motioned for Elda to continue on into Ed's office. There, Ed was sitting with Charlie and Jackson gathered around Ed's desk, all three staring at Ed's computer screen. A small man was sitting quietly

163

typing on his laptop in the corner of the office. Jackson's legs were wrapped around the legs of his chair and his long body was bent forward. Elda was always intrigued that he never fell over from that position. Spotting Elda, Ed gestured for her to sit in the empty chair by his desk.

"What are we looking at?" inquired Elda as she sat.

"This." Ed pointed to a picture of three men sitting on adjacent benches in Lincoln Park in DC.

"Oh isn't that special…Yuri, Doug Clark, and John Clark, sitting and eating ice cream in the park. Any idea of what is going on?"

Jackson responded, "Unfortunately there is no microphone nearby, but I pieced together what I could, from reading their lips. As we know, Doug is asking his father to get some information. Yuri is reminding John of certain incriminating photographs."

Elda smiled broadly, "So John is playing along?"

"It appears so. I certainly hope so," Ed replied.

"When was this?" demanded Elda.

Ed replied, "This morning, which is why I asked you to pop down today."

"Okay. Thanks, Ed. Did you give John instructions on how long to wait before giving them the information?" Elda inquired.

Ed responded, "No. He knows his son best. And I want to limit the number of times I contact him. We'll just wait for it to appear in Russia."

"And who is that?" asked Elda, pointing at the man sitting in the corner of Ed's office, who answered, "I am Ashok Bhatt, computer wizard at your service." He returned to his typing.

Elda nodded and remarked, "Good, we can use someone as good as Stas on our side."

Ashok looked up and gave Elda a wide grin. "I am much better. You will be delighted by how good I am." Elda respected his boyish charm and confidence, but hoped he could live up to it and he wasn't just all bluster.

Chapter Thirteen

Elda huddled with Charlie and Jackson on a small brown faux leather couch in the corner of Ed's office. She noted that Ashok kept up his work on the other side of the office. *The kid's got great concentration.* She added that to her mental list of Ashok's attributes.

Elda tapped Jackson's arm and inquired, "Jackson, can you show me the footage from Trader Joes?"

"Sure, Elda. I'd appreciate your eye on it." Jackson typed quickly on his laptop, pausing frequently to brush the strands of his salt and pepper hair that were falling in front of his hazel eyes. Finally, showing her exasperation, Elda reached over and gathered his hair in one hand. Twisting it together she clipped it to the top of his head with a paperclip. Jackson stopped and stared at Elda. She smiled her sweetest smile at him and declared, "It's you." Jackson rolled his eyes and went back to replaying the footage.

Elda noticed Charlie shaking her head in apparent amazement. Charlie blurted out, "Elda, I've only been observing you for a short while but I feel already I am learning so much.”

“Like what?” asked Elda, curious to get a better read on Charlie too.

Charlie responded, “Your confidence that Jackson would accept your intervention and the ease of the interplay between you and Jackson. But you are both so very serious about the job. It is professional but so human too.”

Elda laughed. She replied to Charlie without taking her eyes from the computer screen. “Being professional doesn’t mean you have to leave your humanness behind, Charlie. This profession does tend to rob you of humor, empathy and some level of the things that make us human. But it’s key that we attempt to hold that off as much as possible. There are times to steel yourself and to compartmentalize in order to do something unaccepted by our cultural norms, such as killing. And there are times when we cannot let down our guard to trust another person. So relish the times when you can be real with another human being.”

Elda grabbed Jackson’s hand. “Wait! Go back a few frames. There. See the large man in a New England Patriots’ Football shirt and cap? The image is rather fuzzy, and he’s not in the same frame as the senator, but…” With her finger, Elda made invisible dashed lines on the screen, "if we extrapolate his route, he would intersect the senator's path in that area." She pointed to an area just out of camera range. "And *that* is a camera dead zone."

Jackson brought a magnifying glass up to the screen and shook his head. "I can't make out any features. Who do you think that is?"

Elda put her hand to her chin and tapped her index finger on her cheek. She bit the cuticle on her middle finger and frowned, studying the picture once again. She responded slowly but confidently, "He's changed his walk and posture, and has a beard and mustache, but I'd put money on that being Anatoly. Can we pull footage from Dulles airport from the day before, both that morning and that evening?"

"Sure." Jackson rapidly typed and busily flipped through a number of applications on his computer.

Just then, Elda looked at her phone and pulled up a secure message from an unknown caller. Opening it, she viewed a photo of John Clark walking though Regents Park with Doug and Yuri. The accompanying message read: *I need to talk with you. S.*

Elda frowned and handed her phone to Jackson.

Jackson read the message and inquired, "Sophia Brown?"

Elda nodded her agreement and responded, "That would be my best guess, Jackson. I need to go to London without MI6 finding out I'm there. Can you continue gathering the information on the senator's death, Jackson. Have them run additional labs on the body. Look for traces of anything that would have caused a heart attack and any small puncture marks. Charlie, are you ready to come with me? We can talk about your role on the way across the pond."

Charlie had been sitting quietly observing the two pros work. She started at her name but answered quickly and enthusiastically, "I wouldn't miss it."

"Good." Elda turned back to Jackson. "Jackson, do you still have all of the files you were analyzing from Operation Bittman?"

Jackson held his hand to his forehead in confusion. Elda was giving everyone whiplash with the sudden change in topics. He responded tentatively, "Yes, I do, Elda. Why are you asking?"

"I have a feeling we missed something there when we were working with Tosh and James. Can you gather the data and give it to me?"

Jackson bristled, "I'm sure I didn't miss anything Elda."

Elda nudged him reassuringly and said calmly, "No, no, no, Jackson. I'm not accusing you of missing anything about Operation Bittman. Your information gathering and analysis was brilliant during that operation. I would like to look at it from a different angle."

Jackson relaxed slightly and inquired, "What's the angle?"

Elda shrugged and held up the palms of her hands. She shook her head. "I'm not sure yet, Jackson, but I will know it when I see it. And then I'll be sure to reach out for your help in analyzing it, Jackson. Anyway, we'll be working with Tosh and dealing with James again, so it wouldn't hurt me at all to be refreshed on their information from our joint mission this past Spring."

Ashok stood and walked over with his laptop. "Excuse me. I may have something of interest…"

Elda encouraged him with, "What is it, Ashok?" Her innate curiosity drove her to measure the new employee. *Can he analyze the information he finds and use it to search for related data or does he stop after finding the first tidbit?*

"There is a lot of chatter about the upcoming elections, of course, but there's also major streams of political and social disinformation which have the signature of the Russian GRU computer experts. There's slander about different candidates, baby snatching, hate groups, minorities, sexual preferences, graft, groups of people out to attack other groups,..."

"Yes, this is nothing new, Ashok," answered Elda, looking at him quizzically.

Ashok nodded and shook his head vehemently, holding up his hand to stop any further interruptions. He rapidly answered her concerns, "Yes, this I know. However, there is also a very small, and hard to find, reference to expecting someone who will bring additional arms to a yet unknown white supremacist group to help sow discord in the United States. Most would have not picked up on this nugget, but this information has the same traces as the data planted by the Russians."

"Interesting…Thanks, Ashok. Stay on top of that one and please keep myself, Ed, and Jackson posted." *Good he uses his brain.*

"Will do, Elda." Ashok bounced confidently back to his station.

Ed wandered from his desk over to the other side of his office where Jackson and Elda were working.

Elda spoke up, "Ed, I have to go to London immediately."

***

"I want to thank you…"

In the cargo plane, Elda cut Charlie off with a wave of her hand. She loosened her shoulder strap and turned in her drop down seat to address Charlie. She raised her voice to be heard over the sound of the engines. "Thank me if you come out of this alive. I'll brief you in detail about each member of the Russian and MI6 teams. I will give you this information once, and you can ask any questions, but I will not repeat myself. In London, to start your training, I want you to tail me in disguise. Each time you give yourself away I will text you, and you will leave the scene. I will let you know what your mistake was and you will try again. Once you can tail me without alerting me you will be ready for the next step. Understand?"

Charlie sat at attention and replied tersely, "Got it. No problem."

"Good. This training may at times seem slow, and it will definitely feel frustrating, but I guarantee that you will walk out of it with valuable new skills.

Now, let me tell you about the Russian team. The most violent person on the team is Anatoly. He has no empathy and loves to kill. His favorite way to dispatch his enemy is up close and personal, but don't let that lull you into complacency if you don't see him. He is also an accomplished long-range sniper. You can keel over from a bullet between your eyes without ever having suspected that he was around."

"Got it."

Elda continued, "The leader and most dangerous of the team is Tosh. Tosh is a skilled operative and a legend in his own right. He can slip in, accomplish his mission and slip out without notice, leaving no trace. It's taken decades to gather any information on him. I worked directly with him and his team last year. Neither he nor his team members are to be underestimated."

Charlie raised her hand. Elda signaled for her to talk. Charlie queried, "Aside from Anatoly, who else is on Tosh's team?"

"Tosh has a select team that he favors. They are top operatives. He dubs them his A Team. His niece, Snezhana, or rather, his grandniece, is still young and a bit rough around the edges, but she learns extremely fast and does not make the same mistake twice. She is a chip off the old block, even down to inheriting Tosh's photographic memory and his ability to slip in and out unrecognized. Whereas Tosh fades into the background, Snezhana exudes a femininity and sexuality that obliviates remembering what she really looks like."

"Interesting. Are there others?"

"The last two on his A Team are Yuri and Stas. Yuri is a genuinely nice guy who loves animals. Don't let that fool you, though. He has no moral compass and will work with anyone without many limits on what he will take on. He is a master of logistics and extremely smart. He worked with me before he joined Tosh's team, so I know him the best."

The plane roughly jostled them as it hit a pocket of turbulence. After ensuring that her seat belt was tight, Charlie prompted Elda to continue, "And Stas?"

Elda nodded, demonstrating appreciation. Charlie was showing a good ability to track the conversation and prompt Elda to resume where she had left off. Elda continued, "Stas is an expert computer geek and hacker. He fits any stereotypes that come to mind when I say those words. He is addicted to technology, skinny and pasty white, introverted and very good at what he does, perhaps one of the best, barring Ashok, *if* Ashok is as good as he professes to be."

Charlie nodded. Satisfied that Charlie was absorbing the information, Elda continued, "All of these people are uniquely skilled at what they do and complement each other nicely. In order to beat them, you will have to be at the top of your game. I have lived longer than many in this career and don't know which mission will be my last one. But I don't want what I know to die with me. So I have brought you on to capture that knowledge and hopefully, be even better than I am at this job. I am a ruthless taskmaster and also very used to operating on my own. I will be short to the point of rude at times and, some days, you will have to just watch, obey, and keep up. This will not be easy for either of us. Are you up for it, Charlie?"

Charlie held up her hand to high five Elda. Elda glared at her. Charlie quickly dropped her hand. She sat at attention and avowed, "I am. Definitely. Lead on."

Elda decided to push Charlie. "Are you willing to forsake *all* else for this? Even to the point of putting your life on the line?" She stared directly into Charlie's eyes, to read her unverbalized response.

Despite the turbulent air, Charlie replied clearly and confidently, "Yes, Elda."

Elda nodded and stated, "Good, because with Tosh and his crew, that's what you will be doing on this mission."

Charlie hesitated and then asked, "You are an ace in your profession. In this briefing you have repeatedly warned me about how dangerous Tosh and his team is."

Elda interrupted, "Yes, so what's the point?"

Charlie filled her lungs with air and then exhaled sharply. She blurted out, "It sounds as if you admire and respect Tosh, but at the same time fear him?"

"That's an excellent observation, Charlie. The name, Tosh, was associated with amazing feats of espionage and assassination. Throughout the years I would hear of this Russian operative who would always disappear without any leads, again and again. We would whisper his name in awe. We feared him and aspired to be as good as he was at our craft."

Charlie was listening with rapt attention. "So can you tell me a Tosh story?"

Elda nodded and continued, "When I was at my half brother's wedding in St. Petersburg, I was asked to look into an assassination of a double agent that had recently happened in that city. The autopsy report was inconclusive. The double agent had been stabbed with a round, sharp object, probably about a foot long, but there was no weapon found at the scene and no tracks around the body. It appeared to be a robbery, but there also had been rumor that the Kremlin had sent an assassin. I dug around and heard that the assassin had been a man called Tosh. He was like a ghost. He slipped in, did his job cleanly, and slipped back out. We never found anything concrete to trace the kill back to the Kremlin."

Looking like a child hearing a bedtime store, Charlie's eyes were wide and her mouth was slightly open. "Did you ever find out it was definitely Tosh?"

Elda smiled at her understudy and answered, "Yes I did. Years later, when working with Tosh, I asked him about this case. He shrugged, said that it was interesting but he had no knowledge of it. He did mention in a following conversation, however, how many icicles there were in St. Petersburg. Amazing! The perfect kill. No weapon. No fingerprints."

All Charlie could say was, "Wow."

Elda continued her storytelling, "Then the rumors stopped and we figured he had become inactive. Either he had finally been killed, which I doubted, or bumped up to be a handler for others. Apparently the latter was true."

Charlie was on the edge of her seat. Clearly she was learning to both admire and fear Tosh. She asked for more of the story, "When did you first meet Tosh?"

Elda took a few deep breaths. Talking about Tosh was wearing her down more than she had suspected it would. However, this was an important lesson for Charlie. She continued., "I met Tosh the first time I was in Russia undercover. He picked me up, took me on a long drive through the snowy streets of Moscow and interrogated me. At the time, I didn't know who he was, but the experience was frightening, especially to a newbie. I then officially met Tosh in Florence when we were working on opposite sides. He reached out since the mission was setting his people up to die needlessly. We worked together to bring down the masterminds behind that operation."

Charlie continued probing, "So what is it about Tosh that is attractive?"

Elda admired Charlie's active mind and went on feeding it with information, "Great question Charlie. Tosh has a moral compass that may not be the same as yours or mine, but he despises being lied to or manipulated. He protects his people with a fierceness of a loving father. When we were in Florence together we discovered a mutual love or art and architecture, and that we both loved the same wooden sculpture of Mary Magdalene by Donatello. We actually had a delightful dinner at an adorable restaurant."

Charlie was listening with her head propped on her hands.

Elda continued, "There was the pull of having found a kindred soul who operated in the same profession, while at the same time knowing that this person could kill you at any moment. I was aware that I had to fight the feeling of comfort and to keep on guard. The man behind the myth lives up to his reputation. He can analyze another as well as I can. His ability to guess what direction you're going in, and, to get to there a few steps in front of you, is scary. Sparring with him is enjoyable. I find few of his caliber."

Above the noise of the cargo plane headed to the UK, Elda continued on to fill Charlie in on more details about Tosh's team and others that they may encounter. The flaps moved and the sound of the engines changed. Elda ordered, "Hold on, Charlie. We're starting our descent."

A few minutes later, the plane landed with a jolt in London.

Elda grabbed her bag. "Game's on."

***

Sophia's green eyes barely cleared the top of Emily Anderson's tall cubicle. She lifted herself up on tiptoes, peered down at Emily and questioned, "Fancy a cup of tea?"

Emily's square face lit up. "I'd be delighted, Sophia. Now?" She ran her fingers through her vintage bob to straighten her dark hair.

"Yes, right away, if you can slip out. There's this fancy new tea shoppe that just opened down the street and I have a desperate hankering for some of their strawberry scones."

"Sounds yummy. Count me in," Emily agreed.

Sophia motioned for Emily to follow her and said, "Brilliant. Let's go."

Emily grabbed her canvas purse from the bottom drawer of her desk and stood on her desk chair to peek over the wall to the adjoining cube. "Jay, I'll be right back. Just popping out for a cuppa. Shall I bring you anything back? No? Righto." She hopped down and followed Sophia out of the building. Once they were out of earshot she asked, "So what's really up, Sophia?

Sophia glanced around. No one was near to overhear. She answered in a quiet voice, "James is acting dodgy. He doesn't want me digging into what the Russians may be up to. Instead he has me buried in realms of paper about China - chasing my tail. But Anatoly was here last week and Yuri is here now. I reached out to Elda. I got this message on the dark web." She held out her phone to Emily.

Emily looked confused and asked, "I thought the dark web wasn't accessible. How did you get this message?"

Sophia answered, "It's not important Emily, but I know you'll perseverate on that and miss what I'm telling you. In a nutshell, the dark web is a part of the internet that isn't indexed by browsers and is only accessible by certain tools. The tools allow anonymous, mostly untraceable messaging. Therefore the dark web is often used for unsavory or clandestine activities. Now *please* look at the message."

Emily glanced at the screen, frowned, shook her head, and stated, "I don't get it."

Sophia turned the phone back to herself, and read the message out loud. "Oh it's pretty clear: *GARY COOPER AT THE O.K. CORRAL FOR BABY BRO SIXTEEN MINUS ONE.* I imagine that means we are to meet her at noon at St James Park tomorrow, the fifteenth of July."

Emily's brown eyes were wide with amazement. She spit out, "Bloody hell, Sophia. How on earth did you conclude *that*?"

Sophia looked shocked that Emily didn't easily get the message. She pointed out, "It's obvious. Elda's American. The movie *Gunfight at the O.K. Corral* is an American movie where Wyatt Earp's younger brother James is killed. One review panned the film, saying it was too derivative of *High Noon*, which is another old American Western, starring Gary Cooper."

"How do you know all *that*?"

"Oliver is an American Westerns buff. So I have learned by osmosis. And Elda knows that Oliver loved these movies as well as how he and I closely share."

Perplexed still, Emily shook her head. Then she cocked her head, put a finger up and knitted her brows together. "Blimey. What if it isn't Elda?"

Sophia shrugged nonchalantly, "It is most likely her. Few others would know that information and anyone who might be able to decode it is probably not in our industry. But if it isn't her, then I'm walking into a trap. Can you back me up?"

Emily's face lit up at the thought of action. "You can count on me."

"Good. Bring a gun."

***

The scene in front of her flickered, blurred and then came in sharply. Elda tapped the side of her glasses to adjust the range of vision. Elda was sitting on a bench near the bandstand in Hyde Park. She had selected the location for its closeness the neighborhood where Nigel had purchased a house for over 10 million Euros. Her team had quickly installed small Bluetooth cameras in multiple locations around her. She appeared to be reading a book, but actually she was watching her surroundings through her mirrored sunglasses which had a computerized screen to show her a 360-degree view. Two men had just entered the park. Facial recognition verified that they were Yuri and Doug.

Elda picked up her phone and sent a text. A nearby jogger stopped, read her phone, shook her head in dismay, and jogged away towards the rose garden. Elda noted with satisfaction that Charlie was getting much more proficient in her disguises.

Although in disguise herself, and despite knowing that seeing through camouflage was not one of Yuri's proficiencies, Elda still held her book up higher and tilted her head down as Yuri walked by with Doug. Doug was waving his hands and shaking his head. As they passed Elda, she overheard Doug say, "I just gave you the information from my father but he is refusing to get me any more information."

"Either you get him to do it or we can persuade him. You won't personally like the latter," Yuri responded.

***

"You can send them home."

Sophia, sitting on a bench in St. James Park, was watching for Elda and also admiring her view of the willows and the water. She jumped and nearly fell off her perch, when a small man with a brown mustache, goatee, and mirrored sunglasses suddenly materialized beside her. She took him in, from his bright orange running shoes, royal blue track outfit, to his hood covered head. The voice, although an octave lower, sounded familiar.

Sophia ventured, "Elda?"

"Yes," answered Elda curtly, "Now please dismiss Oliver and Emily, before they give us away by their undisguised presence."

Sophia gave the thumbs up signal and waved to dismiss her backup team. A nearby bush shook.

Emily popped out from behind it and joined Oliver, who had been walking along slowly and feeding the pigeons. Together, they walked out of the park. Elda typed in a text on her phone and a custodian wheeled his trash cart out of the park.

"Let's walk." Elda moved off and Sophia fell into pace with her. Elda looked down, hiding her lips from any observer, and inquired, "What's this all about, Sophia? Why the subterfuge?"

Sophia held up a hand to her mouth and responded from behind it, "I am suspicious of James. He won't listen, but I think Tosh and the gang are running an op in London."

Elda looked away from Sophia and said out of the corner of her mouth, "You're right, they are."

Sophia, shocked at the confirmation, stopped in her tracks. Forgetting to hide her face or lower her voice, she blurted out, "What?"

Elda looked around her. She scratched her nose in a way that her hand covered her mouth from any surveillance and lowered her voice even further. "I can't fill you in on it all here, but here's the address of the flat I've rented." She slipped Sophia a piece of paper. "Meet me there at 18:00 tonight. Bring Oliver and Emily. But, if you come, you all have to commit to be working with me and on my side, even if it puts you in a bind because James is your boss."

Sophia flinched, "Yes Elda, he is my boss. I don't know if I can work against him. And I am loyal to my country."

Elda nodded and replied, "As you should be. What if your boss is a mole? We're not doing this just because he's a pompous ass, you know."

Sophia frowned and said, "I didn't think you were, Elda. I will admit I think he is going in the wrong direction, but that in itself isn't proof that he is a mole."

Impatient to get Sophia on board, Elda quickly thought for a way to get her to work with Elda. "Ok, Sophia. What if you worked with us under the auspice that you were going to help clear his name and prove that he isn't a mole? You know we were never sure we had found all the moles in Operation Bittman."

Sophia acknowledged that she was on board, "That was a smart move, Elda. Yes, I can do that." She glanced at the paper and handed it back to Elda.

Elda popped the paper in her mouth, chewed vigorously and swallowed hard, followed by a large swig from her water bottle. Sophia looked at her with a grimace on her face. Elda coughed, "Damn, I wish I'd selected a flavored paper. Edible, my foot! So are you in?"

Sophia nodded vigorously. "I'm in. Things wrapped up rather conveniently during the last op. You're right. I wasn't convinced we had found the last mole in MI6."

"Nor am I. I'll have the teapot heated. Bring some of those scones I saw you pick up earlier."

"You've been watching me."

"Of course. I had to be sure of you." Elda glanced around. The coast was still clear. She suddenly dashed away.

***

Charlie sat dejectedly on the edge of the bed in Elda's London flat with her head in her hands. "So, what gave me away?"

Elda stood, feet hip width apart, hands on hips, in her school teacher stance and gave Charlie her observations: "When you were in your jogging disguise in Hyde Park, I spotted you from your distinctive run. Your right leg kicks out slightly and you hold your right shoulder high when you swing your arm."

Charlie nodded. The feedback recorded. "And my custodian disguise?"

Elda smiled and shook her finger in approval. She demonstrated the movements as she spoke, "Ah, that one was quite good. But when you reached in to grab the trash bag, your movement had a hitch to it and wasn't as smooth as it would be from many hours of doing that job. When in disguise you have to also get into the mindset of someone who does it for a living day after day." Elda demonstrated the move for Charlie. "So you were either new at the job or not a custodian. Your clothing was not new, which led support for the latter theory. And then when you scanned the area, you looked around at eye level, not on the ground for more trash."

Charlie frowned and slapped her thigh. "Damn."

Elda held out her hand to calm her and continued with the training, "When in character, go there completely. Submerse yourself into every detail that person would think, do, feel, or see." She walked across the room and with a smooth motion, grabbed the bag from the wastebasket. She swiftly collected bits of paper from the desk and lint from the floor while walking back to Charlie. She tied the bag with a flourish and handed it to Charlie. Charlie bowed in admiration. "Now you do it," Elda ordered. Elda drilled Charlie until she had the moves perfected.

"OK, Elda. Got it. I won't make those mistakes again."

Elda paced in front of Charlie to deliver her final point, "I'm sure you won't. But there are always new errors to make. Rehearse your disguises in your mind and try to pre-think any new mistakes and then just don't make them."

Charlie looked confused and scratched her head, asking, "But how will I know they are errors?"

Elda gave a small smile at Charlie's confusion and reassured her, "I know that sounds impossible. You'll know. Always try to think through what you don't know and plan for it."

With a knitted brow and scrunched face, Charlie responded, "Really?"

"Yes. You'll get the feel for it after a while." Elda walked over to a rolling white board she had placed in the living room and beckoned to Charlie to join her, "Now let's talk over this operation. I welcome your perspective."

Shortly after Elda finished briefing Charlie, Olivia, Sophia and Emily showed up at Elda's sparsely furnished flat in London. Having been introduced, all but Elda sat on milk crates on the living room floor. Elda sat perched on a side table.

"Blimey, Elda, couldn't the United States government pay for some chairs?" complained Oliver, his long legs coming nearly up to his chin.

Elda rolled her eyes and admonished Oliver, "Hush Oliver. With our current deficit in the United States, we're lucky to have the milk crates. Anyway, I don't expect to be here very long. We can all use this flat as a safe house and meeting place during this operation. I have made you each a spare key."

"So what's the plan, Elda?" inquired Emily eagerly. Sliding her milk crate to one side, Sophia moved to sit cross legged on the floor next to Oliver. She reached over and took his hand in hers.

Elda stood to address the group, "First of all I have to know you're all in. Oliver, I know you are taking time off from MI6. Are you sure you want in on this?"

Oliver stretched out his legs in front of him with a painful grimace before responding, "Yes I do, Elda. I think that bastard James sold us down the river on our last mission. I want to get even with him and permanently remove him from MI6." Sophia released Oliver's hand so he could massage his legs. She leaned over and grabbed her crate and handed it to him. He stood and stacked it on top of his crate and sat back down, "Whew. Thanks love."

Elda nodded, "I totally agree with that thinking, Oliver, and considering your severe injuries from that time, he's yours." She pointed at the others and asked, "Emily, Sophia – in?"

"Yes!"

"Righto!"

Elda walked into the bedroom and grabbed a pillow from the bed. Returning, she threw it at Oliver, who gratefully put it under his backside. Elda grasped one end of the rolling white board and pulled it over so all could see what she was drawing. She picked up a marker and started writing names and assignments as she talked. "OK. I want to set up a sting. The bugs I planted in James' office last year are probably there and just need to be reactivated. That will be your job, Sophia. You will also need to reassure him that you are no longer interested in the Russian operatives in London. Can you do that?"

"I definitely can. Elda. He thinks I'm a *juggins* anyway. Treats me like I haven't a brain in my head."

"Good. He'll regret that." Elda pointed at Oliver and snapped out, "Oliver, how good are you at disguises? That limp of yours should help. They have not seen you out of a wheelchair since the shooting. I'd like for you to help me locate where Anatoly and

Yuri are staying and, if possible, bug their rooms. Can you help me with that?"

Oliver stuck his thumb up and replied, "Bob's your uncle, Elda."

"Great. Thanks." Elda turned towards Emily, stating, "Emily. You're also an unknown. I would like for you to get closer to Nigel and Doug and we can improvise on next steps once you have established contact. Can you do that?"

Emily nearly fell off her crate with excitement at being included in their spy game. She nodded energetically and raised her hand.

Elda looked at Emily quizzically and inquired, "Yes, Emily."

Emily gushed, "I just wanted to thank you. I will do my job well."

Elda raised her eyebrows, her left eye twitched, and her mouth quivered in response. She managed to choke out, "Ah, thanks Emily. It really isn't necessary to raise your hand to speak though, okay?"

"Oh, right-o."

Elda looked to Charlie. "Charlie, you're with me. I will need you to help smoke out James more. Let's strategize on that one. He is a dangerous man."

Charlie nodded in response.

"OK, guys, what have I forgotten?"

Surprised at being asked, they all sat mute.

Elda clapped her hands loudly and raised her voice, "Come on, gang! We're a team now. Teams help their leader with ideas. Brainstorm! Think!"

Silence.

Elda said softly, "Blighters. Go home and sleep on it."

They sat still.

Elda glared at them and said in an even tone, "We are done for tonight. Dismissed."

Chapter Fourteen

Sophia strode into James' office. "Thanks for taking the time to see me sir."

"Anytime, Sophia," said James in a flat tone of voice. "What can I do for you?" He half swiveled his chair towards her, ready to turn his back to her and gaze out his window.

Sophia took out her cell phone and appeared to fumble to get the picture up on her screen. She immediately dismissed the message, ACTIVATED, that had appeared in response to a few of her keystrokes and held the phone out. "Here, James. I took a snap of one of the messages coming between China and North Korea. I think it may be worth digging into. What do you think?"

James turned fully towards her, smiled and nodded at her. He said cloyingly, "Now that's a good girl. Exactly the type of intel you should be bringing me." He gestured dismissively at her phone and stated approvingly, "I trust your judgement implicitly. Go dig into that more."

Sophia put her phone back into her pocket and said, "Thank you sir." She forced a cheery smile onto her mouth. Her eyes stayed cold and void of emotion.

James leaned forward with his chin on his fingertips and probed further, "So you are no longer interested in pursuing the Russian operatives?"

Sophia waved his words away, signifying how silly that had been of her. "No sir. I mean yes sir. That is, I am no longer interested in the Russians here in the UK. You really got me to thinking after our last conversation about how I was too obsessed with them after their superiors orchestrated the attack on Oliver, and from having worked closely with Tosh's team on that mission. I *do* need to let that go. You were right. Thank you." She put on a countenance that she hoped conveyed obedience and gratitude, without going overboard.

James puffed up with importance. "Excellent. You know you can always confide in me."

"Oh yes James. I so appreciate that." Sophia turned sharply and shut the door gently, but firmly, behind her.

***

Through her earphones, Elda heard the door shut and, slightly after that, the sound of a desk drawer opening and closing again, followed by a series of faint clicks. She was listening so intently that she jumped at the booming sound of James' voice.

"No worries. She has been successfully distracted….. Yes, China. The rascals, hey? There will be no interference."

***

There was that feeling again. Anatoly looked behind him and saw nothing untoward. He took a sharp turn and ran down the stairs into the Okhotny Ryad shopping center. No footsteps followed him. He dashed to the center of the mall and jogged up the half circle of white stairs, pausing at the top to survey the crowd below. He recognized no one. He decided he would not catch the train at the Okhotny Ryad, but would instead take off at a slow jog and take a few turns on his way to the Kremlin, in case someone was following him. He zigged left and then right and paused at the Marshal Zhukov monument. Again, no one. Why couldn't he shake this feeling? By the time he passed by the State Historical Museum, the hair on the back of his neck was standing up.

Certain that someone was following him, Anatoly took a sharp left and sped off at a run along Nikolskaya Street. He dashed through the GUM department store, pushing shoppers to one side, his feet pounding on the marble floor. He darted through

196

the vaulted halls and out into Red Square. He sprinted around a crowd of tourists who were taking snaps of Lenin's Tomb and dashed into the Kremlin. He didn't stop running until he was safely inside Tosh's building. Once inside the door, he waited until his breath calmed, then marched to Tosh's office to report to Tosh, as ordered.

"From whom were you running?" Tosh's pale grey eyes roved the dampness along Anatoly's hairline and his slightly flushed cheeks.

Anatoly looked chagrinned at being caught running away from something and embarrassed that Tosh might perceive it as a weakness. He announced uncertainly, "I don't know *ser*. Someone is following me again."

"Well, I know who is." Tosh threw a piece of paper down on the desk in front of Anatoly.

Anatoly picked the picture up. His eyes narrowed and his nostrils flared. He snarled, "That little bitch," and tossed her picture back to Tosh.

Just then Snezhana swept into Tosh's office. "*Privet, ser. Privet* Anatoly." She sat and gracefully crossed her long legs and automatically threw her head back to straighten the long brown ponytail that was no longer there. Her blue eyes assessed

Anatoly's subtle dishevelment. "Did something happen that I should know about?"

Anatoly snorted. He kicked back his chair and grabbed a sochniki from a bag on Tosh's sideboard. Powdered sugar flew off the pastry as he savagely bit into it. Snezhana threw a napkin at him. She then glanced at Tosh expectantly.

Tosh replied, "Yes, niece. I have a mission for you."

Snezhana raised one eyebrow and remarked, "Niece? So this is off the books, *ser*?"

Tosh stood up, poured himself a cup of tea and returned to his desk before answering. "*Da*, Snezhana. We have some unfinished business from our last operation with the Americans. Angelina Rodin is following Anatoly. I am guessing that she wants to settle the score from the last time they met. She is an accomplished assassin and *very* elusive. Few have ever gotten the better of her, as Anatoly did."

Anatoly slammed his fist into his thigh. "*Der'mo*. I should have killed her. We didn't get any information from her in the end."

Tosh held up his hand. "True, Anatoly, but that's all in the past. Let's focus on today and how to get her off your tail."

Anatoly growled, "*Da. Khorosho.*"

Tosh addressed his niece, "Snezhana, Angelina has never met you. I would like you to discretely tail Anatoly and see if you can spot her. We need to know if she's still here and if she is serious about taking Anatoly out. If so, we will make a plan to do away with her. If the opportunity arises, feel free to kill her, but keep in mind that she has eluded death or capture for many years now, so respect that experience."

"*Da, uncle.*"

Tosh pushed an orange folder across his desk for Snezhana. "This is all we know about her. Memorize it and leave it here."

Snezhana picked up and leafed through the slender folder. Shutting it, she placed it back on Tosh's desk and looked at him expectantly.

"That is all."

***

Tosh sat calmly in Adrik's office. The analog clock displayed 11:15. Tosh, in the fifteen minutes he was waiting, had quickly memorized any changes in the office and was now looking out the window, scanning faces of those who were walking outdoors and comparing them to his internal database. He briefly considered going back to the anteroom, to ask Adrik's secretary if they needed to reschedule, when the door opened and Adrik lumbered in. He visually inspected his office. Nothing was out of place. He remarked, "Your patience and lack of curiosity is admirable, Tosh."

Tosh shrugged. "No need to be curious, ser. You will tell me anything I need to know."

Adrik narrowed his eyes, staring at Tosh's impassive face. Tosh returned Adrik's gaze without blinking. Adrik perhaps trusting Tosh, for now, responded, "True. I will give you whatever information you need, no more, no less. Your first mission with Senator Clark has been very successful."

"*Spasibo, ser.*"

"You should keep that team in place, in case we have a further need for them, but I have a second assignment for you to start now."

Tosh leaned forward to show interest, "*Da ser?*"

Adrik adjusted his bulk in his chair and looked down at a brown folder on his desk. He opened the folder, read the top sheet of paper, and instructed Tosh, "You will have one of your people join a white supremacist group in the United States to sow chaos and discord. We will even give you a cache of untraceable weapons to garner favor with these people." He passed the paper over to Tosh who quickly scanned it and handed it back.

Tosh drew a deep breath before answering carefully, "*Ser*, although I will follow your orders, I must inform you that this type of operation is not what my team normally does. We are highly trained intelligence operatives, spies and assassins. You might do better by using someone more suited to this type of work."

Adrik drew himself up in his chair and said in a viciously low growl, "Do you doubt my knowledge of your team? Or do you see it as beneath you and your team to do *this type of work*?" Adrik's hand twitched on the arm of his chair.

Tosh stayed silent.

Adrik continued to berate Tosh, "Or are you afraid that your team is not up to the job and you will finally fail?"

Silence.

Adrik barked, "Well?"

Tosh said slowly and clearly, "My team is trained to be invisible. They discretely obtain the needed information or terminate an enemy agent and quickly disappear. Each having complimentary skills, they work together, as needed, to obtain the mission's goals. They have also been trained to think and act independently."

Adrik snorted and responded, "This type of operation where we spread information and rabble rouse a large group of individuals is the future, Tosh. You and your team's way of operating in the shadows is the past. I am giving you a chance to move forward with me. *Ponymayesh*'?" Adrik leaned forward, his eyes boring into Tosh's. "Is your team incapable of doing overt action? Do I need to replace you? And them?"

Tosh looked at Adrik impassively and answered calmly, "*Nyet ser. Ya ponimayu*. Will these weapons already be in the United States or are we to bring them in?"

Adrik grunted at Tosh's question, "Do you know nothing? Of course we have taken care of obtaining the weapons in the States. It is very easy to get assault style weapons there. Your team's role is to ensure the group gets the guns and uses them to create discord and violence in America."

Adrik scribbled a name down on a flimsy piece of paper and gave it to Tosh. Tosh glanced at it. "Is the paper edible, *ser*?"

"*Da*. Do please memorize it and dispose of it." Tosh crumpled the paper up and shoved it in the side of his cheek to moisten it before chewing and swallowing. Adrik continued filling Tosh in on the mission, "You will also have someone infiltrate one of the QAnon groups to help distribute disinformation."

Tosh spoke around the all too slowly disintegrating paper in his mouth, "*Da ser*. Are we to supply them with weapons too?" Adrik reached into his drawer and pulled out a bottle of water which he passed to Tosh. "*Spasibo, ser*." Tosh took a sip, quickly chewed the rest of the paper and swallowed it, followed by a generous swig from the bottle.

Once Tosh was finished, Adrik explained slowly, as if speaking to an obtuse child, "*Nyet*. There is no need to supply the QAnon groups with weapons. These groups are fringe conspiracy groups, mainly backed by quack discredited doctors. They have wild ideas such as space laser beams, injection of microchips, and a government run by baby killers. Most of them have traumatic backgrounds, making them very susceptible to magical thinking and conspiracy theories. We will capitalize on their emotional instability and use them to our advantage to help sow disinformation throughout the United States. Have your agent learn their ideas and help disseminate these ideas. This will help Russia continue to undermine the democracy in the United States. *Vy ponimayete?*"

"*Da ser. Ya ponimayu.*"

Adrik slowly rose from his chair and dismissively asked. "Any other questions?"

"*Nyet.*" Tosh pushed back his chair and stood at attention, waiting to be let go.

"*Khorosho.* Leave."

Tosh turned and vanished from the office, leaving no trace of ever having been there, not even a scent.

***

Yaromir Kozlov sat like a bear, his square muscular bulk overflowing a chair in Tosh's office. His dark eyes were shaded by heavy brows and the dark stubble of his beard blended into the stubble of his shaved haircut. His forearms were furlike covered in hair, and his biceps and pecs strained the material of his black t-shirt. His very muscular legs were covered by tight fitting black jeans and his feet were encased in black, steel-tipped motorcycle boots.

Although rather crude in his approaches at times, Yaromir had been highly successful in his assigned missions. He had failed in his mission against Elda, but Tosh believed in giving second chances to all of his people, as long as they did not repeat the same mistake. He expected that each member of his team would take their job as their number one priority and devote their lives to improving and serving him and Mother Russia. Those who could not, paid a steep price.

Next to Yaromir, with a blank expression on her face, sat Nadia Belov. Nadia with her pale white skin and blond hair had an imposing presence, but her looks could not be called beautiful or even pretty. She was in some ways handsome, with her intense blue eyes and long nose and rugged chin, but a bout of chicken pox in her youth had left scars on her cheeks and on closer inspection, her eyes were just a tad too close together and her mouth a bit too wide for her face. She crossed and uncrossed her legs, as if impatient to leave.

Nadia had recently joined Tosh's group, having been assigned by the Kremlin. Her background in seduction and misinformation was welcomed by Tosh. However, he still was taking Nadia's measure and was glad to have a mission to test her sills and dedication out on. Tosh had dug further into Nadia's background and activities outside of the office when she was first assigned, and did not approve of what he found. Suspicious of her ethics, he spied on her and found that his suspicions were most likely true. *I think she has killed at least one person outside of any missions and that Yaromir has helped her dispose of the body. I suspect she may be having random sex with strangers. Clever of her to ensure she gets rid of the evidence but it leaves her open to criminal prosecution if she's found out.*

He narrowed his eyes as he assessed her. He noticed her interaction with Yaromir. *Ah yes, they have a much deeper relationship outside the office.*

Tosh sat behind his desk with a small stack of manilla folders and assorted papers in front of him. He selected a few of the papers and placed them inside one of the folders. "Yaromir, here is your identification and your plane tickets. You are to fly to the United States of America to meet up with the man identified in this folder." Tosh slipped the folder across to Yaromir. "He's already a member of the Virginia branch of a large white supremacist group. He'll bring you into the organization and together you two will find ways to help tear apart the United States. You will instigate riots, protests, fights, and ensure that there is violence, theft and burning buildings. But do not be caught as the one igniting those flames. *Khorosho*?"?

Yaromir nodded his acceptance of his mission.

"We will arrange for you to receive an arms shipment once you are settled in. This will help raise your position within the group and potentially give you more say over its movements."

"*Da, ser.*" Yaromir read and memorized the folder and passed it back to Tosh.

"You will also contact this senator." Tosh laid down a piece of paper on his desk with a snapshot of Senator Glass. "He has access to some interesting information that we want. We'd like to compromise him—more than just through the pictures we took of his nights here in Moscow—by having him transfer some sensitive information to you. You will then send it on to us via this man…," Tosh slipped a second photo with name on top of the first, "…Doug, when he visits his father. He will be your courier. He's already been flying back and forth from the UK to the US to gather information for us. *Khorosho?*"

Yaromir signified his understanding with an affirmative grunt.

"You have been training since your last mission and have attended many classes on America and smoothed your accent. I expect that you will be able to fit in. Any concerns with that?"

Yaromir with a slight smile answered, "Nope. I gotcha. It's not rocket science. It's right up my alley. I'm on it like white on rice. I'll be drinking iced tea, eating apple pie and shooting the breeze the whole time."

Tosh, hiding his smile at Yaromir's progress, turned his attention to Nadia and addressed her, "Nadia, you will join QAnon using your computer skills to distribute misinformation through Twitter, Reddit, Facebook and similar right-wing social media. We have learned that Senator Madison Barrett is most open to helping us. We have the Moscow photos from his night of sex with the prostitute at the hotel. We also have discovered that he is deeply in debt from his gambling addiction. You will contact him and get him to help spread disinformation that you create through his social media accounts as well as on Capitol Hill. This spreading of disinformation will pay him handsomely. We will arrange a bank account for him and will back these efforts for up to one million American dollars. We will also arrange a bank account for you to tap while you're there. All money must be strictly accounted for and any excess returned. Khorosho?"

Nadia exhaled loudly and said in a bored tone, "*Khorosho.*"

"That would be *khorosho ser*, Nadia," Tosh said icily.

"*Khorosho, ser*," Nadia responded automatically.

Tosh continued, "We have given you a medical degree as a doctor of pharmacy. Your bachelors in chemistry and computer science should allow you to pass and call yourself doctor. You also have a sad story of having lost your only child through a bad vaccination. Memorize it and make it your own." Tosh handed her a manila folder. "This folder cannot leave this office."

Nadia sighed, tossed her hair, sat back and leafed through the folder, closing her eyes and repeating what she had just read under her breath as she memorized her cover story.

Tosh turned back to Yaromir. "Yaromir, this is your story. The FBI killed your brother in error. You believe that the establishment has gone far left, caters to minorities, and whites are left to fend for themselves. The white male especially is losing status and control. You believe passionately that it is time for the citizens to take up arms and take back the United States from non-white, non-Christian, immigrants." Tosh passed a second folder to Yaromir.

Yaromir studied the folder. When he was done, he placed it on the desk and looked at Tosh. Nadia put her folder next to Yaromir's.

Tosh rose from his chair to end the meeting and commanded, "Get into character quickly. You leave tomorrow. I need to speak with each one of you separately. Yaromir, please wait outside."

***

Nadia sat examining her nails while Yaromir walked out of the office. After the door closed, Tosh stated. "I know what you have been up to."

Nadia's head snapped up and she eyed Tosh nervously. *What does he really know? Is he pretending to know something just to get me to confess?*

"Do you have anything to say for yourself?" demanded Tosh.

"*Nyet ser.*" She held her breath, wondering what he really knew.

Tosh continued, "If I didn't need your skills on this mission, you'd be sidelined already." Nadia eyed him and inhaled deeply. *He had nothing.*

Tosh looked at her folder, opened it and shuffled a few papers. Nadia waited in silence. Finally, he

210

snapped out in a terse low voice, "I do not tolerate disloyalty."

Govno. What does he know? Her mind raced to answer. She sat mute.

"I will be watching you closely"

Nadia inhaled again. She relaxed slightly. No details were forthcoming. Then the shoe dropped.

"Adrik will not get you what you want, you know. He is just using you. You are a patsy in a game that you don't completely understand."

Nadia opened her mouth, shut it again and then finally spit out, "*Da, ser.*"

Tosh continued, "And, …" The word hung in the air. Nadia wondered what else was coming.

Tosh stated firmly, "I've noticed that there has been a decrease in the male population in Moscow lately."

"*Govno.*" *Oh shit*, thought Nadia. *That slipped out. What is he going to do with me?*

Tosh shook his finger at her and commanded sternly, "*Da, govno.* You'll be shit if activities don't stop *immediately. Khorosho?*"

What does that mean he'll do? Nadia felt the sweat pool down her sides from her armpits. She wiped her upper lip on her hand and replied, "*Da, ser.*"

Tosh showed her the door with a perfunctory wave of his hand and ordered, "Send Yaromir in. You are dismissed."

***

Yaromir sat at attention in the chair across from Tosh's desk. He felt secure that he had done nothing that Tosh would reprimand him for.

Tosh picked up papers from his desk and filed them as the tension grew in the room. Finally he turned and stated, "There's conspiracy and then there's acquiescence. Which is it on your part?"

Oh crap. Is he referring to me having sex with Nadia? Yaromir decided to come clean about that. *I wonder if he is also referring to me disposing of Nadia's kills for her? I'll leave that vague in my answer.* "It is more acquiescence, *ser*, to get good sex with someone who is secure to associate with, *ser*."

Tosh nodded. "If I asked, would you kill her?"

Without hesitation Yaromir answered, "*Da, ser.*"

Tosh directed him, "Stand by then. You are dismissed"

Chapter Fifteen

Elda scowled and drummed her fingers on the makeshift desk in her London flat. The planks of wood, which were balanced on milk crates to make the desk top, reverberated with the unconscious rhythmic beat of her finger movements. She spoke into her phone, "It's time to narrow the pipeline and get some action from these Russians, Ed. Can we plant more information that only John would have access to?" Elda pressed on her earphones to hear Ed more clearly. "Is someone else in the room with you, Ed?"

Ed's voice came more clearly through her headset, "Sorry Elda. I was multitasking. Let me put you on speaker now. I have Jackson here and I have just filled him in."

Elda stood and started pacing back and forth. She snapped, "We really need to move more quickly here, gentlemen."

His voice sounding tinny through the speaker and headset, Jackson piped up. "I think I know a way. There is an internal server that only the Chair of the Intelligence Committee would have access to. Ashok can create the file to place there. There is no internet connection to the server, so it would have to be accessed by John, or, of course, the one IT person with clearance, who is on our payroll. Through him we can check the logs and monitor any data transfer from the server to ensure no one else picks it up."

Elda nodded at her phone. "Good." She commanded, "Let's set that up. It's time to remove the Russians from London, but we will need to catch them red-handed."

Jackson spoke again, asking, "Elda, did you find anything from those files I gave you?"

Ed broke in addressing Jackson, "What files did you give Elda?"

Jackson stated, "She wanted my research on operation Bittman."

"Operation Bittman? Why would she want that?" mused Ed.

Elda cleared her throat. "Yoo-hoo… I'm here on the phone still guys. And Ed, for your information, I was thinking that our last mission ended up too cleanly with us finding all the bad guys, except potentially, James. Now we are pretty confident that James is working for the Kremlin. Who else may be hidden as a Russian asset? And who in the Kremlin is pulling the strings? We received intel shortly after the operation that Alexei Alexeev, Tosh's boss, had disappeared. I'm suspecting that Tosh or one of his team took him out for having betrayed the team. But would years of planting and operating a deep mole involve just the handful of folks in power that we eliminated? I think not. I suspect there are more."

Ed said sharply, "Elda, that's not this mission. Stand down on that."

"I don't think it's wise, Ed," Elda admonished.

Ed repeated sternly, "Stand down on that. Digging into something that could be that big would not be wise for you, Elda. And you have a relationship to repair."

Elda was silent.

"Don't you?" Ed queried more gently.

Elda inhaled deeply and pronounced sadly, "I've been trying, Ed. And Dawn is so worth it. She's wonderful."

Ed broke in, "Wonderful, Elda? Are you speaking of the same woman who for years has harassed you about the job you do?"

"She has come a long way in accepting who I am and what I do."

"Really Elda? I haven't seen that." Ed stated.

"She didn't tantrum when I told her I had to come to DC," Elda explained.

"Is that sufficient, Elda?" Ed probed.

"I tell myself it has to be, but, …" Elda paused

"But, …?"

"But that's it, Ed. She puts up with me."

Ed didn't let Elda off the hook, "But, …?"

Silence. Ed's question hung in the air.

Finally Elda answered, "I'm still not sure that I can be who she wants me to be. And I know that I don't want to give up this work."

"Someday you will have to, Elda," Ed said firmly.

Elda stood still and looked sadly at the phone in her hand. Then she angrily drew her hand back as if to throw it away. Stopping herself, she brought it up to her face and answered Ed, "I know. That's why I'm training Charlie. But even if America doesn't acknowledge it, the Cold War is still here, and although it is heavily invested in cyberterrorism, there is a strong need for old-style spies to ferret out folks like James."

"I know, Elda. But you also know that most others believe that it can be taken care of through technology."

"Then perhaps they need to see that they are wrong," Elda stated bitterly.

Ed pleaded, "Please, Elda. Don't go off book on this mission."

"Don't worry, Ed. This one will be played by the book. My book, though."

Ed sighed. His voice came through softly, "Try not to get killed, okay?"

Elda cut the connection. She picked up her laptop and poured through the heavily redacted files she had received from Jackson. "Someone is hiding something." She stood and paced around her sparsely furnished London flat. She stopped suddenly and pointed her finer in the air and exclaimed, "Aha! That's what I'll do." She scrolled to a favorite picture on her computer. "Ah, there you are, milady." She printed it out on paper that she had kept from her stay at the Hotel Brunelleschi in Florence, Italy. She scribbled a few lines on the photo and then put it in an envelope, also from the hotel. She sealed it closed and added a wax stamp on the back, whispering, "Travel safely, milady."

Elda then addressed and put postage on the envelope before finally putting it in a second envelope with a short note. On the second envelope she wrote the name of her contact in Germany. He would certainly do her the small favor of forwarding on the inner message since she had done a larger favor for him in a previous mission and had his horrid boss removed.

"Hopefully, he will understand the message." She licked the envelope and sealed it.

***

Emily snaked her way through the crowd to the bar and flagged down a bartender. She ordered a shanty and looked around the full pub for a place to sit. Spying Doug and Nigel sitting together at a table, she made her way over to them. Smiling broadly at Doug, she asked, "May I sit with you two gentlemen?" Doug nearly dropped his beer, sloshing foam over the side as he thumped the mug down on the table. He knocked his glasses off his face in his rush to stand up. Nigel quickly popped up from his chair and reached over to pull over a third chair, knocking over his beer in the process. He clumsily mopped at the liquid with his small cocktail napkin, increasing the rate at which it dripped down the table and onto his shoes.

Emily pulled out the proffered chair and sat down. Nigel leaned towards her, put on his most engaging smile and asked, "Come here often?" He then placed his hand flirtatiously on his chin, putting shirt sleeve squarely in the remaining pool of beer. "Blimey!" He recoiled. "Pardon me." He jumped up to go clean up in the men's room.

Tears were forming in Emily's eyes. Her chin was quivering in an attempt to hold back a smile. She blinked back both the tears and the stifled laughter. Doug mopped up the remaining beer from the table with his napkins and retrieved his eyeglasses from the floor. "Please don't be sad. We're most always this bad at speaking to women," he said with a slight lisp as the words passed through his crooked and oddly spaced teeth.

Emily smiled at his homely sincerity. She glanced at the Newcastle United game on the television behind the bar and exclaimed, "Oh I love that team."

Doug excitedly replied, "I do too! Did you see the goal they scored at home in St. James Park last week?"

"Did I?! It was simply brilliant."

When Nigel returned from the men's room, Doug and Emily were deep in conversation about their mutual love of football. Nigel had no knowledge of or love for the game himself and nothing to add to the conversation. Left out of their chat and ignored, he spit out, "Doug, fuck it. I've had enough of this place. Are you coming with me?"

Doug replied, without taking his eyes off of Emily, "I'll meet you at home later."

Nigel stomped away.

After another hour of spirited conversation, Doug and Emily left the pub. They paused outside the door and Doug shyly handed Emily a piece of paper with his number written on it. Emily accepted the piece of paper and said with a smile, "You do know, Doug, that you're supposed to ask the girl for her number?" Doug blushed and stammered. Emily patted him on his arm. "That's fine. And here." She ripped off the blank, lower part of the paper he had handed her and scribbled her number on it. He reached awkwardly to give her a hug, but she had already turned to walk away. He shoved her number in his pants pocket and happily ran back to Nigel's house.

Doug entered the house humming, but stopped mid-note, when he viewed Anatoly sitting on the couch next to Nigel.

Anatoly spoke in a low, threatening tone, "We were waiting for you."

***

"How was your time with Doug last night, Emily?" inquired Sophia, handing Emily a scone from the paper bag she was holding. Sophia reached back into the bag and threw some small pieces of scone at the mallard duck that was waddling around nearby the park bench they were sitting on.

"I really had a good time with him!" Emily took a large bite of her scone effectively avoiding further questions.

"Charming, but what information did you discover?" chimed in a jogger, who had come out of nowhere and was stretching at the back of their bench.

"Bloody hell, Elda! How do you do that?" cried out Emily, nearly choking on her scone and holding her hand to her chest. Sophia shook her head, adding, "I'd really like you to teach me that someday, Elda. So, Emily…?"

Elda and Sophia leaned in, waiting for Emily to finish chewing and speak. Finally Sophia broke the silence, "So, did you find out anything interesting?"

Emily looked sad.

Elda spoke up, "So you really like the guy and feel like you're betraying him by telling us about your conversation?"

Emily looked shocked that Elda had read her mind.

Elda commanded sternly, "You're a spy, Emily, like it or not. And Doug is your mark. Your allegiance *has* to be to us and not to him. So spill."

Emily nodded, but didn't brighten. "I know. I know. This is just the first time I have done anything like this. I do want to be a spy, but I've only been trained to be a clerk in MI6 right now."

Elda made a motion with her hand for Emily to speed it up.

"You're right, Elda, he is a nice guy and we had a great conversation about football. In different circumstances I might even date him for real."

Elda groaned and raised her eyebrows at Emily. Sophia scowled at Emily.

Emily continued reluctantly, "OK, I get it. No attachments."

Elda prompted, "So…?"

Emily murmured, "All right, all right… He told me he is going to the United States on a regular basis to see his father and will probably be going again in a few days. He said that his father never really loved him and he has found a way to get even with him. He added that his father was resisting, but that would change."

"Nice guy," snarled Elda, "Real date material."

Sophia added compassionately, "Em, your taste in men has always been bad, you know?"

Emily rolled her eyes sadly and said remorsefully, "I know. I am always attracted to the sociopaths and narcissists."

"I think we need to find you a good secure therapist to help get you through this mission, Emily." Elda wrote a phone number down and handed it to Emily. "Please memorize this and eat the paper."

Emily looked at Elda wide eyed and exclaimed, "Eat the paper? Is that a real thing?"

Elda patted her on the shoulder and asserted, "Yes, that one isn't too bad. I think it's banana flavored." Elda turned to Sophia asking, "Sophia, isn't Oliver completely out of the game now? I was surprised he showed up before with you two."

"We're waiting on the surrogate to confirm she's pregnant. He's set up most of the nursery, repainted it, and is just waiting for the furniture to arrive, so I think he's a bit bored right now."

"Good, I have an idea to smoke James out more." Elda frowned, spotting an old man hobbling along and pushing a Zimmer frame. She quickly typed a text, then lowered her voice and explained what she wanted Sophia to do.

Elda reached into Sophia's bag and threw another piece of scone at the ducks. Both Sophia and Emily tracked the projectile, watching as it flew over the walk and was caught by the duck. They applauded the duck's successful catch. Turning back, Elda was gone.

"Blimey!"

***

Charlie sat despondently on the floor of Elda's London flat. "What on earth gave me away in the park, Elda?"

Elda sat on the desk boards which creaked ominously as she swung her legs back and forth. She jumped off and leaned on the desk to demonstrate as she spoke, "Your arms, Charlie. Old people have no muscles and depend on the walker to support their weight as they shuffle along. Your way of holding and pushing the walker implied too much body strength.”

“Damn.”

***

Nervous sweat beaded on his forehead and dropped off his chin onto the coffee table. Doug speed dialed a number on his phone and waited for his father to pick up. He looked down at the script that Anatoly had handed him.

“Dad? Yes it’s me, Doug. No, no, please don’t hang up. You *must* listen to me. It’s *very* important.” Doug exhaled a large sigh of relief and nodded at Anatoly, who lowered his gun. Doug continued speaking with his father, “I know. I know. But this will be the last time. *I promise.*” He winced and held the phone away from his ear to let Nigel and Anatoly hear his father shouting. He pleaded, “Dad, Dad, please stop. I know I said that it was only once, and I believed that, Dad, but that was only a test of us, apparently. I didn’t know. This will be the real one. Please Dad. I really need you to help me.” Doug’s voice had reached an unappealing whiney pitch. Doug listened to his father who apparently, from his lack of yelling, was starting to give in. “Yes Dad. I will owe you.”

Anatoly tapped the piece of paper with the barrel of his gun. Doug continued, "Dad, I will meet you in two days in the States, at the same spot as before. Tomorrow morning, you will take a walk there at 9am Eastern time. Wear a jacket with large external pockets. You will be bumped into and the instructions will be transferred to your coat pocket. Then you will give me the information requested on those instruction, when I see you. It's that simple."

Doug listened to his father again. "Yes, yes, I promise. This is it. They have assured me of that. Thanks."

He hung up and glared at Nigel, who was sitting perched on the edge of his chair, anxiously following the conversation. He addressed Nigel, "You are a bastard." Nigel shrugged. Doug looked at Anatoly and inquired, "This is probably not the last time, is it?"

"*Nyet*. Probably not."

***

Okay Sophia, get this one over with. Sophia reached for the doorknob and urged herself to open the door. She marched into James' office and stood patiently waiting for him to hang up the phone. James waved her to an office chair and continued his conversation.

"I specifically asked for no starch, but my shirts are stiff and yellowed from too much starch." James was scowling and his bottom lip was sticking out in a pout.

Sophia thought, *It is a very unattractive look for him.*

He ran his free hand through his salt and pepper hair which was in disarray. "Yes, that will do. I will expect the replacement shirts in my next delivery." James put the receiver back onto his desk phone, composed himself and swirled his leather office chair around to face Sophia. He addressed her sternly, "You said you had run across some intriguing information. I hope this is not about the Russians again. You had assured me that you let that go."

Sophia made a patting motion in the air with her hand and smiled broadly to reassure James. "Oh no, James. Don't worry. I took your words to heart and I'm no longer concerned about those operatives. But I was chasing the thread on those messages between China and North Korea, and found an interesting snippet. As we suspected, they are working together, sharing data about America. They have found data that implies the United States Intelligence Committee has obtained information that could be potentially interesting to us and could also be damaging to the Russians."

James sat forward in his chair. "Interesting Sophia. Tell me more." He placed his forefinger on his bottom lip and his chin on his thumb and looked directly at Sophia.

Sophia shrugged and replied sincerely, "I wish I could tell you more James, but I can't get at the information. Apparently it is on a server that isn't connected to the internet." She looked at him sadly and batted her eyelashes. *I may puke. I hate acting like a femme. But he is so easy to manipulate.*

James frowned and ran his fingers through his hair. "Then who has access to that server?"

"Excellent question, James. You always get to the root of the issue!" Sophia laying the flattery on strongly, continued, "It's my understanding that only the IT folks and a few of the Intelligence Committee members have access. But you have higher placed connections than I do in the United States. I was wondering if perhaps you could find out more?"

James smiled an unpleasant grin. "Don't you worry any more about this one, Sophia. You have come to the right person. I'll take it from here. Due to the high level of my connections, my inquiries will have to be handled sensitively and I won't be able to let you know how this turns out. But rest assured, I *will* get to the bottom of this one."

Sophia smiled and stood. "You always make me so relieved, James. Thank you." James dismissed her with a wave at the door and turned away from her. She turned and marched out.

***

To the closed door James muttered, "Excellent. You may be useful after all. These women are so easy to manipulate."

Sliding open his bottom desk drawer, James took out a cell phone. He spoke quietly into it, "*Privet*, Adrik. The United States has documents that could be damaging to Russia. It is on an internal server only accessible by the Intelligence Committee." He listened and replied. "Yes, it's safe to use London as a transfer point for the information. My agents are coincidently distracted by the threat from China."

He hung up and tossed the phone into the drawer and closed it with his foot. He slid open the other bottom drawer and took out a bottle of Triple Distilled Kremlyovskaya Vodka and poured two fingers worth into a small goblet. He held it up, swirled the liquid, admiring the clarity of the liquid and took a sip. Raising his glass again he said softly, "To the Motherland."

***

Elda took off her headphones and hissed angrily to her computer, "You bastard." She typed rapidly, bundling up the MP4 of the audio from James' office along with a .doc file with her notes. She compressed and encrypted the file and sent it via a secure link to Ed. She reached out and snatched up her water bottle. Raising it to *her* lips she declared, "To America," and took a large sip of water. In a fierce tone she exclaimed, "Your days are numbered, James."

***

A duck splashed down in the nearby water. A skittish John jumped sideways and nearly knocked Ed down. Ed reached out a hand to steady John. "Breathe deeply, John. You need to stay composed."

John mopped his brow with his white handkerchief and lowered his voice to a whisper. "It's all set. I'm meeting with him in two days. Are you sure it's safe to give him this information, Ed?" The two men were walking side by side along the banks of the Potomac River, near where they had first met.

Out of the side of his mouth, barely moving his lips, Ed responded, "Yes, John, it's subtly misleading and will not harm US Intelligence in any way. We suspect that the Russians have a spy in the American Embassy in London. We falsified a message from him to MI6 that leaks classified Russian information.

If he is a spy, this should result in his removal from the embassy. We had our agent in MI6 forward it on to the Americans but also embedded it in Intelligence Committee briefing so it would not get lost. You should officially see it today."

John wiped his brow again and asked, "What will become of that spy?"

"He may end up dead or in Siberia for all we care. It's not our problem. What's important is that the information could have easily been obtained by him so we are not putting any of our own agents in peril. So, where are you meeting Doug?"

"The same spot as before."

"Perfect. We will set up additional microphones and cameras so we should be able to hear everything. If you spot any of them, do *not* react. Did he say if he was coming alone or not?"

John stopped in his tracks and gazed wide eyed at Ed. He said loudly, "Drat. No. Should I have asked him that?"

Ed held up a hand to calm John down. "Shh. Let's keep our voices down. No, it's fine. We'll assume he'll have his handler with him."

John spat out, "This is the last time, Ed."

"If you value your life, do not tell your son that. But John, look at it this way – you have the opportunity to help us mislead the Russians. Once you are set up with them we can funnel all sorts of misinformation their way."

"I am not a spy, Ed."

"You are now."

***

"Ashok, is there any way we can improve the sound quality?" Jackson asked, straining to hear through his headset. He frowned and cocked his head and pressed his Bose earphones tighter to his ears.

Ashok, fingers flying over the keyboard, sat in front of three monitors. He pulled up the sound waves of the incoming data and boosted certain frequencies. He then removed the static and screened out the background sounds. "Better?"

"Yes, much, thanks." Jackson relaxed his hands and peered at the monitor. "Those birds were driving me crazy! Can we get a clearer picture too?"

Ashok, fiddled with the camera settings, zoomed in with camera number 1, de-speckled the picture from camera number 2, then asked, "How's that?"

"Much better. Thanks." Jackson watched as John walked into the park and lowered himself down onto a park bench. "I wish we could have miked John."

Ed walked into the communication room and responded, "Too risky, Jackson. If they suspected he was wired, then the game would be over. And John's not an operative. His face would give away the fact that someone was talking in his ear."

"I know, Ed, but it would be so much easier than this." Jackson tipped his chair forward and leaned closer to the monitors.

Ashok smiled and shook his head. "You know that doesn't help you hear them any better?" Jackson scowled at Ashok. Ashok continued, "Would you like for me to put the meeting on speaker for you, Ed?"

"Yes, please do."

The speakers crackled to life. Ashok adjusted the volume and continued tweaking settings to ensure the conversation came in clearly. He pressed the record button when Yuri and Doug approached the bench.

"Hello, Dad."

"Hello, son. Hello large familiar nameless one."

Yuri remained silent.

"Do you have it, Dad?"

"Yes I do. Before I give it to you, can you reassure me that this *is* the last time we do this?"

Doug did not answer. His father shook his head. "You can't say it, can you? You know in your heart that this will never end."

Doug dropped his head and looked at his feet.

John put the thumb drive on the bench and stood to storm away. Before he left he turned and looked at his only son with disgust plainly on his face.

"You have no backbone. You have no ethics. You have no love for me. You only use me when you need something and now are willing to risk my career to save your own neck. Damn you."

Chapter Sixteen

Yaromir unzipped his tote bag and lifted up an AR-57 semi-automatic. He noticed that the ammo clips he had stashed in the bag were missing. He recalled Nadia had checked his bag and wondered if she had mistakenly removed them. He would have a talk with her when he returned. Without the ammo to show off, he would have to think quickly in order to not blow the deal.

He jogged at a quick pace over to the warehouse where they were meeting. He met his contact at the door and was ushered in. He walked directly to a card table that was set up and laid out the first weapon.

"Wow, baby, that's the ticket," exclaimed a bald, heavily tattooed man, reaching for the rifle. Yaromir grinned, showing his gold fillings, and slapped the man's hand away. The man reached into his jacket but was stopped by Yaromir's glare. Yaromir reached into his bag again and pulled out a KRISS Vector SMG submachine gun. He placed both guns on the table, stood back, and gestured that they could now inspect the guns. The tattooed man and a second man with a scraggly beard stepped up to admire and check out the weapons.

The tattooed man turned to Yaromir and inquired, "Where is the ammo?"

Yaromir growled, "Don't sweat it. These are just samples."

The bearded man looked at Yaromir wide-eyed in admiration and asked, "Can you get us more?"

Yaromir said with a sneer, "It depends."

The bald man took a step backwards, squinched his eyes and looked at Yaromir suspiciously. "On what?"

Yaromir stated assertively, "It depends on you. I want these arms used against the FBI and the Socialistic government. I want get rid of the immigrants and to return America to us, the Alpha males. Are you Alphas? Are you ready to rise up and take back America?"

A fourth man, who was lingering in the room behind Yaromir, stepped forward and put his hand on Yaromir's back. "He's the real deal, my friends. The FBI killed his brother. He sees how the control is being ripped away from the rightful owners of American land. How heathens and non-whites have taken over America. I welcome him to fight alongside of me. Do we accept him into this proud organization?"

"Hell yes, man." The bald guy held up his hand to high five Yaromir who stared him down until he dropped his arm.

The bearded man spoke again, "Get us more, including the ammunition, and we will give you a voice as to how they will be deployed."

***

Nadia absentmindedly picked at an acne scar on her face while she watched the doorway of Senator Madison Barrett's house. She had studied his weekly routine and noted that he went out jogging at least three days a week, usually on the same days and at the same time. She had learned that he was recently separated from his wife. The front door opened, the senator emerged, and he started running on the side of the road up the hill in front of his house. Nadia easily fell into step behind him. As his pace faltered near the top of the incline, Nadia accelerated and caught up with him. She gave him a friendly smile when she reached his side.

"I haven't seen you on my route before," remarked the senator, in between breaths.

"I'm new to the neighborhood. May I join you in your run?" Nadia asked engagingly.

Nadia watched Madison take her in, his eyes running up and down her svelte body. He readily agreed. As they jogged along, he inquired, "So what do you do?" His face showed that he was mentally kicking himself for such a lame opening.

Nadia gave him a flirtatious smile and said rather breathily, "I am a doctor, but not practicing currently. My passion is helping people find their way in this mixed-up world. There is much that needs correcting. I've taken a sabbatical to help move my ideas forward. Timing is critical and the time is now."

The senator requested, "Tell me more about your ideas."

Assuming a sad and wistful look, she replied, "I was once married and lost my only child to a bad vaccine. This changed my entire view of life and science. I've deeply researched the misinformation around the vaccinations."

Madison inquired, "What type of misinformation?"

Nadia smiled and winked at Madison. She replied, "I can tell you're an intelligent man from the questions you ask. There is a push to vaccinate the world with numerous vaccines. We are being told that these vaccines are safe. Various people on high are helping spread this dangerous information too."

Pleased by her compliment, but frowning in confusion, a puzzled Madison asked, "Why is that a problem?"

Stopping and turning to him, Nadia, replied, earnestly, "Look at what happened with the Covid vaccines. Those vaccines were developed in warp speed under the command of our government. The original patent for one of the vaccines was contributed to by a member of the NIH. His information was based on only eight years of isolated research. But the truth behind the push to vaccinate is deeply buried. They are hoping to keep us under control and compliant by inserting microchips via the vaccines. China has already started doing this. They use it to keep tabs on their people. The chips will allow them to track us and gather our personal data. We *cannot* let this happen in the United States. We need more people in power who can help stop this and preserve our democracy."

Madison looked her up and down, and declared, "I'm interested in hearing even more. But first, I am so sorry to hear about your loss. How long ago did that happen?"

Nadia waved her hand dismissively and looked steadily into his brown eyes with her piecing teary blue ones. She avowed, "That is all past. I need to now to help others from suffering the same loss I did."

Madison put a hand on her arm and entreated, "You are so brave. Let me help you. I am a United States senator. I have a following and a broad reach."

Nadia put her hand on his arm and declared, "You are? What a fortunate meeting this is. How wonderful that would be. I've got all the research and just need a little help getting it out there."

Madison puffed up and put his arm around her shoulders, sending a direct message of interest. "Can we discuss this further? Perhaps tonight over dinner?"

Nadia leaned into him and breathed deeply. She breathlessly replied, "Yes, that would be wonderful. I know of a nice restaurant, the Bistro Cacao over on Massachusetts Avenue. I can reserve a quiet booth for us. Shall we meet there, perhaps at 6:30pm?"

"I will be there with bells on."

***

"Where and who were you today?" quizzed Elda, standing in her London flat. The evening sun outside peeked through the thickening clouds and faded daylight dappled on the wooden floor.

Charlie answered, delight sounding in her voice, "I was the old lady feeding the birds in the park. You were talking to Sophia and Emily. You had your jogging disguise on. By the way, it's a good disguise. I only knew it was you because you left the apartment in those clothes." Elda held back a smile at Charlie's youthful enthusiasm. Her eyes crinkled as she observed Charlie standing in the middle of the living room, her hands clasped at her chin, her eyes wide, so eagerly awaiting Elda's answer.

Elda looked up and to the left as if to replay the park scene in her head. "Ah, yes. Excellent job, Charlie. You were muttering to yourself and nearly falling off the bench each time you threw some bread crumbs. Your nose was running and you kept dabbing at it with a dingy, crumpled, hanky that you kept in the end of your sleeve. Your grey hair was tinged with hints of past color and was therefore more realistic than most wigs or dye jobs. Your eyebrows matched well. Your eyes were a nondescript blue clouded by cataracts. You smacked your lips periodically as some old people do. Perhaps a touch of dehydration. Your body shape could only be described as dumpy and your hands shook as you reached into the bag for more crumbs. Your height seemed to be about two inches shorter than you really are and you had dowager's neck. Excellent job, Charlie. You really owned that character. Congratulations. You have passed this stage of training."

Just then Elda's phone rang. She picked it up from the eraser tray of the whiteboard, and, while listening, made a motion for Charlie not to leave. "Hi Ed. What's up?"

"It's started," Ed replied.

Elda brightened and said, "So the bait was taken? Good. Don't hang up yet, Ed. I have an idea to get more on James and to also ferret out any more assets planted in MI6. I'd like to use Charlie. Can we add some tidbits to her service record. Nothing bad enough to get her kicked out – just a pattern of a disgruntled American who might be turned...?" Elda put her phone on speaker to include Charlie in the conversation.

Ed inquired, "So you are thinking of a way to get more incriminating information on James?"

"Yes, yes, exactly what I was thinking, Ed. We see if James will try to turn Charlie." Charlie's eyes went wide.

"Okay, Elda. I'll put Ashok right on it."

"Thanks, Ed."

Elda hung up, turned to the wide-eyed Charlie, and answered her unspoken objective, "Don't worry. You're ready. I will brief you fully."

After Charlie left, Elda picked up her burner phone and then put it back down on the desk. She nervously paced around her small flat in London. Picking the phone back up, she dialed quickly, before she could lose her courage. She adjusted the volume, put the phone on speaker, carefully placed it on the desk and backed away, so she wouldn't hang it up before connecting. The ringing echoed in her head.

"Hello?" Dawn's disembodied voice floated up from the phone.

"Hi honey, it's me." Elda leaned forward and held her breath for Dawn's answer.

Dawn spoke, "Elda?! You never call from a mission. Are you back in Maine? What number is this? Is this really you?"

Elda felt her heart beat faster and she was short of breath as she answered Dawn, "I know, I know. Yes it's me. And no, I'm not back. I'm still working."

"Are you well? You never call." Elda heard the skepticism and anger in Dawn's voice.

"I just wanted you to know, honey, that I am hoping to be able to get home in a few weeks." Elda checked the timer she had started on her watch. "I have to make this short, but I didn't want you to worry."

"OMG. Who is this really and what have you done with Elda?"

Elda's eyes teared up. This sarcastic response was so typical of Dawn. She realized why she never called home. It was too much of a distraction to the mission at hand. She steeled herself and tried to quickly explain her new behavior, "I realize that disappearing for months is totally unfair to you. It's what I need to do, but I had a phone that needs to be destroyed and a moment to spare, so I just wanted to let you know that I'm okay."

Dawn's voice came plaintively over the speaker, "I miss you, Elda. But I am afraid of giving us another try. I'd like to continue therapy, because it's helping me see who you are and giving me closure. I have loved our life together, but in order to go forward, I need to spend more time with you. It would need you to change and fully retire. Can we restart in that way?"

Checking her timer, Elda spoke rapidly, "Oh honey, I miss you so very much. I do know that you want to see more of me at home. Let's talk more about what that looks like for both of us. It may not be full retirement." Elda glanced at her watch and saw that she was fast running out of time on the phone call. "I have to go now, Dawn."

"I don't understand why you can't call me, Elda. I want you home."

"I won't be able to call again. It imperils both of us. I have to hang up *now* so this can't be traced. I hope we can talk more. Know that I do love you."

The timer went off. Elda abruptly cut the connection. *This doesn't work for me. I really can't be that person.*

Chapter Seventeen

Lost in thought, Senator Glass walked east down Independence Avenue SW in DC. Suddenly Yaromir approached him from the side and started walking in step with him. Unsettled, the senator stopped and demanded, "Excuse me? May I help you?"

Yaromir smiled broadly. The sun glinted off his gold fillings. He replied in a melodramatic voice, "I am hoping you can, Senator Glass. I would love to chat with you about your most recent trip to Moscow. Perhaps you have time to have coffee with me?"

The senator glared at Yaromir and snapped, "I certainly do *not*. That was a classified trip and none of your business."

Yaromir bared his teeth again and growled, "Ah, but it is most certainly my business. And I think you will want to hear what I have to say." He reached into his inside jacket pocket. The senator jumped back and exclaimed, "Don't shoot!" Yaromir gently handed the senator a photograph of Senator Glass in bed with two prostitutes, one male, one female.

Senator Glass dropped the picture in shock, and then scrambled to catch it before it blew away. He crumpled it up and shoved it into his coat pocket. He demanded, "Who are you? And where did that photo come from?"

"Who *I* am is of no consequence, but I think *we* can have a lovely partnership. Do you *now* have time for that coffee?" He took the senator tightly by his arm to steer him towards Le Bon Café and said mockingly, "We can sit outside on the patio and have a lovely little chat. If you're a good boy, then perhaps I'll even treat you to a croissant." *Good he's coming along without resistance. Success."*

Arriving at the café, Yaromir pushed the senator into a chair and sat across from him. Yaromir rested his large hands and hairy forearms on the table. Senator Glass stared at Yaromir's hands. Yaromir's bulk shaded the senator from the sunlight streaming around the patio umbrella and onto the table.

Yaromir leaned in and started the conversation, "So you are on the Defense Budget Committee, *da*?"

Fearful of where this would head, Senator Glass hesitated in answering.

Yaromir squinted and lowered his voice into a threatening growl. "Are you aware of what we can do to you, your reputation, and your career? Your conservative voters will abandon you. You have a strong religious base right now. *That* will disappear."

The senator took out an albuterol inhaler and took a quick puff, bringing the medicine deeply into his bronchial tubes. "Yes, yes, I am. And yes, I am on the budget committee."

Yaromir sat back and commented, "*Khorosho.* Much better. You are a quick learner. So this should be a simple request. You will obtain an electronic copy of any data being submitted from the Department of Defense for next year's budget. This needs to be a detailed list, not a high-level summary. You will download the information to this fob." Yaromir passed a small thumb drive across the table to the senator who nervously snatched it and shoved it into his pocket to hide it from view. "I will give you the place and time to meet and you will give me, or another assigned courier, that flash drive holding the downloaded budget input. This is all we will need you to do."

The senator shook his head. "This information is hard to obtain. I will not do this."

Yaromir continued. "Of course it is. We wouldn't ask if it was already in the budget and public domain. We want to see behind the scenes. This will show us where the deficits are. When the budget is approved, what didn't get approved are potential weaknesses in your security."

The senator shook his head no. "I will not do it."

"Your wife's name is Natalie, isn't it?" inquired Yaromir.

The senator looked at Yaromir in horror.

Yaromir glanced down at his cell phone, pulled up a picture and turned the phone to show it to the senator. He smoothly commented, "She is a lovely woman. You've been married for 20 years, haven't you?"

The senator's eyes grew wider.

"It would be such a shock to her to see those pictures, don't you think."

The senator sat there mutely and then stated, "She will understand. I cannot do this."

Yaromir opened and closed his fist and continued, "And your son's name is Sean, isn't it?"

The senator started to shake. Yaromir continued to pressure him. "I understand Sean just got his driver's license. You know how accident-prone teens are when they first start to drive," Yaromir insinuated.

Senator Glass took another hit of his inhaler. Tears were streaming down his cheeks. He spoke haltingly, "I will cooperate. Please leave my family out of it."

"*Khorosho*. Get that information and then stand by for your instructions."

Yaromir stood and flexed his shoulder muscles, looking much like a bear about to pounce on its prey. His shadow completely engulfed the senator. He bared his teeth in what may have been a smile, turned and walked away.

***

Madison sat at a table in the Bistro Cacao, reviewing the wine list while waiting for Nadia to appear. He appreciated the privacy of the booth with the draping red curtains that helped shield them from prying eyes. It wouldn't be advantageous for his side of the divorce proceedings if his wife found out he was dating. He studied the wine list and wondered if she would like red or white wine. He flagged down the waiter and took a chance on red and ordered the Château Les Grands Maréchaux Merlot Blend.

Madison checked his watch. It was exactly 6:30 pm. He looked up to see Nadia dressed in a sleek black form fitting dress with a simple accent of pearls approaching the table. He took his napkin off his lap and stood to greet her, kissing her on the cheek. "I'm glad you picked this place, Nadia. Their menu looks wonderful." Madison pulled out Nadia's chair for her.

Sitting, Nadia responded warmly, "So wonderful to see you again, Madison. I highly recommend the salmon, but their beef dishes are also wonderful. The Filet Mignon cuts with a fork and melts in your mouth. And this dinner is on me. I will write it off as a business expense."

Madison inwardly breathed a sigh of relief. Due to his gambling, his money for the month was already running low. "Well, thank you. I will accept that from a beautiful woman. I hope you don't mind, but I took the liberty of ordering a bottle of red, but if you are a white wine drinker, we can send it back when it comes."

Nadia beamed at him, and gushed, "I adore red wine. That will be perfect."

The waiter materialized at that moment and poured a taste of the red for Madison. He sipped and approved the bottle. The waiter poured their glasses and disappeared.

"*Salute*." Madison raised his glass, his eyes roaming across Nadia's chest.

"*Prosit*." Nadia took a sip. "Excellent. You have good taste."

"It's nice to be with someone who appreciates my taste."

Nadia reached across the small table and touched his hand. She stated with innuendo, "I think we can have a lovely association here, Madison. Shall we discuss business first and then we can relax and find out more about the other?"

Madison raised an eyebrow and queried coyly, "*What* are you proposing, Nadia?"

Nadia held up her hand, palm facing Madison. "Business first," she commanded, and continued, "If you want to partner with me in disseminating this information I have, I know it will be a definite money maker for you and your campaign."

"*Really*?" Madison sat forward with interest. "How?"

Nadia rolled her eyes, emphasizing the simplicity of her scheme. She presented her plan in an alluring tone, "First of all, we create a list for you of a large number of people. We will mix this list with actual people's names of those who will donate to your campaign because they believe you are on the right side and protecting them. These donations will automatically renew every month unless the donor explicitly opts out. There will be a steady stream of money in addition to the real donations that I can ensure will be funneled through the right channels to be untraceable." She patted her décolletage with her napkin, drawing Madison's eyes back to her cleavage.

"How much money are we talking?" Madison was licking his lips. Small beads of sweat appeared on his brow.

"An extra $250K a year guaranteed with a minimum of $50K up front." Nadia nodded and winked. Madison sat wide-eyed in reaction to her statement.

Madison did some quick calculations. He was in debt for over $100K right now. That $50,000 would immediately cut his debts in half and hold off his 'creditors.' The extra $250K would mean he would be debt free by the end of the year. "Count me in. How do we start?"

Nadia smiled at him and put her hand on his. "You just did. Leave the rest to me. I will set up a bank account for you so the money is accessible but not tied to your identity. You will be able to buy even nicer bottles of wine and perhaps go on a special vacation with a friend..." She winked at him again and gave his hand a suggestive squeeze.

Madison gulped. It was hard to believe his good fortune. He gave her what he hoped was his most sexy look and asked, "Are you free after dinner?"

Nadia replied, "Oh I'm not free tonight, but there *will* be a time for us. Keep the sheets fresh."

Madison gulped again and took a large sip of wine.

***

Anatoly stood watching the door of Nigel's house with his MP-412 REX .357 Magnum revolver drawn. The door opened and Yuri marched in, followed by Doug. Anatoly put his gun back in the holster inside his pants.

"Did he give you the information?" Yuri handed Anatoly a 1G thumb drive. "*Khorosho*." Anatoly slipped the drive into his jean's front pocket, grabbed his weapons kit and go-bag and pointed his index finger, as if it were a gun, at Nigel's forehead. He warned Nigel, "Be good," and then slapped Yuri on the shoulder and took off for Moscow.

Nigel wiped the sweat off his brow and exhaled the breath he had been holding. "That's one scary chap."

"You think *he's* scary?" laughed Yuri, "We have worse. So, as he said, 'Be good.' I'll be back tomorrow." Yuri turned and left.

Inside the front door hallway, Doug faced Nigel, shook his finger at him and demanded, "This *has* to stop, Nigel. I can't take the stress. It's not worth the money."

Nigel laughed at Doug. "It's no longer about money, Doug. Haven't you figured it out yet? Our lives are on the line. There is no way out."

Doug stomped his foot. "Damn you, Nigel. If we survive this, you better not darken my doorstep again."

"Says the man who is living in my house." Nigel said, placing the tip of the thumb behind his front teeth and flicking his thumb forward at Doug. He then swiveled and sauntered away.

Doug muttered to Nigel's back, "When you're dead, this house will be mine."

***

Securely clipped in with cleats holding onto the wood, an electrician looked down from near the top of a pole on Nigel's street. He took out of his bag a small metal box and quickly affixed it to the pole, with the spyhole facing Nigel's front door. Humming in a tuneless contralto, he connected the wires from the box to a small device he had clipped around the cable line. He tapped his earphone and spoke softly.

"It's in place. Are you receiving the feed, Charlie?"

A whisper came back over the earpiece. "Yes, Elda. It's coming in clearly."

Elda chortled. "You know *you* don't have to whisper, don't you?"

"Ooops. Ah yes." Charlie spoke in a normal volume. "So, is it okay for me to just put this on record and leave it?"

"You got it. Thanks." Elda tapped her earpiece to disconnect and was about to descend when she saw Anatoly stride out of the house with his go-bag in his hand.

Elda whispered to herself, "I hope this thing works, Ashok, and I hope Anatoly doesn't know that there are few flying insects in London this time of year." She pointed a screwdriver at Anatoly's bag and pressed a button on the side to target the bug and another button to let the small listening device go. Anatoly paused to check for any tails and then started off again. The black fly sized bug made contact with the outside of his bag, secreted a glue like substance and stuck there..

Elda started down the pole again and then stopped, as Yuri came popped out of the front door. She pressed the earpiece in her other ear and spoke softly, "He's on his way out, Oliver." She watched as Yuri crossed the street and passed under her pole without an upwards glance.

An hour and 10 minutes later, Elda was back in her London flat in a secure videoconference with Ed. She informed him, "According to the tracker, Anatoly is back in Moscow, so that we can assume the information has been delivered." Elda adjusted the volume and stepped back from the cell phone she had set up on a tripod. In the viewer, a tiny version of Ed was shuffling papers on his desk.

"When on earth are you going to get rid of some of that junk on your desk, Ed? It's worse than mine, and that's saying something!" Elda was teasing Ed, since his pile of papers was small compared the stack on her desk in her home office. She never seemed to find the time to file and had resorted to labeling cardboard boxes and tossing the papers into them. Elda refused to computerize her documents, since, with her years deep into the bowels of computers, she recognized that nothing was secure once it was connected to the internet.

Ed threw up his hands with papers in them and a shower of documents flew through the air. "It's driving me completely crazy, Elda. I've got everything else under control in my life, except for this desk." He looked at the papers lying around on the desk and now the floor and contritely remarked, "I've made it worse now, haven't I?"

Elda teased, "You'll need a dump truck soon, Ed. I don't know how you got that much paper in one place."

Ed looked up. He looked chagrined. "Can you come back yet, Elda? This operation is taking far too long. And I need to form a team to handle some things here in the United States."

Elda shook her head and stated definitively, "I can't return yet, Ed."

Ed frowned at her, "*Can't* or don't want to?"

Although she knew his meaning, but hoping to avoid an in-depth conversation, Elda inquired, "Are you referring to Dawn?"

Ed rolled his eyes and answered, "Yes, you know I am."

Resigned, Elda explained, "She has come so far in accepting who I am and what I do but I know she still wants me to give this all up and just stay home with her. I *can't* do that, Ed. I tried to contact her while away and realized it not only put her at risk but puts me and my mission in jeopardy." Deflecting the conversation away from her personal life, Elda continued, "And anyway, I'd like to get a bulletproof case against James so we can get him locked up. You know his superiors will not act on partial information."

Ed shook his head and reasoned, "You also know they'll just exchange him for some other prisoner or a favor."

Elda sighed and sadly said, "I know, Ed. But it's not like we can have a shoot-out."

Ed put his finger to his lips. A moment passed before he stated in a quiet voice, "It would be efficient if you could. But I never said that."

"He doesn't seem the type, Ed."

Ed shrugged, "You never know…"

Briefly covering her ears and then her eyes with her hands, Elda quipped, "I heard nothing, I saw nothing…"

"Good." The application window with Ed in it disappeared.

Chapter Eighteen

Tosh tapped the envelope thoughtfully on his desk. The missive delivered to his office had no return address. He had scanned it for any known fingerprints and as expected, it was clean. He knew there would be no useful DNA on it.

He dropped it, and picked up the letter again. Although he had memorized the message the first time, he reread it, and then took out an ashtray and a lighter from his top drawer and set fire to the paper. He dropped it into the ashtray before it burned his fingers and then followed with the envelope. He searched through the ashes to ensure nothing large enough to examine had survived the flames.

He looked up at his ceiling, deep in thought. Finally he snapped to and scrolled through his computer files. Speaking to himself as he typed, he muttered, "It has to be an appropriate response that would only be known by her." He stopped his mouse and clicked open a file and exclaimed, *"Aga!"* He exclaimed again, "Aha! Osteria Santo Spirito! That's the one."

He printed the picture of the menu. Putting on gloves, he picked it up and without any additional messaging, enclosed it in an envelope. "*Govno.* Where to send it?...*Aga!* Of course." He addressed it to her c/o the Hotel Brunelleschi.

***

She yawned.

Snezhana was in Moscow, jogging a block behind Anatoly, keeping him in her view. Tailing him was getting rather boring for Snezhana. She had seen no sign of Angelina, and Anatoly was *very* predictable in his routines. She thought that Anatoly may have been imagining things. Perhaps it was time for Tosh to have a good talk with him and at the very least encourage Anatoly to vary his routines.

Suddenly another jogger appeared at her elbow, keeping in step with her.

"Who are you?" the short, dark haired-woman demanded.

"*Izvinite?*" Snezhana countered "Who are *you*? And why are you disturbing my morning jog?"

"I am often referred to as Angelina. For you, however, I will be the angel of death if you do not answer my questions. *Vy ponimayete?"* She pointed at Anatoly, and inquired, "Are you following that man?"

Snezhana replied emphatically, "Yes, I *am*. And, although it's none of your business, he runs at the same time I do and has a very nice stride. I like to use him as a pacer. And he's easy on the eyes too." Out of the corner of her eye Snezhana glanced at Angelina's hands to ensure they were empty. As she did, Angelina hip checked her into a parked car.

Ouch! That really hurt! Snezhana teared up and held her now bruised hip. "*Blayad'*! Why did you do that?" Although every bone in her body wanted to attack the woman, she remembered Tosh's warning and her own current lack of weapons. She made her lips quiver and tears rolled down her cheeks.

Angelina hissed, "That was a gentle warning, *suka*. Make sure you stay out of my way. Don't get invested in that man. He's mine."

"You're *bezumnyy*, lady. Totally nuts." Snezhana forced her legs to move backwards to disengage. "What are you, his stalker?"

Angelina sneered at Snezhana, "Suffice to say I know where he lives, and, if you mess with me, I will soon know where *you* live too."

"*Blayad'*. You can have him!" Snezhana turned her back on Angelina and with an exaggerated limp, hobbled away in the opposite direction. When she was sure she was out of earshot, she removed her cell phone from her water bottle holder and dialed Anatoly.

"It's definitely Angelina. She's behind you and looking to kill you."

***

Anatoly shoved his phone into the side pocket of his running shorts and increased his speed. He could hear the footsteps of another runner behind him. He cursed not having a gun with him. Deciding that he still could take her, he wheeled around and started running directly at Angelina.

Angelina stopped in her tracks, then lunged at Anatoly. Anatoly dove and rolled to one side of her and kicked out sharply, connecting solidly with her legs, throwing her out into a heap in the curb gutter. He strode to pick her up and finish her off when she suddenly leapt up brandishing a knife. He inhaled and bent quickly enough to have the knife narrowly miss his abs. With a growl he broadsided her with the side of his arm, sending her slamming into a parked car. Unable to beat him quickly, she shouted at him, "This is not over," as she bounced off, twirled, and ran across the street, brakes squealing and horns blaring at her.

"No it isn't," muttered Anatoly to her departing form.

***

Furious, Snezhana paced back and forth in front of Tosh's desk.

Tosh addressed her in a calming tone, "Well done, my niece. Please sit."

Snezhana sat, crossed her legs, winced, and re-crossed them. She shook her fist in the air. "I will kill her if I see her again, *dyddya*."

"Then let's get you prepared with some weapons you can take jogging." Tosh reached into his bottom desk drawer, took out a large box, and handed it to Snezhana. He inquired with concern, "How's your hip?"

Grimacing, Snezhana rubbed her hip and responded, "Sore, but nothing is broken. It will remind mc of her for a while, however."

Tosh reached up and rubbed his arm where his bruise from Angelina had been. "I know what you mean."

Snezhana opened the box, and with a look of pleasure, examined each item inside. "These are *chudesno*! Just *wonderful*! Where did you get them?" She held up a pair of running shoes with a retractable blade in the toes, activated by clicking the heels together. She bent over and put them on. Lacing them up she jogged in a circle, sat down, and reached back into the box. She pulled out and put on a wrist sweatband that unrolled to double as a strangulation device, and a MP3 player that doubled as a one-shot gun.

Tosh shrugged. "You know that Anatoly has his own set of custom-made devices. I thought you should too. When we were on that last mission and in the Spy Museum in DC, I snagged a few Cold War devices to copy and upgrade to more modern technology. I have additional accessories being made that will go with your everyday attire, as well as others to accessorize your more formal wear."

Just then a showered and changed Anatoly entered Tosh's office. His dark blue t-shirt strained at his neck and clung to his abs.

"Are those Yuri's clothes or are you cleaning out your teenage clothes?" jested Snezhana, noting the tightness of his t-shirt.

Anatoly grabbed at the shirt fabric in disgust. "*Der'mo*. They *are* Yuri's. I decided that since

Angelina was probably heading to my apartment, I would go to Yuri's apartment instead and steal some clothing." Anatoly plucked at the neck of the t-shirt that was nearly strangling him. Tosh handed him a pair of scissors. Anatoly ripped off the shirt and started hacking away pieces of the neck.

"Here, let me." Snezhana snatched the shirt and scissors and evened out the cuts, She threw the shirt back at him.

"*Spasibo*, Snez." Anatoly pulled back on the shirt and flexed his muscles watching as the fabric strained around them. "Hum, not a bad effect. I may keep this now. I probably wear it better than Yuri ever did."

Tosh cleared his throat to get their attention. Anatoly dropped into a chair next to Snezhana. Tosh addressed him, "Thanks for dropping off the drive yesterday, Anatoly. Adrik has informed me that it has a great amount of information on it and is exactly what they were looking for. He will have more instructions about our next steps tomorrow. I'll send someone to your apartment to gather your go-bag and clothes. You can sleep in the barracks here tonight."

"*Spasibo, ser.*"

"What about Yuri?" inquired Snezhana.

"I'll call him soon and tell him to wait in place. I'll send you back to the UK, Anatoly, in case we need to terminate the asset."

***

Despite the cover of the background noise in the Kensington, England pub, Sophia leaned in over the table top and whispered, "He's as crooked as the day is long, Elda."

Elda replied in sotto voice, "Clearly, from the conversations we've heard from the bug in his office. And we've traced the information being passed to London and then couriered by the Russian operatives back to Moscow."

Sophia picked up her glass of ale and spoke over the rim, "So what are we to do?"

Elda lifted her mug and held it in front of her mouth to reply, "We've recorded that he is working to protect Tosh's team's operation here in London, but I'd like to see how deep his deception goes and who else, if anyone, is working with him. I'd love be able to put him away forever." Elda placed her barely touched half pint of Guinness and motioned to the door. "Let's walk back to the flat, Sophia, and have the rest meet us there. I have some ideas for how to get more incriminating information on him."

Sophia pointed at the glass in horror. "You're leaving a perfectly good beer there!"

Elda scowled at the beer. "It's too cold. I hate that you Brits discovered ice."

***

Elda, Charlie, Sophia, Emily and Oliver sat huddled on milk crates in Elda's London flat. "Wait. Let's back up." Emily held up her hand and furrowed her brow, "So let me get this straight. Elda. You will give me a sealed encrypted note to give to James. The encryption used will be that day's code that Russia is using. So if he can read it, it will further implicate him. I tell James that a young woman with a closely shaved haircut gave it to me and told me it was *For James' Eyes Only*. That's all I need to do?"

Elda agreed, "Yes. That's all you need to do, Emily."

"And he'll believe me?" inquired Emily incredulously, with a slight note of panic in her voice.

Elda said in a calming tone, "Sure he will. James is ego driven. He believes in his own importance. He wouldn't question that someone is trying to contact him."

Emily looked at Elda with wide eyes and stammered, "I'm not sure I can do this, Elda."

Elda chuckled reassuringly, stating, "Sure you can Emily. This is right up your alley. If in doubt, play the dumb woman and he'll not bother to ask you many questions. It's a great way to break into the spy game."

Looking calmer, Emily nodded her assent.

Elda continued, "The backstory is that Charlie is looking to find a way to get back at the Americans. Her career at the FBI has stalled, even though she graduated top of her class and has been highly successful at everything she's done. On the surface it will appear as if she is looking to see what career opportunities might exist for her with MI6, but her extreme anger at the FBI and America will make her a useful member of James' secret team. And if we read it right, he lost most, if not all, of his planted assets in the last go-round, so he will need to restaff his moles."

Charlie asked for clarification, "How long a play is this, Elda?"

Shrugging Elda answered, "I don't know, Charlie. I would love for it to play out quickly. It really depends on how desperate James is to rebuild his team. All I do know for certain is that it will be dangerous. Those that have worked for James tend to die mysteriously. We believe that James personally disposed of Henry Davies, Nigel's dad, but we have no proof. Arabella, who worked for Henry also suddenly disappeared, which also could have been arranged by James."

"And what about the rest of us?" asked Sophia.

Elda ruffled her hair and shrugged as she answered, "Unfortunately Anatoly and Yuri know both you and Oliver, but they have never met Emily or Charlie. So we have to use them as primaries for anything close-up in the UK operation. But don't worry, I will have roles for you to play too. By the way, Emily, did you call that number I gave you?"

Emily reported, "Yes, Elda and I've already had a session."

Elda nodded and quickly added, "Good, then I'd like for you to get more information from Doug. Anything you can find out about their planned trips would be great."

Oliver stood and stretched and then refolded a towel he had placed on top of the milkcrate and sat back down, asking, "Anything else for me, Elda?"

"Not right now, Oliver." Elda pointed at Charlie and stated, "Charlie, you have your assignment.

Before you go on it, however, I want to do a bit more training." Charlie groaned theatrically.

Elda then turned to Sophia, saying, "Sophia, I need your brains working with Ashok to fill in any gaps in what we know about Tosh and his operatives as well as whatever they are up to here in both the UK and the United States. Are you okay flying to America to work side by side with Ashok to dig out some information for us?"

While glaring at Oliver, Sophia stated pointedly, "Only if everyone here protects Oliver from himself."

Charlie stood and assumed a military pose in front of Oliver. "I'll guard him with my life, Sophia."

Sophia smiled briefly and then frowned at Oliver, "Thanks Charlie. You may have to, with this prat's history of heroic antics." Charlie sat back down on her milk crate.

Oliver gave Sophia his most engaging, boyish grin. "Don't worry, love. The last mission taught me the foolishness of my ways."

"Just don't be a silly blighter on this one, darling." Sophia walked over and gave Oliver a long passionate kiss.

"Jesus guys! Get a room." Charlie bopped the two of them on their heads with a rolled-up newspaper.

Elda clapped her hands and ordered, "Okay guys, let's roll. We know how lethal this team can be, so caution at all times. Charlie, come with me. We have a training exercise to do."

***

Three hours later in a large building on the Alconbury RAF base, Elda looked down at the assortment of weapons laid across the long table. She quickly selected a knife and a rappelling kit. She left the room so that Charlie could choose hers in secret. The goal of the exercise was to replicate real life as much as possible and to not know what weapons each one of them had.

She waited in the main room while Charlie walked in and then walk back out. Elda noted a few new bulges in Charlie's waistband.

Charlie looked around the sparsely furnished room that had no pictures or identifying logos. She queried, "What is this place, Elda? And why was I blindfolded with earplugs for the ride here?"

Elda dismissed Charlie's curiosity with a brief description that gave nothing away. "It's a secret training area that the US and UK use. And right now we have some training to do. Are you ready?"

Charlie appeared slightly nervous, but stated confidently, "As ready as I ever will be."

Elda stared at her and let that sentence hang before answering, "I hope not. After today you will be far more prepared than before. Here's the rules. Of the weapons we just selected, the guns shoot an electronic signal that gets recorded as a hit or miss. Shots can knock the weapon out of your hand from a remote-control device. The knives appear real but will not cut or stab. They can leave a nasty bruise, however, and will record the extent of the injury that was inflicted. Aside from those weapons, you have your feet and hands. The only rule there is to not maim or kill the other person."

Charlie swallowed hard and replied, "Okay."

Elda gestured to the closed metal door in the far side of the room and continued her instructions, "Behind that door there is an abandoned section of the base with old buildings and junk cars. It has many areas in which to hide and ambush. I will give you a head start to get familiarized with the area and to find out where you want to be when I come through that door. Get ready to go on my command. Any questions?"

Charlie hesitated for a beat and then replied, "Ah, no."

Elda looked at Charlie assessing her readiness. Satisfied, she nodded her approval and continued, "When we finish this exercise we will roll into the next one. At the far end of the new area there will be a rack of paintball rifles. You will take one and run through the door next to the rifles. I will follow in five minutes. Got it?"

"Yes, Elda."

"Go!"

***

Charlie ran through the door.

Where to hide?

Disoriented, she skidded to a stop and quickly took in her surroundings. There was a street in front of her. She glanced back at the façade of the building she had just exited. Realizing she had to quickly move, she took off at a jog. She decided to run for the taller building, hoping to get up to the roof in time to see Elda enter the area.

Her breath was heavy in her ears as she flew up the stairs. She paused halfway to listen for any noises behind her. How big a head start had Elda given her?

Did she also have five minutes to get settled here? She slammed the roof door open and dashed out onto the roof.

Something caught her feet. She immediately realized that it was a wire that had been run across the bottom of the doorway, but couldn't catch herself in time. She skidded across the roof on her belly. "Damn!" She grunted as Elda leapt onto her, swiftly removed Charlie's gun and knives from her belt, and flung them over the side. Charlie rolled to dislodge Elda, only to find that the woman had already jumped off and clear. *How on earth had Elda beaten me to the roof?*

Elda stood by the corner of the roof and addressed her, "Clear your mind, Charlie. Stop trying to figure things out and just act." With that, Elda took a step over the edge and disappeared. Charlie ran to the edge to see Elda unclipping herself from a rope that she had used to rappel down off the roof.

Without the equipment to rappel, Charlie bolted for the roof stairs and hurled down them. She paused before the exit door. *Will Elda be there to ambush me?* Deciding not to take a chance, she headed for a nearby window which she slowly opened and cautiously looked outside. *The coast is clear.* She opened the window the entire way and stuck her right arm and leg out. Immediately, hands had her and she found herself yanked out the rest of the way. "Where did you come from?" she shouted as she was thrown down onto the ground. Again she rolled to get away. She rose to engage to find no-one there. She shouted in frustration, "Damn it!"

Charlie looked at the ground and found faint traces where Elda's footsteps had disturbed the dust. She headed in that direction. Her mind raced to try and get the advantage on someone who was proving to be very hard to catch. She spied movement out of the corner of her eye and threw herself at the body hurtling towards her. The two women crashed to the ground with a whoosh of air being exhaled as the wind was knocked out of both of them. They rolled, arms and legs trying to pin the other. Charlie's mind recorded Elda's moves and anticipated her next ones. It seemed as if Elda was probing for the extent of Charlie's hand-to-hand knowledge and her weaknesses. The two were well matched. Finally Elda, pinned facedown under Charlie, managed to bend her knees, plant her toes and, with a sudden thrust, pushed Charlie off her.

Charlie hurtled herself back at Elda. Elda sidestepped and Charlie's momentum carried her past Elda. The two warriors turned to face each other and circled warily. Charlie made the first move and grabbed Elda's arm to twist it backwards. Twirling her body, Elda ended up behind Charlie with Charlie's arm now in her grasp.

Charlie pushed with all her force to topple them both backwards. Elda landed on her butt with Charlie on top of her. Elda's grip did not lessen, and her legs came up to grasp Charlie firmly around her waist, pinning her body to Elda's. Charlie tried to reach up with her free arm to grasp Elda's hair but her fingers slipped on the gel Elda had in it. The pressure of Elda's legs were making it hard for Charlie to breathe.

Coughing, Charlie twisted to flip the two of them over onto one side. With her one arm and her legs, she came up onto her elbow. She then pushed up into a straight arm and brought her knees up, turning one leg to push herself up. Charlie stood, wobbling. Elda was still attached on Charlie's back, her body weight threatening to drag the two of them back down. *My god, what does it take to shake her off?*

Elda readjusted her grip on Charlie's arm and her other arm circled Charlie's neck. *I have to get her off me before she chokes me!* Charlie ran backwards, and crashed forcefully into a nearby building. She was rewarded by a grunt and Elda loosening her hold. Charlie suddenly dropped down and twirled and reclaimed her other arm. She thrust her elbow backwards and felt it solidly connect. Air rushed back into her lungs as Elda jumped off.

Smirking Charlie asked, "Uncle, Elda?" *I won that one!* Smiling, Charlie stood up straight and started to turn away when her feet were knocked out from under her. She hit the ground hard and winced as she was painfully kicked in her side. *Ouch! She's not holding back!"*

"Don't worry. Nothing's broken. As you were saying Charlie?" Elda stood slightly out of reach, grinning. Charlie slowly stood and rubbed her side. She was not used to being bested especially by a woman, and an older one at that. She rushed at Elda, only to find herself flat on her face again with Elda on her back holding her head back by her hair and a knife at her throat. "If this knife was real, you would be bleeding out right now."

"Damn."

"Game over. You're good, but you still have much to learn." Elda stood up and held out her hand to help Charlie up.

Charlie accepted Elda's hand and rose.

"Let's recap. First of all, never trust your opponent when they say they are giving you any sort of advantage. Secondly, never let down your guard until your foe is dead or has run away. Thirdly, do not underestimate someone because they are a female or because of their age or outward appearance."

Charlie nodded and took Elda's rebuke to heart. "I'm sorry, Elda."

Elda waved that statement away with, "Don't be sorry. Just learn from this. It's not personal."

"How on earth did you get to the roof before me, Elda?"

Elda answered with, "I left right after you and took the fire escape. You paused to listen for a pursuer and that gave me the advantage. Ready for part two?"

Charlie bowed in respect and commanded, "Bring it on, Sensei."

***

Ten minutes later, Charlie was back in the first room with the weapons. She ran to the gun rack, picked up a rifle and checked to see that it was loaded with a paint canister. She looked around. The door they used before had a DO NOT ENTER sign on it. *Where do I go?* Charlie turned 180 degrees and spotted a second door with a sign on it that said THIS WAY, CHARLIE.

She opened the door and slammed it shut behind her. Her foot sunk into mud. In front of her was an expanse of greenery, no buildings for as far as she could see. *Where was she? How big was this place?* She recalled Elda's caution to act and not think and willed herself to move forward. The light from above was filtered through the trees. Dense shrubs impeded her progress. The noise of her movements seemed almost deafening. She knew she was making an easy target for Elda to track and slowed her pace to move more consciously through the spacing in the undergrowth.

Charlie sniffed the air as she moved deeper into the woods. The smell of the outdoors wasn't quite right. She stopped to listen. The sounds of birds and a variety of animals were distant with none around her. She moved to step over a small stream and noticed that the water was crystal clear. There was something off. Something not quite real. The landscape seemed to shift slightly. Charlie reminded herself that it didn't matter where she was. What mattered was to find Elda and shoot her.

Crack. Someone was over there. Charlie spun around and headed for the sound. The foliage was thick in that area. She crouched down as she moved forward and raised her gun to her shoulder to be ready to shoot.

Crash. Charlie fell forward into a recently dug pit covered by branches. The bottom of the pit had been covered in leaves to soften her fall. A note was pinned to the side of the hole with a branch. Charlie plucked it off and read, *Watch where you're going. If this had been Vietnam, you would already be impaled.* Charlie crawled out of the hole and shook the leaves off. She stood silently, listening for her next clue to track Elda.

Splat! Red paint covered her chest. She dropped her gun and raised her arms. Elda emerged from a nearby tree and addressed her. "Not too bad but you got disoriented and sloppy towards the end. Let's go have a cool one and debrief." Elda put a hood over Charlie's head and led her away.

Ten minutes later Elda sat Charlie down in a chair and removed the hood. She placed a cold bottle of water in front of Charlie.

"Where am I?" asked Charlie.

Elda and Charlie sat across a small table in a windowless room that had a whiteboard on one wall, a cot at one end and a sink and toilet at the other. Charlie looked down at the hooks riveted to the table and the chains leading off of them.

Elda said firmly, "Where you are doesn't matter, Charlie. That's part of the issue with your performance today. In the second exercise, you did well in recognizing something was out of place, but you allowed yourself to be distracted by where you were and lost focus on why you were there. I killed you twice, and that is two times too many. I know you can do better than that. Had we more time I would keep you here until you were able to quickly kill me. Unfortunately we do not have that luxury so today will have to suffice for now."

Elda walked to the whiteboard and started diagramming the first area. She drew much like a football coach would do to show potential areas of attack. She diagrammed a number of plays with different outcomes as Charlie periodically interrupted to ask clarifying questions. When she was done with the first scenario, Elda erased the board, paused and asked, "Got it?"

Charlie, looking sheepish, nodded.

"Good. Let's continue." Elda drew the forested area.

Charlie blurted out, "But that is too small. It looks like an oversized hanger, but I was in a much larger area that was all forested."

Elda chuckled, "Yes you were, but it wasn't all real. Didn't you notice that it felt *off*?"

"I did."

"Good," Elda responded. "It was partially mocked up and partially projected. The ground beneath you was moveable so I had you going in a large slow circle. You felt like you were going a great distance but it all fit within the hanger."

Elda mapped out their interactions and added in a few other potential plays and outcomes. Elda could see that Charlie, with her jaw and fists clenched, was clearly mentally beating herself up. Elda didn't let her off the hook and ended with, "This is life and death, Charlie. You will run into many who are not as good as I am but also those who are much better. You need to be alert at all times, planning your attack as well as your escape. Being able to disappear well is an art form. Perfect it. Now let's get the sting going on James. If my suspicions are correct, he often does his dirty work himself and in remote areas. Hopefully if you end up in that situation, you can get out of it."

***

Emily ran up the stairs at MI6 and dashed around the corner of the hallway, slamming right into James, knocking the folder and coffee cup out of his hands and onto the brightly polished linoleum tiles.

"Blimey, Emily."

"Oh James, I am so very sorry. Let me help you pick this up." She gathered the scattered papers, shoved them back into the manilla folder, and placed it into his hand while curling his fingers around it. She noted that as she did, that the papers were from an operation Sophia and Oliver had been on in the winter of 2018. She picked up his now empty coffee cup and held it out to him. "Would you like for me to get you some more coffee, James?"

"No. You've done enough," James said, stomping away.

Emily called after him. "But James. Wait. I was looking for you."

James turned around scowling and growled, "What?"

"I was walking through Vauxhall Park when this woman jogged up to me, asking if I worked at MI6 and if I knew you."

James stepped up close to Emily and said, "What did you say?"

Intimidated by James' nose being so close to hers and feeling his angry breath on her face, Emily took a step backwards. She stuttered, "W-why yes, of c-c-course. I figured that if she was asking for you by name it had to be something very important."

James stepped in again and interrogated, "Yes, that's probably true. And, …?"

"She gave me this." Emily handed James a legal sized envelope that had *For James Richardson's Eyes Only* in bold on the front and a wax stamp sealing it in the back. She quickly stepped back again.

James turned the envelope over in his hands, studying both sides before responding sarcastically, "Interesting. You took this from some random woman in the park? What did she look like?"

Emily looked at James with deer in the headlight eyes and said softly, "Oh dear. Oh dear. Ah, well, she looked very presentable. Maybe American or Canadian. You know these assertive types."

James exhaled a frustrated snort and barked, "Yes, Emily, but what color was her hair, her eyes and how tall was she? Did you notice any of those particulars?"

"Oh dear. Well, she had very closely cropped hair. I'd say perhaps it was brown? I'd guess brown eyes too. And when I reached to get the envelope our hands were at the same level, so I would say she was about my height." Emily beamed a satisfied smile at James.

James rolled his eyes and gnashed his teeth together. "Blimey, Emily. I am glad you are not a spy. Your main talent appears to be running into people."

Emily nodded vigorously, "Yes, you could say that, hey? And I am quite good at that, aren't I?"

James uttered through gritted teeth, "Is that all?"

Emily pronounced cheerily, "She said you should read it today while the code is still valid. I'm not sure what she meant by that."

James turned on his heel and strode away without another word.

***

James buzzed his secretary. "I am not to be disturbed." He leaned back in his chair and studied the envelope before opening it. There was little distinguishing about it, but the seal looked familiar. He grabbed a magnifying glass and peered closer. He saw a shape that looked like the batman symbol. Wondering why the GRU would select this method of contacting him, he ripped open the letter and read: *The seal is your hint.* The rest of the letter was indecipherable, obviously encoded. Taking a piece of paper off of a nearby pad he translated the text using that day's code from Russia. *I am more useful than my current employer believes. I would love to explore career opportunities and ways I can help you. Call the number below if you are interested. This offer expires in 24 hours.*

James sat back and tapped the letter with the end of his pen. He was definitely intrigued. He slid open his bottom drawer, extracted a burner phone and dialed the number. It was picked up on the second ring.

"Hello?"

James put his phone on speaker, leaned over his desk, tapped his pen on his desk blotter and scribbled randomly on the paper covering. "I read your letter. Who are you?"

A low-pitched female voice came clearly over the speaker, "I am Charlie Burlamachi."

James looked down at his scribbles and saw that he had drawn bat shaped icons. He dropped his pen and sat upright. "Why did you choose that seal and how did you get that code?"

"I thought it would get your attention."

"It did," James acknowledged. "However, you didn't answer the second part of my question. Where did you get that code from?"

Charlie had information from Ed that a lowly Russian courier had been intercepted that morning so that there would be a cover for how Charlie had that day's code. It would be common knowledge at the Kremlin by now and James could verify what she said with them. Nothing else was liable to raise suspicion since the information that the courier was ferrying was of little value.

Charlie answered James casually, "The Americans took the code this morning from a Russian courier."

James demanded, "For whom do you work?"

"I work for the FBI, but my career here is totally stalled and I want to be more than a desk jockey. I have heard MI6 is much more generous in their assignments to females and am wondering if there's an opportunity for me to help *you* out in some way?"

James picked up his pen and started tapping again. He paused while he thought and then responded, "That could be difficult if you aren't a British citizen."

"I happen to hold dual citizenship. My mother was British."

James sat back in his chair and put his feet up on his desk. He ran his hands through his hair and then massaged his chin while forming an idea. Satisfied with what he had devised, he spoke up, "Well then, that opens up possibilities even without you joining MI6. There may be some synergies with you staying in DC. I have need periodically for information that I can't obtain through regular channels. Perhaps you could help me there?"

Charlie blurted out plaintively, "But I was hoping to get out of DC."

James answered condescendingly, "When you join me here at MI6 I will be able to help you and your career, but it's best for both of us if you stay in DC for now. Are you willing to do that? Your work for me will be very interesting. And it will have wide impact, as well as help you get back at those who have held you down."

There was a lengthy pause, as if Charlie was thinking it through. She finally asked, "Shall we meet and talk more about it?"

James swung his feet off his desk and checked his calendar on his computer. "Are you still in London?"

"Yes."

"Excellent. Meet me in Vauxell Park at 15:00."
While he spoke, James entered a fake meeting for
that time into his calendar.

"This afternoon?" Charlie replied hesitantly.

James eyeballed the phone, ready to take the
offensive. "Yes. Will there be a problem with that?"
he queried.

Charlie confidently answered, "Not at all."

Done with the conversation, James cut the
connection, took out the SIM card and slipped it into
his pocket. He put a new card into the burner phone
and threw it back into the lower drawer. *Excellent.
Perhaps this Charlie person will be my mole in the
United States. That should increase my value to the
Kremlin.*

James dialed another number. "I have some
interesting information and a potential lead. Meet me
at the same place." He hung up.

***

Elda took off her headphones and checked to
ensure she had successfully recorded the phone
conversation, as well as the office noises.

"You bastard."

Chapter Nineteen

Madison rolled off of Nadia, collapsing onto his back. Nadia rolled her eyes and lay silently for a moment, then took a deep breath and exhaled, "Wow."

Wiping the sweat from his face with his hand, Madison lay tangled in the sheets with a happy grin on his face. He sighed contentedly, then echoed, "Yes, wow. You are amazing."

"Oh Madison. *You* are the man. It is *all you* that I am reacting to." Madison was starting to rise again. Nadia said softly, "Ah, but we are not yet done," and lowered her head to help him along. She then helped prop the completely sated Madison up on two pillows and covered his body with the sheet, rose, and went off into the bathroom. Upon her return, she started to dress. Madison looked at her and said weakly, "Already?"

Nadia shook her finger at him, "Oh you naughty boy. You will wear me out. And we do have to talk business. Let me make some coffee and a snack while you shower."

Relieved that he would not have to perform again, and risk failure, Madison staggered off to the shower. When he returned, the smell of toast and coffee wafted into the bedroom. He dressed quickly and strolled to the kitchen.

"There you are!" Nadia rose from her chair and gave him a peck on the cheek. She motioned for him to sit, put butter and jam on a piece of toast, and slid it on a plate across the table to him. He ate ravenously. She motioned for his plate and put a second slice on it. "Now you fantastic lover, let's see if we can keep out of the bed long enough to plan our steps for making you a lot of money."

Madison perked up and rubbed his hands together at the mention of money. He asked her, "What do I do?"

"Oh it's very simple, Madison. Here's a script for you to follow. There are different versions for your Facebook, your Instagram and your Twitter feeds. There are five pages there with different dates on them. All you have to do is to post that information on those dates."

Madison glanced at the first page and stated, "Looks easy enough. What else?"

Nadia passed another set of papers to him. "Here are your talking points in case anyone asks about your social media posts."

Madison looked at the first page and nodded. Confused he inquired, "But how do I make money?"

"Think of it like advertising, Madison. My company will pay me money for disseminating this information and I will pass 80% of it on to you, since it is really you who are doing the hard work of getting it out there."

Madison cocked his head. "Your company? Didn't you say you weren't practicing right now?"

"How observant you are!" exclaimed Nadia. "Yes, I am not practicing as a doctor, but to get my messages out I needed more funding, so I have joined forces with those who are like minded. A number of these people are well heeled. I call it *my company* for convenience sake. We are like a company, but unlike this arrangement with you that has so many side benefits. Being well funded has allowed me to come to the United States and to meet you! How fortunate is that? I never would have been working with you had I been practicing medicine and that would have been so distressing. I would have hated to have missed out on *our* relationship."

Refueled, Madison looked at Nadia with lust in his eyes. "Shall we deepen our relationship?" He cocked his head towards the bedroom.

"Oh yes."

***

The marchers' feet slapped down onto the pavement in unison. Their fists cut through the air as they pumped them in time to their chants. Scattered groups of men yelled derisively as they passed by. Standing in a group of burly men, Yaromir groused, "Look at those assholes with the protest signs. The country belongs to us, not them." Yaromir punctuated his statement by slapping on the back one of the group's members who was standing next to him.

The man stopped himself from falling over and agreed with Yaromir, "Bastards, we should send them back to where they came from." A small chorus of assent came from the others around him.

"Do you want to stir things up?" inquired Yaromir, handing the man a metal baseball bat.

The man warily looked at Yaromir and the bat, and asked, "How?"

Yaromir pointed to the glass fronted jewelry store. "Just go bash that window in and back away.

294

Let's see how quickly these snowflakes forget their high values and start looting."

Grinning, the man ran away from Yaromir screaming "The Right Ones are here!" Yaromir heard the crash of the broken glass as he disappeared into the crowd of spectators and protestors.

A short way away from the looting, Yaromir slipped into a group of angry white men. He said to no one in particular, "Damn lefties. They are looting under the cover of this march. We patriots need to stop them and break up this march before they come for our families."

A chorus of, "Yeah!" and, "Stop them," surrounded Yaromir. He opened a bag to display rocks and Molotov Cocktails. Hands greedily grabbed at the weapons and started hurling rocks at the marchers. A Molotov Cocktail flew through the air, lightening up the darkening sky. Yaromir opened another bag that contained tear gas canisters and instructed, "Wait until the police come and throw these at them from inside the crowd of protesters. Then run away before the police retaliate." Yaromir stepped to one side to avoid the scramble for the canisters. He pivoted and slipped quickly away.

An hour later, Yaromir stood in the middle of a field in Maryland holding an AR-57 semi-automatic. The group training was about to commence. An abandoned car was sitting at one end of the field and bales of hay with cardboard cutouts of men holding guns were propped in front of each bale. Yaromir shouted, "Men! They have abducted children and have them in the trunk of that car. We need to kill all of them and free the hostages." He put his weapon to his shoulder and riddled a target with bullets, causing the head to drop off. Shots rang out as the others engaged their weapons and followed suit. When they were done, clouds of dust and hay particles floated in the air. Half of the targets were decimated. The car was thoroughly aerated with light shining through holes in the doors, windows shattered and the truck hood popped open.

Yaromir signaled for the men to drop their weapons and marched over to inspect the damage. One man reached into the trunk and pulled out a child-sized dummy that was completely shot up. He reached in and pulled out another, and another, …, same results. There was a stunned silence. Yaromir stepped up and patted the man who was holding the dummy on his shoulder. He addressed all of them, "We couldn't save these children but we stopped the operation and therefore saved many others. They never should have put these kids in harm's way."

The men cheered.

***

"You're crazy."

"I don't care. I won't do it."

Madison sat quietly sipping his glass of wine, listening to the others argue. The air in the small conference room in the DC Hotel was close and filled with electricity and anger behind the words. The closed doors made him feel trapped.

Three of the senators who had visited Moscow with Madison were debating loudly. A fourth one hushed them, saying, "Please lower your voices. We don't want any of this to be heard outside this room."

A portly senator glared at him and retorted, "We are all like lambs being led to the slaughter. I don't care what they can do to us. I, for one, am not going to give in to any demands they may make."

Senator Ronald Glass implored him, "Hank, we don't all have the same luxury of being able to kick back at them as you do. It was a honey pot trap. And we all walked into it willingly. But we have to own what we have done and not betray our country while keeping ourselves safe."

The fourth senator added, "And now that they know our weaknesses, they could try the trap again."

Madison suddenly put his wine glass down. As he swallowed, the liquid was becoming thicker and sticking in his throat.

Another senator snickered and stated, "Ah, but what a way to go."

Hank Baker, the chubby senator, replied, "Nothing would make me betray my oath of office."

Ronald Glass snapped at him, "Jesus, Hank, it's just a job. They could kill you."

Hank laughed, "I'm dying already, Ron. They'd do me a favor."

Senator Glass suggested, "Why don't we go to the FBI?"

No! Then my gambling debts might get exposed. I have to stop that now. Madison coughed and spoke up, "Not a good idea. They would kill us for sure."

Ron Glass countered with. "But there's always the witness protection program. They could hide us for a while."

Madison argued back, "And for how long? Would it ever be safe to come back? And what will we do while in the program? Work at the local hardware store perhaps? No, it's best to play along. They'll get what they want and then leave us alone."

Just then the food that they had ordered was delivered. Madison found that he was no longer hungry.

***

Elda, sitting in her London flat, pleaded with Ed over her secure video chat, "He's a bastard, Ed. My gut says he's the one who betrayed us in Operation Bittman. If we can't report him and have him removed, then let's remove him ourselves." She glanced down at her phone, wishing they had started the conversation on her computer where she could enlarge the picture.

The tiny image of Ed shook his head. "First of all we have no proof. Secondly, we can't remove him, Elda. There will be too many ramifications if it is traced back to us. We need more on him than a chat with the Russians to convince his superiors to act and to justify any actions we might take."

Elda, frustrated at the equipment and at Ed's hesitation, swore, "More! Damnit, Ed. He's a treasonous S.O.B." She pounded her fist on her makeshift desk only to be rewarded with a sore hand and a vibrating desk.

Ed shook his head and countered with, "That, in itself, will not remove him from the scene. You know the hoops we would have to jump through. We need solid proof of his treason, like catching him holding a gun to someone's head or something similarly egregious. Otherwise no-one will take action on him."

Elda hissed, "He's a mole, Ed. There are probably more too." She started pacing.

Looking sad, Ed shrugged her off with, "We have too many other problems in our faces right now to worry about that, Elda. Russian cyberattacks and disinformation are ripping America apart. I have to build a team to counter those attacks. Our Cold War spy vs. spy techniques are being actively discouraged. I have had to fight to keep this mission on the books."

Elda parried, "Ed, you know how much damage one well-placed mole can do."

Agreeing, but undeterred, Ed commented, "Yes, Elda, I do. We have both seen that. And the longer they go undetected and unchallenged, the worse that damage can be. There is nothing officially that we can do about this situation. And I fear that my ability to support you longer term is being hampered."

Elda stopped her pacing and pleaded with Ed, "We can't let this happen, Ed. Once we take our eyes off the ball here, the game is over for America."

Ed concurred, but continued unchanged. He said amiably, "I know, Elda. There is nothing I can do, though. I'll keep you posted. And support you as long as I can."

Elda replied sarcastically, "Thanks Ed. There aren't many jobs advertising for my skills," and terminated the video chat. She slumped to the floor, lying staring up at the ceiling for answers. She wondered how she could get rid of James without Ed's support and keep her job.

Chapter Twenty

"What?!"

"I was heading to MI6 when I spotted Anatoly. I followed him for a while, but I've lost him."

Elda's voice came angrily over Charlie's cell phone speaker, "Charlie, you know you know you have your assignment. Ignore Anatoly and get over to MI6 and ask for James. It's important you keep James off balance and set your own schedule with him."

"Yes, Elda." Charlie placed her phone into her pocket, turned and picked up the pace to make up for lost time.

A few blocks later, she felt a sizeable presence slip in beside her and heard a quiet voice in her ear, "There's a .357 Magnum pointed at you."

Surprised by his sudden appearance, Charlie looked up at the large man who was walking next to her, matching her stride. She noted his hand was in his pocket and there appeared to be the outline of a pistol barrel pointed her way. "What do you want? I have no money," she replied evenly, as she stopped and put her hands in the air.

Anatoly growled at her, "Put your hands down. You'll call attention to us. I only aim to kill *you* and not involve innocent bystanders. You *know* I don't want your money. I want to know why you have been following me."

Charlie lowered her arms and started walking again. "You're terribly mistaken. I'm a tourist in London and have gotten horribly turned around and hopelessly lost. Perhaps you can put the gun away and direct me to the Houses of Parliament?"

Anatoly barked at her, "*Eto khrenovaya chush'.* Stop slinging it and tell me the truth. Come with me or I'll throw your dead body in the river *now*."

River! Charlie brought up a map of the area in her mind. The river was only a few blocks away. She whirled around Anatoly and raced off in that direction, calculating that Anatoly would prefer to capture her for information, rather than to kill her on the spot.

"Der'mo!" Anatoly holstered his weapon and quickly accelerated to a speed greater than Charlie's. Coming up behind her, using an Aikido technique, he dove down to the side of her onto a bended knee. He grabbed her calf and waist, forcing her over onto

her back. Charlie twisted her torso and half rose to punch him in the side of his head. Anatoly's grip loosened and she punched him again. She twisted free, sprang up, dashed away, coming within sight of the river.

Charlie looked over at the Thames and saw two powerboats, a Cigarette and a Donzi, tied up at the Vauxhall St George Wharf Pier. She turned sharply, narrowly evading Anatoly, who was barreling straight at her, and sped off at a run.

"*Der'mo!*" Anatoly skidded to a halt and then turned to take off after her. Charlie flew down the ramp. She had seen the sun glistening off the keys in the ignition of the Donzi, so she ripped the rope off the mooring for that boat and leapt in. She dove for the ignition and opened the throttle wide. The boat flew away from the pier. Anatoly jumped into the other boat, cursing each second it took him to hotwire it. Within minutes he was speeding off after Charlie.

The throaty roar of the performance engines filled the air as the two boats sped down the river. Charlie noticed that Anatoly was steadily gaining on her. She looked back and saw him draw his gun. As she zigzagged up the river, shots rang over her head. She figured that she had been correct. If Anatoly had wanted to kill her, she would be already dead. She knew, from Elda's comments and from his file, what a good shot he was.

The spray behind each boat formed rainbows in the sunlight. A white trail of water showed the zigzag pattern each was making. Charlie calculated how much distance she was losing over time and waited until Anatoly was closing in. Suddenly, she spun the wheel and headed her boat directly into Anatoly's. She grabbed a gas can and poured gas over her deck and then dove for the water with a rope in her hand. She kicked herself downward and held her breath, waiting for Anatoly's boat to pass over. As it did, she threw the rope so it wrapped around the propeller. She surfaced quickly to just draw a breath and dove back down.

***

Anatoly fired into the spot where she had disappeared. He sneered, "What a childish attempt to ram me," and turned his wheel to avoid the abandoned boat, when his motor seized and his boat stalled, dead in the water.

"*Der'mo!*" Anatoly leapt into the water just as the two boats collided. The collision ignited the spilled gasoline. The ball of fire could be seen from both shores. Anatoly surfaced and struck out to shore to get as far away as possible from the boats before the police arrived. As he climbed, dripping, out of the river, he looked back. The Thames had apparently swallowed his foe.

***

"What happened to you?" Yuri looked in amazement as a sopping wet Anatoly trudged into their hotel room. "Was it Elda again?"

Anatoly glared and snarled at Yuri, "*Nyet*. It was someone new."

"*Another* secret admirer? You got a bouquet of flowers delivered to you while you were out. I picked it up at the front desk."

Anatoly snarled and snatched the card from the bouquet and read out loud, "Brush your teeth before you sleep. I'm coming for them. -A"

Yuri commented, "She's getting rather bold, isn't she?"

"*Malen'kaya suchka.*" Anatoly threw a dripping boot at Yuri who fielded it with one hand and dropped it on the floor.

Yuri teased Anatoly, "Who are you calling a little bitch?"

A second boot followed the first one. A trail of soggy clothing marked Anatoly's path into the

306

bathroom. Yuri walked behind and gathered the mess, dropping the clothes into the shower behind Anatoly. He ripped off his socks and threw in the pair on top of the pile and tossed Anatoly a bottle of laundry detergent. "Do the laundry while you're in there." He was rewarded by a growl.

Yuri's phone rang. "He's in the shower, Tosh. I think his phone probably isn't working. No, I don't have the story. I'll put you on speaker." A wet sock came flying out of the shower and hit Yuri on the head. He caught and sniffed it. "Clean! Thanks Anatoly. May I have the other?" A second sock landed on Yuri's head.

From his office in Moscow, Tosh's voice came clearly through the speaker, "What is going on in London!? Anatoly? It's unlike you to shower at this time of day. What happened?"

Anatoly turned the water off and emerged from the shower. Yuri handed him a bath towel. He wrapped it around his waist. "There's someone new in the game, Tosh. I was followed. I stopped her and we ended up playing chicken with boats on the river. What beautiful boats they were too."

Tosh demanded, "Where is she now?"

Anatoly answered ruefully, "I don't know, Tosh. I shot at her a number of times, including right after she entered the water. I saw no sign of life in that river. It may take a few days for the body to appear."

Tosh commented, "Or not." He inquired, "Do you think it's someone working with Angelina?"

Anatoly shook his head at his speaker phone. The silence that followed prompted him to answer verbally, "No I don't, Tosh. She didn't try to kill me. I'm guessing from her accent and from the way she moved that she was American."

Yuri rubbed his chin and narrowed his eyes, "This doesn't add up, though. We know Elda works alone. She'll team up with other agents if ordered, but we haven't received any information that there is a coordinated mission going on."

Tosh remarked, "I'll have Stas doublecheck and I'll also see if Adrik has any information. What else did you notice, Anatoly?"

Anatoly rattled off his list of observations, "This woman is definitely a professional. I told her I had a gun on her and she didn't flinch. She just played along while she calculated her move. She is fast and has a strong build. She had a very short haircut, which may be personal preference, but also points to the professional angle. She moves as if she has had military training. And the way she handled that boat shows experience with equipment and coolness under pressure."

Tosh directed sternly, "There are too many players in the mix, Anatoly. We need some time together. I would like you to come back here to Moscow and give me a full briefing on everything so that we can develop a plan of action. You can return the next day. If needed, I will send Snezhana to the UK to assist you. With Elda there, Angelina, and now this woman, you have my permission to terminate anyone who gets in your way. But make it look like an accident. Even with our protection there, I don't want to have to read about you in the London Times. *Khorosho*?"

Anatoly assented, "*Da. Khorosho.*" He added, snarling, "Now I have three I wish to kill."

"Chose carefully, Anatoly. You may only have opportunity for one shot. And remember, I really would like Elda to be mine."

***

The next day Snezhana and Anatoly sat in silence in Tosh's Moscow office, waiting. Snezhana was still and looking straight ahead, hands folded in her lap. Anatoly, having been summoned back from the UK, looked downcast.

Finally, Tosh broke the ice. "This mission is not going well, Anatoly. There are too many players running after you. You did well handling the asset, and we got the information to Moscow, so Adrik is pleased. However, he has no inkling of the mess in the background. I plan to keep it that way. And you *will* follow my instructions and ensure we keep it that way. Understand?"

"*Khorosho, ser.*" Anatoly sat tensely with his fist clenched. "*Ser*?"

Tosh said encouragingly, "Yes? Do you have something to add, Anatoly?"

Anatoly rubbed his forehead and inquired, "*Da, ser*. Has Stas dug out any information on the third woman or why Elda is in London?"

Tosh shook his head gravely, "No, not yet. But he is searching through the airport and metro feeds now. It would be helpful if we had a photograph…"

Anatoly hit himself in the head and exclaimed, "*Der'mo*. I should have thought of that." Tosh held up his hand to calm Anatoly who slammed his fist into his thigh, and continued consolingly, "… but I understand how you weren't able to get one. You had no time, Anatoly. Don't beat yourself up."

Snezhana sat primly, her head swiveling as she watched the interplay between her uncle and Anatoly. Finally she drew herself up into attention, and interjected, "How can I help, *ser*?"

Tosh turned to address her, "I recalled you so there would be no electronic or paper trace of these orders. These are my instructions, not Adrik's. We need to discretely get rid the noise from this mission. I plan on sending you back to the UK to help Anatoly quiet things down."

Alerted to the possibility of using his real skills as an assassin, Anatoly inquired hopefully, "How quiet should things be, Tosh?"

Tosh replied gravely, "Read the scene. Try to ensure you don't create an international incident. And make sure nothing can be traced to either of you."

Anatoly hopefully asked, "But we can make things as still as death?"

Tosh nodded. "Yes. Do what is needed.

***

Charlie walked out of the bathroom in Elda's London flat and caught a pile of dry clothing that came flying through the air. She dressed quickly while addressing Elda, "Damn that water was cold."

Elda threw Charlie a blanket from the bed. "Get warm. So you decided to follow Anatoly?"

Charlie wrapped the blanket around herself and admitted ruefully, "Yes, I am sorry, but he was right there. And I thought if I could find out where he was staying, it would make things easier for us. I don't know how he made me. I was careful."

Elda sighed and put her hand to her forehead. She spoke in an even tone, "I'm sure you were, Charlie, but Anatoly has many more years in the game than you have. Too bad, you were one person they didn't know yet, but they now will remember you. You are distinctive and stand out. We will have to get you some more disguises. I'll take care of that while you handle James. It's too late to intercept him at MI6 headquarters, so you'll have to make the arranged 15:00 meeting in Vauxell Park. I want you to be armed."

Charlie pointed to the weapons pile on the bed next to her soggy clothing on the floor. "I am, Elda. I have my SIG P226, as well as a Bowen Belt knife, an auto spike, and a pepper spray pen. I won't disappoint you, really."

Charlie looked downcast.

"Here, you may enjoy these too." Elda handed Charlie a packet of metal-edged throwing cards and a push dagger with a lanyard. "The lanyard can be used as a strangulation device."

Charlie immediately perked up. "Oh, excellent. New toys! Thanks Elda!" Charlie took out one of the cards and flung it, embedding it into the wall.

Elda snapped at Charlie, "Be careful there, Charlie. I have a security deposit on this flat that the U.S. government would like back."

Charlie looked embarrassed. She retrieved the card and inspected the spot where it had gone in. She carefully brushed the area and used spit to tack the wallpaper together. "Hardly a nick there."

Elda shook her head and set her mouth. She spoke carefully, "True, Charlie, but I will have to report it and offer to pay for it. We may be spies, but we play by the rules. All actions have consequences. Think carefully before acting. I may not always be around to remind you or to clean up after."

Elda's phone suddenly buzzed. She put it on speaker so Charlie could also hear the conversation. "Yes? Oh hello, Oliver. What's the status?"

"I located their hotel. The Royal Lancaster near Hyde Park."

"Well done, Oliver. Okay, report back here immediately and we'll brainstorm next steps. I'll call

Emily in too." Elda hung up without waiting for Oliver to sign off.

Elda next dialed Emily, "Emily. Oliver has located them. They are staying at the Royal Lancaster at Hyde Park. Do you know where that is?"

"No, I don't, Elda."

"... No? Okay, Google it and then pop over there, get familiar with the layout, and then come back to headquarters.

"Where is headquarters?" Emily asked.

"… The flat, Emily. That's our headquarters." Elda terminate the conversation.

Elda put her phone away and turned to Charlie. "No more diversions. Go meet James. Push him as needed, but also play into his ego. You want him to sign you on. And, be careful. He's dangerous. There's a reason he's survived undetected as a mole for this many years. He eliminates those who get suspicious of him."

***

Charlie strode confidently over to James who was sitting on a bench in Vauxell Park in London. "May I join you James?"

James glanced up at her and icily replied, "You have the advantage of me, but I assume you are… *Charlie*?"

"Yes." Charlie stood waiting for James' next move.

James looked her up and down and then gestured to the space next to him on the wooden bench. "Please do sit. You know that Charlie is usually a man's name, don't you? Do you go by Charlie, Chuck, or Charles, or is it really *Charlotte*?"

Still standing, Charlie narrowed her eyes and spoke through clenched teeth, "Charlie will do, James. Do you prefer James, or do you go by Jim, Jimmy, or is it really Jane?"

James glared at Charlie and snapped, "I'd watch your snark, young lady. It is *you* who has come to me for a job. Sit down."

"Sorry, sir. It's automatic. I'll watch it in the future." Appearing chastised, Charlie lowered herself down on the bench.

James puffed up and patted her hand, which was resting on the bench near him. "Good. Now that you know your place, I *can* see where you may have picked up some of your arrogance. You have a stellar record at the FBI, but according to your records, you have also been known to shoot your mouth off when displeased. Perhaps if you learn to shut it more, or at least show more respect to your superiors, you would not be desk bound." He was quiet and they both sat watching as a small man with a dog jogged towards their bench.

Charlie kept her face impassive, breathed in deeply and exhaled. She then looked pleadingly at James, "Is that the only way a woman can get ahead, James? What about competence?"

James snorted, "Competence! That doesn't matter, Charlie. What matters is having a man who is climbing the ranks as your mentor and advocate, someone who will bring you along with him."

Charlie's jaw muscles tensed. She calmly replied, "Are you looking to *bring someone along*, sir? You seem like someone I could learn from, and you have done well in your career."

James reached over and patted her knee. Charlie clenched her fists and looked away. A short man in a dapper tweed cap and jacket walked towards them swinging his cane jauntily. She breathed deeply.

"Yes. I have done well," his tone pompous. "And yes, *I* could be that *man* for you. But I would need you to be absolutely obedient to me, above country, mission or personal safety. Could you be that person,

Charlie? I can show you a *better* way." He smiled at the intended innuendo.

Charlie took a moment to massage her popping neck and jaw muscles. She then flashed James a brilliant smile, and answered, "If it's worth my while too, and going to get me up the ladder also, yes, I *could* be interested."

"What about your loyalty to the United States and the FBI?"

Charlie waved her hand dismissively and shook her head vehemently. "I'm not a die for my country type of gal, James. I do what pragmatically makes sense for me. I saw the FBI as a way to get out of my small hometown and travel, while doing exciting work. Instead I'm stuck at a desk job in DC, pushing papers. Washington may seem large, but in its politics, it is very small town. *Look at me, James*, I don't fit in anywhere, so I have to make my own path." She looked across the park. The jogger was lapping around the park and coming towards them again.

James studied Charlie, who was sitting silently. Satisfied, he told her, "Good. Well then, let me think on a proper mission for you to prove yourself to me. You will report to me and talk of this to *no-one*. I need you to stay at your job in DC and wait for my instructions. If you do well, then we can talk about future opportunities. Fail me and I *will* ruin you."

***

"Which one were you?" Charlie said, sitting on a milkcrate on the floor of Elda's living room, sipping a glass of red wine.

Elda walked by, lifted the glass out of her hand, took a small taste, and handed it back. "Oh, lovely, a Jumilla?"

"Yes, would you like some?" Charlie held up the bottle to show the label. "I can get you a glass. We do have a second clean water glass. It's the finest hotel crystal."

"Not right now. Thanks. Which one was I in the park?"

"Yes. I know you had to be there somewhere. I saw a male jogger and a man with a very nice matching jacket and cap on. Were you either of them?"

Elda gave a self-satisfied smile. "I was both."

Charlie slapped her free hand on her leg and the wine sloshed perilously close to the rim of the glass she was holding in her other hand. "Damn it! Both?! How did you do that?"

"Don't spill that good wine." Elda chuckled at Charlie's amazement. "It's easy with jogging clothes to quickly slip another outfit on over them. It also changes the body type slightly. I had a bag of clothes secreted in the bushes and I did a quick-change once I had jogged out of your sight."

Charlie took a generous swallow of her wine. "How many people could you have been at once?"

Elda rolled the whiteboard over and assumed her professorial stance. She drew a diagram of the park. "Here are the paths and the areas that are obscured from sight from where you were sitting." Elda drew a big X to indicate Charlie's location and circled areas on the path that were out of visual range from that area. "These circled areas are where the quick changes happened. I had shorts on under the jogging pants, the jogging jacket was also reversible, plus I had different colored shoe coverings. The man's jacket was reversible and I had stashed another matching cap, so if the conversation had continued, I could have come by again. That would make at least 4 different disguises."

Charlie thought a moment and exclaimed, "But wait! Where on earth did you get the dog?"

Elda smiled smugly and replied, "That was just a fortunate accident. A man was struggling with his dog. I paid him to borrow the dog for a short while.

He was happy to sit on a bench on the other side of the park while I gave the dog a bit of a run. Actually I think he would have been happy if I had kept the dog. He did mention that the silly blighter was his wife's and he couldn't understand why she liked the critter. I also had my eye on an older woman with a small Bichon, but the elderly are more reluctant to let you borrow their fur baby."

Charlie bowed to Elda with her palms held together chest high. "I have much to learn, sensei."

"Ah, Grasshopper, you will learn it all. Right now do pour me a glass of wine and let's go over our plans for tomorrow."

***

"I desperately need help and you are the only person I can turn to."

The thud of a dart hitting the bristle dartboard in the London pub filled the sudden silence. Turning, Emily noticed that whomever had thrown it had doubled in. She then turned back to stare at Doug across the small wooden pub table and took a sip of her shanty, before cautiously inquiring, "What do you need from me?"

A flush grew over his pink cherubic face. He opened and closed his mouth, displaying his crooked teeth, stuttered aimlessly, and then, taking a deep breath, said rapidly, "I need a place to stay for a while. Can I stay at your flat?" He slammed his mouth shut and stared at her with a wide-eyed look of terror.

Emily nearly spit her shanty out in response, but managed to swallow it despite sputtering and coughing. "My place?" she asked incredulously.

"N-n-n-no, i-i-it's n-n-nnot l-l-like th-th-that," stammered Doug in reply. "I-I'll…" He inhaled to his capacity and continued rapidly, "I'll bring a sleeping bag and stay on your floor, or your couch, if you have one. It will only be until I figure a way to leave town without being followed." He stopped, wheezing, short of breath.

Emily lowered her voice and leaned in closer. "What are you running from?" she inquired, staring directly into his eyes.

Emily saw that he looked uncomfortable, as if he were ashamed of his actions, Doug looked down at the table and then back at Emily with a beseeching look in his eyes. "It's complicated and will take a while to tell."

Emily coughed as she inhaled deeply and then nodded, "All right then." She took a napkin and wrote her address on it. "I will leave a key under the mat."

"Tttthank you. I may not be there tonight, but when I can get there, I will tell you everything."

"You better."

Chapter Twenty-One

The moonlight shown in, filtered by the DC hotel curtains. In the dim light, Nadia rolled over and reached beneath the covers. Then, she rolled her naked body on top of Madison as she stroked him. When he was hard, she inserted him into her, and, using her vaginal muscles, squeezed and released as she moved slowly up and down on him. Madison, now fully awake, came quickly. Nadia rolled off of him.

Sated, Madison immediately fell back asleep. Nadia quickly got up, washed herself, dressed, and made herself a cup of coffee. The smell of the coffee brewing brought Madison back awake. She sat down on the side of the bed with a cup of coffee in her hand.

"Leaving already?" Madison mumbled groggily.

"I have a lot to do to continue our campaign. You are receiving the money that is being deposited?"

"Yes, I, …, yes, I am, but, …," Madison hesitated to continue.

Nadia asked sharply, "But?"

He eyed her beseechingly and tentatively queried, "Are you absolutely sure that this is all untraceable? I *cannot* lose my career."

Nadia patted his arm, "Don't you worry about any of that. Leave it to me. You will like the results. And I also think you like the side benefits."

Madison's mouth smiled, but his eyes were dead as he answered her, "Oh yes, this…," he gestured to sweep in her whole body, "… is lovely." He hesitated again and then continued, "I just wonder at times what I have gotten myself into."

Nadia answered tersely, "You should have wondered that before you gambled your money away and destroyed your marriage." Nadia put the half-finished cup of coffee on the side table and stalked out of the bedroom.

Madison heard the door close, turned his face to the wall, and quietly wept.

***

"You look tired, Ed." Sitting on a milk crate in her London flat, Elda studied the face being displayed by the secure video chat application on her cell phone.

In his DC office, Ed ruffled his spikey black hair and rubbed his chin, appearing unsure of how to answer to a subordinate who was also a friend. "There's a lot of balls in the air right now, Elda. I've got to tell you, I'm very glad you came back. There aren't a lot of very senior agents I can rely upon."

Elda fake frowned at Ed, and replied in an aged quivering voice, "Senior? You better not mean old, young man." She shook her finger at him in mock anger.

Ed, smiled, which was the reaction Elda was hoping to get from him. "You know what I mean, Elda. I just wind you up and off you go."

Elda acknowledged that statement with a wry grin, "And sometimes you wish you had a string to reel me back too."

"Yeah, that's valid. But the results always are there." Ed's face was more relaxed than at the start of the conversation and he appeared to have lost a few years after offloading to Elda. "Thanks, Elda."

"No problem, Mr. Ed." Elda whinnied, and Ed rolled his eyes at her old joke. She turned serious and inquired, "How are we doing on the Moscow invasion of London mission?"

Ed able to report out more happily on a successful mission, told Elda, "We're good, Elda. Enough information has made it to Moscow and we have it fully traced. But now there's rumor of increased Russian activity here in the United States. And, although it's not his usual M.O., we suspect it may also be coming from Tosh's unit. I'd like to have you two back over here. So can you tie it up there?"

Elda frowned. "What type of activity?"

Ed hesitated and then avoided fully answering the question by saying, "Riots and fights that we think are being driven by Russian disinformation."

Elda shook her head, "But that's not worth my time, Ed. You have others who can trace that."

Sheepishly Ed admitted, "Yes I do, Elda, but it's a way to keep you on the books."

Elda queried sharply, "By doing lower-level work that takes only a brain cell or two to figure out?"

"It buys us time, Elda, while we read the political tea leaves," Ed cajoled.

Elda rubbed the back of her neck while thinking, then said, "Can I bring some of the MI6 players with me?"

Apparently pleased to avoid a fight, Ed readily agreed, "Whomever you deem necessary. Let me know and I'll clear it after the matter is done. The paperwork may be delayed in its long journey over the pond."

Elda smiled at her boss and friend. She was glad he knew when the rules needed to be bent and when to adhere to them. "Thanks. I admire your style. So, can we shut this part of the operation down and send the Russians back to Moscow?"

"Yes, Elda, *pergra*."

Elda grinned at his military slang for permission granted. She envisioned invisible days on her mental calendar and added up her schedule to give Ed an estimation on timeframe. "OK, give me a couple of weeks and I should be able to get there."

Ed frowned. "I'm not sure we have that long, Elda."

"It's a lot to clean up here in the UK, Ed," stated Elda unapologetically.

"Come as quickly as you can."

***

327

Shortly after Elda's conversation with Ed, Emily, standing outside the Royal Lancaster Hotel, in London, received a phone call from Elda.

Elda ordered, "Emily, come back and join us for a meeting at the flat."

"I'll be right there, Elda." Emily turned to leave her observation site and almost knocked over the woman behind her. "I'm sorry." Emily startled and stared at Snezhana with dread, hoping the Russian woman would think her harmless.

Snezhana stood inches away from Emily, causing her to back up. Snezhana advanced again. "You *will* be sorry. Whom did you just speak with?"

Emily drew herself up and answered haughtily, "Pardon? That's none of your business."

Snezhana gave her a chilling smile, "Ah, but yes it is my business. I saw you following my coworker, Anatoly. And then I just overheard you speaking with someone you called Elda. That means you must be a new member of that team, and I'm guessing from your accent, MI6?"

"I don't know what you're talking about," denied Emily, desperately trying to figure a way out of this situation.

Snezhana shifted her overnight bag into her left hand and opened her jacket with her right one, to show Emily a nine mm PYa pistol in a built-in arm holster. "This is not my only weapon. I also have a knife that I can shoot into you from a forearm holder, a poison needle I can stab you with in my shoe, and a garrot that is wrapped around my head as a headband. In addition, I could, and would, also kill you with my bare hands right here if you do not come quietly with me."

Emily looked frantically around at the near empty street. Snezhana took her not-too-gently by the arm. "If you cry out, I will kill you instantly."

Resigned, Emily walked with Snezhana through the side door and up the stairs to Anatoly's hotel room.

Anatoly looked up as Snezhana walked in with Emily, "*Der'mo*! Who is that?"

Snezhana shrugged, replying, "*Ya ne Znayu*. She was following you. I think she is working with Elda."

"*Der'mo*!" Anatoly frowned and then commanded, "Find out what you can and then dispose of her. We have too many loose ends in this operation. And I have too many women following me."

Emily's heart sank.

***

"One peep and I'll kill you right now." Snezhana pushed and pulled Emily down the hall, finally using her master key to enter a room. Snezhana dumped Emily's bag on the bed, roughly threw Emily into a desk chair, and then said, "Talk. Who sent you?"

Emily spat at Snezhana. "Why should I say anything? You're going to kill me anyway."

Snezhana sighed and shook her head, "Stupid, stupid… Defiance will get you nowhere. I can't believe you are forcing me to do this. Okay, it's the hard way then."

Snezhana took a Kleenex and wiped the spit from her shirt. "You're lucky this does not need dry cleaning," she sneered. "And yes, I am going to kill you anyway, but you have a choice as to how you go. You can go quickly and painlessly or the last long moments of your life will be agonizing torture."

"I'm only a clerk and don't have any information that would interest you," Emily said.

Snezhana grabbed a face cloth from the top of the bureau, shoved it into Emily's mouth, and duct taped it to her face. Then Snezhana pulled her up off the chair by her neck, spun her around and duct taped her arms together. Emily's eyes grew large.

"Come with me, stupid one." Snezhana grabbed Emily by the hair and dragged her into the bathroom. She turned on the water and filled up the sink, while Emily vainly struggled to get loose. Snezhana shoved Emily's face into the sink full of water, kicking a bath towel under the sink to catch the overflow. She brought Emily's head up to catch a breath of air. Emily snorted water out her nose and gagged on the towel.

Snezhana ripped the tape off and removed the towel. Emily gasped for air. Blood dripped down Emily's face from where the tape was.

"I am losing my patience, stupid one. Who sent you? With whom are you working?"

Emily was silent. Snezhana pushed Emily's head back into the sink.

Snezhana held Emily's head up by her hair and asked, "Now? I have plenty of time to do this."

Emily sobbed.

"With whom are you working?" Snezhana demanded and slapped Emily's face. "Voz?"

Crying, Emily coughed out, "Elda."

Finally! Snezhana dragged Emily back into her chair. "See, that wasn't so hard, was it?" Emily sobbed in response. Snezhana slapped her. "Focus. Who else is there?"

Emily stuttered, "I d-d-don't know. Elda came to me because she needed someone you wouldn't recognize and who wasn't officially a MI6 agent."

"Why not MI6?" interrogated Snezhana.

A drop of blood fell from Emily's face and into her lap. She hesitated before answering. "She suspects a mole."

Snezhana patted Emily on the shoulder. "You are really getting the hang of this. Who does Elda suspect?"

Emily shook her head negatively, winced and stated, "I really don't know. She doesn't give out much information."

Snezhana stared at Emily. Emily stared pleadingly back. Finally Snezhana said, "Yes, that fits. Elda is a loner. You are just a convenient fool for her to play against us. Thank you." Snezhana pulled out a silenced pistol and shot Emily between the eyes. "You were good. You got a quick death," Snezhana told the corpse. She duct taped a towel around Emily's head to control the spread of blood.

Then she dragged the body into the tub to catch any seepage. Snezhana shook her finger at the body and commanded, "Stay there."

Snezhana left the room in search of a laundry cart.

***

Huddled in the laundry room of the Royal Lancaster Hotel in London, Elda hissed at Oliver and Sophia, "Where is Emily?"

Sophia whispered back, "We don't know, Elda. That's what we were trying to tell you. She hasn't answered her cell; it appears to be shut off. We could track it using more sophisticated equipment to grab a history of where she's been, but we don't dare use MI6 facilities to do so. We were wondering if you could have Ashok try and locate it?"

Elda paused before answering them. *Man oh man. I thought they were more capable than this. Do I have to do everything? I am getting tired of this part of the job. Sometimes I wish I could leave my whole life behind.* She looked quizzically at Sophia and Oliver. "Did you go to her flat?"

Oliver and Sophia looked at Elda like deer caught in headlights. Oliver slapped himself on his forehead while Sophia opened her mouth and uttered, "Ah, …"

Elda raised her hands in disbelief. "Oh my god. You two twits. After this is done, go to her flat and see if she's there. If she's not, treat it as a crime scene and do not disturb anything. Got it?"

Oliver kept shaking his head and slapping his palm on his forehead. Sophia reached over and grabbed his hand. "Stop that, dear." She then turned to Elda and stated, "I can't believe we didn't think of the most obvious place. Yes, we will, but will you also have Ashok try and locate her, in case she's not at her apartment?"

Elda waved at her impatiently, "Yes, of course." She typed a brief message on her phone then said, "Done. Now let's get going and send Yuri on a little trip. Are you guys all set on your end with the logistics?"

Oliver spoke up. "Yes, we even arranged at the other end to have all his expenses paid for two weeks, and we can extend that if we need to. I think he'll enjoy his *vacation* there."

"I certainly hope so, because I would hate to dispose of Yuri permanently. He's really a good guy." Sophia and Oliver raised their eyebrows at each other. "Stop that you guys. I will gladly eliminate anyone who is trying to kill me, but if they are not, and there is a better way to clear the decks, then that's the way to do it. There's a lot to be said for having an enemy in your debt. The spy game is so much more than chase scenes and shoot outs. It's subtly played with small moves. In fact, at times it's long and drawn out, like a well-matched chess game Watching what we really do on TV would often be very boring."

Sophia put her hand on Elda's arm and asked, "Are you sure you're not too attached to Yuri?"

My god! These children are questioning my actions! Elda shook off Sophia's hand. *Okay breathe, explain it to them. You don't always have the answers and you need others. You're just tired.* Elda took a deep breath and responded, "I *am* sure. Yuri is not a killer, however. He's got too soft a heart. He has been useful to me in the past and may be useful again in the future. There's no need to violently remove him in this case."

"We'll be sure to put hearts and flowers on his pillow," Oliver commented dryly.

Twit. Elda glared at him. "He's out to dinner so it may be a while. Leave after me and wait with the crate in the room across the hall from Yuri's."

Elda stomped out of the room, resisting the impulse to slam the door behind her.

***

Snezhana waited for a group of chatty tourists to pass her in the hallway of the Royal Lancaster Hotel. She quickly let herself into the laundry room. Suddenly, she paused and looked around. There was a familiar scent in the room, not perfume, not laundry detergent but a human musk mingled with others. She stored it in her memory to sort out later. Grabbing a large cart, she pulled a pile of bath towels off the shelf and tossed them into the cart. Then she donned a cleaning service white coat that she spied hanging on a peg and pushed the cart out of the room.

***

Having slipped into Yuri's hotel room a few floors up, Elda waited for him to return. She quickly searched the room and noted that there was only one set of toiletries and assumed that Anatoly was staying in a separate room. She prayed that Anatoly would not check in on Yuri before she finished her mission here.

The hallway floor creaked and Elda moved into position behind the door. Yuri entered, shutting the door behind him. Elda kicked his legs out from under him, and he came crashing down to the floor. She quickly had him gagged and zip tied.

She patted his back and apologized, "So sorry, Yuri." Then she injected him with the contents of a syringe. "It's time you took a little trip." He slumped on the floor. She checked his pulse. Satisfied, she dialed a number, and spoke softly into her phone, "OK, it's time to send Yuri on his vacation. I do hope he sends us a postcard."

A few minutes later, Oliver and Sophia appeared, dressed in the uniform of a local cleaning company. They rolled Yuri into a large box on wheels, put an oxygen mask on him, and started the flow from a large tank that was tucked inside the box. They checked his pulse and oxygen level and gave a thumbs up. Sophia informed Elda, "We'll ensure he's checked at the transfer point." They securely locked and then taped and labeled the box.

Elda glanced at the mailing label. "Bermuda. Perfect. I hope you put on enough postage. And *please* make sure he gets there alive."

Elda slipped out the door and down the side stairs.

***

Oliver and Sophia rolled their cart down to the service elevator, across from the passenger lift and stairway. Entering the elevator, Oliver pressed CLOSE to hurry the doors. Through the slit of the disappearing view of the hallway, Oliver spied Anatoly exiting the stairs that Elda had just gone down.

"I sure hope she made it out," whispered Oliver to Sophia.

***

In the hallway two floors below Oliver and Sophia's position, Elda willed herself not to sneeze or cough. Just thinking about it made the urges stronger. Standing in the hallway with her back against the stairwell door, Elda held her breath and prayed that Anatoly's room was on the same floor as Yuri's. She had recognized his footsteps and she darted through the nearest hallway exit door. She heard his feet thump by her landing and silently let out her breath. After waiting a beat, she threw herself through the door and dashed down the stairs.

***

Having reached Nigel's house in London, an enraged Anatoly picked up and threw the glass across the room, shattering the glass covering a painting

338

hanging on the opposite wall. "*Der'mo*! What do you mean he's missing?" he shouted.

Nigel peeked over the top of the coffee table that he was trying to hide behind. Doug backed further away from Anatoly.

Anatoly shouted, "Answer me! *Seychas*!"

"H-h-he told us he would be back in the m-morning and then he just n-n-never showed up," said Doug haltingly.

"And?!" Anatoly picked Nigel up by his neck with one hand. Nigel's legs kicked futilely. Gagging, his eyes bulging, he slapped at Anatoly's arms and made bleating noises.

"T-t-t-that's it. He never s-s-s-showed up," stuttered Doug.

Anatoly dropped Nigel with a thud on the floor. "*Der'mo*! Do not leave this house!" He stomped out.

Doug picked up a sleeping bag and an overnight duffel from inside the front door.

"What are you doing?!" croaked Nigel, rubbing his neck.

Holding the strap of the duffel, Doug threw it over his back and opened the front door. He answered over his shoulder, "I'm out of here."

"They will kill you."

"I'm a dead man either way. They will kill me if I stay. This way they will need to find me first." The door swung shut with an anticlimactic soft click.

***

Elda spied Anatoly storming furiously back towards the Royal Lancaster Hotel. Slipping out from behind a parked van across from Nigel's house, Elda followed Anatoly at a safe distance, ducking between cars every few streets to change aspects of her disguise. She needn't have bothered, since in his anger, Anatoly was not checking behind him.

Nearing the hotel, as Anatoly passed a side street, Elda spied a short dark-haired woman hiding in the shadows, raising a gun, about to get the drop on Anatoly. *My god! That's that little bitch, Angelina!* Elda shouted, "Behind you Anatoly!"

Anatoly swiveled around and drew his weapon. Angelina turned to the yell, and, hissed, "You…" and fired at Elda. Both Elda and Anatoly fired back. Angelina somersaulted, diving behind a car and jumped onto the running board of a passing truck, holding onto the open window with a gun on the driver who, at her command, sped away.

Anatoly turned his pistol on Elda. Feeling confident that Tosh had instructed his team not to kill her, Elda holstered hers and held up her hands. She walked towards Anatoly until she was just a few feet away.

Anatoly barked, "Stop or I will shoot you."

Elda shook her head at him and informed him, "If you were going to kill me, you would have already. Plus you can't kill me now, Anatoly. Moscow rules still hold true: *Pick the time and place for action.* This is not the time nor the place for us. I just saved your life, so you owe me one. Leave here now. I'll stay to explain the shots. That will make a favor that you owe me."

"*Da. Tol'ko odin.*" He lowered his piece. "I'll save your life now and that will make us even."

Elda laughed and countered, "You weren't going to kill me so you still owe me one."

Anatoly growled, put his gun away and quickly vanished from the scene.

***

In his London hotel room, Anatoly shook his head at the phone, stating, "I can't find any trace of him, Tosh." Anatoly and Snezhana had finished scouring Yuri's hotel room. Snezhana, having returned from dumping Emily's body, was sitting on a bed, scrolling through the security footage, without picking up any clues. He looked across the room at the hole he had punched in the wall. "Yes, *ser*. I can access the airport security footage. I have a contact in London who has helped me with that before." Anatoly put his phone on speaker so he could crack his knuckles.

Tosh's calming voice came through clearly. "Please reserve another room there. I'm sending Stas over immediately to help you."

Anatoly hesitated and then mentioned, "One more thing, *ser*."

Anatoly could imagine Tosh's eyes narrowing as he responded, "*Da?*"

"Angelina's here in London…," Anatoly paused.

"What aren't you telling me?" demanded Tosh gently, but icily.

"She almost got the drop on me, …," Anatoly took a deep breath and blurted out, "but Elda saved me."

Much to Anatoly's relief, a chuckle came through the phone. "*Chto*?! Elda?! You buried the lead there, Anatoly. Now we know what probably happened to Yuri. I am actually glad to hear that she is there. It may mean that Yuri is alive."

"How can you be sure that Elda is involved with his disappearance?" quizzed Anatoly, rubbing his hand over his buzz cut, as he tried to figure out Tosh's line of thought.

"I know Elda," replied Tosh confidently. "Keep a lookout for her. Let me know the moment you spot her and I'll immediately fly over. I look forward to a rematch with her."

***

Meanwhile, on the street outside Emily's London apartment complex, Sophia held out her arm to stop Oliver. "What?" he snapped.

Sophia pointed up at Emily's window. "There's a light on in her flat."

"Knowing Emily, she probably dropped her phone in the loo again," chuckled Oliver.

Sophia joined in, "Oh that was a great incident. We let her have it for days after that. I bet she did and is ashamed to tell us."

Oliver wryly acknowledged that truth, "I would be afraid to tell us after the hard time we gave her."

"You're lucky you two go way back, Oliver. Let's go up, but be cautious just in case. No heroics."

Oliver clapped his palm to his forehead and grimaced, "Ouch. Will you ever let *that* one go?"

Sophia snapped back, "You played hero while on missions twice and the second time you nearly died. So no. I will tell our children about it."

Oliver brightened up. "*Children*, hey? How many do you want, dear?" He smiled his crooked grin at Sophia and winked.

Sophia leaned in and kissed him and then quickly retreated. She fanned her face and held up her hand at an advancing Oliver. "Enough! Let's verify that Emily is okay and then we can discuss that. However, you are taking care of any kids we have, right?"

"Bob's your uncle I am."

"And we will have them all by surrogate, correct?"

"Righto, love."

"Good. Follow me." Sophia led the way up the inside stairs that opened across from Emily's flat. She noticed a pair of men's Wellingtons outside the door. She looked at Oliver in disgust. "Cor. She's brought a man home. And I bet it's that Douglas creature. Her choices are so bad. I was hoping that therapist was helping."

"Perhaps we should just leave them be, darling. It's been a while since *we* last rolled around. She'll call when they surface for food." Oliver grinned wickedly at Sophia. She shook her head and frowned in return. "No, it's not like Emily to keep something like this quiet. We should verify and, if true, retreat." She reached out and rang the doorbell and put her ear to the door. "Chair pushing back, footsteps, lock being undone, …" She straightened up just as the door opened to reveal Doug in an open robe and boxers. "Oh dear me," she exclaimed, "Is Emily home?"

"G-g-g-gosh, n-n-n-no. Sh-sh-she h-h-has-s-s-s-en't b-b-b-b-been b-b-back here f-for d-d-d-days," stuttered Doug.

"Blimey!" Sophia pushed Doug back into the flat and pulled Oliver in behind her. Oliver shut the door. "You two stay here." She drew her gun and did a quick tour of the apartment. There was no sign of Emily but her bathroom items were still there, as was her luggage. But her phone and wallet were missing. Sophia returned to the living room and pointed the gun at Doug and demanded, "How did you get in? Why are you here?"

Chapter Twenty-Two

Light shone brightly in as the top of the crate was pried off. Yuri closed his eyes and shook his head to try and figure out where he was. A head peeked over the top of the crate, and said in a cheery and proper British accent, "Good morning sir. I hope you enjoyed your flight. Let's get you out of there and into your room. I'm sure you are in need of a nice hot shower and a robust breakfast."

The side of the crate dropped open and Yuri rolled out. A hand lifted the O2 mask off his face. Another hand extended down to help Yuri up. Yuri accepted the hand and stood, shakily. The first man handed Yuri a pair of sunglasses, which he gratefully put on.

Yuri looked blearily around the loading dock. The white sand and teal water sparkled in the sun. "Where am I?"

"Allow me to introduce myself. I am the concierge here at the Grotto Bay Beach Resort & Spa, sir. All your expenses have been paid for your stay. Meals and extras are included. It looks as if you may want to try our spa for a massage."

Yuri stared at the man in confusion. "Yes, but what part of England am I in?"

The concierge shook his head and corrected Yuri, "England?! Oh sir, you are not in England at all. You are in Bermuda."

Yuri scratched his head and despite the glasses, squinted in the bright sunlight. "*Chert*. Really?" A balmy sea breeze informed him that the man was telling the truth.

"Yes sir. Please follow me to your room. I will send up a meal and book your spa appointment for this afternoon."

"Are you sure I haven't died and gone to heaven?"

The man smiled at Yuri. "It will seem like that, but no, you are really at a resort. I have instructions to take good care of you and in a few weeks, send you back home."

"Home?"

"Oh yes, to Moscow."

Yuri set his jaw and queried, "So are you saying I can't leave before then?"

"Unfortunately, yes. That is the case. But we will take good care of you," dryly replied the concierge who was standing next to Yuri. He pointed at the second man. "Michael will ensure that you do not want for anything while here, as well as make sure you do not leave prematurely." Michael, who rivaled Yuri in size, opened his jacket slightly so Yuri could see his holstered sidearm.

Yuri nodded to acknowledge his predicament and his cooperation. He then cocked his head as if remembering something, then asked, "You said you had instructions - whose instructions?"

"Unfortunately we are not allowed to give out that sort of information to our guests, sir. But they did pay for the premium package. With a provision to extend it, should we get instructions to do so."

"*Chert.*"

***

Ashok triumphantly marched into Ed's office without knocking. He was holding up his computer in his right hand, like the staff of a victorious returning warrior. He declared, "It's Tosh's operation here in DC."

Ed, used to Ashok's theatrics by now, calmy inquired, "How can you be so sure?"

With a flourish, Ashok put his laptop on Ed's desk and turned it to face Ed.

"Look at these texts. They have tried to mask the source and have added metadata to obscure their origination. The routing has been very tricky. This is most difficult to figure out. But you know Ashok is the best. Look here at this byte of data."

Ed stared blankly at the character codes on the screen and shook his head. "I'm sorry, Ashok, but you are going to have to explain it to me."

Ashok pursed his lips and stared at Ed in disbelief. "It's so obvious. They all match up with this byte of data."

Ed ruffled his hair, making it stand up on end. He took a deep breath and patiently asked, "Yes?..."

Ashok looked at Ed with a surprised expression and exclaimed, "You don't remember? This is a message we intercepted early on and correlated with the activities around Doug and his father."

The penny dropped for Ed and he exclaimed, "And we assumed that that message came from Tosh or Stas."

Ashok shook his head and pumped his fist in the air. "Correct. Most excellent!"

Ed leaned forward in his chair and asked, "So what does this all mean? Do you have enough data to tie together a picture of who from their team is over here?"

"Yes, that is what is so delightful about finding that byte. I have been able to tie together a bigger picture." Ashok sat and smiled at Ed. The pause filled the air.

Ed inhaled deeply. "And, …"

Ashok pressed a key to pop up another window displaying cryptic metadata. He pointed at a line approximately one third of the way down the screen and happily stated, "There are two Russian operatives. One is called Yaromir and another is called Nadia."

Ed looked at the ceiling and down to his toes and then closed his eyes to focus on taking calming breaths. He then opened his eyes and stared at Ashok who was sitting, nodding and smiling a satisfied grin at Ed.

"And do we know what they are doing here?" Ed asked, his tone patient.

Ashok nodded, "No, we most definitely don't. But I intend to find out with the upmost speed. You will be delighted at the amount of information I will so quickly bring you."

"Thank you, Ashok. That would be most excellent. Even more so, if you could get me pictures of these operatives and their areas of operation by the end of today." Ed waved his hand to dismiss Ashok.

"It is done." With that, Ashok gathered up his laptop and trotted out the door.

***

Sitting across from Madison at a restaurant in DC, Nadia glared at him. She calmly took a sip of her wine and told him, "You can't stop now, you know."

"Why can't I?" Madison shouted at her angrily. "I've done everything you asked. Is it you who are asking, by the way, or are you working for someone? I feel as if I am being played."

Nadia held her hand up. "No need to shout, Madison. I'm on your side. The only place you are being played, Madison, is in the bedroom. And, I thought you enjoyed those games. The rest is benefiting you, as well as me. Look at your bank account. It is growing rapidly, as is my own. You have held off your creditors and will be in the black again by the end of the year. And your political star is rising. Have you seen the number of followers you have on Twitter?"

Madison cast his eyes downward and mumbled, "Yes, yes, I've seen that." Nadia drummed her fingers on the table. Madison looked back up at her, stared directly into her eyes, and blurted out, "Are you working for a foreign government?"

Nadia laughed and trilled, "*Good God*, Madison! Whatever made you think *that*?"

"I saw a text on your phone. It was in another language with strange characters," Madison quickly looked back down again and missed Nadia's furious glare.

Eyes narrowed, she asked quietly and sweetly, "Why on earth were you looking at my phone, Madison?"

"I needed to know what was going on and if I could trust you, Nadia. My entire future is in your hands."

Her left hand in her lap, Nadia clenched and unclenched her fist under the table. She put on a false smile and said, "Yes, I guess you could say that, Madison. Let's go back to your place and I can show you how I can hold you in my hands...."

***

Night had fallen. Anatoly and Snezhana were prowling the streets of London, searching for Elda. Anatoly stopped and scowled at Snezhana who was shadowing his every move. He grumbled, "We'll cover more territory if we split up, Snezhana."

Snezhana stopped, faced Anatoly and looked at him seriously, asking, "Do you think that's wise, Anatoly, with Angelina stalking you? You really should have backup nearby."

Anatoly acknowledged, "You're correct, but I need more space. I work best alone. Let's at least do a grid search so we are at most only a few blocks away from each other. If we run into either Elda or Angelina, we can signal each other with our phones. You go left and I'll go right."

"*Khorosho.*" Snezhana took off with long purposeful strides.

Crash! "*Kakogo khrena.* What the fuck??!" Snezhana felt the metal handlebars of a bicycle dig into her arm and the rider's foot slam into her side. The wheel hub grazed her leg, drawing blood. The impact threw Snezhana into a row of nearby trashcans. Staggering, Snezhana wheeled to face the bike rider who had leapt off her bike. *Damn it, it's Angelina!*

Angelina grabbed at Snezhana's neck, gripping it tightly. Snezhana thrust her arm violently around and down, breaking the choke hold. Snezhana gave a side kick and thrust the smaller woman backwards.

Angelina continued her momentum and backwards somersaulted over a trash can. She smoothly picked the trash can up and threw it at Snezhana, all moves integrated as part of her roll.

Snezhana easily batted the can away and shouted, "You'll have to do better than that you little bitch!" Angelina picked up another can and, holding it out in front of her like a battering ram, came running at Snezhana. Snezhana sidestepped Angelina and slammed the woman in the middle of her back with her fists. Unfazed, Angelina turned and slammed the can into Snezhana, who staggered to the side. *Ouch! That one hurt! Angelina's like a rock.*

Dropping the can, Angelina kicked out at Snezhana, connecting with her shin. *Chert! That hurt!* Snezhana grabbed Angelina's leg before she could draw it away and spun Angelina into the pile of cans, jumping in on top of her. Both women now on the ground, Angelina put her legs around Snezhana's waist and butted her forehead into Snezhana's. "Chert!" Snezhana shook her head in reaction to the blow.

Snezhana bashed Angelina in the face with her fist. She rolled over onto her back with Angelina hanging on with her legs. Snezhana had one of Angelina's arms twisted behind her. Angelina was attempting squeeze Snezhana's neck with one hand. Their breath intermingled as they fought for dominance.

Snezhana channeled her intense anger. Using her free hand to push herself upwards and bending one leg beneath her for leverage, She rose up and stood. Struggling from the load of Angelina hanging onto her, she rammed Angelina into a wall, shaking her up enough that Angelina's legs loosened their grip. Angelina fell off of Snezhana.

Snezhana quickly backed up and drew her gun. Before she could fire it, Angelina rolled away and, rising, threw a can at Snezhana. She whirled around and leapt into the street to grab the side of a passing truck.

"Oh no, you don't do that trick of jumping on a truck again, you *malen'kaya suchka*." Furious with her adrenaline pumping, Snezhana sprinted and jumped to catch the tailgate with her free hand and the hitch with her right foot. She pulled herself up and over the tailgate, landing with a thump in the back of the truck.

From where she had been hanging on outside the truck, Angelina threw herself over the side, into the truck bed, and landed on top of Snezhana. She grabbed for Snezhana's hair, but her hand slipped off from the gel that Snezhana had put in it that morning. Angelina crashed backwards against the inside of the truck, but, although shaken and winded, she managed to pull her gun out.

Still on her back, Snezhana drew her feet back and forcefully kicked the weapon out of Angelina's hand. The gun went skidding across the bed. The driver glanced in the rearview mirror and started slowing the truck down to pull over to the side of the road. Angelina dove for her pistol, only to be yanked back by her hair. Angelina pulled a knife out of her calf knife sheath and stabbed Snezhana in her hand. Fully in fight mode, immune to pain, blood drawn away from her limbs, Snezhana grabbed the knife hilt with her other hand and yanked it from Angelina's grasp.

Enraged, Snezhana kicked out at Angelina's calf with her shoe knife and connected soundly, thrusting upwards to widen the wound. "Take that you bitch."

Angelina fell over, bleeding from her leg. She rolled to her feet and hurtled over the tailgate and onto the road. Horns blaring as she landed on her feet and wove her way across the street and down a side alley.

Damn it! I can't believe she can run like that on that leg. Ignoring the oozing blood from her hand, Snezhana jumped off the now completely stopped truck and ran after Angelina.

***

Frustrated, Anatoly stopped near the Royal Lancaster Hotel. "*Der'mo.* This wandering the streets is not working for me. I need a way to do this more quickly. Let me see what Stas can come up with" A passing man looked warily at the large man speaking to himself. Anatoly barked at him, "Who are you looking at?" The man dashed between the cars and scurried across to the other side of the street. Anatoly turned the corner and bounded into the hotel and up the stairs to Stas' room.

He burst in and announced "I need you to scan the video for flights in and out of Heathrow. Then Gatwick."

Stas looked up from his computer and stated plaintively, "It will take me a while to access Heathrow's system, Anatoly. It's not an easy one to get into. And, anyway, how did you get in?"

Anatoly said curtly, "I have a passkey." Surprised that Stas was fallible, he asked, "You can't immediately get into the airport systems?"

Stas shook his head. "*Nyet*."

Anatoly wheeled around and pulled on Stas' arm. "*Khorosho*. We don't have time to fool around with you trying to crack those systems. Stop what you're doing. I know of a quicker way. Come with me, Stas." Stas quickly and deftly bundled his laptop into his backpack with his other hand.

Outside, Anatoly flagged down a cab to take them to Finsbury Park in London. Dropped off in front of a row of connected houses, Anatoly, stopped to scratch his head. "It's one of these basement flats," he told Stas. "What is? Why are we here?" Stas questioned.

"*Aga*! This one!" Anatoly immediately headed to the center of the row of houses and knocked on the door of the basement flat. The hacker opened the door a crack and sprang back in fright when he saw Anatoly. Anatoly pushed his way into the dark windowless room. "Hello hacker. Miss me? It's time to get to work again." The hacker backed up in trepidation. Anatoly held out an envelope of money. "There's more when you finish showing me the footage from Heathrow. Here's the dates of interest."

Anatoly threw the money and a paper onto the table next to the row of computers.

Shaking, the hacker motioned for Anatoly to sit in front of one of the monitors. Stas stood over his shoulder and watched the hacker as he broke into Heathrow's camera systems and replayed the footage from Heathrow.

Quickly losing patience, Anatoly thumped his fist on his leg as he watched the hacker slowly scroll through the scenes. He shouted, "Nothing! *Der'mo!*" The hacker edged his chair a few more inches away from Anatoly. Anatoly grabbed the mouse and scrolled more quickly forward and then back again through the footage. "Where is she? *Der'mo!*" He pounded his fist on the table.

"P-p-p-please. Those are sensitive machines," stuttered the scared hacker.

Appearing to agree with the hacker and showing concern for the machines, Stas grabbed Anatoly's arm. "We can leave now, Anatoly."

Anatoly looked at the skinny shaking hacker with disgust. He tossed the money onto the table. As Anatoly's arm moved, the hacker dove under the table. Anatoly shook his head. "Grow a pair, man." He followed Stas out of the flat, slamming the door behind them.

***

Anatoly, Stas and Snezhana sat huddled in Anatoly's hotel room. Stas was running the footage back and forth trying to see what they may have missed while at the hacker's flat. Anatoly handed Snezhana a glass of water and two Tylenol. After she had gulped those down, he gently started examining Snezhana's hand. He folded over a gauze pad and applied a temporary bandage to her hand. Snezhana held an icepack to her forehead with her other hand.

"Ouch! That hurts, Anatoly."

Anatoly poured two shots of vodka and handed it to her. "Drink this," he commanded.

Snezhana put down the icepack and downed the vodka. She could feel it burning as it dulled the peripheral pain. Anatoly poured her another. Feeling a warm glow from the first, Snezhana protested, "Anatoly – I don't need more."

"You will for this." Anatoly held up the medical kit and proclaimed, "You need stitches."

Snezhana glanced at her hand that Anatoly had temporarily bandaged and saw the blood seeping through. She downed the second glass of vodka.

Anatoly folded another gauze pad and handed it to Snezhana. "Bite on this," he directed.

361

"What no bullet?" Snezhana quipped and then gasped with tears coming to her eyes as Anatoly started the first stitch. She bit down hard on the gauze.

After he was done stitching, Anatoly handed Snezhana another shot of vodka. She gratefully took it and tossed it back. Anatoly started rebandaging her hand.

Somewhat inebriated, Snezhana lamented, "*Blyad*"! I can't believe I lost her."

"Hold still, Snezhana," commanded Anatoly. "Stas, how did you get into the Heathrow systems? I thought you couldn't, which was why we went to the hacker."

"I couldn't before we went to the hacker's, but I memorized his keystrokes as he broke in. So now I have access any time we need it," declared Stas.

Anatoly growled, "God, I detest hackers!" Stas looked at Anatoly sharply. Anatoly reassured him, "*Nyet, nyet*. Present company excluded. *Ya lyublyu svoyego khaker*. I love my hacker."

Snezhana pointed at the screen, taking Anatoly's hand and the gauze roll with her. "Stop moving, Snezhana," Anatoly commanded.

Ignoring Anatoly, Snezhana waved her gauzed draped hand at the screen and commanded Stas, "There. Go back. Can you zoom in?"

"*Nyet, izviniti*," Stas said apologetically, freezing the screen at that frame.

Anatoly gently, but firmly, held Snezhana's arm with one hand. "*Der'mo*! Hold still Snezhana or I *will* slap you." She looked at him in surprise and he nodded an affirmative. Chastised, Snezhana turned sideways and let Anatoly tend to her hand. She continued to direct Stas through the footage.

"Those two baggage handlers seem familiar. Go back farther, Stas. I want to see them walk."

"Who are they, Snezhana?" queried Anatoly, as he finished bandaging her up.

"I'd swear that's Oliver and Sophia rolling that large crate over to the baggage check-in."

Anatoly leaned in to see the screen better. "*Der'mo*! That looks large enough to hold Yuri."

"It does," acknowledged Stas, holding his finger up to the crate and measuring it against the figures in the picture.

Snezhana inquired excitedly, "*Otlichno*! Great! How do we trace that, Stas?"

Stas was rapidly typing and screens of code flew by on the screen. He stated, "Already started. *Pozhaluysta,* give me some time and I'll find out where it went."

"*Der'mo.* He better be alive or someone will pay dearly." Anatoly slammed his fist on his thigh.

Snezhana patted him on his shoulder. "Trust Tosh, Anatoly. He knows Elda well. She would not harm Yuri unless it was absolutely necessary."

"It's time I had a talk with her." Anatoly stood up preparing to storm out of the room.

Stas looked up from his computer. "Perhaps we should locate Elda first?"

"*Der'mo!*" Anatoly stopped mid-stride. He marched over to where Stas, sitting on the couch with his laptop on his knees, was rapidly typing. He spoke sharply to Stas, "Well?"

Stas glared back at Anatoly and patiently answered, "That's the third time in an hour that you've interrupted me, Anatoly. In order to go faster, I'll need to increase my computing power here. If I have more servers to spin up then I can parallel process and increase my search area for Elda."

"Well do it. *Idti!* All that *komp'yuter goverit* means you need more money right?"

Stas held out his hand, and replied, "*Pozhaluysta*."

Anatoly pulled a roll out of his pocket, peeled off a number of bills and handed them to Stas. Stas snorted, "I'm buying heavy duty computer equipment, not some child's game."

Anatoly took a deep breath and extended his hand to Stas. Stas grabbed the bills. "*Chert! Vor*! You took it all!"

Stas said dismissively, "I know you have another stash hidden, Anatoly, and I'll bring back the change."

Anatoly growled and sneered at Stas.

Unfazed, Stas commented, "I'll be back in a couple of hours." Stas powered down and shut his computer and carefully placed it into his padded backpack. He happily strolled out of the hotel room and shut the door behind him.

"Where are you going?" Anatoly belated remembered to ask as the door clicked closed.

***

Slap! The eraser hit and harmlessly bounced off the wall in Elda's London flat. Oliver sank to his crate and buried his head in his hands. Elda looked at

Sophia quizzically. Sophia put her hands gently on Oliver's shoulders and answered Elda's unspoken question, "There's still no sign of Emily. Doug had no information to give us. Emily has never gone a day without at least texting Oliver a picture of her breakfast. It's been a running joke between the two of them for years. Oliver is a big believer of a proper English breakfast and Emily will eat whatever is on hand such as cold Indian food or even chocolate cake. We have not received any texts from her for three days now."

Oliver's shoulder's shook as he sobbed.

Sophia added, "It's quite a loss. Oliver and she were best mates since Year 1 in Primary school. She was the only one who still called him Ollie."

Elda nodded and then walked over and gently lifted Oliver's chin so his eyes met hers. She asked quietly but firmly, "Are you up to continuing, Oliver?"

Oliver nodded.

Elda continued to stare him in the eyes and reprimanded him, "I'll need a verbal confirmation. Oliver. You cannot have any doubt in your mind or hesitation in your actions."

Oliver gave her a direct gaze back and stated decisively, "Yes, ma'am," before breaking his eye contact.

Satisfied, Elda walked over to the whiteboard to map out the next phase of the operation. She verbalized the plans as she drew, "Okay. Yuri was an easy mark. Of the three remaining, Anatoly and Snezhana are the two most dangerous. Snezhana is still relatively new to the field, whereas Anatoly is an experienced assassin. Therefore, we'll leave him for last. We will remove Stas next." She drew a map of London and put an X on the location of the Royal Lancaster Hotel. "I expect them to move their location shortly, so we need to move fast. There is a CeX computer store nearby." Elda marked a second X on the road lines she had drawn. "We know how much of a computer geek Stas is and I am making a bet that he will gather more equipment prior to their relocation. I have obtained a van and had the CeX logo applied to it. Oliver will drive the van, and Sophia will draw Stas to the van. We know from training with him that Stas is not a fighter unless you try to separate him from his equipment, so make sure you send him back with his precious computer. Okay?"

Both Sophia and Oliver nodded. Elda continued, "It's up to you guys to plan the rest of the operation to fit your styles." Elda turned to Charlie and added, "Let's go for a walk and plan our U.S. operation."

Charlie hung back and asked, "I thought you weren't keen on going back over there and leaving this?"

"I'm not," Elda agreed. "But it's a good way to get you established with Ed."

Charlie frowned and inquired, "But what about you?"

"Don't worry about me, Charlie. I will continue on my own terms," Elda said dismissively. Her sentence lacked conviction in delivery. Elda glanced away from Charlie.

Charlie stated, "Or?"

Elda straightened her shoulders, winked at Charlie and added with a wry smile. "Or, not at all." She opened the door and motioned Charlie out ahead of her.

***

Stas bounced along the street on his way to CeX on Queensbury street in London, humming in anticipation of the equipment he would see and play with. A stout matronly woman was standing at the bus stop along his way. She took out her cell phone and texted.

"Young man," the woman called out to Stas, who stopped and turned. She continued in an aged, quivering voice, "These buses never run on time, do they?" Stas internally rolled his eyes but nodded and replied politely, "No ma'am, they don't." He started to walk, eager to be on his way again. She drew nearer to him, pushing her shopping cart. "I just texted my grandson for a ride but he didn't answer. I don't live far from here, in fact, just down the street, but these days it's just not safe to be on one's own, you know? Do you mind if I walk with you?"

Stas's eyes and mouth twitched as he gazed at her dowdy housedress and plump figure. "*Nyet* ma'am. I mean, *da* ma'am. Ah, *da, pozhaluysta*, do walk with me."

The grandmother waddled along next to him. "That language you were speaking. It is so pretty. Where do you come from, lad?"

"Russia, but I am here now," stated Stas.

She responded with an extra quiver in her voice, "Well, *yes*, you are young man. Do you plan on staying long?" Before Stas could answer, a van pulled up next to them. The driver beeped his horn and yelled, "Pardon me. I'm a bit turned around. I'm looking for CeX on Queensbury. Am I headed in the right direction?"

Stas brightened, "*Da*. I'm heading there too. I can show you the way." He looked forward to being relieved of the burden of escorting the old lady.

The driver responded, "*Ta* mate. I'd appreciate that."

In a trembling voice, the woman addressed Stas, "Oh dear. You're leaving me alone in this neighborhood? Could I possibly get a lift from the driver too?" Her lips quivered.

Oh please don't cry, thought Stas. He looked at the lost look on her face and reluctantly asked the driver, "Can you take her too?"

The driver sighed heavily protesting, "I'm not even supposed to take any passengers but I'm very turned around. Where do you live lady?"

"Just a few blocks down this road on the right," she answered.

"All right," the driver grudgingly agreed.

The old woman smiled warmly at the driver, "That would be ducky. I don't live far from there. Thank you."

The driver pulled the van all the way over to the curb. He got out and addressed Stas, "There's really only room for one in the front, mate. You'll have to ride in the back."

"That's great!" replied Stas, eager to ride with the equipment.

The driver put his arm around Stas' shoulders and guided him to the back of the van. The woman moved in behind the two of them.

The driver opened the van door to reveal a compartment that was empty except for a large crate. A disappointed Stas wheeled around, only to face the woman holding a gun on him. "Get in now," she commanded. Stas obediently jumped into the back of the van. She leapt in after him and tore off his backpack. Stas reached over to get it back. She threw him down and gagged him. She then put his backpack against his chest and zip tied his hands in front of him, holding his backpack. She then duct taped everything to his body. Finally, she bound his ankles together.

Stas lay in dismay as the driver slammed the door shut, started the truck, and pulled away from the curb. He saw the driver through the grill in the partition that separated the cab from the cargo area and heard him inquire, "All set back there, honey?"

Honey?

"Yes, he's secure. Thanks, love."

Love?

"I rather like the matronly you, dear."

Dear? Is this part of their mating ritual?

She threw the roll of duct tape against the grill and snapped, "Just find a place to pull over so you can help me get the package ready for Tosh in Moscow."

Tosh? Moscow? Who are these people? Stas stared wide eyed and struggled against his bonds.

"Relax Stas. It's not first class, but it will be a quick flight for you. And when you get to Moscow, do not come back to London or we will kill you."

Stas gulped and closed his eyes. *And I never got to buy my equipment at CeX.*

Chapter Twenty-Three

In Moscow, Tosh strode into the anteroom of Adrik's office and enquired of the secretary, "Is he in? He has summoned me."

The secretary looked up from her typing and replied, "*Da.* He is expecting you. Please go in." She then pressed a button on her desk and spoke into the intercom, "Tosh is here to see you, *ser.*"

A disembodied voice crackled back over the speaker, "Send him in."

Tosh opened the inner door and marched into Adrik's office.

Adrik raised his bulk from his chair and motioned Tosh to a seat. He then sat back down heavily. Silence filled the room. Tosh sat patiently with a neutral expression on his face.

"You have done well in the UK, Tosh." Adrik's tone and words were discordant, and he looked angry.

"*Spasibo, ser,*" Tosh replied flatly. "I aim to please."

Adrik sneered, "Your ways are still old-fashioned."

Tosh replied evenly, "But apparently effective, *ser*."

Adrik snorted, "Apparently, on easy cases… We have the information from our first asset, John Clark, and he is firmly under our control. Now we need to milk the others. You have informed me that, what is his name, the man who set this up, is no longer needed? It has taken you long enough to figure *that* one out."

Tosh breathed in deeply to lower his blood pressure. "*Da ser*. We have all the information from Nigel we will get and do not need him any more as a go between."

Adrik pointed a finger at Tosh and demanded, "Clean up after yourself then. Dispose of him and any others you need to remove. Do not get caught. Then focus on the DC operation. You should find that more of a challenge for your archaic skills."

"*Da, ser*."

***

Sitting at his computer in his office, Tosh glowered at Nadia who was in the hotel room in the United States. The heat of his disapproval could be felt through her computer screen. He spoke softly but Nadia detected an edge to his voice. "I have not received a report from you this week, Nadia."

Careful not to anger him more, Nadia smiled sweetly at his image on her phone. "I am so very sorry, Tosh. I was so busy turning Madison that it completely dropped from my mind."

Clearly unmollified, Tosh stated, "These reports are important and necessary. I am recording this call. Report *now*." He shook his finger at her in reprimand.

Wanting to drag things out in the comfort of the United States, Nadia's mind raced as she worked up a story full enough to satisfy Tosh and gain her a delay. "He was not as cooperative as I had at first hoped."

Tosh snapped back, "You told me he was an easy mark."

Nadia put on her most sincere face and replied, "Yes, yes, I *did*. And I *did* think that at first. But he is hesitant to go forward. He still has loyalty to his wife."

Tosh snorted, "I find that hard to believe, Nadia, since we caught him in the honey trap in Moscow. Plus you have the *kompromat* from that operation, including all the pictures, to use to turn him. Try again."

Nadia looked away from the video chat, replying, "Yes, yes, that is all true, Tosh. But you know how men can make what they consider as a mistake and then regret it giving them more fortitude and resistance against a second one."

Tosh fixed her with his steely glare and snarled softly, "So don't be a mistake. Plus I have seen some of the disinformation being distributed through his accounts already. Do *not* lie to me, Nadia."

"*Da, Ser.*"

"Look at me when you say that," demanded Tosh.

Keeping her face impassive, Nadia thought, *I wish he'd get off his high horse. I can run rings around this old fool. These men are all alike with their overinflated egos.*

Tosh instructed, "I expect that he will be *fully* cooperative by next week."

"But that may be too soon," Nadia said. More than anything she wanted to draw this mission out as long as possible. She was enjoying her time in the United States. She glanced at her phone and gave it her most endearing look.

Unmoved, Tosh barked at her, "Then I will replace you. Do your job."

The screen went blank.

Nadia slammed down the lid of her laptop. *I am so sick of these men. If I had my way I'd get rid of them all.*

***

The pounding on the door brought the London veterinarian to the front door of the clinic. He yelled through the door, "The clinic is closed."

An angry voice screamed back, "Open it now! You have an emergency."

The vet stared out the glass door at a young woman with blood soaking through her pant leg. He took out his cell phone.

The woman yelled, "If you use that to call anyone, your family is dead."

He hesitated and nervously asked, "How do you know my family?"

"You are originally from Moscow. Your lovely British wife, Heather, and you have two strapping sons, Vlad and Boris. Your father is dead, but your mother is still alive and living in Moscow. You are

377

hoping to bring her to the UK, but she likes Russia. We would hope that she continues to enjoy living there."

Shaken and convinced, the veterinarian yanked open the door. She limped in and commanded, "First clean up that mess before anyone sees it," pointing to the blood that had dripped where she had been standing.

The doctor grabbed a rag and a spray bottle of cleanser and wiped clean her tracks outside the front door. Finishing, he quickly shut and locked the door behind her. "You need to go to the hospital," he told her.

She gave him a death stare and retorted, "*Nyet. You* need to fix me up here. And you will speak of this to no-one. *Vy ponimayete?*"

"Who are you?"

"Some call me Angelina. For you that name can be a death sentence or a future favor. Your choice."

The vet gulped, then nodded and led Angelina back into the operating area.

Chapter Twenty-Four

Two workmen in grey overalls wheeled a large box on a 4-wheeled dolly into Tosh's Kremlin office and asked, *"Gde ty khochesh' etogo?"*

Tosh, deep into reading the contents of a folder, answered them with a wave to the far side of his office. Hearing the thump of the box roll off the dolly onto the floor, he looked up and asked, *"Eto chto?"*

"We don't know what it is. Sign for it here." The taller of the workmen held out a clipboard with a lading invoice on it. Tosh scribbled a signature where they indicated. They gave him a crumpled copy, picked up the trolly, and marched out of the door.

Tosh grabbed his bug tracker from his desk drawer and went over to the box. He examined the box for any signs of explosives and scanned it with the bug tracker. He noticed that the TO field in the address label had been correctly filled out with his full name, Toshchiy Chelovek, but the FROM field had been left blank except for three x's. He reached into his office tool box and pulled out a pry bar. He carefully inserted the bar between the side and the top of the crate. The top splintered off with loud cracking noises as portions of it fell to the floor. Inside, Stas was curled up around his backpack with an oxygen tank hose affixed to his nose.

"*Chert*!" Tosh reached in and gently removed the O2 nosepiece, cut the tie wraps and duct tape, and then, with two hands, helped a stiffened and cramped Stas up and to his feet. When he was sure Stas could stand, Tosh put the pieces of the top back into the crate, the bar back into his toolbox, and the scanner back into his desk drawer. He waved Stas to a chair. "*Kto eto sdelal*, Stas? Who did this?" he asked.

Stas sat with his head in his hands and replied, "I don't know, Tosh."

Tosh gently probed, "Then tell me what you remember. What happened?"

Stas filled Tosh in on the entire abduction scene. Tosh repeated back to him, "A man and a woman? The woman was short and stout? They threw you in the back of an electronics van and then injected you with what was probably a sedative, crated you and mailed you to me? This has all the marks of an Elda operation."

Stas disagreed, "*Nyet*. She didn't sound like Elda, though Tosh. She had a British accent."

"Trust me, Stas. This has Elda's fingerprints all over it."

***

Nadia sat in Yaromir's rented DC apartment with her feet up on his coffee table. Yaromir slapped them off and in their place set down a vodka bottle and two shot glasses. Nadia reached out and poured each of them a shot and quaffed hers in one gulp. Yaromir followed suit. She reached to pour again but Yaromir caught her arm. "*Nyet*. We have to report to Tosh first."

Nadia sneered at Yaromir and retorted, "He'll never know. What are you afraid of?" She reached for the bottle.

Yaromir grabbed her arm again, only very roughly this time. "You are in my apartment. My rules. And by the way, Nadia, I found the lock missing from the rented storage unit door. You were the last one in there. Any idea where it went?" Yaromir stared accusingly at Nadia.

Nadia shook his arm off and glared at him. She snapped, "*Nyet*. What does it matter anyway? Such a puny padlock wouldn't keep anyone out."

Yaromir took Nadia's hands in his and gently squeezed them, increasing the pressure as he spoke,

"If the weapons had been stolen, my operation would have been compromised and shut down. Be sloppy on your own time but keep your hands off of my stuff. *Khorosho*?" He released her hands.

Nadia shook out her hands and rolled her eyes, and responded sulkily, "*Da. Khorosho.*"

Yaromir moved the bottle out of her reach and hid the shot glasses from the laptop camera's view. He slowly typed in a number of commands and a secure video chat was initiated with Moscow. Tosh's face appeared, filling the screen.

Yaromir flinched and asked, "*Ser*. Could you move back from the camera? You are very close." Nadia looked on with disinterest.

Tosh adjusted his distance from the camera and said tersely, "Report."

Yaromir quickly filled Tosh in on his progress. Tosh summarized, "So you have made great progress, Yaromir. They took the bait on the guns and you have incited a number of riots over there. *Otlichnaya rabota*! You are on track with that. How about the other part of your mission with Senator Glass?"

"*Da, ser*. It is also going well. I made the initial contact and I'm sure of his full cooperation."

"*Khorosho*, Yaromir." Tosh turned his gaze to Nadia and inquired sharply, "Nadia, how are you doing on *your* mission?"

Nadia had leaned back on the couch and was examining her nails. She spoke up laconically, "It is, how do you say it in American—*tort progulka*—a cake walk. These men are so easy. I show a little leg at dinner and then they are in my palm."

Tosh narrowed his eyes and said icily, "Are you bored, Nadia? If so, I'm sure I can ask Yaromir to make things more interesting for you there."

A trace of fear flickered in Nadia's eyes, but she responded coolly, "No, Tosh. There is no need for that. This is like pulling wings off of flies and watching them slowly die. I much prefer to squash them and see the guts squeeze out. But I have it under control."

"*Ser*." Tosh tersely reminded her.

Nadia sat up and responded, "I have it under control, *ser*."

Tosh replied in a steely tone, "You better. It's much nicer being the fly swatter than the fly."

Tosh's screen went dark.

Nadia stood and retrieved the vodka bottle and poured two shots, downing both of them. She then poured two more and gave the second to Yaromir. "He's awfully touchy today. I don't think he realizes what an asset I am to this team."

Yaromir grabbed the bottle, doubled his shot and then glugged it. "Don't get too confident there, Nadia. Anyone is dispensable."

Nadia crossed her legs showing a long, bare leg. She smiled knowingly at Yaromir and taunted him, "You wouldn't. You would lose this."

Yaromir sat next to her and ran his hand up the inside of her leg and shoved his finger inside her. She gasped. He kissed her passionately and then removed and licked his finger. He grabbed her legs, removed her panties, and unzipped his pants. As he drove into her he whispered, "Oh, I would and I could."

***

Nadia, in bed with Madison in a DC hotel room, stuck her head up from under the covers. "What is wrong, Madison? This has never happened with us." She rolled over and crawled up to face him in bed.

Tears welled up in his eyes as he replied, "I know. I'm so sorry. I just can't."

Madison held his hands over his face. Nadia looked at him with narrowing eyes. "Is there something on your mind?"

Madison uncovered his face and sat up in bed. Nadia followed his lead. The covers slipped off her upper body, eliciting no response from Madison. Nadia scowled at him. She pressed her lips together and stuck her bottom lip out in a pout, a look that Madison had often found appealing.

Madison undeterred, accused Nadia, "You thought I was sleeping, but I heard you talking to another man on the phone."

"Really…," Nadia said slowly, "And what did you hear?"

Madison shrugged, "Nothing that made sense to me. You mentioned you'd see him soon and that he shouldn't worry about Tosh. Your tone sounded as if you knew him well."

Nadia laughed, "You silly fool. Of course it did. He's my brother. He's having a problem and I am trying to help him work through it. Were you jealous?"

Madison nodded, "Why yes. I thought you were sleeping with him."

Nadia shook her head. "Men! You're all alike. So insecure. Let me get you a drink and then perhaps we can try again?" She stood up and wiggled her ass at him as she walked to the bureau to grab the bottle of scotch. Part way there, she turned towards the bathroom. "One minute though. I have to use the little room here." Madison lay with his hands behind his head watching her. An erection was starting to grow.

He called after her, "Don't be too long."

Nadia returned in a few minutes, poured his scotch and handed it to him and then poured a couple of fingers for herself. Madison downed his scotch and reached for Nadia. She stood looking down at him with a slight smile on her face. He grimaced and rubbed his chest with his right hand. Nadia studied him, asking, "Are you all right?"

Madison's color was draining from his face. His pained expression indicated that he obviously wasn't well. Nadia watched him as he grabbed his chest with both hands. His body jerked in a sudden convulsion and the smell in the room was not pleasant. Nadia checked his pulse at his throat and then reached up and closed his eyes. Putting on gloves, she retrieved his scotch glass, washed it thoroughly, splashed a jigger of scotch in it and placed it by the bed. She washed her glass and placed it inside her purse. She thoroughly wiped down Madison's skin and anything in the room that she may have touched. After cleaning the bathroom she walked around the bedroom to ensure she had left no trace. She looked down at the peaceful corpse.

You knew too much about me, Madison. And your feeble attempts at lovemaking were tedious at best. I was sick of sucking your ugly short cock. It was time for you to go. Don't worry, the autopsy will show that you died from a massive heart attack. Your reputation will remain intact. The bank account will disappear. I thank you for adding to my retirement funds.

Wiping surfaces and doorknobs as she left, Nadia quietly shut his front door and strolled away.

***

The sun shone brightly in Bermuda.

"Another vodka, sir?"

Yuri looked up at the waiter over the top of his mirrored sunglasses. Yuri lay on a double width sand chair with his arm around a pretty brunette. A blond was sitting at his feet and a red hair woman had her lounge chair pulled up close to his side, in order to join the conversations. Yuri replied in a broad British accent, "Why yes, my good man, another vodka with

387

a water chaser and please put on my tab whatever these lovely ladies want."

"Certainly sir." The waiter made a few notes on his order pad and walked over to the next set of chairs.

Yuri turned his attention back to the women, "Where were we?"

***

In his London hotel room, Anatoly dialed the number for the sixth time. No answer. "*Der'mo!*" He threw the cell phone across the room where it landed unharmed on the bed. He stomped over to it and punched in a new number. He snarled into the phone, "Stas is missing, Snezhana. He's been gone for over seven hours, and he said he'd only be gone for a couple at most. It can't take that long for him to pick out his *sumasshedshaya komp'yuternaya tekhnika*." He listened to Snezhana ask, "Where did he go to get his equipment?" and snapped tersely, "*Nyet*, I don't know where he went."

Snezhana yelled, "How could you not know that?"

Anatoly held the phone away from his ear and when he returned it there was only the buzz of the

388

dial tone on the line. He threw the phone at the bed again.

The hotel room door opened and Snezhana barged in.

"How did you get in, Snezhana?" Anatoly demanded.

Snezhana glared at Anatoly. "Tell me everything you know."

"My room, how did you get in?" Anatoly demanded again.

"*Glupyy*, I have a pass key, of course. Now what did Stas say before he left?"

"He said he needed more power and servers and so was buying more junk. He took a lot of money for it too. And then he walked out."

Snezhana looked around the room. "*Govno*!" She exclaimed, "He took his computer with him, so we can't trace him that way. You didn't mention that," she accused Anatoly, slapping him on the arm. He drew back his fist and dropped it when he saw the look in her eyes. It was scarily like Tosh's expression when he was furious.

Snezhana took out her iPhone and powered up an application on it. Curious, Anatoly asked, "What's that?"

Snezhana paused in her typing to answer Anatoly. "I had Stas install trackers on all our computers after Yuri went missing. We can find him from those. And if he's not where his computer is, we can assume he is dead. Stas would never abandon his precious laptop."

"*Der'mo*," Anatoly said sadly.

Snezhana rapidly typed on her phone and then stopped and stared at her screen. She cursed, "*Blyad'*."

Anatoly attempted to view her screen over her shoulder. "*Kakiye*? Where is he?"

Snezhana pointed at her phone. "He's in Moscow."

Anatoly rapid fired his questions at her: "Moscow?! What's he doing there? Can you determine where in Moscow?"

"*Da*." Snezhana typed a bit more, stopped, looked puzzled and shook her head in disbelief.

Anatoly scowled at her and barked, "Well?"

"He's in Tosh's office."

Anatoly and Snezhana turned and stared at each other.

***

Anatoly and Snezhana shut down the secure connection with Tosh. Anatoly addressed Snezhana, "You heard him, Snezhana, it's time to close down this London operation. The little weasel, Nigel, is mine. I'll take him out. Then we can search together for the rest of the players. As Tosh requested, we'll notify Tosh when we locate Elda."

Snezhana readily agreed with Anatoly, "*Da.* You do that and I'll call Stas and get a search for Elda started by him. I'll feed Tosh whatever information he needs from here." Snezhana started typing into her laptop.

Anatoly checked his bag and slipped a silenced MP-412 REX .357 Magnum revolver inside his jacket, and a garrot and a 9 centimeter switchblade into his pockets. "I'll be back soon." He shut the door quietly behind him and slipped down the back stairway and out of the hotel. He fell into a comfortable jog, feeling the pleasant anticipation of a kill.

Anatoly slowed his pace as he approached Nigel's house. He was pleased to see Nigel's Mini parked in the driveway. He stormed up the walkway and into the house without knocking.

Nigel looked up from his seat on the couch. He took a sip of his beer and laconically inquired, "Oh, hello strong man, to what do I owe this pleasure of a visit?"

Antony growled at him, "Where is your friend?"

"I don't know, mate. He took off. Would you like a beer?" Nigel put his beer on the table and stood to walk to the kitchen to get Anatoly a beer, and asked, "What's our next job?"

Anatoly narrowed his eyes and replied, "There is none. This operation is over."

Nigel's lips trembled. His shoulders drooped. Trembling, Nigel turned to Anatoly and pleaded, "No, no. There is so much more information I can get you."

Anatoly sneered at Nigel, "You little *kher*. We have no use for you. Your only use was connecting us to Doug. And now he's disappeared."

"Wait, wait! I can get him back." Nigel sank to his knees in front of Anatoly. "Please, I'll do anything for you. Just let me live."

"Stand up, you sorry excuse of a man," Anatoly snapped at Nigel.

Nigel slowly stood. Anatoly took a step in closer to Nigel and looked down into Nigel's tear-soaked eyes. He could feel Nigel's rapid breath. He stepped in even closer until their bodies touched. Nigel stood submissively. Anatoly reached up and put his hands around Nigel's neck and started squeezing, watching as Nigel's eyes grew wide with panic. Nigel reached up and tried to pry Anatoly's fingers off his neck. Anatoly's thumbs dug in deeper. Nigel gasped for air, his body shaking with terror.

Anatoly watched as Nigel's eyes registered final acceptance and rolled up. His body sagged into Anatoly. Anatoly held him there, still choking him, to ensure the deed was done. He then lowered the body to the floor and reached down and closed the man's eyes. Anatoly took out a wet wipe and wiped any trace of his prints from Nigel's neck. He breathed freely as his heart rate returned to normal. All the tension had drained from his body. Only his erection remained to register the pleasant moment of death.

Chapter Twenty-Five

Tension electrified the air. Elda, in her London apartment, glared at the image on her phone and snapped, "You know I'm more valuable here, Ed."

Ed scowled back at Elda and rejoined, "I need you back in DC *now*, Elda. We have reliable information that Tosh has dispatched operatives to DC to infiltrate hate groups and to shake down more members of the Senate."

Elda gritted her teeth and retorted, "You can do that with another operative. It doesn't require my skills."

Ed took a deep breath and deescalated by admitting, "I've been instructed to use you and your team on this."

Elda narrowed her eyes and stated, "Do you see anything strange about that, Ed?"

Ed shook his head and said confidently, "It makes sense. You have the most experience with Tosh and his team."

Ed is far too trusting. Someone wants us gone from London. Is it James or someone else? Elda paused for a moment, breathed deeply, and then responded, "OK, Ed. I'll play along with whatever is driving this request. We've put a dent in their operation here. However, no matter where we are in the DC mission, I will return in a few days to shut the UK Op down completely. I'll be there in DC by tomorrow night and will bring Charlie. It will be a good operation to break her in on. She's ready."

***

Thud. Crash.

Yaromir brushed the capped vodka bottle and glasses off the table in his DC living room with a sweep of his arm. He shouted, "Why on earth did you do that, Nadia?"

Nadia, reclining in a robe on Yaromir's couch, cackled, "Relax Yaromir, it's all untraceable. The poison will have completely disappeared from his system. They'll think, poor hardworking Madison, so young to die. He must have been broken hearted from his separation." She rose and picked up the vodka bottle, uncapped it, and took a healthy swig. Then she reached for the two shot glasses, placed them on the table, and refilled them.

Yaromir grabbed a glass and tossed back his shot. He persisted in a calmer tone, "I'm sure you handled the kill with competence, Nadia. That's *not* the point. Tosh will not be pleased that you terminated the asset so quickly. There was so much more information to be obtained and misinformation to be passed on. *Whatever* got into you?" Yaromir topped off their shot glasses.

Nadia lifted her glass, threw the vodka at the back of her throat, swallowed hard, and heavily thumped the glass down onto the table. She sneered and said disparagingly, "He was a nothing, Yaromir. I can get us another asset to work. He was so terribly boring."

Yaromir pounded the table with his fist and shouted, "You are missing the point. We had a mission and *he* was your assigned target."

Nadia flicked a crumb off the table. "If I had my way, Yaromir, I'd kill them all. They are useless walking penisses. All they want to do is fuck us. I've been fucked by men since I was eight years old. I'm sick of taking it."

Yaromir shook his finger at her. "Nadia, I know your history, but you have to get these urges to wipe the male species off the earth under control. It's affecting your ability to do your job. You can't go off book like this. Tosh will have your head when you return."

Nadia snickered, "Don't worry your muddled head about it, Yaromir. Tosh is old and won't be in control long. I'm not worried what he thinks."

Yaromir rejoined softly, "You should be."

***

The door slammed open. Elda turned to see Ashok burst into Ed's office interrupting Ed's briefing to herself and Charlie. "This is most excellent. I have something."

Ed scowled at the interruption but kept silent.

Aware of the game that needed to be played here, Elda inquired, "Wonderful. What is it, Ashok?"

Ashok puffed up and answered, "I was scanning the video feeds from around the Capitol building and I found this." Ashok put his laptop on Ed's desk and motioned for the three to view it.

Elda patted Ashok on the shoulder. "Yes, most excellent, Ashok. You did use the description of Yaromir that I gave you well. That's him."

"Ah yes, so it is, Elda. And thinking that it might be, I extrapolated his course and pulled these feeds." Ashok popped up pictures of Yaromir meeting and walking with another man. He pointed at the man and

397

stated, "This is one of the senators that was in Moscow. Senator Glass."

"A very good job, Ashok," praised Elda. "Do we have anything else of interest?"

"Ah yes, that is where Ashok is so clever and you will agree." Ashok turned the computer around, typed in some commands, and turned it back to Elda and the rest. "See?"

Elda smiled at Ashok. She felt his boyish need for approval was charming and decided to ham it up for his ego, "Ashok, you are very clever. You downloaded the senator's personal calendar. He is meeting with *Bear Man* tomorrow. And he even put in the time and location. Perfect!"

Ashok beamed. "I have more, Elda."

Elda, enjoying the game they were playing, smiled back at Ashok and prodded, "More Ashok? You are truly clever. What?"

"I wrote a program that takes the various intelligence video feeds and uses facial recognition to compare the pictures of the female Russian agents we know. One of these agents works for Tosh and is called Nadia Belov."

Ed barked impatiently, "So?"

Elda added more calmly, "Please go on Ashok."

"I have located a picture of the woman, Nadia, dining out with another senator." Ashok turned his laptop around so Elda and the others could see.

Ed leaned in and frowned and inquired, "That man looks familiar. Who is he, Ashok?"

"He is Senator Madison Barrett." Ashok sat back and waited.

Ed nodded and said, "Oh yes, he was one of the senators that visited Moscow and has just been found in his home dead of a heart attack. Please pull the autopsy report, Ashok. Thank you."

***

Charlie, turning a page in her novel, peered through her mirrored sunglasses at Senator Glass nervously walking into the park in DC. She moved her finger along the text on the page while her eyes tracked the senator. She covered her mouth with a Kleenex and coughed into it, receiving two clicks in her earpiece in response.

A burly man approached the senator from the other direction, bumped into him and reached out to steady the senator.

399

Charlie coughed again into a Kleenex, causing a woman who was about to sit next to her to frown and scurry away. In Charlie's ear piece she received the command, "Take that large man down. His name is Yaromir and he's a Russian operative."

Charlie waited until the senator was out of range and Yaromir was closing in on her position. She rose from her bench just as he was passing by her. He turned to check her out and she lunged up, stabbing him in the side of his neck with a hypodermic needle and plunging the contents into him. He roared and picked her up off the ground by her neck. She grabbed at his massive arms, trying to get enough air in to fight him. Her legs kicked ineffectually at him.

Elda lightly padded up from behind him and waited patiently, watching to see if Charlie could get herself out of her predicament. Charlie tried to pry his fingers off her neck and butted the side of his face with her forehead, neither of which changed the situation. As Charlie's movements started to slow and her eyes signaled desperation, Elda stuck Yaromir with a hypodermic needle in the other side of his neck.

He fell like a redwood on top of Charlie. Elda rolled him off of Charlie and reclaimed the two syringes. Charlie lay there gasping for breath.

"Ah, Yaromir. We meet again." Elda quickly frisked Yaromir. Finding in his front pants pocket the fob drive he had taken from the senator, she took a picture of both sides of it and sent the photos in a message to Jackson. She then removed Yaromir's wallet, socks, shoes and belt. She turned and helped a still coughing Charlie up on her feet. "It takes two injections to fell these big guys, Charlie. Always carry a second one." Charlie nodded her understanding and coughed again. Elda examined Charlie closely and said, "Your color is returning. You'll live."

Just then, a drone swooped in carrying a bottle of beer and a small pen drive and landed at Elda's feet. Elda removed the hard drive from the drone and attached the one she had taken from Yaromir. She then removed the bottle and opener from the other side of the drone and sent it flying back. She slipped the replacement USB flash drive into Yaromir's pocket and said to Charlie, "Help me move him."

The two of them dragged Yaromir over to the side of the path and propped him up against the bench. Elda then opened the beer, poured it over him, and put the empty in his hand. "There, that will hold him for a while. Let's go."

***

Senator Glass walked rapidly towards the park entrance. He had decided that it would be better to flee his country than betray it. *I can take a leave from the Senate and come back when it's safe.* Mentally he calculated an escape route. He just needed to pop by his safe deposit box and pull the money and documents he had stashed there. He picked up his pace, anxious to be away from the madness he had fallen into.

A man in a dark suit and sunglasses fell in step beside the senator. Soon he was joined by a second one on the other side. The senator's heart skipped a beat. He felt the sweat start to gather on his brow.

"You will come quietly with us, Senator."

Fearful of the answer, the senator inquired, "Who are you?"

"FBI. If you cooperate, things will go better for you and your family. We can assure a quiet resignation and limited jail time, or perhaps even just probation. Otherwise all this goes public."

"Shit."

***

Yaromir woke up with a very dry mouth and a headache. He looked down at his feet to see that his shoes were gone. He quickly patted his pockets and was relieved to find that the fob was still there but was dismayed to discover his wallet and all of his money and credit cards were gone, along with his cell phone. He sniffed and wrinkled his nose at the smell of stale beer that emanated from his clothing. A tourist stopped at pointed at him, nudging his friend. "Look the homeless are all over DC!"

Yaromir snarled at them and they quickly ran away from him. He set off in stocking feet. Soon his feet were sore and he was cursing DC's efforts to remove homeless encampments where he would easily be able to snag a pair of shoes from some weakling. Hobbling through another park, he spied a homeless man sleeping on a bench. He walked slowly up to him and calculated that his sneakers were about the right size and they looked relatively new. He shook the man on his shoulder to wake him up. "I need your shoes."

"What? No way? Get your own pair." The man rolled over and turned his back to Yaromir.

"I definitely plan to get my own." Yaromir sat on the edge of the bench and placed his elbow hard on the man's neck, effectively holding him down and at the same time, squeezing his airway. The man attempted to rise but couldn't. Soon he went limp. Yaromir removed his shoes and laced them up. He picked through the corpse's pockets and found

$23.45 in wadded one-dollar bills and coins, which he placed into his own pocket. His head was pounding from the lingering effects of the drugs he had been given. He set off at a brisk pace to return to his rented room, collect money and a pair of his own shoes, and go back out to buy a new cell phone and report in to Tosh.

***

"Get back to Moscow now. You've been burned," Tosh said. Opening his desk drawer, he took out his blood pressure cuff, pumped it up, and waited for the reading.

Yaromir's voice came clearly over his speaker phone, "*Nyet*, Tosh. I was mugged in the park. You know how much crime there is here in America."

Tosh shook his head at his blood pressure reading, took number of deep breaths, and pumped the cuff up again. He calmly explained, "Yaromir. Do you see any parallelism between what happened here in America and what happened on your previous mission in Newcastle, England?" He frowned at the second reading and put the cuff away.

There was a pause and Yaromir asked, "*Kak*? When Elda stuck me with that drug and rolled me, taking my phone and shoes?"

"Yes," Tosh patiently answered, waiting for the light to dawn.

Again a lengthy period of silence ensued. Finally Yaromir said softly in shame, "*Oy.*"

***

"What's up Mister Ed?" Edla inquired flippantly. She was sitting on a stool in Ed's DC office, next to Charlie, Sophia and Ashok.

Ed replied, "We have permission to remove all the Russian operatives from the DC area."

Elda raised her hand.

Ed rolled his eyes, "Yes, Elda?"

Elda gleefully inquired, "By 'remove,' is that an *ask no questions and permanently remove* or a *ship back in a crate* remove?"

Ed raised an eyebrow and replied, "By any and all means possible. Just be discrete." He winked at Elda. Elda nodded, acknowledging Ed's unspoken message to ensure that nothing could be traced back to him and that he would deny the team was on a mission if they were caught.

Charlie inquired, "Do we know if Yaromir is still in the DC area?"

Ed spoke first, "I haven't received any information to the contrary."

Ashok chimed in, "I think not, Mister Ed."

Ed rolled his eyes again and ground his fist into his forehead. He hissed, "People, you have to work with me! Keep me in the loop."

Ashok cast his eyes down and said penitently, "I'm sorry Mr. Ed. I just discovered it this morning."

Elda patiently prodded, "Why do you think he has left the country, Ashok?"

Ashok expounded happily, "When I was searching the various data feeds, I had automatic facial identification software also working in the background. Through that, I have found pictures of him leaving the country on an Aeroflot flight to Moscow."

Ed muttered, "It would be really nice if you called...," and then, in a normal tone, addressed Ashok, "Okay. That's one operative down. Please verify his arrival in Moscow, Ashok, and we can cross him off our list for now."

Ashok typed into his laptop and brought up a screen. "I also have a location on the female operative, Nadia, who has been spreading the QAnon silliness through the Senate."

Elda narrowed her eyes in thought and inquired, "Ashok, did we ever find any evidence that she killed Senator Barrett?"

"Not directly, Elda. There were no traces of poison in his bloodstream, and no evidence of a second person in the house, but the Nadia woman was caught walking in that area on a doorbell video feed."

Ed put his fingers to his forehead and mused out loud, "We don't have a case on her so we can't extradite her or have the FBI move in. But if she killed one senator, she'll kill another. We can't let this spread. It would be best to remove her."

Pressing to find out which side Ed was on, Elda piped up, "Extract and send home? Or dispose of?"

Ed replied, "I would postulate that someone who is destructive to national security and killing innocent senators needs to be disposed of. But, you know I'm *just* thinking out loud and *never* would order that."

Elda turned and pointed at Sophia. "Sophia, she's yours."

***

"Ashok, where did you last locate her again?" Sophia pressed her earpiece into her ear more so she could better hear his answer over the city traffic.

Ashok answered from his command center in Ed's conference room, "There's an apartment building on 10th Street NW. It looks like #825. The Apartments at City Center. I keep picking her up on camera feeds near there. Perhaps she's staying there?"

"Thanks Ashok. I'll call if I need more help."

Sophia hung up and plugged the address into her phone map app. She checked her location on the map and cursed, "Bloody Hell. I've walked too far. I'm almost at Freedom Plaza."

She turned around and headed north on 12th street. Passing by the G Street Metro Center station, she glanced at the passengers heading into the station and could hardly believe her luck. *There she is!* Sophia texted Ashok. *I have eyes on her. G St Metro Station.* She picked up her pace to follow Nadia.

Sophia held back as the train approached the platform and watched to see if Nadia got on. The woman entered the car and Sophia rushed to jump on just before the doors closed. She noted that Nadia had looked up and down the car surveying the other passengers. Sophia quickly looked down at her cell phone. Nadia appeared to relax in her seat, but Sophia noticed she was using her phone to survey the front and back of the car. The man in front of Sophia blocked Sophia from Nadia's view.

The train pulled up to the Federal Triangle stop. Anticipating that Nadia might get off the train, Sophia exited the train immediately after it pulled in. She used the computerized glasses she was wearing to view the crowd as she walked slowly away from the platform. Nadia rushed out of the train just before the doors closed.

After exiting the station, Sophia stood on 12th Street NW, consulting Google Maps on her phone. She looked up and down the street as if a lost tourist and saw Nadia emerge and head north on 12th. Taking a gamble, Sophia headed south on 12th and then turned left onto Constitution Ave and jogged up 10th St NW and headed west on E St NW. She was gratified to catch a glimpse of Nadia crossing E St. Sophia stopped, turned her jacket inside out and reached into her bag and put on a black wig. She followed Nadia back to the metro station.

Nadia stood at the edge of the platform in the crowd at the station. Sophia slowly wove her way through the crowd until she was standing immediately behind Nadia. Nadia gave Sophia a glance. Sophia had her head down and was scrolling through Twitter on her iPhone, her head bouncing to loud tunes leaking outward from her earbuds. Apparently dismissing Sophia as a threat, Nadia turned to scan the crowd on the other side of her.

The arrival sign stated that the Federal Triangle train was approaching. Just before the cars pulled in, Sophia reached out and nudged Nadia off the platform onto the tracks. A yell from a waiting passenger over to the right of Sophia set off a panicked response from the crowd.

Sophia watched as the train ran over Nadia. The smell and noise of the screeching brakes and the screaming from the crowd filled the air. Nadia's bloody arm and foot were over to one side of the track. Her body was crushed beneath the train.

Unnoticed in the ensuing hubbub, Sophia quickly disappeared from the immediate area. She deftly removed her jacket and wig and tossed them in a trash can and jogged up the exit stairs.

Chapter Twenty-Six

Sophia walked happily into Ed's office, pleased with her part in the DC operation. Her smile faded when she saw Elda and Charlie there, as well as the looks on their faces.

"What's wrong? Is it Oliver?" she demanded.

Elda held up a calming hand. "Oliver is fine Sophia, but you may want to sit down."

Sophia lowered herself to the couch and stated warily, "It's Emily, isn't it?"

Elda nodded and answered, "Yes, it is. Her body was found."

Sophia shouted, "Bollocks!" and punched her fist into the couch arm. "What happened?"

"It appears that it was a quick death; a single shot between the eyes." Elda walked over and sat next to Sophia on the couch. "I'm sorry, Sophia."

Sophia looked at Elda with tears streaming down her cheeks. "Does Oliver know yet?"

Elda shook her head. "No, Sophia. We haven't told him. I thought you would want to be there for him when we did. I have taken the liberty of booking you a flight for this evening."

Sophia looked at Elda with gratitude and grabbed her arm. "Thank you so much, Elda."

Sophia was surprised that Elda looked unsure of what to do next. After a long pause, Elda stood up and inquired gently, "It may not be easy to focus, but we need to tie up your mission here. Can you update me on that?"

Sophia shook her head and dried her eyes. She took a large sip of water from her water bottle and replied in a shaky voice, "Oh yes, quite right. No worries. Glad to have work to focus on. Nadia is very dead."

"Oh! Good. What happened?"

"She got in the way of a metro train."

***

Elda stated dryly, "What an unfortunate accident." She added, "Job well done, Sophia. Next we will need to finish up the details in the UK. Will you be able to help us with that? Or will you need to focus on Oliver? In any case, Charlie and I will be flying over with you." Elda inspected Sophia for any signs that she might not be up to continuing the mission.

Sophia snapped angrily, "Bloody Hell, Elda. Of course I will. I'm not some fragile shrinking violet. And anyway, Emily was my friend too, but it's Oliver who will need the support more than I will. He'll be gutted. I want revenge. I'm certain he will too. It's time we at least got James."

Satisfied that Sophia was shaken out of any shock over Emily's death, Elda continued. "Good. And I do not consider you fragile, Sophia. Quite the contrary. You are a very strong and capable woman and agent. I am so pleased to have you as a temporary part of my team. So let's plan some next steps here. We still have Snezhana and Anatoly to deal with, as well as potentially Tosh. If Tosh comes to the UK, he is mine, understand?"

Sophia waved her hand at Elda's reminder and responded, "Righto. Definitely."

Elda pressed on, "And James should be dispatched by Oliver. Would you agree?"

Sophia nodded impatiently, "Yes. Definitely."

Elda went on, "I think we should find out who killed Emily before we decide the final disposition of Anatoly and Snezhana."

Charlie shook her head in disagreement and blurted out, "But they'll just show up again."

Elda carried on. "So true. It's the devils we know though. We know their identities. We know their habits. We know their weaknesses."

"And they know ours," countered Charlie.

Elda acknowledged Charlie's point and went on to spell things out even more clearly, "True, that does level the playing field a bit, but these agents play by the Cold War rules. Others may not. And the learning curve could be costly for us."

The penny dropped. Charlie responded, "Brill. Thanks for explaining that."

"OK, so that leaves the little rat, Nigel and his pawn, Doug."

***

Shall I kill him? Tosh wondered.

Tosh looked up at his office ceiling and felt the edge of his knife with his thumb. He glanced at his watch.

He will be here in a few minutes.

There was a rap at his door. Tosh opened the side draw of his desk and threw the knife in on top, leaving the drawer open. "*Voyti*," he commanded.

Yaromir marched in and stood at attention in Tosh's office. Tosh glowered at him, and Yaromir hung his head.

"How could you be taken twice the same way?" Tosh asked. "You know I don't mind mistakes, but I only ask that you do not make the same one twice."

Eyes downcast, Yaromir replied penitently, "I know, *ser*. I have no excuse, *ser*."

"Look at me, Yaromir." Yaromir raised his eyes to meet Tosh's steely gray ones. Tosh continued to reprimand him, "They took your money, your phone and your shoes, and yet they let you keep the fob."

"*Da, ser*," answered Yaromir blithely, his tone and eyes indicating that he was still missing Tosh's point.

Tosh continued drilling him to get him to think through the situation, "And you did *what* with the fob?"

Straightening his shoulders and still at attention, Yaromir declared proudly, "I passed it in to my contact at Control."

Tosh tapped his finger on his desk while he pointed out to Yaromir, "You were supposed to pass it to Doug."

"*Da ser*, but I decided it would be better for me to leave the country quickly so I left with it."

Tosh sighed heavily. "Yaromir, you have, except for the two operations where Elda has been involved, been very successful. Unlike Nadia, you have been very loyal to me, and that has immense value. If I tell my superior that you have may have passed on misleading information, he will have you immediately executed. And, he may also do the same with me."

Yaromir stared wide-eyed at Tosh. "Misleading information, *ser*? I don't understand. It was the same fob that I picked up."

Tosh held his fingers to his forehead, gritted his teeth, and said skeptically, "I doubt that it was, Yaromir."

Yaromir argued defensively, "It even had the same scratch on the side, *ser*."

Breathing deeply, Tosh said flatly, "I'm sure it did." He then sternly instructed Yaromir, "Here's what's going to happen now. You are going to go back to training for an intensified course. Should you survive this course, you will be operating on trained reflexes and less likely to make these types of mistakes in future missions."

Yaromir's shoulders slumped with obvious relief at being allowed to live. "*Da, ser. Spasibo.*"

Tosh waved his thanks away. "When did you last see Nadia?"

Yaromir frowned. The topic had suddenly shifted. He looked down, then looked back at Tosh. "It has been days, *ser*. Why are you asking?" Yaromir said.

Having decided he could leverage Yaromir's willingness to get back into his good graces, Tosh informed him, "She had contacted my superior a few weeks ago about replacing me. If there is any sighting of her in Russia, I will pull you out of school to find her and do away with her. Will your personal feelings about her get in the way of doing so?" Tosh narrowed his eyes as he studied Yaromir's face.

Yaromir quickly and confidently answered, "*Nyet, ser.*"

Satisfied that Yaromir would obey, Tosh added, "*Khorosho.* And when you do kill her, make it slow and painful."

"*Da ser.*"

Yaromir turned to leave. Tosh interjected, "And Yaromir,…"

Yaromir turned back to face Tosh. *"Da, ser?..."*

Tosh pointed his finger at Yaromir and said menacingly, "One more failure on a mission and I will eliminate you."

"Da ser. As you should."

***

"Nyet! We need the US operation to continue." Tosh, sitting in Adrik's office, did not flinch as Adrik pounded his desk with his fist to emphasize his words.

Tosh raised his index finger and inquired cautiously, *"Ser.* If I may speak?"

"Speak!" Adrik commanded. He pressed the record button for his hidden recorder. His electronics team could later modify the transcript in any way that he ordered.

Tosh spoke softly and calmly, "There is a slim possibility that one of our agents may have been compromised. Out of an abundance of caution I have pulled the agent who was identified."

Still angry, but being mollified by Tosh's subservient attitude, Adrik queried, "How did *that* happen?"

Tosh replied levelly, "It was a very unfortunate accident, *ser*. He ran into an American agent from a previous operation. It was a chance meeting that was very unlikely to happen, since we had intel that the American was not operating in that area. There was no sign that the American recognized him. But we do not want to take any further chances and risk that the mission may be discovered, so I felt it was better to take him out of the picture."

Adrik thought for a moment. This sudden change in the operation might benefit his goal to remove Tosh from his job. His smile was frightening as he responded, "That is good thinking, Tosh."

Tosh added, "The operation had been very well done up to now. We got excellent information and the seeds of discord that the agent planted are still growing strong."

Wanting to force Tosh to be the one who shut the operation down, Adrik inquired, "So do you feel he needs to be replaced?"

"*Nyet*. Not at this moment, *ser*. I feel that he accomplished what we asked him to do."

"Excellent then!" Adrik sat back and placed his hands on his belly, looking like a contented cat who had just stole the salmon from the grill.

Tosh suggested, "I am thinking that it might be wise, *ser*, to shut down the entire operation. What do you think? I know you are a very cautious leader when it comes to things like this."

"You are advising pulling the woman too?" Adrik could not believe his luck that Tosh was playing so well into his hands.

Agreeing, Tosh stated, "*Da, ser.* They were working together to support each other, since they were both operating remotely. Her operation had started well, however, it may be best to watch and see where we are most needed. Then we can send her back in when we have more information."

Adrik sat back in self-satisfaction and said gloatingly, "So are you admitting defeat on this unfinished mission? That isn't like you, Tosh."

Tosh quickly responded with, "Oh no, *ser*. You can report a successful completion on both operations at this point. That, of course would be much better than having to report anything else, should either of them be detected as a Russian spy."

Delighted that he could report the operation as Tosh's failure, Adrik thought for a moment and replied, "This was a critical operation. We were only one small part, but we did succeed in our part, and that will look good on my record. And you and your operatives get to live to save the day in the future." He thought again and then spoke, "Tosh, due to the successful completion of this operation, I am allowing you to shut down your two operatives in the United States." He folded his hands over the girth of his stomach and smiled a self-satisfied grin.

Tosh looked at Adrik's face for a few moments before commenting, "*Spasibo, ser*. I will send you the full report with my decision to shut it down contingent on your approval. In my report I will celebrate your foresight in ensuring our agents did not get caught by the Americans and your success in designing the operation and in directing me in this mission." Tosh pushed back his chair and stood to be dismissed.

Frowning, Adrik held up his hand to have Tosh wait. He asked in a threatening tone, "Tosh, your words are pleasant, but I must inquire: Are you still competent at your age to be doing these operations?"

Tosh gave Adrik a subservient half bow and replied confidently, "*Da ser*. When I am no longer able to perform my job I will turn in my gun to you personally. I know why you are thinking this, *ser*."

Adrik raised an eyebrow and said slowly, "And,…"

Tosh volunteered, "I disciplined the female agent for getting too personally involved in a case. She was not happy that I demoted her. She is now looking to get back at me and contacted you to seed doubt about my abilities. It would be your folly if you listened to this clearly discredited agent."

Hearing that Tosh was sending him a message, and wondering if Tosh intended to remove Adrik's mole, Adrik scowled and queried, "And what do *you* plan to do about this problem of yours, Tosh?"

Tosh stood tall at attention. He stated flatly, "I am having her permanently removed from the service. This will protect you, *ser*. Also, our jobs require absolute loyalty. I intend to send that message."

Adrik crossed his hands over his large belly and sat back in his chair. He cocked his head and, with a slight smile on his face, declared ominously, "Yes they do, Tosh. I am glad you think that way. I assume that goes for *you* also?"

Tosh answered confidently, "*Da ser.*" Adrik felt Tosh's eyes bore into him. It was as if Tosh could see inside Adrik and knew his plans.

Adrik warned sternly, "Don't forget this." He terminated the discussion, "Dismissed."

Once Tosh was out of his office, Adrik pulled open his bottom desk drawer and pulled out a package of Kurabie biscuits and shoved two of them into his mouth. He chewed, spitting crumbs while opening his top drawer for his burner phone. He dialed a number from memory. Swallowing, he roared, "Is everything on track in the UK?..."

The unexpected answer of, "Yes, I assume so," came over the phone receiver.

"You assume so? *Assume?*" Adrik's body jiggled with his rage. He lowered his voice so as not to be heard outside his office and commanded, "Well, check on it. And find a way to *oblazhat'sya.*"

There was a pause and then Adrik heard, "To do what?"

"*What?* Have you forgotten all your Russian? *Screw it up*, now!" Adrik slammed the phone down on his desk and then tossed it back into the drawer. Fuming, he shoved a handful of cookies in his mouth, only to choke on the dryness and coughing spitting the cookies out onto his desk.

"*Der'mo!*"

***

"Bloody hell! *Oblazhat'sya*, my ass. I have no-one to use on this friggin' operation." James threw his burner phone across his office and sat stewing. Finally he decided, *Well, I took his father out. I will just have to remove the son too. That should put a spanner in the works.* James left his office and set out for Nigel's house.

The house was still; shades drawn down in the front. James walked up to the front door, jiggled the handle, and muttered, "Bloody hell. It's locked." He walked around to the back door with the same result. After five minutes of effort he managed to pick the lock. He opened the door to be regaled by the unmistakable stench of a dead body. He put covers on his shoes and walked through to the living room where Nigel lay, obviously dead.

What a fortunate accident. But I can't let the police find this. James took out his official cell phone and dialed. "Send a cleanup crew immediately. This is an undercover operation, so be disguised and make no record of this call." He gave Nigel's address and then went outside to wait. The smell of death had invaded his nostrils and settled in.

***

Tosh impatiently drummed his fingers on his desk and stared at Stas who was rapidly typing on his keyboard. He demanded, "Where is she, Stas? She hasn't reported in again. She had better be dead."

Stas shrugged as he typed rapidly on his laptop keyboard. "*Ya ne znayu, ser*. There were a number of deaths in the DC area last month. I have weeded out any who were identified, all males, all children and any old people."

Tosh held his fingers to his neck and checked his pulse while contemplating Stas' reply. Deep in thought, he looked up at his ceiling, then pointed at Stas and demanded, "Who died accidentally, and how did they die?"

Stas brought up his database containing the results of his search and ran his finger down the screen. He stated, "We have shootings, drownings, heart attacks, motor vehicle accidents, and one crushed by a train."

Tosh perked up. "Crushed by a train? Really…? Tell me more about that one."

"It was rush hour. The station was packed. The body is mincemeat but they identified it as a female."

Tosh commanded, "Get me video from that station."

Stas nodded with satisfaction. "Already done, *ser*. I thought that one was of interest too." He cued up the station video on his screen and passed the computer over to Tosh. Tosh ran the video feed forward and backwards and then sat with his eyes closed, scanning his memory banks. His eyes popped open and he stated decisively, "Sophia."

Stas looked confused and asked. "*Ser*? What about Sophia?"

"It was Sophia who did me a favor. I will have to thank her."

Stas stared wide-eyed at Tosh. "How do you know that?"

Tosh patiently explained, "She was at the station at the same time. See?"

Tosh slid the laptop back to Stas who played the clip again and shook his head. "*Nyet, ser*. I don't see her."

Tosh came around the desk and forwarded the video to a scene of a group of passengers walking down the platform. He pointed out one woman who was bobbing her head in time to whatever was playing in her earbuds. *"Tam."*

Stas wondered, "That's Sophia?"

Confidently Tosh pointed to the screen. *"Da.* Look at how she holds her body, the shape of the back of her neck, the size and slope of her shoulders. That's Sophia. There's no other person who matches anyone we know at the station at that time. I'll bet you a thousand rubles it's her."

Stas held up his hand to ward off Tosh's proposal. *"Nyet ser.* Although I could cover that bet, I won't throw my money away. So what now?"

"Find Sophia. Sophia will lead us to Elda."

Chapter Twenty-Seven

Doug nervously parked his scooter a few blocks away from Nigel's house. He snuck in over the back bushes and scurried to the back door. He reached under a nearby rock and retrieved the backdoor key and let himself in. The house smelled stale and in need of airing out. He locked the back door behind himself and tiptoed through the house calling softly for Nigel. He wove through every room and upstairs, finding each one empty. Nigel's toiletries were in the bathroom still and his luggage was in his closet. Doug returned to the kitchen and opened the refrigerator and quickly closed it again. He dragged a wastebasket over and opened the door and started tossing spoiled food from the fridge. *He must have been gone for a while.*

Doug returned upstairs and dug through Nigel's closet until he located his safe. He spun the dial to various numbers from Nigel's social security number, then he tried Nigel's license plate. Each time he tried the handle, the safe refused to open. Doug felt his face grow red and blotchy from his frustration.

Finally he turned the dial using the digits of Nigel's birthday and turned the handle. The door opened revealing stacks of money and a key that he recognized as belonging to a safe deposit box. "Cor, I'm bloody flush!" He looked around sharply to ensure there was no-one to hear his exclamation. Inside the safe was also the deed to the house and the Vehicle Registration Certificate for Nigel's car. Doug removed the certificate and peeled off half of one of the stacks of bills and then closed and relocked the safe.

Returning downstairs, Doug powered up his laptop and navigated to the DVLA website and typed in the 11-digit Document Reference Number for Nigel's car and quickly transferred ownership to himself. He tore off the bottom of the V5C document and filled out the final transfer of the car to himself. He then called a slightly shady lawyer he knew to start the process of transferring the deed of the house to his name.

That will do for now. Doug poured himself a Glenfiddich neat, sat on the couch, put his feet up on the living room table and toasted to his good fortune.

***

"Honey, I'm home!" Elda walked into Sophia's flat followed by Sophia and Charlie.

"In here," Oliver yelled back from the room they were turning into a nursery He looked up from the floor at the three standing in the doorway. "Perfect timing. I'm trying to put this bloody crib together and I think they forgot a few parts."

Charlie walked over and sat on the floor next to him, taking the screwdriver from his hand. "Let me work on this while you guys go into the living room."

The yellow walls reflected a cheer that was notably absent. Oliver, looked at Sophia and startled and asked, "What happened? Sophia? This is not a social call, is it, Elda?"

Elda replied gently, "No, Oliver, it isn't. Let's go sit in the other room."

Oliver followed them and sat heavily on the couch. In a wooden voice, he said, "It's Em, isn't it? She's dead, right? I was so hoping that she was still alive."

Sophia lowered herself next to him and put her arm around his shoulder. "Yes, hon, she is." She placed a glass containing two fingers of whisky on the table in front of him.

Oliver reached forward and took a sip from the glass, then he glugged the rest. "Shame to do that with single malt," he commented idly, placing the glass back on the table with a shaky hand. "Cor. What happened?"

Elda watched Oliver carefully as she spoke, "We don't know yet, but it was a single shot between the eyes at close range. Obviously it was a professional assassination and her death would have been instantaneous."

Sophia poured another splash into his glass and Oliver drank it before replying, "*Thank God* for that, at least. Were there any signs of torture?"

Elda responded again in her most professional tone, "Could have been some. There was some water in her lungs, but not enough to indicate any prolonged submersion. It was obvious that the killer had duct taped her hands together and also used tape over her mouth to keep her silent. But all things considered, she received a merciful death. Luckily she did not have a lot of information to give, but now whomever killed her will now come after us."

"Let them bloody well try. Come and get me arsehole. I *will* get you first." Oliver crashed his fist down onto the table causing the glass and bottle to jump. Sophia grabbed the bottle before it could topple over.

"I'm with you, Oliver," stated Sophia. A background chorus of "Me too" came from Elda.

Elda pointed at Oliver and solemnly avowed, "OK, Oliver, we *will* help you avenge Emily's death, but *first* let's clear out any remaining obvious characters and ship them back to Moscow. All except James. I think it's time to remove him permanently. Are you up to that Oliver?"

"Bloody hell I am," responded Oliver through clenched teeth, "My body still hurts when it rains from my injuries I got in the last mission that bastard ran against us." He rubbed the scar on his leg where the bullets had ripped into him.

"Then that will be your job, Oliver. Because, push comes to shove, if we can't find out exactly who did pull the trigger, we know that James enabled it. Kill him and you will get justice."

***

Anatoly and Snezhana stood in the empty flat near Hyde park in London.

"*Chert*. There's not even a chair here," complained Anatoly. He took off and wiped his horn-rimmed glasses on his shirt and scratched the brown stubble on his chin that matched his current hair color.

"You'll scratch your glasses that way, you know," stated Snezhana, flipping back the long black bangs from her forehead and unbuttoning her suit jacket.

Anatoly glared at her and then inquired testily, "When will the furniture arrive?"

"In a couple of hours," answered Snezhana calmly. She threw a paper bag at Anatoly who deftly caught it with his right hand. He peered in to see an assortment of scones and Chelsea buns. "Where's the jam?" Snezhana threw another bag that Anatoly snagged with his left hand. He looked around for somewhere to eat the goodies. Snorting, he sat on the floor with his legs extended in front of him. Extracting the napkins, jam and plastic knife, he spread the now empty bag out flat on his lap and placed a scone on it. He quickly cut the scone open and liberally spread strawberry jam on it. He hummed tunelessly as he prepared his snack.

Snezhana bantered, "I like your hazel eye color, Mr. Jones."

Clearly in an improved mood from the food, Anatoly replied, "It matches yours, Mrs. Jones, wife and main squeeze."

In a more serious tone, Snezhana led into a discussion about their next steps, "I paid cash for the furniture and this complex doesn't have security cameras, so we should be untraceable for now, but we need to keep switching disguises."

Anatoly opined, "Unfortunately it's hard to hide my height and bulk, but this baggy clothing and shoe lifts should make it harder for any recognition software to quickly match me. Once this beard grows out it will *really* change my appearance."

Snezhana continued to direct their mission, giving further details, "So now we have to find Elda. She was last seen here in London and I would bet that Oliver and Sophia from MI6 are working with her too."

"Does Stas have any leads yet?"

"*Nyet.*"

"And so we wait…" Anatoly ripped off a bite of Chelsea bun.

***

Having scattered her team across various areas of London, Elda assumed a disguise and set out to help them find Anatoly and Snezhana. Soon a small man in a suit holding a cane and topped off by a bowler hat brought his hand up to his right ear and tapped his hearing aid. He spoke softly, "Have you found any trace of them yet?"

Elda envisioned the team members in the disguises and locations as they checked in. A hunched over elderly man leaning heavily on and pushing a wheeled Zimmer frame clicked in and replied, "Nothing here on Clifton Place, Elda."

"Thanks Charlie. Sophia, where are you?"

An old lady sitting on a park bench by the Italian gardens adjusted her earpiece and said in a low tone, "I'm in Hyde Park, Elda. No sign of them here or when I was enroute to here."

"Thanks Sophia. Oliver, please check in."

A telephone repair man up a pole on Bayswater Road adjusted his computerized glasses to zoom in down the street both ways. "No luck here either, Elda."

"OK then. It's time to branch out. They've obviously moved from the hotel. That's smart. I would too."

Sophia broke in, "There's too many hotels to cover them all, Elda. Plus, what if they've rented a flat like you did. That would be *impossible* to trace in any short amount of time."

Elda twirled her cane as she thought through the possibilities. Having her own answers, she decided to use this as a training opportunity and then responded, "True Sophia. But why would they stay in London at all?"

Charlie piped up, "To eliminate us as payback for ruining their operation."

Elda paced and twirled and then asked, "Where would each one of you stay if you were cleaning up loose ends?"

Oliver stated, "Well, Nigel is one loose end. So I would stay near where he lived."

Charlie added, "And they may believe that we would return to the hotel looking for them."

"Exactly," Elda exclaimed, "Let's reconvene at the flat. I'll ask Ashok to gather information on all flats around this area that have been rented in the last 72 hours. Oliver, you can call each rental company or owner on the list to see if anyone paid cash. Charlie, you and I will gear up and go see Nigel. Sophia, can you arrange for a place for us to bring Nigel to, once we snag him?"

"Definitely, Elda," answered Sophia with certainty.

Elda clapped her hands to signal the end of the conversation and the beginning of action. "OK. Let's go then. See you at the flat. If you spot anyone along the way, do *not* engage. We want to lure everyone into our trap."

***

Charlie and Elda cautiously approached Nigel's house from the back and the front, respectively. "Wait!" Elda's whispered command came clearly over Charlie's earpiece. "Get into position and proceed on my command." Charlie stopped to look and listen for signs of life.

Elda whispered, "I see a shadow in the living room. Approach cautiously." Charlie answered Elda with the affirmative two clicks.

Charlie padded silently up to the back door and quietly picked the lock. She gave two clicks to Elda. Elda clicked back. Charlie tiptoed into the kitchen, clicked and waited again.

While Elda crept up to the front door and silently picked that lock, Charlie sent two clicks to signify she was in position and received Elda's acknowledging two clicks back. Without a sound, Charlie carefully dashed through the empty kitchen and into the living room. Doug, sitting on the couch eating popcorn, threw his hands up in the air, upending the popcorn all over himself and the couch.

Elda burst in through the front door. Charlie was holding a gun on a frightened, popcorn covered, Doug. He was sitting on the couch with his hands up, breathing heavily through his mouth.

"Where's Nigel?" demanded Elda, leveling her gun at his face.

"I-I-I d-d-don't kn-n-n-now," stuttered Doug in terror.

Elda lowered her gun, but signaled to Charlie to keep hers aimed at Doug. "What do you know, Doug?" she asked in a kindly, but authoritative, voice.

Doug took a deep breath. His face was bright red, and sweat mingled with tears poured down his chubby cheeks. He opened his mouth, but could only wheeze and stutter.

Elda motioned to Charlie to guard Doug and left the living room, heading towards the kitchen. Returning with a glass of water she handed it to Doug.

"Drink up and try to relax. We're here for Nigel, not you. We need your information."

"I-I-I, …" Doug drank a large gulp of water and took in some calming breaths. He wiped his face on the tail of his shirt, momentarily exposing a chubby and hairy belly. He spoke rapidly, "I was at Emily's house. I returned here to find that Nigel was gone. The house was very clean except the milk and some other food in the refrigerator that had spoiled. But none of Nigel's travel kit was missing. It was if he had disappeared into thin air. I figured that they had killed him and removed the body."

Elda asked, "They?"

"The large Russians."

Charlie interjected, "Why stay here?"

"I don't have any other place to go. And this is much nicer than where I had been living. Plus if they want to kill me, they will kill me wherever I am. Here I have a house and money."

Elda waved her hand at Charlie, who lowered her weapon, but kept alertly focused on Doug and the hallway. Elda addressed Doug, "You're correct, Doug. If they want you dead, they will kill you no matter where you are. Their reach is long. And by staying here you will know sooner rather than later if you will be allowed to live. For your information, Emily is dead. We suspect that they killed her."

Doug started weeping. Between sobs Doug blabbered, "She was so good to me. We really hit it off."

Elda commanded, "Then in Emily's memory, stay out of trouble. You were a traitor to your country, but we would have to involve MI6 to prosecute you and extradition would be a long process. We will do that if we have to. However, overall you were an unwitting pawn in this game. So I'm willing to let you go this once. But don't let me catch you ever fucking with the United States again."

Doug looked at Elda with his bloodshot, teary eyes and asked, "Or, …?"

Her eyes bore into him as she replied steely, "Or I will personally kill you. And it will not be a merciful death."

***

Charlie, Oliver and Sophia were with Elda in her London flat. They had discussed the mission to date. After presenting her ideas for ways to move forward, Elda waited for the team to react.

"Elda, you know that that removing his agents from London will definitely lead to a faceoff with Tosh, right? And if we dare to hurt Snezhana, he will most likely kill you."

Elda had been standing at the whiteboard but now sat on a milkcrate and stared to her left.

"So what do you do?"

"I'm a student at the university," he answered. "So what do you do?"

"I'm a teacher. We probably have a lot in common."

He chuckled a throaty laugh. "Touché."

"Elda!" Charlie's voice brought Elda out of her memories. Elda shuddered at the thought of being on Tosh's wrong side again.

She blinked and the fog in the room cleared. She sharply snipped back, "What?"

"You are uncharacteristically distracted." Charlie offered, "We can help, you know?"

"Yes, yes,…" said Elda distractedly, her mind racing to come up with a plan.

Charlie gently prompted, "And, …"

"Let's get some information." Elda dialed Ed's office and put him on speaker phone. "Did you get me the warehouse in London that I asked you to?"

Ed answered, "Well *hello* to you too, Elda. Yes, and, as you requested, Ashok has arranged it so that it *can* be traced back to you with a small amount of effort."

Elda rapid fired back, "Was everything backdated?"

Ed responded calmly, "Yes, just as you asked."

Elda acknowledged with a nod and then realizing Ed couldn't see her, added, "Thank you. And Hello back, Ed. And please do thank Ashok for the work he did with Oliver." Elda hung up and made some notes on a notepad. She stopped as her mind wandered to Florence. She could feel Tosh's presence at her side as they walked along under the moonlight. He was a formidable foe and unmatched as a sparring partner. She actually enjoyed their interplay.

"Did you like being in the KGB?"

"Why are you part of the CIA?"

She wondered if he would go back to Moscow willingly or if she would have to kill him. Or if he would end up finally killing her. She knew that the final battle between the two of them was not far off.

Charlie cleared her throat. Elda stood up from her milkcrate and rolled the whiteboard to the front. She projected a map of the extended area around Hyde Park onto the board. "Ashok and Oliver narrowed the possibilities to these three places." She circled three smaller areas on the map and went on, "Although the fastest way to narrow it down would be to go into each one with guns blazing, the Brits take offense at us killing innocent people, so of course we cannot go that route. Instead, we will set up surveillance on each one and keep in close contact. We will check in every half hour. Sophia, I want to use you as bait, so no disguises for you. Charlie, you will gear up and shadow her. And, *all* of you, no heroics. We call for backup if we spot them. This especially means *you*, Oliver."

Oliver rolled his eyes and sighed, "Will anyone ever believe that I have learned my lesson?" A chorus of "no" answered him. Sophia leaned in and gave him a kiss.

Elda wrote their names by each target location and ordered, "Let's get going."

***

Snezhana and Anatoly had set up a temporary workspace in their unfurnished flat near Hyde park in London using milk crates and lengths of wood. Snezhana looked up from her computer and stated, "They are here."

"Where?" demanded Anatoly.

"Definitely in this area." Snezhana motioned him over and pointed at her screen. "Look at this snapshot that Stas discovered from a doorbell camera. The angle is poor and we only have a snippet of the action. The rest is obscured by a delivery to that address."

Anatoly stomped to the desk where Snezhana was working and leaned in over her shoulder. "It's an electrical truck stopping to pick up an old lady."

Snezhana punched him in the arm. "Exactly. That's odd. Money on her being one of the agents."

Anatoly rubbed his buzzcut, then shrugged, asking, "So what now?"

"We go out undisguised and lure them into a trap."

***

Anatoly pivoted to avoid running Snezhana down as she suddenly stopped in front of him. "*Der'mo!* What the fuck, Snezhana?"

"Anatoly, it will be best if you and I split up to methodically search this area of London for Elda and the rest. It will increase our chances of finding them."

"What are you suggesting?" Anatoly growled, anxious to be going again.

Snezhana pointed at the cross road and suggested, "I think we should prowl a street apart, heading in the same direction."

Agreeing, Anatoly jogged quickly away from Snezhana.

***

Oliver, driving a CeX truck passed Anatoly on Gilbert Street and turned left onto Brook St. He sent the GPS location, with one accompanying word, *Anatoly,* to the rest of the team. Soon Oliver spied Sophia, with Charlie disguised as a letter carrier behind her, turning the corner onto Gilbert from Weighhouse St. Snezhana was tailing the two agents.

***

Elda, driving a telephone repair truck on Davies Street spotted Snezhana about to take a left on St. Anselm's Place. Elda pulled the truck over to the side, leapt out and headed to intercept her.

***

"Tam!" Anatoly pointed at Sophia with his phone camera and sent a picture to Snezhana, who took off at a run to help bring Sophia down. Anatoly started jogging towards Sophia, but stopped in his tracks. She was standing strangely still. He yelled at Snezhana, who had just come around the corner,

445

"*Prervat*! Abort! It's a trap!" He wheeled and took off at a run, lowering his shoulder and knocking down Elda, who was running towards him. Charlie sped after Snezhana and tackled her.

***

Charlie had Snezhana's legs tightly in her arms. Snezhana struggled to rise. "No, Snezhana, you are not going to get away from me." Charlie crawled her way up Snezhana's body and as Snezhana moved her torso to flip Charlie off, Charlie slammed Snezhana back down with a blow between her shoulders. Snezhana's head hit the sidewalk. "Come on, Snez, give it up," Charlie commanded, "I don't want to hurt you."

"*Khuy tebe*!"

"Really Snezhana? Can we be a bit more professional than saying *fuck you*?" Charlie sighed. *This was going to take longer than she had hoped. I will try not to hurt her too badly.*

Blood streamed down Snezhana's face as she tried to shake the burden on her back and rolled the two of them over. Charlie let go to get a better grasp. Snezhana jumped to her feet, whirled and kicked at Charlie, who was still on the ground.

Charlie caught Snezhana's foot and pulled, causing Snezhana to go down hard on her back. She lay there winded while Charlie rose and approached cautiously and entreated, "Okay, Snezhana. How about if you just peacefully come with me and we can see what Elda wants to do with you?" Charlie held out her hand to Snezhana.

Snezhana kicked out and caught Charlie on her kneecap. Charlie went down.

"Ouch! That hurt! Okay, Snezhana. Gloves are off." Charlie rubbed her knee while watching to see what Snezhana would do next.

Snezhana wobbled up and threw herself on top of Charlie. Charlie grabbed Snezhana in a bear grip, put her legs around Snezhana's lower body and tightened her arms around Snezhana's ribs. Snezhana pushed against the ground and pulled her upper torso and head as far back as she could, while wiggling to try and get out of Charlie's grasp. Charlie brought her head up to slam her forehead into Snezhana's injury. Blood dripped on Charlie from Snezhana's head. Unconscious, she slumped against Charlie.

"Sorry, Snez," Charlie stated. She slipped out from beneath Snezhana. Gently rolling Snezhana on her side, Charlie checked her pulse. Satisfied that Snezhana was going to be okay, Charlie zip tied her wrists and fastened her ankles.

"Oliver can you make a pickup with the CeX truck? I have Snezhana ready to go."

***

Sophia spotted Elda running after Anatoly who was running down a line of cabs to get the front one. As she came near, she saw him toss the driver out into the street, jump in and speed off. Then she watched Elda hand a wad of bills to the driver of the second taxi in line, take his car, and speed off after Anatoly.

Sophia flashed her MI6 badge and consoled the driver of the first vehicle, assuring him he will get it back and be compensated for his troubles. She slipped him a sizeable amount of money for the taxi "rental." Horns blowing from down the street informed her that the chase was on.

Since Elda was chasing Anatoly, and Sophia was unsure that she could help out in any way, she ran back to where she left Charlie. Oliver was there with the CeX truck. Sophia jumped in the back of the truck where Charlie was bandaging a snarling Snezhana's head.

"Is she hurt?" Sophia asked Charlie.

"There doesn't appear to be any permanent damage, Sophia, although we should monitor her for a concussion."

"Righto, Charlie. Let's get her to the warehouse."

***

Elda wove in and out of traffic following Anatoly's cab. She sped up Grosvenor Street and circled around Grosvenor Square. She rounded the Marble Arch and followed Anatoly entering the wrong way onto A4202. "My god, Anatoly! Are you trying to get us killed?" Horns bleated; the scenery was blurry as she sped by. A lorry, unable to swerve fast enough clipped Anatoly's vehicle and he spun out off the side of the highway.

"Serves you right, you twit!" Elda hit her brakes and pulled over as far as she could off the highway. She jumped out and ran back to Anatoly's taxi. The door was open and he was gone. She looked around to see which direction he had headed in but there was no sign of him.

"Damn."

***

Tosh put down his office phone and stared at his ceiling. Snezhana was missing, probably taken by

Elda and MI6. Anatoly had escaped but had reported in that he was still searching for them.

Tosh picked up his phone and dialed Stas. "Get in here. *Seychas*!" Stas was sitting in Tosh's office within five minutes.

Tosh barked uncharacteristically at Stas, "What do you have on Elda's whereabouts?"

"I'm not sure exactly, Tosh, but I did find a shell company that rented a warehouse in London approximately one month ago. This company has in the past been associated with United States Operations in foreign lands."

Tosh demanded, "Get me the address. We'll be on the next flight to London."

Stas looked down at his computer and then up at Tosh.

"*Kakiye*?" snapped Tosh, drumming his fingers on his desk. Then he softened and inquired, "Why the worried look, Stas?"

Stas said hesitantly, "I know it's Snez who's missing, but, …"

"But what?" Tosh said sharply.

Stas took a deep breath and blurted out, "They said they'd kill me if I ever showed up in London again. I was wondering if I could support you from Moscow?"

Tosh exhaled noisily and said more calmly, "Of course, Stas, although, it was most likely a hollow threat to scare you away. And, I'm sorry I was brisk with you. You know what Snezhana means to me. If it wasn't Elda who took her, then she may be in grave danger. Can you cover my tracks electronically so no-one knows I have flown to London?"

Already typing at his computer, Stas answered, "Certainly, *ser*. That will take a bit longer. Can you fly out tomorrow instead?"

Tosh paused to take three deep breaths before agreeing, "Yes. That would be better. It will give me time to plan as well as to secure some equipment. Get in touch with Anatoly. Tell him to expect me in a day or two. Set up a secure channel for the three of us to use. And tell me immediately when you have a fix on Elda's location. I don't care what time of day or night it is."

Stas marched out of the office. Tosh opened his bottom drawer and took out a blood pressure cuff, put it on and took his reading.

"*Govno.*"

***

"Pridurki! Khuy Tebe! Blyad'!" Colorful screams reached their ears from the warehouse room where Elda had stashed Snezhana. Charlie sat holding a bag of ice to her head. Elda peeked under the icebag and commented dryly, "You'll have quite the welt there, Charlie. Any dizziness?"

"No, I'm good." Charlie started to shake her head and then stopped immediately. "Ouch."

Elda continued her exam and probing, "Nausea? Headache?"

Charlie replied cautiously, "No nausea. No headache. It hurts at the bump but no-where else. Except when I shake my head."

Elda shone a penlight in Charlie's eyes and then commanded, "Stand up."

Charlie stood, still holding the icepack on the bruise.

Elda directed, "Stand heel to toe."

Charlie complied, grinned and stood perfectly without a wobble.

"Switch."

Charlie's balance held true.

452

"Name, rank and serial number?"

Charlie answered.

"What town are we in?"

"London and it's not a town. It's a city in the United Kingdom," Charlie said, snickering.

Elda rolled her eyes and waved her hand dismissively at Charlie, and said, "OK, you're obviously good to go for now. Let me know if you get any delayed onset of confusion, dizziness, increased headache, or nausea."

Sophia glanced at her buzzing cellphone and exclaimed, "Bollocks, it's James."

Elda instructed her, "Answer it. And smile as you do so."

"Why should I smile?" Sophia pouted.

"So you don't sound as petulant as you look right now," responded Elda, continuing, "It's a standard customer support technique to sound friendly and upbeat."

Sophia gave Elda an exaggerated grimace and then put a smile on her face.

"That's good." Elda gave her a thumbs up.

Sophia pressed answer. "Hello, James. … Where am I? I'm in London, of course. Such a beautiful day, I thought I'd take a stroll at lunch. … What? No one has seen me in the office today? Check the logs. You'll see I signed in this morning and out again for lunch. … Pardon? In the States? What a silly rumor. No, I haven't been."

Sophia listened to James for a while before answering, "No, James I have not seen any of the Russians. I thought we weren't taking an interest in them anymore? You'd like to see me after lunch? Certainly. I'll be there with bells on. Ta." Sophia hung up. She turned to Elda and said, "I think he's suspicious."

Elda smiled a not too pleasant grin and replied, "Good. That means we have leverage to get him to the warehouse."

***

At his home in Moscow, Tosh rolled over in his bed and glanced at his watch. It was 02:01. He quickly answered his vibrating burner phone. "*Da?*"

Stas' voice came over the speaker, "*Privet*, Tosh. I know it's 2am but you said to call you if I had any more information on Elda's whereabouts…"

"Hold on." Tosh, now fully awake, crawled out of bed, careful not to wake the other occupant of the double bed. He looked back at his partner. Their sex-life had been non-existent lately and Tosh felt lonely. It added to Tosh's feeling of being old.

Tosh slipped on his robe and slippers and tiptoed to the kitchen to continue the conversation. Holding the phone between his shoulder and ear, he filled the tea kettle and sat down in a straight-backed wooden chair at the small kitchen table. He took the phone back into his left hand and prompted Stas to continue, "*Da. Gde ona*?" inquired Tosh.

"I'm assuming that she's at the warehouse address I gave you."

Checking his pulse at the side of his neck and breathing deeply before answering, Tosh probed, "Assuming? On what basis?"

"I have video footage which shows Elda nearby that address. And I have traced the ownership documents further. It's got many layers of misdirection, but it finally has Elda as the one who signed the original paperwork in London."

"*Khorosho*, Stas. *Spasibo*. Can you send me the video feed?"

"*Vot.*"

Tosh's phone pinged and a video link arrived as a secure text message. He pressed PLAY and viewed Elda walking down an alley in the direction of the warehouse. His eyes narrowed. "Something seems off here, Stas."

"*Ser*? It's the original video. It hasn't been modified."

Tosh played the video through again before replying, "No. It's not the video. It's Elda. She's hiding her face, but it's as if she knows where the camera is and that we will be seeing this. She's play acting. There's a message in this somewhere. I wonder what her game is…" Tosh disconnected from the call.

I have an idea. It will be interesting if this pans out. Tosh picked up his phone and dialed an office number. "Go out and buy a small chess set immediately. You will have further instructions waiting in your office when you get back." Tosh disconnected from the call.

***

Her hip pocket was vibrating. Elda took out her burner phone and glanced down. She had a package at the Hotel Brunelleschi in Florence, Italy. She texted her contact to see if he could chat. He could.

Elda waited on the line while he carefully scanned the package for bugs and bombs, and then opened it.

"No note, just a small chess game. The Black King and White Queen are taped on the outside of the game box."

"What positions are the two chess pieces in?"

"Facing each other," her contact replied.

"Thanks so much. Wait a second…" *Ah yes, the King and Queen face each other in chess. Are you wondering what the next move is, my friend?*

"Okay, I would like you to pick up a large sea shell and then insert a smaller shell inside of that. Then place the shells with the White Queen and Black King together side by side into a box, wrap it up, and send it off. "

"Any particular type of shells?" her contact inquired.

"No. Thank you." Elda hung up.

***

The mannequin in the corner crashed to the floor. Charlie, Oliver and Sophia all jumped up from the crates they were sitting on in Elda's flat. Elda

457

lowered her silenced pistol. Charlie shouted, "What the fuck, Elda?"

Elda said casually, "Don't worry, Charlie. The bullet won't go any further than the mannequin. It should be captured by the vest. Will you go check?"

Charlie stomped over to the corner, muttering, "You yell at me when I throw a tiny blade at the wall, and yet you shoot a gun in an apartment building." She pulled aside the dummy's jacket and plucked off a flattened bullet from the chest area. "Wow! What's this got on?" She lifted up the shirt to display a black formfitting corset-bra covering the model's hourglass chest and abdomen area.

"Whoa, I'd date her!" Oliver walked over and leered.

Elda rolled her eyes and shook her head, commenting, "Down you two. Sophia, you have to leave soon to see James. I'm going to fit you with this very lightweight vest. It's the latest thing in full coverage bras. Just out of our labs. Really more of a skin tight tank top. It's a very lightweight, but fully bullet resistant material."

"Ah, …resistant?" Sophia asked with doubt in her voice.

Elda dismissed her worries with a wave of her hand, stating, "Well, it's better than nothing, right? There's also a small transponder sewn into it so we can track your whereabouts at any time. Here's a set of special ear pods for your phone. We'll be able to communicate through them as long as he doesn't distrust you and have you remove them. I would draw attention to them deliberately, which will help disarm his suspicions. Perhaps gush over how great they stream Pandora without needing your phone, what a great deal they were and how fantastic the sound quality is. You can even hand them to him to show off the sound quality. Blast some of that head bobbing music you like."

Sophia walked over and closely examined the divot left by the bullet. "Thanks, Elda. I think…"

Elda waved her hand to motion Charlie to follow her and Sophia. "Charlie, come help me get Sophia kitted out. Oliver, feel free to watch from the door," she stated with a seductive grin and wink.

"Bob's your uncle, Elda," Oliver said, trotting after them.

Sophia stripped off her shirt and bra, causing Oliver to lean further into the room. The sound of Velcro being adjusted accompanied Elda's words, "OK, Oliver. We are going to lure James to the warehouse. He will be yours to dispose of. Follow my lead. Understood?"

"Righto. Thanks, Elda."

Elda picked up Sophia's shirt and handed it to her to put on. Oliver cleared his throat to catch Sophia's eye. He flashed his crooked smile at her, causing her to miss a couple of buttons on her shirt. Charlie stepped in and helped her correct the mismatched holes and buttons. "Oliver, focus," reprimanded Elda.

Oliver replied coyly, "I am, Elda."

"On the mission, boy," Elda commanded, continuing the briefing, "Now, we also need to have Tosh and Anatoly join us at the warehouse. We will figure that one out before they arrive in London. Once they are at the warehouse, we'll trade them Snezhana for them dropping the op and leaving the UK. If there is any action, Tosh is mine to take out. Am I clear on that?"

The other three replied in unison, "Yes, Elda."

She continued her directions, "Good. When they agree to cooperate with you, gather all their weapons and secure them in a lock box. Mail the key to Tosh's office. Anatoly is very attached to his kit. I arranged to have a chopper meet us on the warehouse roof.

Place the Russians with their weapon box on the helicopter. Cuff them for the chopper ride and remove the handcuffs only after they are seated on the plane at the airport. Understand?"

Elda received a chorus in response, "Yes, Elda."

"Charlie, you are now second in command. If anything happens to me, carry on and ensure the Russians get their ride home." Elda passed Charlie a piece of paper. "Here's the contact information for the chopper. They will arrive at the arranged time unless you tell them otherwise. They are aware that you are authorized to give them orders."

Sophia interjected, "I have to go now, Elda."

"Yes, Sophia. How's that feel?" Elda pointed to Sophia's torso.

Sophia turned slightly to the left and then to the right and rubbed her hands along her sides, replying, "Like a corset from the dark ages." She drew in a deep breath and coughed.

"At least it isn't a metal corset," said Elda, dismissively.

Sophia sighed and murmured, "Why don't I find that helpful?"

Elda continued the instructions, "OK. Ashok is going to plant additional information that leads to the warehouse and he will release it for them to find on my command. First we move on *Operation James*. Go. And Sophia,…"

Sophia turned at the door and replied, "Yes Elda?"

"Please try to not get maimed or killed before we can rescue you, okay?"

***

In James' office, Sophia sat, as directed by James, in the chair directly across from him. The air felt heavy with things yet to be said. Sophia swallowed heavily and made an effort to remain calm and non-threatening. She put a smile on her face and then broke the silence with a perky, "Hello, James. What's up?"

"What's up? You tell me, Sophia," James said in a menacing tone, tossing a photo across his shiny mahogany desk to her.

The picture slid to a stop and Sophia slowly picked it up. It was a shot of herself chatting with Elda. She shrugged casually. "It's just Elda, James. She's here on holiday and rang me up." She casually threw the picture back down onto his desk and gazed expectantly at him.

"Really?" James passed a second picture across to Sophia. She glanced down at a scene of Elda fleeing in a cab, with a crashed taxi in view in the far corner of the picture. "I checked on this *accident* and the driver of the cab that crashed said that a female MI6 officer had paid him for the use of his cab. The other driver said that the woman who took his cab had paid handsomely for it."

Sophia shrugged. She stated flatly, "How very interesting, James. It must mean that Elda lied to me.' Raising her voice she added, "And that they are posing as MI6 officers. Don't you think this incident warrants looking into closer, James? We can't have that!" Sophia declared indignantly.

James narrowed his eyes, "No, we *can't* have that, Sophia. So are you willing to find and arrest Elda?"

Sophia drew herself up and stated firmly, "Of course, James. I am loyal to MI6 and will protect our country."

James looked quizzically at Sophia. Sophia willed herself to stay calm. She suspected he was wondering if she was telling the truth or not. Silence hung in the air between them. Suddenly he threw at her, "So where is she, Sophia?"

"I have an address that she gave me." Sophia wrote it on a piece of paper and handed it to James. He briefly glanced at it. It was the same address that the Kremlin had found for Elda. Sophia inquired helpfully, "Shall I go there and arrest her for the commotion she caused?"

James sat back in his chair.

Silence hung threateningly.

Is he wondering when and how to kill me? Sophia wondered. *Or am I still useful in helping him get Elda?*

"No, no. You shouldn't go alone," he said. "I will accompany you. Let me get some gear and you meet me at the motor pool."

Whew! At least he isn't going to shoot me now. Sophia relaxed slightly.

Then James ordered, "Leave your cell phone here with me."

Sophia startled, "My cell phone?" *Blimey...*

James smiled and stated, "You wouldn't want anyone tracking us, would you?"

Sophia passed the phone over to James. He placed it in his top drawer, planning to search the messages and addresses when he was back in his office. "And you won't be needing those earbuds without your phone, will you?"

Sophia briefly kicked herself for not having made a show of why she needed them as Elda had suggested. *Bloody fool, Sophia…Now would be too late to explain how they worked streaming music without her phone.* She popped each one out and handed them to James. He threw them in with the phone and closed the drawer. Standing, he motioned to her to leave the office before him. "They will be right there for you when we return. Let's go."

***

At the motor pool, James demanded curtly, "Give me your weapon."

Sophia stopped walking towards James' car and sputtered, "What? Why?! No! I'll need it in case the confrontation with Elda goes south. First you take my cell phone and now my weapon? What's going on here James?"

James rolled his eyes at her and said gently, "Calm down, Sophia. Why are women so emotional? Of course you will need it. Nothing's going on. I'm just putting it in the gun box with mine for the ride.

You know MI6 has strict rules about riding around London with loaded weapons."

Sophia wheedled, "But James, you know nobody follows those silly rules."

James stated authoritatively, "Yes, I am aware of that. However, I have to follow them, Sophia. I am in charge and I have to enforce those standards."

Sophia nodded, but countered with, "I'll feel naked without it, James. Would it be all right if I just give you the clip from it? We'll be compliant with the regulations that way too."

James smiled at her broadly and held out his hand, replying, "Certainly, my dear. We just have to follow regs."

Sophia popped out the ammo clip and placed it into James' palm. He opened the boot of his car and deposited the clip into a lock box. Sophia silently noted that he did not place his gun inside. On her way around the car to the passenger seat and out of James' range of vision, she quickly replaced her clip with a spare one and slipped her gun back into her shoulder holster.

James started the car and smoothly navigated out of the tight parking garage. As he pulled onto the street, he mentioned, "I have one stop I'd like to make while I'm out before we get there. It's a bit out of the way, but I am supposed to check on a safe house outside of London on a weekly basis and have not had a chance to do so. This is the perfect opportunity. Do you mind? Also I don't think you've seen this place, and it would be a good one for you to know about."

"Certainly James. You're in control here." She looked out of the window and watched as they whipped by cars on the Motorway. Silently Sophia prayed that the tracking device Elda had put on her was working. She had a hunch that James was heading to the same spot where they had found Nigel's dad Henry's, body. She kept staring out the window so that James could not read her face.

James remarked, "You're rather intent on that window view, Sophia. Looking for something?"

"It's such a treat to be driven, James. I am always the driver. Things look so much different when you're a passenger, don't they?" Sophia turned to James with a wide-eyed innocent gaze. He visibly relaxed and sped on.

***

The red dot moved out of London north along the A10. Elda's earpiece crackled to life, Charlie's voice came clearly into her left ear, "Good guess, Elda. It looks as if heading to Waltham Cross was a good call.”

Unused to anyone commenting on her decisions, Elda decided to use it as a teaching moment. She explained, “I figured James to be a creature of habit. He’s a bureaucrat and not very creative. Either he was going to head to the warehouse with Sophia to come and get me, or he was going to dispose of her first. Therefore, for him to return to where we suspect he offed Henry Davies seemed logical. I’ll head into the forest a bit, ditch the car, and go the rest of the way on foot.”

Oliver broke in, worry dripping off his words, “That’s a lot of guessing, Elda. What if you’re wrong?”

Elda retorted tersely, “Analyzing data and human habits is what I do best. I won’t be wrong.”

Oliver snipped back at her, “I hope for Sophia’s and my sake you’re right about that.”

***

Wheels spinning on the gravel, James veered off of route 121 near the Epping Forest and parked the car. He threw the car into park and cut the ignition. “We have to walk from here to safe house.”

"Lead the way, James," Sophia said with a cheery tone.

Good. She has no suspicions, thought James. He strode off with Sophia close behind. He glanced over his shoulder to ensure she was there. The gravel of the path crunched beneath their feet as they silently strode along. After a short distance, James proclaimed, "Oh dear. You'll have to excuse me, Sophia, but it was a long ride and nature calls. Turn your head and watch the path for me."

"Certainly, James."

James took one step past a tree and a quiet voice whispered in his ear, "Put your hands above your head."

James hesitated. Elda stepped out from behind the tree and shouted, "Now!"

As James raised his hands from his sides he snagged his pistol from his pant holster. Wheeling around, he hastily fired a shot at Elda and missed.

Elda reprimanded him, "Bad move, James. Never miss with your first shot." She slashed her hands down and chopped James' wrist hard, knocking his gun out of his hand. James punched at Elda with his other hand, clipping the side of her head. She whipped her fist into the side of his head causing his head to snap to one side. James staggered backwards, and then ran at her with his head down.

My god. This man just doesn't know when to call it quits. Elda sidestepped his advance and stuck out her foot, bringing him down. James rolled and rose while Elda watched him carefully. *He's stupidly egotistical enough to try another attack.* "James, just quit now before I hurt you," she entreated, knowing that she had to keep James alive since she had promised Oliver he could be the one that killed James.

James walked up to Elda with his hands in the air. *I don't trust him. Let's see what he tries next.* She stood waiting. Once close enough, he kicked out at Elda, who intercepted his leg with hers and brought him crashing down to the ground. He rolled and reached for his gun, only to have it kicked away by Elda's steel toed boots.

He scrambled on his hands and knees to reach his gun.

"Sorry James. No weapons for you." Elda's boot caught him in his side with a crunching noise, signifying a cracked rib or two. He yelled in pain and grabbed at his side.

"I warned you." Elda lashed out again with her foot and caught him squarely on the jaw, snapping his head back. He collapsed onto the ground and moaned. Sophia picked up his gun from beneath the brush and pressed the barrel against the nape of his neck. A sobbing James croaked, "OK, I'm not fighting anymore." Elda grabbed his right hand and cuffed it and then brought his left one down to join the right in cuffs. She reached into the back of his pants and deftly removed his second gun from the internal holster. She rolled him over onto his side, and, after checking to ensure he had no other weapons or further injuries, with Sophia's help, stood him up and leaned him against the tree.

James sneered at Elda and wheezed, "You'll pay dearly for this, Elda."

Elda patted his upper arm and retorted, "Ha! No, I won't James. But I do need you to come with me like a good boy." She pointed her weapon at his forehead. She reached into James' pocket and extracted his car keys. Throwing them at Sophia, she instructed, "Drive his car back to the warehouse."

James glared at Sophia and, coughing and wincing, snarled, "You'll get the gallows for this, Sophia."

Sophia smiled sweetly at James and motioned with her gun for him to go onto the path, stating, "After you, James."

Elda drove back to London with James cuffed in the backseat. Arriving at the warehouse, she dragged him out by his cuffs and not too gently shoved him into a small room located on the side of the warehouse area. She waved at the rest of the team and shut the door behind herself and James.

"You'll bloody well pay for this, Elda," James sputtered feebly, "Damn Yank."

Elda laughed at James and said with contempt, "Stop pretending, James. We know you aren't British."

Hands still bound, he lunged at her. "You're an insane twit."

Elda punched him in his cracked ribs. He bent over and threw up.

"Gads. Talk about being a twit. Now you have to be in this room with the smell of your own puke." She turned and exited the room, locking the door behind her.

"Cleanup in aisle three," Elda said. Oliver looked at her in confusion. Charlie started laughing. Elda pointed at her and said, "Don't laugh too hard, my little understudy. You get the honor of visiting Snezhana to see how she's doing. Watch it. She can be a wildcat."

Elda followed Charlie into the room where Snezhana was firmly cuffed and chained to a chair.

"*Khuy tebe!*" Snezhana spit at Charlie, landing a glob on her cheek.

"Excellent aim, Snezhana," Charlie said, as she wiped the spit off onto her sleeve. "And although your offer of carnal relations is somewhat appealing, I think we'll just stick with more of the bondage angle."

Elda stared with disapproving amusement at Charlie, who shrugged and winked at Elda. Elda motioned for her to leave and yelled after her, "Two coffees?"

Charlie's reply came floating back to Elda, "Certainly. Cream, no sugar for you. What does twinkle toes take?"

Elda yelled, "Just bring the cream and sugar on the side, plus a water. We don't want her to dehydrate. Spitting is her only weapon."

Snezhana struggled in vain against her restraints and sneered, "Blyad' My uncle will kill you for this."

Elda frowned at Snezhana and said coolly, "*Nyet*, Snezhana. He won't. But he and I will need to settle our dispute once and for all, and you're the leverage to get him here."

Elda reached over and examined Snezhana's wrists, which were red and bruised from her attempts to slip the cuffs off. "But it would not do to have you returned to him damaged in any way. After you and I have a little chat and coffee, we will remove your restraints for a while. You can see that this room has been converted into a very nice cell for you, complete with a toilet. All the comforts of home. Unfortunately we can't provide you with anything you could use as a weapon, so you do not get a sheet or a blanket to go on that mattress. Nor can we afford to give you complete privacy. We are monitoring the cell 24 hours via cameras and our own vigilance. Hopefully your uncle will find you soon so you will not have many days to stay here."

Snezhana tried to lurch forward, but her chair was bolted to the ground. She sneered, *"Malen'kaya suchka!"*

Elda nodded and said, "Well, I'd much rather be a little bitch than a big bitch."

Just then Charlie walked in with a tray with coffee and scones. Snezhana's stomach growled at the sight of the food.

"That's a good sign," Elda observed. "I'm going to ask some questions to ensure you don't have a concussion."

Snezhana spit at Elda but missed.

"Charlie, I think our prisoner needs some time alone to calm down. You're going to have to ask Snezhana the questions later. I do want to ensure she's healthy, however. For now we'll just monitor her condition. Help me change her cuffs. And please, after I leave, rub some arnica on those bruises of hers."

Elda and Charlie walked to either side of Snezhana. They quickly and deftly unlocked one of the cuffs. Then they moved her hands to the front and locked the cuffs back on Snezhana's wrists to a chain that was attached to the chair, while bolting another chain around her waist. Snezhana tried again to lunge and strike out but was held solidly to the chair.

"Come on, Snezhana. Be reasonable. You know we have the upper hand for now. Settle down, eat, regain your strength. At least give yourself time to think of how to get out of this instead of being reactive. You know that leading with your emotions will just defeat you in the end."

Elda's words echoed things both Tosh and Elda had told Snezhana in the past. Snezhana inhaled deeply and said, "*Da*, Elda. You are right. But you will pay for this someday."

Elda raised her eyebrows and retorted, "We'll see. This is not something you want to be vindictive about, Snezhana. It's just the game. Play along and live to see another day."

Snezhana sneered, "Cold War rules?"

"Yes. Old spy rules. Just ask your uncle the next time you guys talk. Having a known enemy who plays by the rules is far better than having one who doesn't. You'd be amazed where cooperation will get you in our profession."

***

Tosh looked with disdain around the small room Anatoly had rented. The shabby rug hid years of encrusted dirt and dead insects. The furniture was far past time to throw into the rubbish bin.

"*Der'mo!*" Anatoly slammed his fist into his leg. Dust flew from the spread on the rickety bed where he was sitting.

"*Uspoykoysya.* Settle down, Anatoly. We will find them."

"*Izvinite, ser*. I just can't believe I haven't located them." Anatoly balled his fists, ready to strike.

Tosh sat on the edge of an old straight back chair, his hands on his knees. "I have an address, but I am suspicious and don't know why." He looked up at the ceiling and instantly regretted doing so. The view of the spider webs and water stains was not conducive to having great thoughts. "How on earth did you find this despicable place, Anatoly? We are getting you out of here and into someplace that will not give both of us a disease."

"*Khorosho*. I won't fight you on that one, ser." Anatoly frowned and inquired, "What did Stas tell you again, Tosh?"

"He said he traced the warehouse to Elda through a series of shell companies and misdirection. He had video footage—which I viewed—of Elda near the warehouse. Although she was shielding her face, she didn't seem to be hiding from the camera. Something seems off." Tosh stood and brushed dust from the back of his pants. "You know Elda. She's better than that." Tosh looked with a frown at the rug beneath his shoes. "We're getting out of here, Anatoly."

Anatoly grabbed his kit bag. "*Khorosho. Ya gotov.* Lead the way." He looked around the grimy room, pointing to each area and repeating, "*Proveryat', Khorosho, Ochistite*," his mantra of "Check, Okay, Clear."

Tosh took out a wipe and opened the door, sanitizing the doorknob and wiping away any prints. He carefully put the used tissue in his pocket.

The two men walked silently down the street, each deep into his own musings on what to do next.

Suddenly Tosh's phone rang. "It's Stas. I wonder if he has anything for us." He answered, "*Da*?"

"*Ser*, there's a package for you here. It's marked, URGENT. OPEN IMMEDIATELY."

"Have you scanned it for explosives?"

"It's clear, *ser.*"

"Open it. *Seychas!*"

Stas said hesitantly, "It's very strange."

"What?" Tosh barked.

"There are two shells, one inside the other, and Queen and King pieces from a chess set."

"How are the pieces positioned?" Tosh demanded.

"They are side by side, *ser.*"

Tosh stopped suddenly, "*Aga*! *Glupyy*! Stupid, stupid. Tosh you *are* getting old."

Anatoly and Stas waited.

Tosh spoke sharply into the phone, "What were the names of the shell companies, Stas?" Tosh heard Stas rapidly typing.

The answer soon came. "Bittman and Donatello, *ser*."

"*Govno*. Of course. *Spasibo*, Stas." Tosh hung up and continued walking.

Anatoly looked at him expectantly, finally breaking the silence, "Well?"

"The first company's name was *Bittman*."

Anatoly rubbed his head and nodded. "*Eto Interestno*. That was the name of the operation we worked with the Americans and British on, wasn't it?"

"Yes." Tosh added, "And, if you remember, the Russians and the British had deeply planted moles that we ferreted out. But we were never sure if we had found them all. We suspect that James Richardson in MI6 is still a Russian plant, which would mean that there is still someone here in the Kremlin running him and perhaps a larger operation that we are not aware of."

"What is the other shell company's name?" Anatoly asked.

"Donatello." Tosh shook his head and muttered, "*Glupyy starik.*"

Anatoly frowned at Tosh. "Please *ser*, stop calling yourself a stupid old man. You run rings around agents half your age still. What on earth does Donatello mean?"

Tosh explained, "Donatello was a Renaissance sculptor. When he was around 60 years old he created the wooden sculpture of Mary Magdalene. Such a beautiful piece, showing the ravages of time and her wasting by fasting and abstinence."

Showing that he was still confused, Anatoly shook his head and asked, "You mean that old bag that you and Elda loved to visit in that museum in Florence?"

Tosh threw Anatoly a glare. "Art is really lost on you, Anatoly, but yes, it is in the Museo dell'Opera del Duomo in Florence."

Anatoly shrugged and asked, "So what does it mean?"

Tosh explained, "Florence was a shared time of commonality between Elda and myself. I strongly suspect the package was from her. The chess pieces are side by side and not opponents. I have a feeling she has a proposition to float by me. I need to talk to her. *Alone.*"

"What if you're wrong?" Anatoly asked.

"Then I could be a dead man for trusting her," Tosh replied

***

Elda and Sophia walked into the windowless room where James was cuffed, hands and feet, and bound by a long chain that ran through his cuffs and down to a metal chair, insuring that he couldn't go far. Sweat poured down his face, and he winced in pain each time he moved.

Elda handed him a pill, which he immediately popped into his mouth. She held a glass of water to his mouth and he gratefully swallowed. "Do you want to know what you just took?" she asked.

James looked at her in horror, realizing that he may have just made a huge error.

"Relax, it was only Tramadol to help with the pain. We taped your ribs while you were passed out, but there is really nothing else we can do for them right now. I suspect, since nothing is sticking out of your chest and you are able to breath and move as well as you can, that you just cracked your ribs and didn't break them. Still, that must be pretty painful. Try not to cough or laugh."

The chains clanked as he reached up and gently touched his jaw, which had started to turn a lovely shade of purple on one side.

Elda commented, "That also doesn't appear to be broken. We rubbed some arnica on your ribs and your jaw to help with the pain. We want you to be able to talk. You're a lucky man, James."

"Lucky?" he managed to spit out as he jangled his chains. "Release me at once," he commanded.

"Don't worry, James. We just want some information from you. Sophia, please leave us alone." Elda laid out a set of surgical knives and dental instruments and pulled on a pair of Latex gloves.

Sophia blanched. James turned white. Shaking he demanded, "Unlock these chains at once."

Elda glared at Sophia and commanded, "Leave now."

Sophia obediently did an about face and left the room, closing the door firmly behind her.

Elda picked up a surgical knife and held it up to a thin sheet of paper. She swiftly sliced the paper in two and leered at James. "Now, it's time for a little chat…"

***

"What?" A half hour later Elda strolled out of the room to be faced by a team of concerned faces.

Oliver spoke out first and said, "Is James still alive? You did tell me he was *mine* to dispose of."

Elda glanced down at her bloody surgical gloves and instruments she was carrying, and replied, "Oh, no, don't worry about that. He's fine. Not a mark on him. I just wanted to get some information out of him. It's all psychological you know? These bullies crack the moment they see blood."

"Whose blood is that, then," asked Sophia with curiosity.

Elda held up a bandaged finger and responded with a grimace, "Unfortunately mine. I nicked myself while sharpening these tools, so I decided to put the ensuing blood to good use and smeared it on the gloves and on a number of the knives."

Charlie spoke up, "What did you find out, Elda?"

Elda shook her head in disappointment and responded, "It appears that the Russians have wisely kept poor James out of the loop so he doesn't even have enough information to save his own life. He's in the dark about any others like him who may be planted within MI6 and doesn't have any Russian contacts aside from Adrik, Tosh's boss, at the Kremlin. Prior to Adrik, he was being handled by Alexei, who is now deceased. So apparently James and any other moles are being run at the levels above Tosh."

Charlie frowned and inquired, "So what does this mean?"

Elda replied, "It means that there is quite probably at least one other high-ranking mole in MI6 and potentially in the other intelligence agencies in the United States and perhaps even in Mossad in Israel. The Russians would not have put all their eggs in this one basket."

Oliver chimed in, "Bollocks. So what do we do?"

"Nothing," Elda said uncharacteristically.

"Nothing?!" the astonished team exclaimed all at once.

Elda explained in her professorial tone, "Face it, no-one will approve sorting this out unless there is a strong reason to do so and a trail of actionable intelligence. And if we tell anyone what we know, we run the risk of being eliminated since we don't know who to trust."

"So we do nothing?" Charlie's frustration showed clearly on her face.

"Correct," Elda stated calmly. "Keep quiet and keep your eyes open. This is deeply rooted. The Cold War is *not* over. And as Ed once told me: Trust no one."

***

Responding to the loud knock, Anatoly jumped up and grabbed his gun. Tosh held out a calming hand.

"We ordered room service. This is either that, or it's them. Either case is welcome. Here, hide that gun with this book." Tosh threw a copy of Gideon's Bible over to Anatoly.

Anatoly held it open over his gun, wryly stating, "Rather a dead giveaway, isn't it? Hardly the type of book *I'd* be reading."

A second, more demanding rap sounded on the door.

Tosh looked out the spyhole and opened the door. "Sorry for the delay," he said sincerely.

"No problem, sir." The waiter put the tray on the coffee table, accepted Tosh's tip, and rapidly left the room.

Anatoly closed the bible and threw it onto the desk. He bounded over to check the pastries on the tray. Selecting one, he paused before taking a bite and confessed, "*Ser*, I'm confused. Shouldn't we be hiding until we have a plan?"

"I have a plan," Tosh replied, asking, "What do you have for weapons?"

Anatoly unzipped his kit bag and rattled off, touching each weapon: "Vityaz-SN submachine gun , MP-412 REX .357 Magnum revolver, VSS Vintorez silent sniper rifle, AK-103 assault rifle, MSS Vul silent pistol and NRS-2 survival kit of a knife and a single-shot noiseless pistol."

Tosh held up his hand and broke in, "Perfect. I want you to visibly wear what you can under a large raincoat. When we get close to the warehouse you'll ditch the coat and come storming up to it, like Rambo. However, there will be no shooting or killing until you get the signal from me or they attack us. Understand?"

Anatoly frowned and cocked his head. He asked, "*Khorosho. No kto Rambo?*"

Tosh looked at Anatoly as if he was from a different planet and exclaimed, "Gads, Anatoly. Don't you ever watch movies?"

"*Nyet.*" Anatoly stated flatly and shrugged, "So what's the rest of the plan?"

"*Elementarnyy*," Tosh explained. "We go to the warehouse and knock on the door. When they open it, we walk in."

"*Der'mo*!" Anatoly exclaimed, "*I* could have devised *that* plan, Tosh! What keeps us from getting killed?"

"I truly believe that Elda wants to talk with me," Tosh declared confidently.

Anatoly slapped his forehead and growled, "That's it? *Der'mo*."

***

Elda quietly paced along the main open area of the warehouse, back and forth past the office doors that they had been using for holding cells and interrogation rooms. Chairs were set up in the center and chains were lying loosely with one end hooked to O rings on the floor. Charlie jumped up off her chair and marched in step beside Elda. Sophia and Oliver sat expectantly, their heads following Elda and Charlie as if watching a tennis match.

Breaking the silence, Charlie inquired, "So what's the plan. Elda?"

"We wait until they show up," Elda declared loudly enough for Oliver and Sophia to hear.

"And, …," prompted Charlie.

Elda asserted, "We play it by ear, Follow my lead. No shooting until I give the signal or they shoot first."

"*That's* your plan?" Charlie's voice rose an octave.

Elda stopped short and faced her. "Yes. It is. Watch and learn."

In a calmer tone, Charlie inquired, "What keeps us from getting shot if they shoot first?"

"I don't believe they will. I think Tosh has gotten my messages," contended Elda.

Charlie frowned and blurted out, "Your messages? We've been with you the entire time. I never saw you send any messages."

"Trust me."

***

Angelina ripped the IV from her arm. The vet ran over and stanched the bleeding. He yelled, "You can't do that."

Angelina demanded, "Just give me some gauze and tape."

"You'll need that for sure." The vet reached for the materials on a nearby tray and applied a wrap to Angelina's arm where the needle had been. "You'll have to wait here until I ensure you are able to go. Let me check the stitches again."

Angelina snarled, "You finished. I suspect you are hoping the police will show up. If they do, you are a dead man, *pozhaluysta*?"

The vet gulped and nodded. Angelina inspected her leg. "You did a good job, *Spasibo*. Remember, you tell no one about this." Angelina stood and limped out of the office.

Once around the corner and out of sight, she stopped to catch her breath and plan her next move. She decided to go back to Moscow for her weapons and a change of clothing from her apartment before she did anything else. Then she determined to get even with Anatoly and end this once and for all. With that decided, she held out her arm for a cab.

Chapter Twenty-Eight

"They are coming!" Oliver ran into the main area from the warehouse security room where he had been viewing the cameras. "And they are tooled up, or as you would say, Elda, loaded for bear." He watched Elda spring into action mode.

"Great!" Elda exclaimed, "As to be expected. Ready your weapons. Sophia, move over to cover Snezhana," Elda directed, pointing at their assigned positions.

Oliver looked around the room. Snezhana was sitting in the center of the warehouse, shackled to a ring on the floor. James was seated on a chair near her, handcuffed with his ankles shackled together. "Where do you want me, Elda?" he asked.

Elda pointed at James and replied to Oliver, "Unshackle him and then stand over to one side where you can get a clear shot on him or the Russians."

Oliver moved quickly to do as he was told. He addressed James, "James. If you move or cause any trouble, I will shoot you. Understand?" James, his hands shaking, nodded his head.

Oliver watched the other players take their positions.

Charlie holding a Sig Sauer P228 had moved in to cover Elda. Elda turned to Charlie and said, "Good positioning, Charlie, but remember that I need to talk to Tosh and, if the shooting begins, he's mine to take out. So perhaps you'd be better used covering Sophia or Oliver."

Charlie shook her head emphatically, "No Elda. I am here to learn from you and intend to keep you alive so I can do that. And, you *know* that this is what *you* would do if you were in my shoes."

Elda sighed and nodded her agreement. "You have learned fast, grasshopper. Soon you will not need me. I am glad I selected you to follow me."

"And I will continue to do so."

"You can't say that, Charlie. We never know the future. Especially in our business. But do feel confident in your ability to handle any situation in the future, even if I am not there." Elda turned away sharply and strolled over to the front door.

Oliver felt his stomach churn as he waited in silence.

A loud knock on the door, followed by rustling and clicks as the team readied their weapons, announced the Russians' arrival. Raising her Smith and Wesson, Elda opened the door, her body shielding the rest of her team. She calmly viewed Tosh's pistol, pointed at her head, and stated, "It was unlocked. Come in." She took a step back, allowing Tosh to enter, followed by Anatoly holding his Vityaz-SN submachine gun. Elda and Tosh each held up their non-dominant hand to signal to their teams to stand down.

Tosh looked first at Snezhana and asked, "Are you all right, Snezhana?"

Crying, Snezhana sniffed back her tears and responded, "Yes, uncle. Nothing is wounded except my pride. They have treated me well."

"Shall we talk, Tosh?" Elda handed him the key to Snezhana's chains and cuffs. Neither Tosh nor Elda had lowered their weapons. Without looking away from Elda, Tosh handed the key over to Anatoly. His grey eyes bore into her brown ones. Finally he assented, "*Da*, Elda. We need to talk." They continued to stand there unflinchingly.

"Just end it and shoot each other already. Or give me your weapon, Elda and I'll take care of him." James stated, starting to take a step forward.

Elda stood rock steady, holding her gun on Tosh. "Stay out of this James," ordered Elda. She looked at Tosh. "May I have a momentary break to take care of a situation?"

Tosh swiveled to point his firearm at James and nodded, "*Konechno.*"

Elda walked over to Oliver who was standing to one side and handed him her gun. "Oliver, I promised you that he would be yours."

James interrupted, "But Elda, Tosh is your nemesis, not Oliver's."

"I wasn't talking about Tosh."

A loud retort echoed in the open area of the warehouse. A bullet hole appeared between James' eyes and he toppled over face first. Oliver handed Elda her pistol back.

"Thank you, Elda."

"No problem Oliver. I had you unshackle him so you wouldn't be shooting a sitting duck. Now please take Snezhana and go join Sophia and Charlie outside. Please ensure that everyone stays friendly while Tosh and I settle our own matter. Then you all will need to clean this mess up." Elda turned to resume her position facing Tosh. He swiveled back to face her.

***

Oliver joined Anatoly, Charlie, and Sophia who were nervously standing guard outside the warehouse door. A short time after Oliver had stepped outdoors, two shots rang out simultaneously within the warehouse. The group stood in fear of going back in. Finally, Anatoly yanked the door open.

"Der'mo!'

Charlie, Sophia and Oliver pushed Anatoly inside and looked around the warehouse. James's body was lying where Oliver had left it. There was no sign of Elda nor Tosh.

Epilogue

Anatoly sat helplessly watching Snezhana cry. He looked desperately around Tosh's office for a hint of how to help her. The sight of the empty chair filled him with a strange feeling. He angrily shouted, "*Der'mo.*" He slammed his fist into his thigh. The absence of Tosh was palatable. He turned to console Snezhana, "He will show up, Snezhana. He always does."

Through her sobs, Snezhana stated angrily, "You don't know that, Anatoly. It's been two weeks already, and the blood found in the warehouse matched his blood type."

"And also Elda's. They had the same type. So until the lab gives us more information we won't know for sure." Anatoly turned away from Snezhana and looked helplessly at the missing Tosh for advice. His eyes rested on the metal file cabinets. "We have to clean out his files before they get taken away. There's so much useful information in them that Tosh never put online. We don't want the next crew to get it. I have a secure place where I can stash them. Will you help me do that today?"

Snezhana nodded and then spit out bitterly, "You know that Adrik will shut this operation down in favor of his cybersecurity teams."

Anatoly shrugged resignedly. His skills would always be in great demand on the black market. "*Da.* Well at least Stas will have a job, if he wants it."

Snezhana put her head in her hands and sobbed again, "What will happen to us?"

***

"You guys really don't have to come to the airport with me, you know?" Charlie stood, with her bag at her side, at the door of the flat that Elda had rented in London. The apartment seemed larger without Elda's presence in it.

Oliver marched over and picked up Charlie's bag. She held back her hand from swatting him and accepted his aid.

"We'll drive you there and see you off," Sophia stated firmly.

Charlie looked sadly around the room, holding back tears. The whiteboard had been thoroughly scrubbed and rolled to one side. Elda's clothing and disguises, along with her cell phone and computer, had been sent back to Ed. No trace of Elda remained.

Finally Charlie declared, "She's not dead. I would know if she were."

Sophia put her hand gently on Charlie's arm and said softly, "I can't believe she is either, but there was a lot of blood at the scene. We'll have to wait for the MI6 lab to let us know whose it is. The probability is high that it could be both Tosh's and Elda's. We heard two shots and both of them were excellent marksmen."

Oliver added sympathetically, "Ed is sending the information on Elda's blood to the MI6 lab. It should be there now. We'll know soon. But we've looked everywhere for them and they seems to have disappeared without a trace. Even the small trail of blood from the warehouse quickly petered out."

"That's the thing!" Charlie exclaimed, "If she were dead, we should have found a body by now. I believe she is alive and we will find her. Can I tap you guys in my search for her?"

Oliver and Sophia looked at each other. Charlie observed a signal pass between them but they both said at once, "Yes, of course, Charlie. Anything you need."

"Good, because I plan on continuing to look for her until either I find her or her body," Charlie avowed.

Sophia reassured her, "We will continue to be on the lookout here in the UK in all the hospitals as well as the morgues."

Charlie shuddered.

***

Anatoly walked to his apartment. *Aga. The small scattering of dust I left on the threshold has been disturbed. I wonder why the wire didn't alert me. Aga! It has been severed.*

Anatoly paused in the hallway, adjusted his sleeve to ensure his wrist knife would not be impeded and took out his single shot, noiseless weapon from his NRS-2 survival kit. He silently backed up and then walked more noisily to his front door and started humming as he unlocked his door and stepped in. A small dark-haired woman jumped on him from behind his door and plunged a large knife into his shoulder. Anatoly shook her off, pulled out the knife with one hand and flung it away. As she rushed at Anatoly again, he shot her neatly between the eyes with the pistol in his other hand. He looked dispassionately at the small lifeless body.

"Didn't you ever learn the saying, Angelina, never bring a knife to a gunfight?"

***

Ed sat at his desk staring at his phone. It had been two months since the end of the London operation and there had been no sign of Elda nor of Tosh. Charlie had dedicated herself to finding Elda and had come up empty handed. All that they had found leading out of the warehouse was blood that matched Elda's and a second pool that had matched Tosh's, but both trails had petered out. No bodies had turned up in the UK. No trace of either of them had shown up anywhere. He was stumped. However, there was no reason to believe either was still alive.

Ed tapped his fingers on his desk, dreading this phone call. Slowly he dialed.

"Hello, Dawn…"